WHITE STONES

KIT DOMINO

Published in 2019 ThornBerry Publishing UK, England

A CIP catalogue record for this book is available from the British
Library.

ISBN 978-1-909734-20-3

ThornBerry Publishing hates typos but occasionally the pesky things
do escape our notice.
We would be grateful to any eagle-eyed readers who spot any and
take the time to email us to let us know at
thornberrypub@gmail.com
in order that we can fix them as soon as possible.

COVER DESIGN
SelfPubBookCovers.com/RLSather

By the same author

Every Step of the Way

My thanks go to my dear Ivy Writers friends: Avis, Tricia, Rosemary P, Brenda, and Rosemary E. Without your friendship, generous encouragement and support I would have given up a long time ago. You ladies are incredible!

Special thanks go also to Faye Avalon and Elizabeth Power for your patient reading of the manuscript and all your invaluable help and suggestions.

This novel is dedicated to Dave, my wonderful husband of many years who has never given up believing in me and my work.
Your love and support knows no bounds.

"He meets, by heavenly chance
the destined maid; some hidden hand
Unveils to him that loveliness which
others cannot understand.
His merits in her presence grow,
to match the promise in her eyes,
And around her happy footsteps flow
the authentic airs of Paradise.
For joy of her he cannot sleep;
her beauty haunts him all the night;
It melts his heart, makes him weep
for wonder, worship, and delight.
Oh, paradox of love, he longs,
most humble when he most aspires,
To suffer scorn and cruel wrongs
from her he honours and desires.
Her graces make him rich and ask
no guerdon; this imperial style
Affronts him; he distains to bask,
the prisoner of her priceless smile.
No smallest boon were bought too dear,
though bartered for his love-sick life;
Yet trusts he, with undaunted cheer,
to vanquish heaven and call her wife."

The Angel in the House
by Coventry Pitmore (1823–1896)

Chapter 1

Disjointed notes faded in and out. Gone one moment, there the next – faint strands of music drifting up from downstairs. Cursing herself for having left the radio on, Penny Cornwall tossed down her book, threw back the duvet and reached for her dressing gown draped across the bottom of the bed.

On opening the bedroom door, the music became a fraction louder. Chords rose and fell, but the bars were incomplete, vague fragments of sound that lacked coherence. Head tilted, she listened for a moment before groping the wall for the light switch. The narrow stairwell flooded with harsh cold light.

As she reached the last few treads, one foot poised in mid-air, the music ceased. Her heart and mood lifted. *He's back!*

"Harry! I didn't expect you home yet. Why didn't you ring? I'd have waited up." She hurried down the remaining stairs. "Harry?"

No answer came. The only sound was the steady ticking of the grandfather clock by the front door.

"Harry? Harry, is that you?"

Skin prickling with fear, all thoughts transformed into the shape of someone lurking in the shadows, ready to pounce on her. Shivering against the cold sweat now trickling down her back, a vision played out in her mind. Of Alex, her estranged husband, creeping about in the darkness. Hiding. Waiting. Ready to pounce. Choosing this night, knowing she was alone, to break in and drag her back to London. Punishment for running out on him.

"Alex? Alex, is that you? Don't do this to me!"

The solid oak front door shook in its frame, straining against a force trying to wrench it open. Her eyes flew first to the top bolt, then to the bottom one. Both were firmly shot.

If it isn't Harry or Alex, then who the hell is it?

"I know you're there, I've got a gun!" Aware of her raw, nervous voice quavering at the bluff, her heart pounding against her ribs.

The door shook again, the brass letterbox beating a tattoo against the unnatural wail forcing its way through the constricted space.

Bitter bile rising from her stomach quelled when she realized with body-sagging relief it was only the wind battering against the door, not some night-time prowler or, heaven forbid, Alex trying to get in. The wind died away allowing the tick...tock of the clock to fill the void once more.

Crossing to the sitting room, she snapped on the overhead light. Everything looked perfectly in order. The television was switched off, with no red standby light showing, unlike the video recorder on the shelf beneath, where the eerie green glow of its digital clock blinked from eleven thirteen to fourteen.

In the bay of the window, the white grand piano stood silent, its lid closed. Behind it, heavy chenille curtains billowed and sank back, but their movement didn't worry her; they always did that when the wind blew up the valley from the west, according to Harry. The room felt cold, the chilled air making her pull the dressing gown even tighter around her waist as she headed into the kitchen.

The fluorescent ceiling tube buzzed loudly before flickering into frigid brightness, showing her that here, too, everything was undisturbed. Not one item out of place, and the radio, perched in its usual position on the worktop by the breadbin, was as she had left it – unplugged.

A loud clanging near the back door made her jump, sending her heart racing again as she took several steps backwards and bumped against the kitchen wall. Her fright dissipated, replaced by a feeling of foolishness when she realized the noise had come from the ancient refrigerator, its clanking motor cutting in. She could sense the house exhale a gasp of relief in unison with her own as everything sank back into familiar normality.

She glared at the fridge now emitting a noisy hum that sounded ten times louder than usual.

Stupid thing, scaring me half to death like that!

Pulling out a chair out from the kitchen table, she sat,

calming herself, at the same time wondering what it was she had heard. It had definitely sounded like music.

Maybe I imagined it? I'm not used to this place yet. I've only been here what... three weeks? Early days. Get a grip, girl, there's no one here.

She sighed, missing Harry like she never thought possible. Wishing he was there. She didn't like being on her own. *Go back to bed. Harry'll be back tomorrow.*

Satisfied everything was okay, she double-checked the back door was locked properly. Not that it would deter anyone if they were that determined to get in, she knew, nor would leaving on all the downstairs lights, but it made her feel better doing so. Safer.

Upstairs, one hand across her eyebrows, nose pressed to the cold glass, she peered out of the bedroom window, seeing nothing through the impenetrable blackness. Even the distant lights of Bristol were obscured.

Lightning chose that moment to rip open the sky, a bright white flash filling the room. Seconds later, a loud clap of thunder shook the house, followed immediately by the sound of rain hurling itself at the window, the noise that of a thousand stones being thrown at the panes. The ill-fitting wooden frame complained against the onslaught, sending a chilling caress across the nape of her neck, causing her to shudder.

Perched on top of the steep escarpment of Stonecott Hill overlooking the River Severn, the centuries-old Cotswold stone walls of Hill House were full of tiny gaps and cavities through which wild winds loved to play and moan during storms, Harry had told her. She'd get used to all the creaks and groans of the place eventually. But tonight they seem worse. Much worse.

She yanked the brocade curtains together to shut out the dark, stormy night, then darted back into bed. Tucking the duvet deep under her chin, her eyes flitted to the bedside clock. Four minutes past midnight. Twelve more hours until Harry was home. Twelve more long hours of being alone.

Heaving a sigh of missing him, she lay back against his feather pillow propped behind her head. From the cotton case came a waft of his spicy aftershave. She pulled the pillow closer, nuzzling into its feathery softness, then picked up her book, determined to ignore the March gale howling up the valley, screeching through the naked branches of swaying oaks and creaking sycamores flanking the driveway.

Engrossed once more in the thriller, her heavy eyelids drooped, but she fought to stay awake, wanting to reach the end of the chapter before turning off the light. The paperback jerked as her arm fell, its weight pulling it down towards the quilt as sleep became victor in the battle. Her head nodded forward, her hand releasing its grip on the book.

A different sound crept into the distant boundaries of her hearing. A faint murmur, scarcely discernible. Senses abruptly awakened, her eyes flew open, sleep vanquished as she struggled to make sense of the intrusion.

Music again! Distant. She turned over, buried her head in the pillow, and tried to ignore it.

Chapter 2

The next day, sheltering in the porch, Harry Winchester shook the rain off his overcoat before letting himself into the house. It was such sweet joy knowing Penny was there, eagerly awaiting his return. He pictured her wiping her hands hurriedly, swiftly checking her hair was tidy before rushing to him with welcoming arms and ardent kisses.

Before Penny, it hadn't been the outside world that had bothered him; it had been the awful loneliness of opening the front door knowing all that would greet him would be stone cold silence. For three years he had endured such emptiness following the accident which had taken away his wife Lorna and their children. But now all that was banished to a past life. Hill House was a home again, somewhere worth returning to. His life worth living.

As he hung up his coat and dropped his car keys into the pottery dish on the hall table, the letterbox clattered. A white envelope fell to the doormat. Through the frosted glass of the front door, he recognized the postman's silhouette retreating down the driveway, his merry whistling fading with his footsteps.

Stooping to pick up the letter, he saw it was addressed to Penny, the franked logo showing it came from her solicitor. He hoped it brought good news this time. News that her bullying husband had finally seen the futility of fighting and arguing over the impending divorce.

As he straightened up, an odour, vaguely familiar, teased his nostrils. It wasn't unpleasant, more an old-fashioned perfume, slightly stale. Lavender? Or was it attar of roses? Lily of the valley? Something floral he couldn't put a name to. Or was it Lorna's scent, as haunting as a melody bringing back wave after wave of memories? In his head he could see her now, hear the sound of her laughter amongst the children's squeals of delight as they raced down the stairs, eager to surround him with cuddles and kisses.

So many times he had tried to blank out these thoughts,

consign all the pain and anguish to that compartment in the back of his brain labelled "history". Lock them away and throw away the key, never to be re-opened. But every now and again some little thing would trigger a memory or three, sapping his resolve. He arched his back, stretched his weary limbs. No, it was the present and future he must focus on now, he reminded himself, chasing away unwanted images. The past must stay buried.

Leaning against the door jamb to the kitchen, his frown melted as he watched Penny unloading the dishwasher. She was humming as she worked, seemingly unaware of his presence. Drinking in the glorious calmness she always instilled in him, he relaxed, allowing the stiffness in his aching muscles to ebb away. Next time, he decided, he and Peter would go by plane, that long up drive from Folkestone was too much hassle. As he loosened his tie and yanked open the neck of his shirt, the top button pinged to the floor.

Penny spun round at the sound, the startled look on her face softening into her beautiful smile when she saw him. Oh, how he'd missed that smile.

"You're back!" Swiftly putting down the plate she held, she rushed across to his outstretched arms.

Her auburn hair was pulled back in a tight ponytail. He wanted to set it loose, tumbling about her shoulders, free and wild and luscious. Eager to hold her close, feel her warmth, and with a mouth hungry for hers, he pulled her tightly to him, not wanting to ever let go.

"How was Paris?" she asked when their lips drew apart from the lingering kiss.

"Fine, except for the rain. God, I've missed you," he whispered.

"And I you."

"I was mad leaving you behind on your own here. Next time, you're coming with me. That's a promise."

Her smile fell a little. "You mean you've got to go back? When?"

"In a few weeks' time. We didn't complete the deal. Jacques Tatterelle wouldn't sign the contract. Reckons he needs at least another fortnight before making up his mind on the footprint changes. Anyone would think we're rebuilding Notre Dame Cathedral instead of designing a new house for him. But that doesn't matter, you're coming with us. We'll make a few days of it. Do some shopping in all the antiques markets. Wander around the artists' quarter. You'll love it there."

"Wonderful. I've always wanted to see Paris."

He remembered the envelope in his hand. "Here, this arrived for you."

She gave the envelope a cursory glance, the gleam in her hazel eyes dimming. With a dismissive shrug, she flipped the letter across to the Welsh dresser.

"Aren't you going to open it?"

"It can wait; it's only about the divorce. Alex is still being awkward and won't sign the papers. I'll read it later. I don't want to spoil things the moment you're home."

The mere mention of her hopefully soon to be ex-husband's persistent delaying tactics made his hackles rise. To his mind, the brute was being difficult for the sheer hell of it. A bully right to the end. Each time the man tried to stall the inevitable, the more it fuelled the intensity of his dislike for Alex-blasted-Cornwall.

Alex had never hit her, Penny had assured him, but he couldn't forget those purple, fresh bruises on her forearm the day she'd arrived at Hill House with nothing more than a single suitcase and a box of CDs. She'd claimed she had knocked her arm on a door handle whilst carrying her things to the car. A minor mishap. Her own clumsiness, she had said, but still he doubted. Penny was never going back to Alex, of that he was sure, but deep down inside he worried something or someone would come along to kick down the walls surrounding his happiness, and he would lose everything again.

He should be grateful to Alex, he supposed, remembering the day he'd first set eyes on Penny. Struggling with one arm encased in plaster, she'd been trying to retrieve the contents of her handbag dropped on the station platform. She was rather accident prone and had fallen down some steps, breaking her arm, she'd explained whilst he'd helped gather up her belongings. Been pushed more like, Harry had later thought; for the more he learned about Alex in the following months, the more convinced he'd become that Alex was the sort of man who preferred using his fist to his mouth. Such was his venom for the way Alex had treated Penny, he'd love to punch the man's lights out if he ever met him. In reality, it was something he knew he would never do, for that would only be reducing himself to that bastard's level.

A despondent sigh escaped her lips. "Alex is determined to stop our marriage being dissolved, certainly not until such time as he deems it so. He's a control freak of the first order, and the sooner he's out of my life, the better. I should have left him years ago."

Aware of how vulnerable Penny still was to her husband's demeaning influence, he felt utterly useless, having to stand back whilst the solicitors fought it out between them. Penny didn't want him drawn into the battle, but he could see the constant hassle and long delays were taking their toll on her. He pulled her back into his arms.

"I feel I should be doing more to help you through all this. If only you'd let me; tell me what I can do. You know I would do everything and anything to protect you."

"You do help, Harry, by loving me and being here for me." She leaned back from him slightly. "Anyway, you're a fine one to talk. Things have been difficult enough for you in the past with what you've been through, but you never loosen up either. If you did, it might chase away those gremlins you still harbour." She wagged a finger at him as he was about to interrupt. "And don't say you don't. You still wake up in the middle of the night from nightmares, and I can't do anything to help you. I don't know what to do because you won't talk to me about it."

She had a valid point, he admitted to himself, but how do you tell someone you love that you were to blame for the deaths of three people? If only he could stop feeling so guilty about what happened that terrible day, he might sleep easier.

He so much wanted to open up, share the pain, but Penny had enough problems of her own to contend with at the moment without his compounding them. His were horrors of his own past, and for now not for sharing.

Chapter 3

Satiated by their lovemaking, Penny stretched out languidly across the crumpled sheet. Harry was in the shower. She could hear his deep baritone voice filling the upper floor of the house. A good singer, but he was unable to hit the high notes of "Nessun Dorma", today's choice. Then, whilst he shaved, she heard him whistling.

How does he manage to do that without cutting himself?

A second strand of music wandered into her head, stray notes plucking in the deepest cavern of her mind; the same curious discords she'd heard the previous night. But she could hardly call it music, these odd notes in harsh disharmony to Harry's singing emanating from the bathroom.

Patting aftershave onto his cheeks, Harry came into the bedroom, the seductive aroma of Pour Homme trailing after him. He shot her a quizzical stare.

"You look pale, are you okay?"

"Yes, I'm fine. You sound happy." She shook her head in a vain attempt to dispel the dissonance, but the clamour inside her head continued. It was hard to ignore.

"Of course I am," he said. "I come home to my beautiful woman waiting for me and sweep her upstairs to make passionate love. Of course, I'm happy." He took a clean blue shirt off its hanger and slipping into it said, "What man wouldn't be? Life's good now that you fill up my world."

She watched him dress, wondering whether to tell him about the music. Perhaps talking about it would make it go away, but as she opened her mouth to speak, the more absurd it all seemed. Inconsequential. Irrelevant. After all, what could she tell him? That she'd heard music in the middle of the night that had vanished with no explanation, even though it was playing inside her head right now.

It was simply unfamiliar noises in a creaky, wind-battered old house, wasn't it? She sought reassurance from her own reasoning, seeking an answer that came bouncing back as a resounding: *Yes, that's all it is. Forget it!*

Harry sat on the edge of the bed to pull on his socks, then leaned across and kissed her cheek. "I'll leave you to dress in peace, sweetheart."

Dear Harry. He was everything she wanted or needed. Considerate. Thoughtful. Loving. Spoiling her in little ways that meant so much. The breakfasts in bed, all the beautiful bunches of flowers he bought her, the gentle way he grabbed hold of her hand when she passed by his chair. How his face lit up with delight when she entered a room - things she wasn't accustomed to. It was hard to believe it was really happening to her. That here she was at thirty-six, starting over, in love with a wonderful man and living in such a beautiful house.

Watching him as he combed his damp hair, she wondered still if she were dreaming all this, dreading the thought of waking up and finding herself back in bed in that pokey terraced house close to Heathrow Airport, with Alex snoring from the next bedroom loud enough to drown out the roar of any jumbo jet. Would she yet wake to find her life was the same dreary pattern as it always had been before Harry had stepped off a train at Paddington Station and into her life?

Her cheeks swelled along with her smile at the memory. How, seeing her predicament when she'd dropped her open handbag - her arm in a sling, such a hindrance - this handsome stranger had rushed to her aid, bought her a coffee. That was eight months ago. Now she was here, in glorious Gloucestershire, having finally moved in with him after weeks of secret meetings whenever he could get to London. After lengthy phone calls during the day when Alex was at work. After talks and kisses slowly persuaded her to get out of a stifling marriage. And bit by bit, day by day, she had fallen more and more in love with Harry.

She filled her head with lyrics and melody of her favourite song, desperate to override the other tune still clinging there. *"Harry makes me smile..."* He certainly did that all right, she thought, and a lot more besides. She held out her arm.

"Pinch me, Harry. Let me know I'm not dreaming all this. I'm so frightened the bubble will burst?"

He laughed as he turned from the dressing table. "Darling, you ask me that every day. If I were to pinch you every time you would be covered in bruises, and I'd be locked up for assault. Wife-battering even!" His smile slipped.

She sensed his regret at mentioning bruises. Probably wanted to kick himself for reminding her. But these little slips were bound to happen sometimes, she told herself. It didn't matter, they were of no consequence.

He blew a kiss from the doorway. "Coffee in fifteen minutes."

In her hand she caught the love token, lay back against the pillow and listened to his retreating footfalls as he took the stairs two at a time, jumping the last two as always.

If someone had told her life could change so rapidly, become so blissfully tranquil and perfect, she once wouldn't have believed them. But it was true. As the days and weeks had slipped by, he had filled each waking moment with pleasure, each hour of darkness with such tender love she thought her heart would burst from so much devotion.

Hounslow seemed a thousand light years away instead of a hundred-odd miles. Ten years of married hell over. Almost over, she reminded herself with a jolt. There was still the matter of the divorce to deal with. But yes, Harry was right. Life was good. Apart from one black cloud forever lurking below the horizon, gripping on at its edge, always threatening to spoil things - Alex.

Like that annoying little tune still duelling with the other inside her head, Alex wouldn't go away. Her thoughts returning to him at inopportune moments, always skulking there in the back of her mind, waiting to pounce.

Why won't he let go of me and let us all get on with our lives?

With every ring of the telephone, each persistent knock on the door, she dreaded it would be him. Each day living in trepidation that he would turn up at the house. It could surely only be a matter of time before he found out where she was, and he would be here, thumping on the door, demanding she come home with him at once.

There had been no remorse in leaving Alex. No pangs of guilt or tinges of sorrow, merely relief when she closed the door on the West London house for the last time. But there were tears. Tears of regret that she hadn't had the courage to do it sooner. When Harry had rushed to her that day she'd arrived at Hill House and pulled her into his arms before she was even fully out of the car, she knew she had done the right thing. Harry would always take care of her. Keep her safe. Love her.

But she feared the repercussions. Revenge was the sort of thing Alex was capable of. He'd pick a fight with Harry, come in with arms flaying, blaming everyone but himself.

This looming threat worried her, not that she had spoken of these fears to Harry. He had his own past to deal with. Her physical wounds and bruises had healed; his were still sore. Emotional scars that would be with him for eternity, so why make him suffer any more than he already had by worrying over the baggage of her past.

If only he would talk about Lorna and little Sam and Elly more, speak about the accident instead of clamming up every time she tentatively broached the subject. They were a part of him she wanted to share yet she knew so little about them. She needed to understand, to know that part she hadn't yet been able to reach.

"Sweetheart, it's nearly brewed." Harry's voice calling from downstairs scattered her thoughts.

"On my way." Extricating herself from the tangled sheets, she headed for the bathroom, a spring in her step as she sang, "Harry is my love..."

Harry was on the landline phone when she came down. Acknowledging her presence at the foot of the stairs, he winked and smiled at her as he continued listening down the receiver. He then gave an animated shrug and exhaled a heavy sigh, as if trying to hold back his annoyance before speaking to the caller.

"I said I would, and I'm not a man to break my word, least of all to you." A pause as he listened again, then, "Yes, for the thousandth time, I will be there." Another pause while the caller spoke.

Penny had never heard Harry sound so rattled when he answered, "Look, will you please stop this. I keep telling you, I'm all right. The last thing I want is some man-hungry, money seeking bimbo hanging on my arm for the entire evening. Apart from which—"

Although curious to know whom he was talking with, Penny headed towards the kitchen at the far end of the hall, wanting to let him finish his conversation without her hovering like some nosey eavesdropper.

With each step she took, the light in the hallway darkened by quickening degrees. By the time she'd reached the kitchen doorway, rain hit the window in a sudden deluge. Amidst the sound of lashing raindrops she thought she could hear music. A tinny, annoying sound playing in the background, like someone's iPod playing on way too loud through headphones. Determining the music must be coming from the telephone, she shook her head in disbelief. Why on earth didn't the caller turn the darned thing down? Better still, turn it off. If she could hear it from this distance, what must it be like at the other end? No wonder Harry sounded crotchety, that row blasting his eardrum.

"No, you don't! You've no bloody idea how I feel," Harry's angry voice bellowed out, causing her to jolt.

She swivelled to see his face flushed, his brow creased in a scowl. Whoever was on the other end of the phone had obviously prodded a raw nerve. That annoyed her. They had no right to upset him like this. She hurried back down the hallway, wanting to give him comfort. When she touched his arm gently to let him know she was there, he pulled her towards him, clutching at her waist and kissing her cheek lightly.

"I lost my entire world," he spoke into the handset, his voice calmer. "How could you know what it feels like to lose your wife and children? ... No! You're wrong. I'd been living in a void ever since, a nothingness, until the day I met—" He stopped, listened, then in a subdued tone, said, "Yes, I know you miss them too, but I do wish you'd understand I'm doing okay as I am. I'm dealing with things at my own pace, and now that—"

The caller interrupted him again. Penny couldn't hear what was said, but it made Harry chuckle, immediately lifting the taut atmosphere in the hallway.

"Look, don't worry, Elaine, I will be there." He paused, listening. "Yes, yes... I'll do my best to look like I'm enjoying myself, I promise." There was a saucy grin on his face as he spoke, all the while his gaze concentrated on her, a mischievous glint in his eyes. "Look, I have to rush. Lots still to do... Seven-thirty. Cabot Room. Top table. Yes, got all that. By the way, I'm bringing someone so please don't arrange—" Another interruption. "For the hundredth time, woman, I won't be late! Now go away and stop fussing."

The call ended, he pulled Penny closer still but instead of kissing her as she'd expected him to do, he wrinkled his nose up and frowned.

"That funny smell's back, Pen, have you noticed? You don't think it's the furniture polish, do you?"

She shook her head. "I shouldn't have thought so, it's a new can. Apart from which, I haven't done any polishing the past few days." She sniffed the air. "I can't smell anything. Really, Harry, I'm beginning to think you imagine it."

"No. I can smell it all around us." He inhaled the air again, his top lip curling slightly in disdain.

On the windowsill sat a small, blue china dish of potpourri. She picked it up and lightly poked the faded flower petals with a finger, then sniffed at the offending bowl.

"Maybe it's this. I'll throw it away. Who was that on the phone?"

He pulled her back to him. "That was the inimitable Elaine Frampton, checking up on me. I've told you about Elaine, haven't I?"

She nodded. "A little."

Elaine was secretary of the Emerson's Trust, set up by Harry with his life-long friend and business partner, Peter Ballantyne, following the Nepal earthquake in 2015. With support from a large number of eminent politicians and celebrities, the Trust had raised considerable sums of money to help fund rebuilding projects there and in other places around the world since. But there was still an awful lot about Elaine she didn't know.

"She was being her usual, highly efficient, highly organized self," Harry explained. "Ringing to make sure I hadn't forgotten about the dinner on Friday evening. A good job she did too, else—" He stopped, head cocked to one side as if listening.

"What's wrong?"

"I thought I could hear something."

"Probably that music still echoing in your ears," she quipped. "Why didn't you ask her to turn it down?"

His eyebrows narrowed, a puzzled look on his face. "What music?"

"That radio or television she had on in the background. I could hear it from the other end of the hall. It's a miracle you could hear anything at all, small wonder you were shouting."

"Was I?" He looked even more puzzled. "But, Penny... there was no music playing. Not that I heard, anyway."

A loud clap of thunder shook the roof, making them both jump. A few petals tumbled from the dish she held and fell to the floor.

"Doesn't it ever stop raining here?" she asked light-heartedly. "It seems like that's all it's done since I arrived. Anyway, what dinner?"

"Sorry, sweetheart, I had forgotten all about it. It's for the Trust, planned ages ago. Elaine was worried in case I didn't turn up. She knows how much I hate these events."

"And she was supposed to be your date for the night?" she teased.

Harry chortled. "You have got to be joking. No way! Elaine isn't my type. Too loud and far too bossy. No, she's forever trying to fix me up with someone even though I'm constantly telling her I'm not interested, I can find my own date, thank you very much. She is a superb organizer, mind, I'll give her that, but she's enough to drive any man to exasperation." He grimaced apologetically. "I know I shouldn't say things like that about her because she was a real brick following the accident. Looking after the house and everything. Making sure I had food in the cupboard and a clean shirt to put on. I'm sure I've told you. She helped to keep me going through the grimmest of days. You must think me most uncharitable towards her," he added.

"Why ever should I think that?"

He shrugged. "There's been times when I've been rather harsh on poor old Elaine. She misses Lorna and the children, you see. She was Sam and Elly's godmother. She loved those two tykes as if they were her own. She took their deaths badly."

"I can understand that."

"Believe me, I've lost count of the number of times I've watched her collapse into heaps of tears at the merest mention of them, the slightest memory setting her off. I found that difficult to deal with. I know it was hard for everyone who knew Lorna and the kids to accept what had happened, but they all had their own fulfilling lives to carry on with, while I had nothing except a large, empty house full of memories and the knowledge that I was partly to blame for what happened." He turned away, staring out through the window, his forehead pressed against the glass.

"Harry, how can you say that? You said yourself Lorna was driving the car, taking the children to school." That and the fact he wasn't even in the car at the time, so how could he hold himself culpable?

Guilt's part of the grieving process, isn't it? Is that what he's still going through, all this blaming himself for all that happened?

She stared at his back, imploring him to turn around and talk about it some more, to free himself of the angst he carried, weighing him down like a concrete block tied to his legs. She couldn't even guess what was going through his mind right now.

"Why don't you want to tell me about what actually happened that day, Harry? It might make things easier for you.

You can't keep hiding your feelings like this from me. It's not good for you. For us." She reached out and gently touched his arm.

At that moment the hallway lit up in dazzling electric white light as the sky ripped itself open with sheet lightning. Seconds later, a thunderous crash exploded overhead. Windows rattled. The thunder continued reverberating and rolling around the hillside for several minutes.

Listening as the roar diminished, on the air she caught a whiff of perfume. The sweet scent of lily of the valley emanating from... she couldn't quite determine. She sniffed the potpourri again. Amongst its dusty overtones of rose and lavender came the merest hint of patchouli. No, that's not it, she thought. As she looked up again, a flicker of movement across the hallway caught the corner of her eye. A shimmer of light, a whisper of gossamer that vanished so quickly, she doubted it had been there at all.

Harry still had his back towards her. His dejected stance tugged again on her heartstrings. Poor man, she thought, he'd been to hell and back whilst, in comparison, her past had been only complicated. A bad marriage, a spiteful bullying husband, the pending divorce. Things that, although painful, were nothing compared to the gut-wrenching devastation of grief he had endured. The death of your partner was bad enough, to have to bury your kids too must be the worst misery of all. God, they were only seven and nine years old! Their lives just beginning. She couldn't begin to imagine what it felt like to lose everyone you loved in one fell swoop.

Finally, he turned to her, his face brightening as a smile formed on his lips, not enough to raise his cheeks but enough to light his eyes and ease the tension in the atmosphere.

"The past has gone now, Pen. It'll always be there, but we have our future together to consider. I don't want to keep looking backwards, and neither must you. Why torture ourselves? Going over old ground, digging up the hurt isn't the way. It's all Elaine talks about whenever I see her. It doesn't help."

Penny sighed. "Promise me one thing..."

He nodded. "Anything."

"That one day you *will* tell me all about it. If we're going to be together, we shouldn't have any secrets. We need to know everything about each other, the good and the bad. Total honesty. I don't want any ghosts of our lives lurking in cupboards, waiting to sneak up and bite either one of us when we're least expecting it. Promise?"

"I promise, sweetheart. When the time's right. When I'm ready. Now, about this dinner..."

Chapter 4

From its place propped against a book on the shelf, Harry lifted down the invitation and reread the gold lettering. The thought of having to listen to all those mundane speeches, no doubt rehearsed over and over again until they'd lost all their spontaneity, filled him with dread. He tucked the invitation into the top pocket of the jacket of his dinner suit laid out on the bed.

Penny was pampering herself in the bathroom; her new black evening dress hanging from the wardrobe door in readiness. He hoped it wouldn't be too dull an evening for her, with all the hand-shaking and air kissing and the be nice to so-and-so because he's made a considerable donation this year palaver.

It might well all be for a good cause but, to him, it seemed an extravagant waste of money putting on such events. It was all such a long way from the organization he and Peter had originally set up, positive in his belief that once all the sums were totted up, the donations would equal the outlay of tonight's bash, and all that would result would be a lot of hangovers.

He shouldn't be so pessimistic, he knew, but it played on his mind, dulling his enthusiasm. As was the fact he hadn't written his own speech yet. He was supposed to deliver the welcome address and introduce the chief guest and speaker, Aaron Lucking MP. Oh well, too late now, he would have to wing it. It was a good job he knew Aaron from their university days together at Oxford; he had several amusing stories he could recount.

Half-dressed, he stood at the dressing table, rummaging through the drawers, hunting for the black leather box containing his treasured gold cufflinks. He caught sight of his face staring back at him from the mirror.

Taking a long, hard, critical look, he studied the furrowed brow, convinced he was no oil painting where good looks were concerned, and at forty-two no young stud either. One or two grey strands were beginning to appear in his jet-black hair. It was a wonder his whole head hadn't turned white after all he'd endured, more than most men in a complete lifetime, he thought, wondering what on earth Penny ever saw in him.

Turning his attention back to the drawer, he found the small box buried under a pile of underpants. Relieved, he opened the lid. The cufflinks were oblong, designed to look like skyscrapers inset with minuscule diamonds fashioned to represent windows. He loved the way their facets caught in the light and sparkled brilliantly, but they were fiddly to put in. In the struggle, one link fell from his grasp.

"Bugger it!" He was on the floor in an instant, crawling around on all fours, feeling through the thick pile of the cream carpet. "Why do they always make the buttonholes too small for these things?" He lay flat on the carpet, peering under the dressing table. "It has to be here," he muttered.

Something lightly touched his cheek. He brushed it away, thinking it a loose hair, a stray cobweb, a fleck of dust, but some deeper instinct told him it was material. Soft satin. Smooth silk. He caught a whiff of perfume. Familiar. Momentarily, he thought it was Lorna who had touched him, letting him know she was still with him. The thought sent a shudder down his back and brought a lump to his throat.

"Here, let me help." Penny was on her knees beside him, a fluffy white bath towel encasing her naked body and a smaller one turbaned around her damp hair. The cufflink recovered, her nimble fingers quickly manipulated the thin gold chain through the buttonhole in his shirt cuff.

"Lorna always had to do them up for me, too. She gave them to me, a birthday present. Her last to me," he blurted out, then wanted to kick himself for being so tactless.

Penny smiled. "She had good taste."

Tenderly, he kissed the top of Penny's head, appreciating how understanding she was. What would he do now without her? She looked utterly ravishing. Unable to resist the urge, he began walking his fingers down her neck slowly towards the bath towel, intent on removing it. The grandfather clock chiming the half-hour interrupted the moment.

"Time's getting on. Aren't we supposed to be there soon?"

The sexy rasp of her voice told him she was as tempted as him to be late. Reluctantly, he let her go.

"Then I'd better get my skates on before Elaine Bossy Boots comes knocking to check I've washed behind my ears. No doubt she'll check you out too; see if you're suitable for me and not simply after my money."

"Let her try," came Penny's jovial retort as she went back into the bathroom.

Was it his imagination, he asked himself a short while later as he pulled on his overcoat, or had the atmosphere in the hallway changed?

He peered through the hall window up at the large black cloud dropping its cargo of rain on the hill. But it did appear to be lifting, he thought, noticing bright streaks of blue appearing above the treetops. The rain was easing too.

A shaft of evening sunlight burst through the cloud and beamed across the flagstone floor. Along its golden length danced a thousand dust motes in time to a tune only they could hear. The evening light streaming in was dazzling. Surreal. His hair bristled, a weird sensation coursing through his body. It felt as if the whole world had tilted on its axis and nothing would ever be the same again.

Hearing a faint rustling sound behind him, a swish of material, he turned, expecting to see Penny coming down the stairs but they were empty, the bedroom door still closed.

The sudden honk of a car horn jolted him.

"The car's here," he called, shrugging off the strange feeling that had come over him.

"Coming!" The bedroom door opened. Penny appeared on the landing.

The sight of her took his breath away. She looked so beautiful. The full-length silk dress shimmered with black sequins as she gracefully took each stair. Her hair, swept back off her face and pinned high to one side of her head with long ringlets tumbling down the other side of her neck and over her bare shoulder, looked stunning. New dangling silver earrings glinted, as did the matching silver and diamond necklace nestled into her décolletage.

Aware the air felt lighter, fresher, he imagined he could see his old life escaping, evaporating now he had let down the barriers, lowered the drawbridge to his isolation and allowed the future to flood into Hill House. He let out a light laugh.

"What? Have I got my dress caught in my knickers or something? It wouldn't be the first time..." She looked about herself, checking.

"No, no. Merely a foolish thought. About me. You look stunning, darling. Then again, you always look ravishing in anything you wear. If you wore jeans and a t-shirt tonight, you'd still be the belle of the ball."

"Charmer! Alex always said I looked fat in jeans."

"Trouble with him is he didn't appreciate what he had. More fool him. His loss. My gain."

When she joined him at the bottom of the stairs, he pulled her into his arms and kissed her, wishing he could take her here, now. He felt himself rising. But he mustn't. It would make them late. The thought of what Elaine would say at their arriving flushed, Penny's hair dishevelled, his suit creased, made him smile widely. He kissed Penny again, reluctant to let go but knew he must.

For a moment Hill House was filled with silence before another brief splatter of rain hit the window. A wild wind rushed through the budding trees outside. Over it, he thought he could hear another sound, something out of place, one that shouldn't be there. He tilted his head, listening, trying to make out what it was.

It was music. Soft, distant notes, drifting on the air.

"I think you've left the CD player on upstairs." As soon as the words left his mouth the music ceased.

Penny shot him a perplexed look. "I can't have done; I didn't have it on."

"Oh! I could have sworn... How odd."

"Certainly is," she agreed. "I thought I heard music the other night when you were away. Thought I'd left the radio on in the kitchen. I hadn't. Goodness knows where it had come from."

"Probably someone driving along the lane with the windows open and blaring music playing."

"But it was raining that night. Who in their right mind would have been driving around in the pouring wet with car windows wound down?"

Settling into the taxi, Penny tried to keep down the nerves bubbling up inside at the prospect of meeting all Harry's friends. Wondering what they would all make of her. Did she look okay? Was her hair okay? Was the dress suitable despite Harry's insistence how stunning she looked? She didn't want to let him down.

"You've gone quiet, Pen. Is everything okay?"

"Just nervous. I won't know anyone there. Not even your business partner. I've never met him."

"What, Peter Ballantyne? But you've spoken to him on the phone countless times. He rings practically every day."

"That's not the same thing."

"You'll be fine, sweetheart." He gave her hand a reassuring squeeze. "And I shall take great delight in introducing you to the gang, especially Elaine. Who knows, with luck she might get off my back now. Don't look so worried, sweetheart, you'll love them to bits, as they will you."

Easy for him to say, she thought, but she wasn't so convinced. It took her time to get to know people and feel comfortable with them.

Here's that old confidence deficit showing through again. Confidence knocked out of me by Alex.

But she did want to meet his friends, they were part of his life, his world, a world she now shared, and she couldn't stay hidden forever.

"Where did you say the dinner's being held?" She hoped it wouldn't be anywhere too fancy, not trusting her habit of knocking over things when nervous, knowing she wouldn't be able to relax and would be on edge all the time. She wanted to be enthusiastic but didn't want to embarrass him in front of anyone. She wanted to make a good impression.

"The Beverley. Best hotel in Bristol. Top notch chef and

top-rate food. You'll dine like a queen... as long as you don't have a big appetite." He winked. "One of those sod-all-on-a-big-plate places, you know the kind."

Her mind conjured up images of dainty morsels of garlicky food served on huge slivers of slate, with tiny dollops of sauce dripped sparingly around the edges by some dizzy chef who thought he was Picasso in another life.

As the taxi sped towards the main road at the foot of the hill, she also wondered what Elaine was like and what Elaine would think of her.

Chapter 5

With his reassuring arm around her waist, Harry escorted her through to the Ambassador suite. A cacophony of wall-to-wall sound greeted them from a sea of strangers, many gathered in groups, everyone chattering at once. Loud bursts of laughter rang through the air, and countless glasses clinked.

She lost count of how many circular tables there were, each neatly draped with starched, white damask tablecloths. At least fifty, she estimated. At each place setting, silver cutlery gleamed and glasses sparkled in flickering candlelight. Pale-blue linen napkins had been folded cleverly into roses, marking each place. At the far end of the room, by the table nearest the raised podium, she recognised Aaron Lucking, the Minister for Foreign Aid, in conversation with a slender woman wearing a figure-hugging dark blue cocktail dress, champagne glass in hand.

"Is that Aaron's wife?" she asked Harry. "She's a lot younger than him."

"No. That's Elaine," Harry uttered when the woman looked in their direction and gave a small wave.

So this was the woman who had held Harry's life together and kept the Emerson's Trust running like clockwork, thought Penny, feeling in awe of the tall, willowy and confident woman who'd immediately excused herself from the guest of honour, set her glass down on the table, and was now striding across the room in their direction, a broad smile set on her face.

"Harry, darling. I'm so relieved you're here." Elaine greeted him with a large kiss on the cheek. "Oops! I've gone and put lipstick over you, naughty me." She rubbed at it with a finger whilst eyeing Penny up and down with caution. "And who's this glorious creature? You never told me you were bringing someone." She held out a hand to Penny. "Elaine Frampton. And you are...?"

Harry removed Elaine's other hand firmly clasping his arm. "This is Penny, the new light in my life. She's recently moved in with me at Hill House." There was a mischievous grin on his face, prompting a look of flustered surprise on Elaine's.

"Oh! But... I thought you... Oh dear, do excuse me a moment. I must go over and say hello to someone." Elaine darted off towards a group of people standing near the bar before either of them could answer.

"Gosh, is she always like that?" Penny asked, watching Elaine now in animated conversation with a slim brunette woman wearing a short, tight-fitting red dress and red painfully thin high heels.

Harry laughed. "Yes, always. But she has a heart of gold."

"I think she fancies you."

Harry looked bemused. "You do? Not a chance... Ah, there's Peter. Come and say hello to him. He's been dying to meet you in the flesh."

The vichyssoise followed by spring lamb noisettes in a tarragon sauce passed Penny's lips without being savoured, so enthralled was she with Harry's conversation to one side of her, and Peter's sparkling chat and wit to her left. She'd taken an instant liking to Peter; he'd made her feel at ease, and within a few minutes of talking with him felt she had known him forever.

"More wine?" he asked, lifting the half-empty bottle.

"Yes, please."

As Peter topped up her glass, she looked across to Elaine in deep conversation with Aaron. Elaine must have felt her gaze, for she turned her head slightly and gave Penny a friendly smile, before turning her attention back to the minister.

"Elaine's done a great job again organizing this shindig," Peter said. "And a great choice of wine too, but then, we wouldn't expect anything less from her."

"It must have taken a lot of work," Penny agreed. She glanced across the table again, admiring Elaine's short blonde hair perfectly coiffed in a layered cut that framed her oval face perfectly. Her hands were equally well manicured, long nails painted dark blue and decorated with gold motifs. Penny looked down at her own hand, fiddling idly with her full wine glass. Short, and lacquered only with clear gloss, she wished now she'd taken the plunge at the hairdressers that afternoon and agreed to have them pampered.

Suddenly, her glass toppled, spilling red wine over the tablecloth.

Harry grabbed at his napkin and began mopping up. "Don't worry, no damage done."

Embarrassed and annoyed with her clumsiness, and feeling everyone's eyes around the table on her as a waiter rushed over to help, she knew her blush went deeper than the merlot staining the damask cloth.

She saw Elaine watching her. Smiling, Elaine nodded slightly. A reassuring nod and a friendly smile, Penny thought. One telling her that all was okay. A smile that made her relax as the waiter removed the sodden napkin and placed a fresh wine glass in front of her.

"I did that last year," Peter whispered, then laughed before saying, "And accidently managed to spill some on Elaine's dress at the same time. She was furious."

"I bet she was," Penny said. She glimpsed across the table again. Elaine still wore a wide smile as she continued talking to Aaron.

Removing her earrings, Penny dropped them onto the hall table, at the same time kicking off her high heels.

"God, my feet are killing me. I don't think I've ever danced so much."

Harry helped her out of her coat, brushed off the slight peppering of rain, then hung it on a peg on the hallstand before divesting himself of his own damp coat and pulling off his bow tie.

"Wasn't too a bad night, was it, Pen? Did you enjoy it?"

"Mmm, very much. I don't know what I was so worried about, they're all lovely people."

Even the food had lived up to his promise, the champagne excellent, and she'd only embarrassed herself once when she'd knocked over her wine glass.

"Elaine seems nice too," she added, "and nowhere near as bad an ogre as you made her out to be. I thought she was rather sweet. Mind you, I did think she was going to go apoplectic when she realized Peter had muddled up her seating plan, swapping all the place names around before everyone arrived."

"He does that every time. His little joke. It was Paddy Olson's suggestion of everyone moving around to different tables after each course that did it finally for me. Poor Elaine took him so seriously at first until she saw he was kidding."

"It was mean of you all. She'd obviously gone to a great deal of effort, and you all should be more gracious and thankful towards her. I wouldn't blame her in the least if she told you where to stick the Trust and walk out on the job. Then where would you all be?"

Seated on the third stair, Harry pulled off his shoes, wriggling his toes in their new-found freedom. "Elaine knows us well enough by now, she's used to a bit of joshing. Takes it all in good fun. Nightcap?"

Penny unpinned her hair and shook it loose, immediately regretting her action as a throbbing pain shot through her skull, making her feel queasy.

"No thanks. I think I've had quite enough to drink tonight. I'm not used to it. How much did I have?"

"I wasn't counting. What did you think of Peter?"

"Utterly charming, and he certainly enjoyed himself dancing all evening. He hardly sat down. Elaine couldn't leave him alone."

"That's because she couldn't get her hands on me. She usually drags me out onto the dance floor as soon as the music starts. Always telling me we have to encourage everyone else to get up because no one likes being first." Giving up the attempt to remove his cufflinks, he held his arms out helplessly.

Penny removed the links deftly and put them next to her earrings on the table. "Peter certainly was a lot of fun; all those rude jokes he told. I haven't laughed so much since I can't remember when. Do you think he'll ever marry again?"

"I do hope so, Pen. He deserves some happiness. His wife was such a lovely lady. Having lost her – Freda died of breast cancer, did I tell you? – he knew precisely what I was going through after the accident. He helped me enormously, as did Elaine. I'm glad you like him. He's besotted with you, you know. I can see I shall have to watch the two of you else he'll be stealing you away from me." His banter was light-hearted, amusement in his eyes.

"It would be nice to invite him over one evening for dinner."

"Good idea," Harry agreed. "We could also invite Elaine and see if we can't pair them off properly."

"Did you see that look on her face when you told her I'd moved in with you? I'm not sure if it was shock, horror, delight or jealousy."

Harry laughed. "Knowing Elaine, probably all four."

"Oh, you!" She punched him playfully in the ribs.

Clutching his middle, much to her horror he doubled over, staying in that position for far longer than someone clowning around.

"Harry? Harry! What is it? What's wrong?" Panic filled her heart, fearing the worst.

When he started laughing, she could see he was messing about. She was about to dig him in the ribs again when he said, "That strange smell's still here."

She sniffed the air. "I can't smell anything. Come on, let's go to bed. It's late." Exhausted but happy, she climbed the stairs. Harry followed.

Halfway up she stopped and looked over her shoulder at him. "Did you hear that?"

He bumped into her, grabbing her by the waist. "Hear what?"

"I thought I heard whispering. From the sitting room. You did turn off the television earlier, didn't you?"

"Of course I did. You daft ha'ppeth, if anyone was in there whispering, you wouldn't have heard them, would you?"

She considered this a moment, then conceded his point

and was about to continue up the stairs when Harry said, "Stay there a moment, I'll go check. What with smells and music and now whispering, this seems to be a night of weird goings-on."

He opened the sitting room door and turned on the light. "It's okay, it's all fine, sweetheart. Everything's off. You must have imagined it." He shut the door again.

"Must have. Sorry," she muttered, but already her mind had moved on, listening instead to music playing in her head – the last catchy dance tune of the evening, the one before the five-piece group played their final slow number. She stumbled up the remaining few stairs. Beneath the refrains of the song, vague undertones of another tune played until the melodies intertwined and became so muddled, she couldn't distinguish one from the other.

Harry unzipped her dress, allowing it to slide gently to the floor. Holding onto his forearm for balance, she side-stepped ungainly out of the crumpled dress, unsteady on her feet.

"I think I'm a little drunk," she confessed, swaying. "Do you know, I can still hear that band playing. They were good. Do *you* ever get that feeling?" She stabbed several times at her ruffled hair. "You hear a song and then it won't go away. Instead, it plays in your head all day."

"Sometimes," he said, helping her into bed, "but it soon stops."

Chapter 6

The ring on the doorbell was insistent. Bleary-eyed from the excesses of the Emerson's Trust dinner the night before, Penny was astonished to see Elaine, looking fresh, radiant and immaculate in a cream trouser suit and peach satin blouse, standing inside the open porch.

"Where's Harry?" Elaine demanded before Penny had fully opened the front door. "I need to speak with him. It's urgent."

No hello, or good morning, or sorry to disturb you. Charming!

"I'm afraid he's not here," Penny told her. "He had to go over to Cheltenham this morning with Peter. To meet a client."

"What? On a Saturday? They never said anything about it last night. I'll wait for him. He won't mind." Elaine pushed by without waiting to be invited in.

But I mind, thought Penny, as she watched Elaine flounce down the hallway, removing her leather driving gloves as she headed straight into the sitting room as if she owned the place. Penny stared after her in disbelief.

Just who does she think she is, barging in like this?

With her head pounding, the effects of a few aspirins and a glass of liver salts to disperse her hangover yet to kick in, the last thing she needed or wanted was company, especially someone as ill-mannered as Elaine behaved this morning. She couldn't believe such a change in character.

By the time Penny caught up with her, Elaine had made herself comfortable on the leather sofa and was flicking through the pages of a magazine from off the coffee table. Appearing uninterested by its content, Elaine slammed the cover shut then tidied the pile and gazed about the room.

"Glad to see you haven't changed things in here," she said. "Lorna wouldn't have liked that. She had a precise place for everything. I do have to say this, and forgive me for being honest, but I was more than shocked when Harry turned up with you last night. He could at least have given me warning."

"He tried. Over the phone, the other day when you called. You didn't give him a chance."

"You mean you were listening in to our conversation? Well, really—"

"I was standing right by him."

Elaine sniffed. "I didn't know what to think, or what to tell Wendy Beckingham. I'd arranged weeks ago for her to accompany Harry. It was embarrassing."

I really don't give a stuff how awkward it was for you! Harry did try to tell you.

Elaine might have been all charm, graciousness and polite conversation yesterday evening, but this morning's attitude showed another, unexpected, side. She may have been too caught up in the spectacle of last night's extravaganza to see it then, but she could certainly see it now. No, that was no smile of reassurance or friendship Elaine had given her over the spilt wine. It was one of smugness. She'd actually enjoyed her embarrassment! But why? Then it dawned on her. Elaine really was in love with Harry and saw her as a threat. She actually resented her relationship with him.

Well, tough, madam! He's mine. I'm here and for good, so get used to it, missy. Harry was right about you, after all.

She was about to ask Elaine to leave and come back later, like next year, then remembered the woman was nevertheless a friend and colleague of Harry's, and he might not appreciate her being uncivil towards this woman who had helped him over his bad times, even if she was behaving in such a snotty manner now. She at least had better offer the unwelcome visitor a drink. With a bit of luck, Elaine would decline.

"Coffee. Black. No sugar."

"No please or thank you, then," Penny muttered under her breath, as she made her way to the kitchen. She half-expected Elaine to follow and oversee she made the coffee correctly. She could well understand now why this woman exasperated Harry if this was how she carried on. She'd have to think of an excuse to get rid of her. She didn't want her in the house a moment longer.

"I don't know how long Harry will be and I've got to go out presently," she called from the kitchen. "He could be gone all day. Perhaps you'd be better giving him a call later."

"No matter, I'm in no rush. I'll wait," Elaine called back. "You run along and do what you have to do. I'm sure I can find something to do to keep me occupied. I know my way around."

I bet you do. Like snooping upstairs or rearranging the kitchen utensils.

Carrying the tray of coffee things into the sitting room, her eyes were drawn immediately to the fireplace. The blue glass vase she had placed on the windowsill because she thought it looked better there where it caught the changing natural daylight, was back in the small alcove by the side of the inglenook. Elaine must have moved it whilst she was out of the room.

Of all the flaming nerve! How dare she?

Penny banged the tray down on the coffee table, then stomped across to the fireplace, picked up the vase and returned it back to its place in the window, setting it down with a forceful thud. She gazed quickly around the room, seeking anything else out of place.

"Excuse me, but this is my house now, and I'll thank you to leave things where I put them."

Elaine scowled through narrowed green eyes. "I do have to say, Penelope... It is Penelope, isn't it?"

"It's Penny."

Unperturbed, Elaine continued, "As I was saying, I for one will be livid if Harry gets hurt again. He's been through hell and back these last few years. He needs stability in his life, he's still vulnerable. I hope you aren't messing with his affections."

"I beg your pardon!" Penny was so taken aback by the hurtful remark she thought she would explode. *The gall of the woman!* What had started as mild annoyance had now risen close to fury. "Now, you look here, Elaine Frampton, I can assure you I have no intention of hurting Harry. For your information, I too haven't had things easy over the years. I would have thought you being his friend, you would be only too glad to see him happy?"

"Do you have children?" Elaine's question was full of insinuation even if her voice had softened slightly.

"What the hell has that got to do with anything? No, I don't have children. Why, do you?"

"Then you obviously do not appreciate how fragile Harry is."

Elaine had avoided answering her question, she noted. However indirect it might have been, it at least warranted an acknowledgement. Ramming the plunger down in the cafetière, venting her anger on the chromium rod instead, Penny wished she had the nerve to throw the whole pot over this irritating woman. Pushing aside these thoughts of all-out warfare, she smiled, tight-lipped, determined she wasn't going to be goaded any further.

"And tell me, Elaine, have you ever been married?" She waited for an answer, at the same time thinking Elaine couldn't help being the way she was and, well, when all was said and done, she had taken care of Harry in the past, and probably only had his best interests at heart. She supposed that did allow her some say on Harry's future wellbeing, no matter how small. Breathing slowly, deeply, determined to calm herself, she poured out the coffee.

A thought struck. In spite of how difficult it would be, if she tried to make conversation, kept on the right side of this woman no matter how infuriating, Elaine might be willing to fill in all the missing gaps about the accident Harry wouldn't talk about. If anything, she would at least like to know where it happened. Not out of morbid curiosity, far from it. It was more a need to know all the facts in order to understand him more, help ease his pain. It didn't mean she had to like the woman. And to think last night she'd been defending her.

Elaine took a sip of coffee, nodding her head slightly in approval; at least Penny hoped that's what it was.

After wiping the corner of her mouth with her little finger, Elaine said, "I've known Harry many years and knew Lorna even longer. We were at school together. I was chief bridesmaid at their wedding, did Harry tell you that? I thought not," she added when Penny shook her head. "Lorna's children were as close to me as any of my own would be. No, I've never married. No man has yet matched up to my expectations."

Penny fought down an irresistible urge to laugh, and through pursed lips uttered, "Yes, I can see you are a person with high standards."

Placing her cup and saucer back down on the table, Elaine took a deep breath before speaking again. "I have seen and felt the heartache this house has suffered and, believe me, to see Harry smiling and laughing again is wonderful. It is good for him that you are here, but..." She hesitated a moment. "How shall I put this...?" Another hesitancy. "You do have to admit it is all rather swift, your moving in with him. You've known each other what... seven, eight months? Not long. I don't want him to suffer any further if you decide you can't hack it here with the memories. After the novelty wears thin and you go swanning off back to London, or wherever it is you come from, *I* shall be the one left to pick up the pieces again."

Penny jumped to her feet. *Enough!*

About to let rip a fervent lashing of words, the telephone ringing in the hallway intercepted the rage ready to effervesce over into a full torrent. She excused herself to go and answer it.

"Sweetheart, I've got Peter with me. Okay to bring him back for a spot of lunch?"

"Of course, it is," Penny spoke quietly into the mouthpiece, shielding her mouth with her hand to prevent her visitor overhearing what she said, sensing Elaine was the kind of person who would be straining her ears, if not standing close to the door, listening to her conversation. "By the way, Elaine's here waiting to see you."

There was silence. She could tell Harry was thinking, the cogs in his brain whirling round.

"In that case, tell her I'm calling to say I won't be home until late this evening, and that I'll call her on Monday. Is she being okay with you?"

Penny lowered her voice to a whisper. "Frankly, no. She really is the most insufferable—"

In the background she could hear a muffled exchange of words, then Peter came on the line.

"Put Elaine on to me," he instructed. "I'll get rid of her for you. I've an errand I need running for the Trust. She won't refuse me."

Fifteen minutes later the phone rang again.

"Is the coast clear?"

Penny laughed. "Yes, you can both come home now. I don't think it was you she wanted to see anyway. I'm sure she came over solely to suss me out and see what changes I'd done to the house; see if they meet with her approval."

"I am sorry, sweetheart. I'll have to have words with her."

"Don't worry, there's no need. She left knowing in no uncertain terms where she stood and what my position is. I hope I haven't upset things between the two of you, though. You see, I wasn't particularly polite, I'm afraid."

Peter Ballantyne pushed his empty plate away with an appreciative look of satisfaction.

"That, my dear, was superb. Harry's a lucky man finding such a good cook."

"Go on with you," Penny dismissed his praise. "It was only a mushroom omelette, with a bit of salad. Anyone can rustle up that."

It had been an enjoyable meal, and along with Peter's witty conversation, banter and endless anecdotes, his relaxed manner made her feel at ease, warming more and more to his delightful company. As she reached out for his empty plate, she realized she knew exceedingly little about their guest.

"Peter, will you tell me something?"

"Of course."

"How did you and Harry meet? He's never said." She sat back down, eager to learn more about him.

Peter rubbed his chin. "Well now, let me see. We do go back a long way, don't we, old boy?" He looked to Harry for agreement.

Harry nodded. "We sure do. We lived next door to each other when we were children growing up in Fulham. We went through junior and senior schools together and to the same university. I studied architecture and urban design, Peter—"

"Mathematical science and technical drawing," Peter interrupted. "We've helped each other through all the happy times and propped up each other during the bad. I don't think I could have coped with losing Freda if Harry hadn't been around. He was best man at my wedding." He gave his lifelong friend a warm smile of kinship.

"And he at mine, but it's more than that," Harry continued. "Peter has always been there for me. Many a night, in the depths of my utter despair and desperation, he would come over, driving like a lunatic in the middle of the night to be with me. Helping me. He got drunk with me, cried with me, and even handed me plates from the cupboard to hurl at the walls during my fits of anger. It was Peter who swept up the pieces of my shattered life. It was also him who hauled me back up when I sank to rock bottom. I owe him far, far more than I will ever be able to pay back."

"I thought it was Elaine who had been your prop and anchor," she threw in with more than a hint of derision. The woman's actions that morning still riled.

"She was, to a degree. She took care of all the necessary things, like cleaning and shopping, making sure I ate, but she couldn't appreciate the rollercoaster of emotions I went through. It's different for a man, plus she's never lost anyone close before. Real close, that is."

Peter nodded. "That's right. You have to have been through it to feel it, but I did no more than what any other friend would have done given the circumstances. Harry and Lorna were there for me during Freda's illness. It's what friendship is all about, isn't it?"

"I wish I had friends," Penny said, feeling pangs of envy. "Real friends, that is. Before, it was no more than the wives of Alex's colleagues at the school where he taught. Superficial acquaintances. I suppose I've always been a bit of a loner. I had hoped Elaine and I could be friends, but after this morning's performance I can't see that's likely now."

Peter caught hold of her hand. "Don't worry about Elaine. She blows hot and cold. Always has, always will. Once she gets to know you better, she'll lighten up. She needs to step back a bit and take a look at what's happening to Harry. Give her time." He winked. "You know, it's that good seeing old Harry happy again, it's made me realize my little pad is far too big for me on my own. Time I uprooted myself and moved on. That place is like a mausoleum. Too many memories in too many rooms."

"Your *little* pad?" Harry queried with raised eyebrows. "Really, Peter...! You ought to see his "little' pad, Pen. Only happens to be one of the oldest and largest country houses this side of Tewkesbury. Huge. If you think Hill House is big, you ain't seen nothing yet."

Peter leaned back, his hands clasped behind his head. "He exaggerates somewhat, but you must get Harry to bring you over soon."

"I'll look forward to it. You've never looked to marry again? Aren't you ever lonely?"

"Sometimes," Peter admitted, a hint of sadness mixed with regret in his voice, "but most times no. I'm too set in my ways now, but I do miss Freda around the house. I'm afraid another woman would find it difficult to handle my idiosyncratic ways and eccentricities. And I have rather got used to my own routine. That's why I admire you so much, Penny. It couldn't have been easy moving into another woman's house with all that went on here."

"Whatever do you mean?" She noticed Harry shoot Peter a warning glance, a look that said: "Don't say any more or I'll throttle you." She wondered what was going on between them.

"What I mean is," Peter hurriedly said, "it must have been hard moving into another woman's home. Like moving in with the mother-in-law. All rather difficult and uncomfortable living amongst her things. Her kitchen. Wondering if it's all right to move this knick-knack there, or safe to throw something out that isn't really yours to discard."

"Oh, Peter, it's not like that at all," she exclaimed, re-minded of Elaine's tactless manoeuvre with the vase. "It's never felt that way. Harry's let me change things around how I want. It's not a problem. Right, time for coffee."

She stood again, quickly gathered up the pile of plates and dishes, then vanished into the kitchen from where the smell of freshly filtered coffee wafted through the open doorway.

Harry leaned across the dining table, his voice low.

"Don't you dare say anything about what happened, Peter Ballantyne."

Peter looked incredulous. "You mean you've not told her about Lorna?"

"Not the gory details, no."

"But you have to tell her," Peter whispered.

"Why? What on earth would it achieve? Absolutely nothing. How do I even start to explain I stood by and watched it all and did nothing?"

"But there was nothing you could have done to save them; the coroner told you that at the inquest. Lorna died instantly. For Christ's sake, man, she'll understand it wasn't your fault. You've got to stop blaming yourself."

"That's the whole point; it *was* my fault."

"Harry, it was an accident. Penny has a right to know," Peter pleaded.

"And I disagree. There's no need for her to know any of it. The horrors are mine to live with, not hers."

"If you don't tell her, someone else will, as sure as eggs are eggs. Then how do you think she'll feel then?"

He glared at Peter. "I'll tell her when I'm good and ready. When the timing's right."

"That's a coward's way out, Harry. There's never a good time, a right time. I should know."

The soft sound of Penny humming could be heard along with the rattle of china in the kitchen.

Harry shrugged. "I'm not a coward. And you of all people should know that I've only her best interest at heart."

"She deserves to know. You *have* to tell her."

"No, and nor will you. It's finished now. Finito!"

"Then you're a bloody fool, Harry Winchester."

Chapter 7

The sound of breaking glass outside the sitting room door sent Harry jumping up from the armchair and dashing into the hallway. Penny hurried after him to see shards of broken glass littering the flagstones and the hall table yet there was no visible sign as to what had caused the damage. No tell-tale stone or brick having been thrown through the window. Not even a stray tennis or football rolling around the floor.

Carefully treading over the debris, Harry went outside to investigate further while Penny fetched the broom and dustpan from the kitchen cupboard.

"You'd better come out here and see this," he called.

On the wet gravel beneath the window lay the motionless body of a cock pheasant, clearly dead, bits of glass scattered over it and the honey-coloured stones. With the back of his hand, Harry brushed away the glass splinters from the creature before picking it up. Its neck and head hung limply over the edge of his outstretched palms, its iridescent feathers damp from the falling rain.

Such a sorry end to a magnificent bird saddened her. "The poor thing must have flown straight into the window," she said.

"Something must have spooked it, probably a car," said Harry. "They're daft creatures, pheasants, always flying directly into danger instead of away from it, and they don't fly high either. I'll board up the window for now as we certainly won't get a glazier up here this evening to fix it. I'll go bury this, unless..." he looked at her, a glimmer of mirth in his eyes, "...unless you want it for the pot? I don't mind plucking and cleaning it."

"No, thanks. From the butcher is one thing; road kill, or in this case, window kill, I can do without."

Harry knotted his tie and slipped on his leather jacket.

"Darling, are you sure you don't mind being here on your own again? I feel awful leaving you behind, but I daren't delay this trip with Peter now that Tatterelle has finally agreed to our proposals. We need to get our signatures on that contract before he changes his mind again."

"Of course I don't mind. It's not your fault I can't come as planned. Sod's law that today of all days is the only time the glazier can get here. Someone has to be here. Leaving the house unattended with a boarded-up ground floor window is asking for trouble; anyone could break in. Besides, I'm sure you two will get more done without me trailing along. I'll be fine. Gives me the chance to do the housework in peace. Blitz the place." She hoped she hid her disappointment well.

"I still don't know why you don't get a cleaner in. You don't have to do it."

"It's my job to look after you now, not someone else's. Anyway, I like cleaning the house. It helps to make it feel more like my home."

"But—"

"You're a man, you have no idea how us women feel about these things. To most men, a house is simply somewhere to live, it doesn't matter who cleans it."

"I'm not like most men," he retorted, then smiled.

She couldn't argue that one. He was indeed a man in a million. A trillion. "Give my love to Paris."

He kissed her goodbye. "I'll take you there soon. I'll make it up to you, I promise."

Of that, she had no doubt, but the moment his car pulled out of the driveway, she carried a nervous uncertainty along with the plastic basket of cleaning paraphernalia as she went from room to room. The unease was something she couldn't quite put her finger on. She couldn't understand why today she felt more of a stranger here than ever, more even than on that first, nervous day after leaving Alex, when she'd swung the car off the road and through the gates of Hill House.

Despite her efforts to concentrate on the housework, she couldn't settle to polishing and dusting, even with the stereo blaring out. Nor could the seductive tenor voice of Andrea Bocelli or a resounding Mozart concerto soothe the overriding pressure of oppression that seemed to engulf her. The house felt bleak and empty, the atmosphere oppressive, made all the more depressing by the incessant rain that hadn't stopped falling for five days.

Ironing became a tedious chore with only a dull, old black-and-white war movie on television to watch whilst doing so. Nor was there anything interesting on the radio to listen to, just some stuffy local politician being interviewed about global warming.

Global warming? "Huh, that's a joke," she huffed, staring through the window, where outside, the rain was attempting to metamorphose into sleet. *God's sake, it's May, not flipping January!*

Giving up after pressing three shirts and a blouse, she went into the study, the intention to catch up on some letter writing. There were still several people she had yet to inform about her recent change of address, including her mother, something she'd been putting off since the day she'd arrived. She had let her sister, Anita, know her whereabouts, and no doubt Anita had told their mother, but she really ought to explain things herself.

She could telephone her, but that would mean too many questions asked, too much probing, and she wasn't ready for that yet. Her mother wasn't into computers let alone the Internet either, a basic mobile phone being as much as she could cope with, according to Anita, so she couldn't even do the deed by email. Harry had suggested on several occasions that they drive over to Buckinghamshire to visit her mother, but she'd always declined.

It wasn't that she had doubts about introducing Harry, far from it, but ever since all those years back when she had first introduced Alex to the family, she and her mother hadn't got on well, a distance growing between them that certainly hadn't been there before. There'd been no falling out, no argument as such, more an acceptance on her part that Mum and Dad disapproved. As a consequence, she was nervous of her mother's reaction to Harry. Stupid, she knew, but she couldn't help the way she felt. She wanted her mother's approval but was frightened she wouldn't get it again.

"Dear Mum, I know I should have let you know sooner, but..."

Biro poised over the pale-blue, lined paper, she stopped. It was as far as she could get, unable to find the right words. How do you admit to your mother she was right all along? That you had indeed made a lousy choice in marrying Alex Cornwall.

Thinking she might do better wording it on the laptop first she switched it on, but her mind was as blank as the white screen in front of her, words failing to form in her head, let alone across the black keyboard. Giving that up as a bad job, she tried playing a game of Patience, which only served to make her lose hers.

Frustrated and uncomfortable, she switched off the machine and stared out of the window, watching hailstones the size of peas bouncing off the path, covering the lawns in a white blanket in a matter of moments.

Feeling chilled suddenly despite the lit fire, she pulled her red cardigan tighter around her and let her mind drift back to the day she came to Hill House, the day she saw this room for the first time.

It was late afternoon, she remembered, a low sun filling the space with a warm golden glow, making it difficult to judge whether the walls were painted yellow or apricot, or if the carpet cream or white. In one corner of the room stood a glass display cabinet full of crystal animals that sparkled and glinted in myriad colours, as if set on fire by the sun.

The large mahogany desk she now sat at was then in the centre of the room, angled towards the marble fireplace. She had run her fingers over the desk's polished surface, noticing how warm the wood felt. Harry had since moved it closer to the French doors, to take advantage of the views out across the rose garden so she could admire their blooms in summer and the magnificent panorama of the valley beyond in its ever-changing seasonal glory. She thought it a perfect room for contemplation and reflection in its calming atmosphere, bathed as it was in the afternoon radiance. In the short time she'd been living here, she had spent many happy hours surrounded by the room's relaxing influence.

But not today. Today she felt like an intruder, as if she had no right being there. More disconcerting was the ever-present feeling creeping over her that its previous owner was still in residence, watching her every move. Even the stones and bricks of the walls seemed to be whispering to each other in secret, making her feel ill at ease, as if they too didn't want her there.

Along the wall opposite the fireplace ran floor-to-ceiling mahogany shelves stacked full of books. She went across to look at a few titles, choose something to read, anything to escape the depression lurking about her. She ran her fingers along the blue, green, and red leather-bound volumes with their intricate gold lettering. The works of Dickens, Brontë, Austen, Thurber. Dictionaries, encyclopedias. Poetry collections and Greek myths. Books all calling out to be read.

From the corner of the room, a flicker of movement caught her eye. She turned but saw nothing other than the wall with its gilt-framed botanic prints hanging in a row across the chimney breast. In the grate a half-burned log crackled and dropped slightly, sending sparks dancing up the chimney.

Restless, needing something to do to keep her busy, anything to fill the empty hours ahead until Harry telephoned, she wandered from room to room, seeking something, but not knowing what. Opening and closing drawers and cupboards for no apparent reason, she languished in idleness while the lonely minutes and hours ticked by, slowly dragging the long day towards evening.

Even the glazier hadn't been a long-enough distraction when he arrived to fix the hall window. He'd refused the offer of a cup of tea, claiming he was far too busy, had lots to do and must get on.

Finding herself now in the sitting room, she wandered over to the white grand piano and ran her fingers over the keys. It had been the first thing she'd noticed upon entering it that first time...

"And you have a piano, how wonderful," she had exclaimed. "I'd always wanted one, but the house in Hounslow wasn't large enough, not even for an upright. But the real reason was that Alex refused to buy one. Said he couldn't afford it. Which I know wasn't true."

"Can you play?" Harry had asked her.

"I used to be quite accomplished at one stage, but I've not played for years. I expect I've gone rusty."

Asking Harry if he played at all, he'd shaken his head, confessing he couldn't tell one note from another although the children had been learning. Elly had been doing well, getting quite proficient, although Sam was rather clumsy apparently. She recalled the image she had garnered in her mind's eye of his two young children seated side-by-side on the piano stool practising their scales.

Lifting the piano lid, she had asked tentatively, "May I?" then, when he'd nodded, ran her fingers across the keyboard, playing the scale of G Major. When she'd struck the black F sharp key, the note was flat. Laughing, she had declared, "I think it needs tuning." True to his word, Harry had called the piano tuner the very next day...

She pulled out the piano stool and sat, flexed her fingers, and began to play "Somewhere in Time", the theme from her favourite film of the same name, but the notes wouldn't play right. She kept missing keys, sending chords crashing into painful disharmonies.

Rachmaninov descended into Scott Joplin, Bach into nursery rhyme jingles. Not knowing what to play next, nothing seemed to fit her mood, serving only to depress her further, she slammed the lid down with a loud crash, the piano shaking. God, how she missed him.

This is silly! Anyone would think I've never been on my own before.

The gloomy isolation manifested into an evening weighed down by morbid ideas that something awful would happen to him and he wouldn't be coming home. Ever. A train crash. A car accident. The Eiffel Tower collapsing on top of him. Another terrorist attack on the French capital. Her head filled with fears and premonitions which compounded in making the hours drag more slowly. She never believed she would miss anyone's company as much as she missed his, longing to feel the comfort of his presence. Please come home safe, she prayed inwardly. Repeatedly.

At eight o'clock Harry telephoned as planned, but the connection was full of interference, she could hardly hear him. Nevertheless, hearing his voice, no matter how faint, gladdened her heart, but also served as a reminder of her uselessness without him.

Had Harry felt like this when he'd first lost Lorna, she wondered, picking at her supper of cold leftovers for which she had no real appetite. He must have felt worse. At least she knew he was coming back, the separation only temporary.

Deciding an early night with a book was the best course of action to while away the evening, she double-checked all the doors were locked securely, all the windows firmly bolted, the radio and television turned off and unplugged, then ran a hot bath.

In a room lit by vanilla-scented candles, wallowing in foamy warm water scented with lavender and ylang-ylang, she relaxed for the first time that day.

She wasn't sure if it was the sound of torrential rain hammering at the window or the music that had roused her from sleep. As it coalesced into a slow, triple-time tune, she recognized it as the one she had heard before, that first night Harry was away.

Da dee dee, da da dee...

Music – there but not quite, snippets of a distant romantic piano melody drifting up from below, making the fine hairs on her body stand up with the beauty of its sound.

Slowly, she eased herself out of bed and crept downstairs, one hand clutching tightly to the banister, a feeling of déjà vu and a hint of fear enveloping her with each tentative footstep.

Halfway down the stairs the music stopped, as it had before, and silence, other than the steady ticking of the grandfather clock, filled Hill House. For several minutes she stood waiting to see if it came back, all the while wondering where on earth the sound had come from.

When it didn't return, she continued down and went into the sitting room, flicking on the light switch with a sharp snap. Everything looked normal. The same in her study. Nothing out of place.

Perplexed, she was about to give up and go back to bed when a sound outside caught her attention. A distant whooshing noise, getting louder, nearer. A faint flash of light streaked across the glass in the front door, the sound slowly diminishing. Tyres on a wet road. A car in the lane. She smiled. Perhaps Harry had been right, the music had come from a car radio. But as she climbed the stairs, she thought his explanation didn't make sense. The music would only have been a momentary burst as the car went by. Certainly not enough to wake her.

In bed, behind closed eyes the music refrain played on, repeating itself again and again until sleep blotted it out.

Chapter 8

Harry turned the blue BMW off the narrow lane and up the gravelled drive to the house. Before he had even unbuckled his seatbelt, Penny was at the car door, pulling it open, clearly relieved he was home.

"You're back sooner than I expected," she said, jubilant, smothering his face in kisses.

"We caught an early flight. Mmm, what a lovely way to be greeted, I shall have to go away more often." Extracting himself from the car, he swept her off her feet and carried her into the house like a new bride.

She squealed in fits of laughter. "Don't you dare go off and leave me again. Now put me down, silly."

"No. I'm frightened if I let you go, you will vanish as miraculously as you appeared that day on the station platform." Lowering her gently to the floor, he caught her hand in his, the wide grin of pleasure never leaving his lips. "It's good to be home and with good news. Tatterelle signed the contract and the mayor's approved the plans. This one's going to make us a lot of money."

Delighted, she threw her arms around him. "That's wonderful. I'm so pleased for you both."

"And it means I can spend more time with you now. I feel I've neglected you over the past few weeks."

"Nonsense, darling. You have to work and make a living to keep me in the style to which I'm quickly becoming accustomed to."

He laughed with her. "Have you missed me?"

"What a silly question, Harry. Of course I have. It's been hell here?"

He looked taken aback, his happy countenance changing rapidly to one of concern. "Why, what's happened."

Realizing her words may have given him the wrong impression, she hurried to clarify. "Nothing really. It's..." She shrugged. "I didn't know what to do with myself, that's all. I'd planned to spend yesterday pottering about in the garden only it hasn't stopped flipping raining."

"Poor you, has it been really grotty here? Only you'd tell me if anything was bothering you, wouldn't you?"

"Everything's fine, darling. Honest." She kissed him again, hoping he couldn't read what was hidden behind her eyes. She didn't want to tell him about the music for it seemed so vague, so inconsequential now. Yet deep down, in the bottom-most recess of her mind, it clung there, not wanting to let go, buzzing around like a trapped fly persistently seeking escape.

As the weeks went by, he couldn't remember a June being as miserable and wet for many a year. The wind had returned with a vengeance, carrying with it torrential rain that rattled on the roof tiles of the barn like a million nails clattering from the sky. Down in the valley, the swollen Severn river had flooded the fields along its banks, a frequent occurrence higher up the river valley around Gloucester in wintertime, but not this far down, and certainly not at this time of year.

A loud rumble of thunder reverberated around the hill, shaking the rafters. The beat of raindrops came faster and faster until such a tremendous downpour burst from the clouds, it gave him cause to wonder if he should start drawing up plans for an ark instead of working up the sketch for his latest assignment, an office complex on the outskirts of Bristol.

Today the wind raged savagely, blowing up the valley direct from the Atlantic, gathering momentum to hit Stonecott Hill and take its preferred short cut directly through the house. Blowing under doors and around windows, finding the slightest gap through which to squeeze. One that would whistle under skirting boards and howl like a banshee across the landing and, if strong enough, lift the carpets inside the house. They would billow up from the floorboards, quiver, and in slow motion sink gently back down. If the carpets hadn't been securely fitted at the edges by metal carpet grippers, he was sure they would rise up completely.

Staring out of the window of his office, watching the trees alongside the drive whip and lean precariously against the forces of nature assaulting the green canopy, a pang of melancholy creased his heart.

He recalled wistfully how, whenever the winds found their way into the house, making the carpets lift, Sam and Elly loved to pretend the Thomas-the-Tank rug on the playroom floor was a magic carpet. Sitting with fingers crossed, believing they only had to wish that little bit harder the next time the billowing draft came so they could be carried off to some far country, flown away on some mythical, magical adventure. Even he and Lorna had joined in their game occasionally, the four of them sitting cross-legged on the mat, wishing and waiting...

Harry's office was a converted barn across from the house, filled with his drawing boards, computers and plotters, keeping his business day separate from the rest of the household. Most times, it was a pleasant, bright place to be in but today the building felt dismal even with all the lights on.

He felt on edge but couldn't understand why today the confines of the office made him feel like a caged animal. He needed to be outside, feel the wind on his face. Where once, in those dark days before Penny, he'd been only too glad to stay indoors, shut off from the world outside, he now craved to be away from its restricted bounds.

He also missed the afternoon walks they had enjoyed during the few warm, drier days of May, rambles across the hill and saunters down to Sodbury Common to watch and enjoy the wildlife.

In urgent need of fresh air in his lungs, he pushed open the barn door and peered out. Rain bounced off the ground by several inches, the gravel more like the bottom of a riverbed than the path to the kitchen door. Deciding to make a dash for it, he ran toward the house in search of Penny. They had to get out today. Blow the work and sod the rain!

Leaping over the puddles, he thought they might drive over to Lechlade, perhaps lunch at the Trout Inn. Unless, of course, there was somewhere else Penny would like to go.

Opening the back door, he froze. Lorna was standing at the sink, her back towards him.

Chapter 9

Of course it's not Lorna, he berated himself. Lorna's dead. But for a brief, single moment, he really thought it had been her. Not because Penny looked anything like his dead wife, but because Penny was humming.

She'd been doing it more and more lately, now he came to think about it. Humming incessantly for the past few weeks; something Lorna was forever doing – always humming half a dozen notes as flat as pancakes, again and again, driving him up the wall.

He watched silently as Penny rinsed out a coffee mug under the hot tap, seemingly unaware of his presence. Eventually, he crossed to the kitchen table and picked out a green apple from the fruit bowl.

Jolted by the sound behind her, she spun around.

"Oh, it's you. You made me jump."

The thunderstorm continued to rage around the hillside, shaking the house to its foundations. She nodded in the direction of the misted windowpane. "Look at it out there, tipping again."

He gave the window a fleeting glance as another bolt of lightning tore open the black sky, lighting up the herb garden that was now little more than a muddy quagmire. Before the summer rains had forced Penny to abandon their cause, the parsley, chives, thyme, mint and oregano were fighting their way through the heavy soil. Now there was little hope of them flourishing in the squishy red soil.

As if thinking the same about her herbs, Penny let out a resigned sigh and shrugged.

"Oh well, nothing I can do about any of it. I've been listening to the news. There's dreadful flooding all over the county. Tewkesbury's virtually cut off. That's not far from here, is it? Do you think Peter's place will be okay?" She picked up a tea towel and, as she wiped dry the mug, started humming again.

"Do you always have to keep making that confounded noise? Or at least try another tune." He hadn't meant to shout, but like the relentless rain of the past few days, it had got to him, the noise grating on his nerves until he snapped.

She stared at him, visibly shocked by his outburst. "I'm sorry, I didn't realize I was doing it."

"You're always at it! And it's getting rather monotonous." It wasn't the humming *per se* that infuriated him; it was the fact that it was always the same blasted refrain over and over again. Never complete. Never whole. A Chinese water torture by music. Death by humming.

She shrugged apologetically. "I'm sorry, but you know how it is. You hear a song, and then you can't get it out of your head no matter how hard you try."

"Put some music on, then. Perhaps that will help to make you stop!" He took a large, angry bite from the apple before stomping back outside, slamming the door as he went.

Sidestepping another deep-looking puddle in the gravel, a wave of déjà vu engulfed him, a remembrance that made his gut wrench. The whole scene played out in the kitchen had happened before, and its memory halted him in his tracks. The realization that it might be happening all over again filled him with dread.

He and Lorna had been arguing about her constant humming the morning she had died. She had stormed out of the kitchen slamming the door behind her, as he had done now. Only then, Lorna had hustled the children into the car, anxious to get them to school on time... they were running late... she'd screeched off into... He screwed his eyes shut, trying to blot out what had happened next.

Opening his eyes again, the nightmare receded. What a complete bastard I am, he said to himself. Now deeply regretting his departing comment to Penny, he wished he could take back those bitter words, but it was too late. He could have kicked himself. *What had got into him?* It wasn't Penny's fault he'd been reminded of Lorna. Nor was it her fault she was humming. Humming was normal. People often hummed when they were happy, didn't they? Why, didn't he whistle, sing even, whenever he felt cheerful? And wasn't humming far more feminine than whistling?

He tossed the barely eaten apple into the beech hedge, knowing the birds and hedgehogs would enjoy it far more than he was doing, before turning and hurrying back to the kitchen. He had to apologize. His own foul mood had brought this on, not Penny. None of this was her doing, and she didn't deserve his outburst.

Penny didn't want to cry, but it always happened when anyone shouted at her; a childhood response that made her avoid confrontation at the best of times. She hated being unable to control this involuntary reaction making her appear weak and spineless. She grabbed a sheet of kitchen paper from the roll on the countertop and, blowing her nose, thought it so unlike Harry, grumpy and growling at her like that. Normally he was cheerful. Happy. Always whistling or singing away to the radio inside the barn as he worked. She couldn't recall him doing either lately.

As she mulled over his outburst, she became conscious she was humming yet again; a few notes, a simple refrain. She pulled herself up sharply, thinking she really must stop doing it, particularly as it annoyed him so much. What was more disconcerting was the fact she didn't even know the tune. It wasn't even a proper one.

She peered through the rivulets of rain sliding down the window to see Harry scurrying back toward the barn. Suddenly, he stopped. Stood still. She saw him throw the apple into the hedge, turn, and sprint back towards the house.

Anxious to show his rant hadn't upset her, she darted across to the kitchen table and pulled out a chair, sitting down just as he burst in through the door.

He rushed across to her, dropped to his knees and took hold of both her hands.

"Sweetheart, I am so, so sorry. I don't know what came over me. I'm ashamed of myself. Look how I've made you cry. Please forgive me."

She sniffed. "No, I'm the one who's sorry. I didn't realize I was so annoying."

"But it's not you, sweetheart, it's me. Whatever can I say?

I acted like a complete jerk. It's this depressing weather getting to me. Come on, grab your coat and let's get out of here for the day?"

"But your project..." she protested.

"Sod the bloody project. It's nothing that can't wait a day or two. Our sanity and well-being are far more important than some towering glass office block that probably won't get past the NIMBY brigade anyway."

Heeding Harry's advice, she kept the radio switched on all day, every day, in the hope that one tune would drown out the other playing continuously inside her head.

It didn't.

Louder and louder she turned up the volume, but the music inside her brain was unremitting. A tune all the more irritating because it was incomplete, and all the more puzzling because it was one she didn't recognize other than being the one she thought she heard in the house whenever she was on her own.

Day in, day out, the music played repeatedly, its tones swaying from chord to disjointed chord. Short phrases and bars that for a moment gelled before scattering in all directions with no pattern or rhythm, turning itself into a niggling, gnawing sound which wouldn't go away. Annoying like a headache that won't manifest itself fully or disappear after a couple of aspirins.

Worse, she couldn't stop humming the dratted thing, time and again pulling herself up short whenever she became aware she was doing it. And each day she felt more swamped by it, biting her lips and the inside of her cheek in an effort to quell the urge to break the progressive habit.

No wonder it got on Harry's nerves; it was getting on hers. She'd even begun to wonder if she were humming it in her sleep – those times she could sleep. Most nights she lay awake waiting for it to stop.

Most nights it didn't.

* * *

Harry awoke with a jolt, instinctively reaching out a hand for Penny. The sheet beneath his palm felt cold. Thinking she'd gone to the bathroom, he lay waiting for her return, waiting to cuddle back up against her warm body, find comfort in her curves when their bodies moulded together.

He listened to the rain falling on the roof, the spitter-spatter against the windowpanes, all the while waiting for the sound of the flush. Five minutes passed. Ten. He sat up in bed. There was no light glowing underneath the bathroom door; she wasn't in there. She must have gone downstairs to make a drink, he thought. He was about to get up and join her when he heard her footsteps padding up the stairs.

"Where have you been?" he whispered, a feeling of un-ease hovering around him as he watched her get back into bed and snuggle down beneath the duvet.

"Go back to sleep, darling, it's still early," she whispered back.

He pulled her close, nuzzling into her soft hair. Her skin beneath his hand felt cold. "Was it another bad dream?"

"No, I think the rain woke me. I can't remember a sum-mer as bad as this. Sorry I disturbed you."

"You didn't." He stared up at the ceiling through the darkness, his head in too much turmoil to go back to sleep. This was the fourth time in a week – no, fifth, he corrected himself – she'd crept downstairs during the middle of the night.

Penny had changed over the last few weeks, he'd noticed. Not in any concrete way he could identify; there was no one thing he could truthfully say had altered. It was more the intense feeling she was keeping something from him. Some little secret she didn't want him to know. That thought hurt. He wanted no hidden thoughts, no secrets, everything out in the open between them. Any worry and concern raised. Huh, that was rich coming from him, he scolded himself, he who didn't want to talk about the past.

What worried him more was that her usual rosy complex-ion had gone, her skin pale and taut, and there were grey shadows under her eyes during the day. Over the past few weeks, she'd been more and more withdrawn, her face set in an absent, far-away expression as if her mind was constantly on other things. Was she still worried that Alex would appear and cause trouble?

Three weeks had passed since his cross words with her about her humming. She'd forgiven him the spat, but he couldn't forget it, nor forgive himself, remorse crawling through him. Forget it, Peter had advised when he'd told him of the incident, it didn't matter how much one was in love, little quirks and habits were bound to irritate sometimes. They were bound to get on each other's nerves a little now and again. All part of life, part of a normal, healthy relationship, according to Peter. But Harry felt it was more than that. As if something intangible had crossed over the boundary and uninvited, had entered Hill House, unwilling to leave.

Lying in the darkness, he'd half-convinced himself it was Lorna's presence around him he could feel. In the bedroom, the hallway. In the garden even. It wasn't Penny's humming that had brought about this absurd feeling, more a pervading atmosphere that hung about the rooms as if trying to tell him something, something akin to the strange perfume that occasionally wafted around the hallway that only he seemed able to smell. And without any other explanation, he didn't know what else to think. Was it Lorna trying to tell him something? Did she not approve of the new love in his life? Even as he thought such a ludicrous notion, he dismissed it. Lorna would be pleased he'd found another love. She wouldn't have wanted him living like a recluse for the rest of his life.

The sleeping shape of Penny lay beside him, the duvet pulled tight to her chin, her breathing steady. In her sleep, she stretched and rolled onto her back, her unfettered hair splayed out across the pillow. He took hold of several strands, stroked them gently, lifting them to his nose and inhaling the luscious scent. At least, for now, she slept soundly. Too often lately she'd awoken from bad dreams, unable to remember enough to tell him anything about them. Fearing she was worrying over the divorce, which wasn't going well - Alex was still being an awkward cuss - he had tried to ease her anxieties. But where her dreaming was concerned, he was completely helpless. There was nothing he could do to stop them. Nor she his.

Maybe it *was* the house? Was Penny having second thoughts about living there? It couldn't be easy moving into someone else's home, and what with all this disturbed sleep, no wonder she looked so... so ill.

Sleep, when it finally carried him away again, took him straight into his own private nightmare in all its vivid, horrific detail. The sounds of metal being crushed, a searing fireball of flames, the silent screams emanating from the mouths of his children. Scenes so raw in his head that would not go away. Even now, after all this time, a vision that will haunt him for the rest of his life.

Dawn's early light had begun to infiltrate into the darkness when he sat bolt upright and, much to his frustration, realized he was crying. He rubbed at his face. Was he never to be free from the memory each time he closed his eyes?

Chapter 10

Summer in its full glory arrived late, interspersed with the odd shower or two that couldn't dampen Harry's determined plans to take Penny on long scenic drives around the glorious Gloucestershire countryside. Along the many narrow, ivy-covered stone-walled lanes, eager to show her pretty villages with odd-sounding names like Slad, Uley, Ampney Crucis, the Slaughters. To picturesque but tourist-filled Bourton-on-the-Water, with its honey-coloured stonework and a shallow stream running through its charming main street.

Excursions further afield were also in order – up through the Forest of Dean and down the Wye Valley. Early morning jaunts to watch the sun rise over the Cotswolds; picnics watching the gliders at Coaley Point and madcap hang-gliders jumping off the high hills. Days in the countryside that filled him with pleasure at seeing her delighted, fascinated face. No man had surely been luckier than to live in such a lovely part of England with such a beautiful, gentle woman at his side.

Much to his relief, Penny seemed wholly relaxed on these days out, back to her bubbly self. Of course, that was probably down to the fact that Alex had finally succumbed and agreed to the terms of the divorce. With no children involved to fight over and their London house only rented, financial implications and custody battles were non-existent. Alex had for many months refused point-blank to accept her claims of mental cruelty, citing instead the irretrievable breakdown of their marriage and claiming desertion on her part. All academic now really. The deed was done, papers signed, but the man had dragged it out unnecessarily. More a case of his solicitor trying to bump up the fees, he concluded. Penny seemed to be sleeping better too. No more waking up and wandering around the house in the dead of night. Best of all, she had stopped that dratted humming.

He smiled broadly as he turned into the pub car park where they were to have lunch.

Life was indeed good again.

* * *

A few weeks on and the wet weather returned, and with it Penny's melancholic mood, not helped by the repeat musical performances playing in the house. In her head.

Yet again, she awoke before dawn to the familiar discordant sounds that, as before, wouldn't go away. Never starting in the same place, always stopping at random mid sequence, over and over. Tossing and turning in bed, trying to shut out the sounds with the pillow clutched tightly against her ears, she gave up trying to go back to sleep.

Quietly, so as not to disturb Harry, she ventured downstairs, walking around the house, opening and closing doors. Listening intently, seeking desperately to pinpoint where the sounds came from, where the music was loudest.

Every time she thought she had located its source, the melody moved to another room. It was teasing her. Playing games. Mind games. Musical rooms. Let's see which room you are in when the music stops. Was she even going a little insane, she wondered. Madness gaining on her like a disease creeping inside her body, worming its way through her system and coiled around her cerebral cortex. Every part of her felt run down and worn out. Empty.

She was tired from broken sleep and tired of the music, any beauty lost in its monotony. She no longer enjoyed living at Hill House; its welcoming charm had been lost in the strains of an unknown melody that persisted in haunting her.

As she prepared breakfast, the local news on the radio only added to her deepening depression. There were numerous reports of more severe flooding around Gloucester, many homes and people's lives ruined, fresh drinking water in short supply, bottled stocks being ferried in. Many roads were impassable or in danger of being swept away altogether. Livestock had been lost, farmers left with no choice but to leave their herds to fend for themselves. Living high up on a hill certainly had one advantage, she mused.

In an effort to lighten her mood, she laughed aloud at one of the disc jockey's anecdotes, and sang along to "Brown Sugar", dancing around the kitchen as she laid the table, gyrating to the music, turning up the volume by degrees to drown out the other music in her head, but still the undercurrent played beneath the surface, spoiling any real enjoyment.

"Glad someone's in a good mood this morning," Harry said brusquely. He settled himself at the table and poured himself a coffee.

"Gosh, you sound grumpy. Bad night?"

He nodded, stirring in the milk.

"No chance of giving the old drawings a miss and we go out, is there?" Not relishing spending time inside Hill House on her own for yet another day, she had asked out of hope. Restless and on edge, she needed his company, wanting to feel the protection and assurance of his presence.

Harry shook his head. "Not today, sweetheart. I must get the plans finished before Peter gets back so he can start on the three-D models." He yawned, stretching wearily in preparation for another day hunched over his computer.

He looks all-in, she thought, knowing he hadn't been sleeping well either, and wondered guiltily if it was her fault he wasn't getting enough rest, if she disturbed him at night by her wanderings. He'd been working solidly on his own for the past fortnight whilst Peter was abroad with Elaine on some mercy mission for the Emerson's Trust. Peter was the engineer in the business, Harry the artist, and between them, they made a good team, but on his own, he seemed to be floundering. He really could do with another pair of eyes and hands, she thought.

She handed him a second slice of hot toast. "How long before the plans have to be submitted?"

"By the end of the month, then we'll have some time off. I'm thinking we might go away for a few weeks once Peter's back. I keep promising you a holiday. We haven't even celebrated the Tatterelle contract properly yet."

"Is there anything I can do to help you?" she offered, knowing she knew nothing about architecture or plans and elevations, or the calculations and sciences needed to design buildings.

"Not unless you know AutoCAD inside out or how to

overlay multi-layers of drawings. Meanwhile, there's nothing you can do other than make me another coffee and bring it out to the office for me, please."

"That isn't what I meant," she snapped. "I was offering to come across to the barn with you. Tidy up. Sharpen your pencils. Keep you company..."

He caught hold of her hand, giving it a gentle squeeze. "I know. I'm sorry, sweetheart. It must be incredibly boring being here all day by yourself, but I need to press on with things. I need Peter's input to bounce a few ideas I have. At the moment I'm struggling to come up with a sound solution to meet the local council's latest round of specification changes."

After clearing up the kitchen, she tiptoed into the barn, put a mug of hot, milky coffee down carefully on his desk, placed a gentle kiss on the top of his bowed head, and crept back out again, closing the door behind her as quietly as she could.

The rain had stopped, the grey sky tinged with pink streaks, circles of blue sky visible. She rushed back indoors. With equal haste, she dashed back out carrying her own mug, and wandered through the garden, under the pergola with its knotted wisteria, its boughs heavy with ripening purple raceme cascades dripping water. A little further along the path, two wide semi-circular stone steps took her down to the lavender walk leading into a walled rose garden where rain-ragged brown blooms hung limp and forlorn.

She seated herself on the damp wooden bench to enjoy her drink. The morning sun, finally making an appearance through the ever-widening gaps appearing in the clouds, felt warm on her face.

From the paths, walls and wooden trellises steam rose, and the green lawns were soon blanketed in a misty haze of rising evaporation. The light was bright, the earth smelled sweet. She could virtually hear the plants sigh with relief now that they were well watered, though many were all but drowned. Now they could get on with their proper business of throwing up glorious blooms for what was left of the summer months ahead.

She loved the garden. It was the kind she'd always wanted, one in which she could entertain friends in style, sipping cocktails on sunny afternoons and warm summer nights, throwing lavish parties and barbeques.

But the garden also held another attraction, one that out-weighed all its other beauty, for it was only outside the house she found relief from the ever-present tune in her head.

The inclement weather had forced her to stay indoors far too frequently lately. The only respites being when they went to fetch groceries or deliver plans or drawings, or when the rain stopped for a brief spell and she could escape into the garden to try to resuscitate the herb patch or pull up a few weeds that dared to grow. Taking advantage of any excuse to leave the confines of the house, to hear the rustle of the wind through the leaves on the oaks or a skylark singing high above the Common, the bleating of sheep rising up from the farm below in the valley. Outside, the only humming was done by the bees. In the garden there was no music in her head.

Harry appeared from around the south side of the house, aiming for his favourite spot on the wooden garden seat facing across the valley to drink in the view and the remains of his coffee. She waved out, smiling with pleasure at his unexpected arrival, and shuffled along the damp seat to make room.

"What's wrong, love?" he asked, settling next to her. "You look rather pale and glum sitting here. I've noticed lately you're not your usual self, I hope you're not sickening for something."

"I'm feeling a bit under par, that's all."

"You've been worrying too much over this divorce, I reckon. At least it's all over now."

She shrugged. "You're probably right. Perhaps this after-noon I'll drive over to Chipping Sodbury and take a look around the shops... I could do with another pair of shoes and some retail therapy. I might even drive over to Westerleigh, to that new garden centre. My herb patch has been washed away, I need to restock it."

"I'll tell you what, how about tomorrow, if the weather

stays fine, we take a picnic and go for a long walk? There's something further along the hill I'd like to show you."

She sighed. "We haven't been for a proper walk for ages because of all this rain and you being so busy. I need a day away from Hill House. It would do you good too to get away from that computer and drawing board for a change. You've been shut in there for days."

He leaned back against the seat. "Ah, so there was more to it this morning than wanting to tidy my office. But why so sad? Is it because I said no?"

She shook her head.

"What then?"

She hesitated, unsure how to explain herself. "It's the house... well... no, that's not it. It's me. It's this bloody tune, it won't go away, Harry. I thought maybe the noise of the radio and the background hum from all your computer equipment, especially that plotter you use, might drive out the continuous music in my head."

"It's still bothering you, then?"

She nodded, sucking in her lips. "Persistently of late."

"Can you hear it now?"

She looked about the garden, smiled, then said, "No, that's the funny thing. Out here there's peace. It's only indoors, once I step over the threshold, that the music comes rushing back. I'm beginning to think the house doesn't like me?"

"That's silly. Houses are bricks and mortar; they don't hold feelings like us. They're inert. Solid."

"Are they, Harry? Do we really know that? I've often heard people say they know immediately if they like a place or not, that they can feel it the moment they step through the door. They can sense it. Understand its aura..."

He shot her a puzzled stare. "And you believe all that?"

She gave him a half-hearted smile. "Yes, I believe I do. It might sound daft to you, but it could well be Hill House has a musical aura and that only I can hear it? But I do wish it would stop. It disturbs my thoughts when I'm awake and invades my dreams at night."

"All the more reason for us to have a day out, then."

"It wouldn't be so bad if I knew what the wretched tune was. Even its title."

"Something you made up?" he suggested.

The question remained unanswered whilst she stared out across the valley once more as Harry finished the remains of his drink and put the earthenware mug down on the ground. It toppled over on the uneven slabs beneath the seat, rolling onto its side, coming to rest on its handle. He reached down and picked it up.

"I think being cooped up indoors with all this rain is depressing me, Harry. I'll be better tomorrow." She tried to sound hopeful.

"That and a good night's sleep. I know you've been sleeping badly again."

"Sorry, have I disturbed you often? I didn't want to worry you; I know you're under pressure and what with Peter being away..."

He pulled her into the crook of his arm. "That's what I'm here for. You should have told me."

"Well, it's all in the open now." She laughed lightly at the funny side of her comment. "Yes, you're right. A day out might be the perfect tonic needed to put this stupid tune to bed once and for all."

Chapter 11

Penny could hear it drifting up from downstairs.

Music... *dum dum, de dee dee...* only louder this time. Much louder.

A look at the bedside clock showed it was a quarter to three in the morning. The steady breathing and gentle snores from Harry told her he was fast asleep. Determined not to disturb him yet again, she slid from the bed and crept downstairs, drawn by the music, unable to resist its hypnotic pull.

On the last but one tread, she sank down on her haunches, listening, enraptured by the gentility and beauty of the sweeping lulls and crescendos. She hadn't heard it so clearly before. It was simply exquisite.

...dee dum dum, da dee dee...

A haunting flute, a sad cello joining in, a gently plucking harp, mellow strings, a piano harmonizing in reply...

...dee dum dum...

The hallway was illuminated by moonlight through the window. In its beam, she caught a glimpse of two people dancing a slow waltz in time to the music, dust motes falling like a thousand tiny glittering snowflakes all around them. A man dressed in a black tuxedo, a dazzling white cravat. There one moment, gone the next, before coming back into her view. Highly polished black shoes reflecting pale layers of peach tulle his partner wore as he spun her around in a graceful turn. In and out of the moonbeam they danced.

She could not see their faces fully. They were shadows, a glimmer in the moonlight, gone for a moment then coming back into focus before disappearing again. A flash of a smile, a sparkle of brown eyes caught in candlelight with the turning of a head.

A tingling sensation ran through her body at the magical scene in front of her as another pair – or was it the same couple? – became visible by the sitting room doorway, waltzing to the melody in perfect syncopation. They, too, evaporated to nothingness, then back again, fading in and out like fuzzy pictures on an old television set whose reception was faulty, the signal disrupted.

Mesmerised, she watched the images dancing before her. She felt fully awake, but a part of her wondered if she were in one of those weird, curious dreams she sometimes experienced, ones where she dreamt she was dreaming in her sleep. Yet her mind told her this was no dream, logic breaking into her thoughts. These dancers weren't real but had been. In the past. And if they weren't real, it could only mean one thing: they were spirits. Ghosts of the past.

But ghosts were meant to be scary, weren't they? Spooky, flitting creatures with no faces that floated through walls and frightened you to death. She didn't feel the least bit afraid. Ghosts can't hurt you, she told herself. There was nothing to be scared of, not when ghosts appeared as fascinating and charming as this spectacle, there was nothing at all threatening in their movements.

Other thoughts crowded her mind. Memories. Memories she knew were not hers, yet somehow...

A pale yellow moon hung low, keeping company with stars twinkling like diamonds scattered over black velvet. Great swirls of snow, whipped into a frenzy by the howling north wind, whirled across the buried expanse of meadows sweeping down the Wilder Kaiser Mountains towards Schloss Altener and the great forest beyond. Across the snow, an orange glow from countless windowpanes shone out into the darkness. Inside the Schloss, hundreds of flickering candles burned, their warmth reflected in the crystal chandeliers beneath which the noble guests of Graf Wilheim von Engels and his family waltzed in triple time to the music of Strauss, gliding in unison across the marble floor of the gilded ballroom.

Liselle bobbed a short curtsey, a balancing act she was well rehearsed in, as another guest helped himself to a glass of champagne from the silver tray she gripped firmly in her hands. In the crowded room, she was bumped into constantly by guests but kept her composure, slithering between them as inconspicuously as she could, whilst at the same time ensuring everyone was served. She was hot, licking her pure and unkissed lips as scarlet as the military jackets the men wore. She would give anything for a sip of wine to moisten her dry mouth.

Her eyes fell upon the young Count Johann, the only son of Graf Wilheim, in whose honour the grand ball was held, for today Count Johann had reached his twentieth birthday. Standing not some six feet away, oblivious to the conversations and attention being thrust upon him as he stood amidst a group of female guests in their flamboyant ball gowns and over-pampered hair, laughing with high-pitched voices, the young Count met her gaze and smiled kindly, his deep, dark eyes alight with fire. She couldn't help but notice how handsome he looked: his broad stance, the strong jawline and narrow nose of his father, the beautifully manicured imperial moustache, dark and waxed.

Blushing, she averted her eyes. It was not done for a servant to stare at the nobility, least of all at the eligible Count. He beckoned her with his finger. Fearing now she would be in trouble for staring at him, she began to quake as she approached.

"Thank you." Count Johann spoke quietly as he took a long-stemmed flute of the sparkling wine from her tray with an appreciative smile.

Thank goodness! He simply wanted a drink. She bobbed again, willing her arms to stop shaking, frightened in case the remaining glassful would topple from the tray. That would never do. One broken glass would be all it would take for her to lose her job and be thrown out, back onto the streets to meet the angry wrath of Uncle Zdenek. He would never forgive her for spoiling such an opportunity as he had arranged for her at the Schloss, and with such a noble family related to the Emperor of Austria himself. Franz Joseph was at the Count's ball tonight, but she had yet to catch even a glimpse of the great man, let alone serve him, for he was always surrounded by his entourage of courtiers and guards.

"Girl!" A voice called to her from behind. "Here."

She smiled slightly at the Count, then turned hastily to serve yet another thirsty guest with the last glass of champagne before hurrying silently from the ballroom to replenish her tray.

"What is it like in there, Liselle?" asked Truda, another servant girl whose duty it was that evening to fetch and carry the dirty glasses between the table outside the ballroom and the kitchens. Her head darted this way and that as she tried to peer inside as Liselle backed out through the heavy door.

"It's hot, but oh, you should see them. All the beautiful sequined dresses. The dazzling jewellery. Such wonderful tiaras and coronets. It's all so magical. And the music! When they dance, it's like something out of a fairy tale. All swirling colours of the rainbow, glints of flashing swords and medals, and sparkling diamonds and rubies." She mopped her brow with the linen napkin she kept tucked into the belt of her starched apron.

"Let me take a peek?" Truda begged. "Just a little look through the doors as you go back inside."

Picking up a full tray of drinks, Liselle hesitated then conceded. "Okay, but be swift. And be careful, or we'll both get into trouble—"

"What are you looking at?"

The gentle voice of Harry beside her caused Penny to turn in his direction. Seeing him there, she smiled, then whispered, "Didn't you see?" She pointed. "Over there, by the wall. It was beautiful, Harry. People were dancing."

He took hold of her hand, gently pulling her to her feet.

"Come on, sleepy head, back to bed with you. I think you've been sleepwalking. Up you come, there's no one there now."

She allowed him to lead her back upstairs without argument, but in her head the dancers still twirled around and around, waltzing across the highly polished floor of a vast candlelit ballroom in some grand palace.

"Why are you rubbing your hand like that?" he asked.

She looked down at her right hand, wiggled her fingers. "I... I don't know. It feels all tingly, like pins-and-needles."

She realized then how cold she felt, shivering uncontrollably as Harry tucked her back into bed.

"They looked so happy," she whispered, as he kissed her forehead lightly.

"Who did?"

"The dancers in the hallway. Blissfully happy. So in love as they danced to the music. The same music that's always in my head but different somehow." She sat up swiftly, her eyes flaring widely. "Harry, am I going insane? Tell me I'm not mad. I know what I saw, I wasn't asleep."

"You're not insane, my love. A little daft maybe, but not mad. You've been worrying too much about things of late, that's all. It was only a dream." He kissed her lips delicately.

She sighed, lay back down and muttered sleepily, "But it's such a lovely tune, the sort of tune people *should* be dancing to."

"Hush now. That's it, close your eyes. Go back to sleep. You'll forget all this by morning."

He pulled her curled body closer until it was nestled against the arc of his own and listened to her slow, steady breathing, wishing he too could fall back into oblivion instead of lying wide awake. Too many thoughts and worries were racing around inside his head preventing him from falling back to sleep.

Bad dreams and a silly song playing in your mind were one thing. Crikey, hadn't he experienced that himself on the odd occasion? Heard a song on the radio and then all day long was all he could hear in his mind. But seeing people who weren't there dancing in the hallway? That was crazy! No, this was more than sleepwalking and vivid dreams. Something had to give. Penny couldn't go on like this. Was it any wonder she looked so exhausted?

In the darkness, he sighed. This wasn't how it was meant to be. Penny must be ill. She needed help, and a whole lot more than he could give. She needed to see a doctor. The more he thought about it, the more certain he became that something was seriously wrong with her. His mind scrambled, searching for answers, reasons and logical explanations, but each time he came back to the same conclusion. His eyes glistened then flowed over with tears. Heaven forbid he should lose her too. He didn't think he could bear that.

A gust of wind whistled around the house, floorboards on the landing creaked.

Perhaps it *was* the house. What if Penny was right and the house didn't like her? Could it even be haunted? And what if it's Lorna? Is it possible? Difficult though it was, no matter how hard he thought about it, how measured and rationale the arguments, he suddenly believed it could be true – Lorna didn't want Penny there. She had returned to haunt the house because of all his doubts and intolerances in the past. And because of her awful death.

Payback time.

Was this what his weary mind was trying to tell him? Don't be stupid, man, he argued with the absurdity of his thinking. There's no such thing as ghosts.

But was there? He couldn't dispel a niggling doubt of un-ease creeping over him. Just because he hadn't seen one, didn't mean to say they didn't exist.

He turned restlessly onto his back. God, it wasn't Penny going mad, it was him losing grip on reality.

Chapter 12

Woken from dreamless sleep to a room blushed by fingers of orange and pink light ushering out the night, Harry turned to pull Penny towards him, but she wasn't there.

He found her downstairs, seated cross-legged on the sitting room floor and surrounded by untidy stacks of CDs. The curtains were still drawn, the lit ceiling lamp casting a cold light and harsh shadows around the room. A sight causing him to shudder, for he'd witnessed the same scene before in the past. Only then it was Lorna he'd found there that morning, her last, doing the same thing as Penny did now. His innards churned, petrified it would all end like it had with Lorna. Constant arguments. Harsh and bitter words spoken in anger and resentment. Perhaps if he told her... No! No, it was too awful an ending; he didn't want to think about it. His horrors had to remain in the past. Hidden. Buried along with the three charred bodies in the grave in the little churchyard at the foot of Stonecott Hill.

"What are you doing, Pen? Surely it's too early for music? It's not even turned six yet?" He kept his voice light-hearted, reminding himself this wasn't the same as before. It couldn't be.

He caught the guilty look of a child found in the act of doing something it shouldn't upon her face as she looked up at the sound of his voice.

"I'm trying to find that piece of music I keep hearing. You must have it on one of yours, Harry, because I know it's not on any of mine. It's got to be here somewhere. I have to find it, play it through properly, then maybe I can get it out of my head once and for all."

Penny had such a fine ear and recall for music, for a moment his heart lifted at the hope there was something in their record collections that would jog her memory.

"Maybe you heard the tune years ago, before you ever came here? Perhaps what you hear isn't so vague and unfamiliar after all, simply forgotten?"

She looked at him as if mulling over his statement before turning her attention back to the plastic jewel case still clutched in her hand, studying the cover in deep concentration.

"I suppose there is the tiniest, incy-winciest possibility," she finally said. "I once read somewhere that so-say experts claim a tune heard as a baby whilst still in the womb will linger somewhere in the deepest recesses of the child's brain, even if it's only played the once. All it takes to be awakened is some event, a few words, or even a smell, to trawl it up from the depths, so I suppose that's a possibility. A slim one, but a possibility nonetheless." With a loud sigh she tossed the last of the CDs onto the haphazard pile on the floor. "No, it's not on any of these. I know them all."

That he could well believe, losing count of the times he'd come into the sitting room to find her tinkling away at the piano, playing a bit of *Elvira Madigan* or *Musetta's Waltz*, or the hard-practised melodies and chords of a Chopin polonaise played with gusto. Each one from memory, learnt by heart, a scoresheet to follow not required. She could improvise well too, he knew, remembering a few nights ago when she'd entertained him, much to his appreciation and delight, with a rendition of Mozart's *Sonata No.15* played jazz-style. A far better pianist than she would ever give herself credit for.

"Perhaps you heard it with Alex, at a concert or something?"

She shook her head vehemently. "You have got to be joking! Alex hated classical music. We never went to concerts or anything remotely connected with music. I love opera, but he detested anything he didn't understand, especially when he couldn't comprehend what was being sung. He couldn't see the point. The most I could get him to listen to was Lesley Garrett, and that was only because he thought she was, to quote his words, "a little belter with a big bosom'. As for sitting through a classical concert..."

Harry pulled back the curtains, letting daylight fill the room. "Are you sure it's a classical piece? Not some modern pop jingle?"

"Positive."

"You might have heard it on the radio or television recently without realizing it." He switched off the overhead light. "They often use classical music on adverts, things like "Going Home" or "The Flower Duet" or some aria from *Madame Butterfly.*"

"No, they're all popular, common pieces. This tune isn't. It's different, it's... Ouch! I'm getting cramp." She stretched out her right leg, then struggled to stand.

He rushed across to help, gripping firmly to her arm and elbow while she hobbled about on the parquet floor, rubbing at her tense calf muscle.

"There are some good record shops in Gloucester, aren't there," she said. "Could we go there today and ask? I'm sure someone will recognize the tune if I hum it to them. I simply have to find out what it is."

"We can certainly try, my sweet, but not today. We have other plans. Remember? We can go on Friday after we've collected the groceries."

She nodded slowly. "Ah, yes, I'd completely forgotten. You know, Harry, I'm absolutely certain I'd never heard the tune before coming here."

She'd not mentioned last night's wanderings, he thought with relief. Hopefully, she couldn't remember anything about her ramblings. Definitely sleepwalking. Not really awake. Dreaming. And like most dreams, forgotten the moment of awakening.

She looked about the room, saying, "No, it's something about this house. In this house. If only I could pinpoint it, figure out where it's coming from..."

"Perhaps it's haunted!" he uttered, half joking, but the moment the words were out of his mouth he regretted saying them. He'd already convinced himself it was Lorna come back to haunt the new mistress of Hill House, as ridiculous as that sounded. For it had to be more than a coincidence both loves in his life hummed, surely? From raised spirit and hope, he plummeted into morbidity.

Penny studied him, a look of incredulity on her face.

"Whatever made you say that? You certainly don't strike me as a man who believes in ghosts, Harry Winchester."

Why am I doing this, he quizzed himself, battling against all the do's and don'ts. Why can't I simply tell her? What's so hard about mentioning how Lorna always hummed some tuneless ditty she didn't know the name of? Humming it to the point of distraction and at great annoyance to everyone else. He *knew* why.

She shook her head. "No, you're probably right, I've heard the piece somewhere and it's got stuck in my brain like a needle caught in a record groove. Give my head a quick thump and knock the needle on to the next track, eh, love?" She attempted a laugh.

He laughed with her as common sense kicked in, telling him it was the right time now to tell her. She needed to know how plagued by a bit of music, Lorna, too, had been unable to find out what the piece was called. A similar fruitless search of CDs, except Lorna played them through track after track after track; she didn't know music as well as Penny. But Lorna had never seen anyone dancing in the hallway in the dead of night. Lorna had never seen ghosts!

Then it hit him. First with triumphant jubilation, then with relief. That's the answer, of course! How could he have been so stupid? If Lorna had been plagued by music then it couldn't be her haunting Hill House. And as for dancers? That definitely meant it wasn't Lorna. Lorna couldn't tell her right foot from her left. She hated dancing.

He rubbed his chin, feeling like Einstein on the verge of some great discovery. Whatever it was Penny heard or saw, or thought she saw floating about the hallway, was none of Lorna's making. He shook a little; feeling weird to the point of touching on complete lunacy, but feeling relieved nonetheless.

But his self-reasoning opened more questions than answers. If it wasn't Lorna, then who or what was causing Penny to hear music? And why couldn't he? ...Or maybe he had? His mind flitted back, remembering the evening they'd gone to the Emerson's dinner, when he was positive Penny had left the radio on. Was it the self-same mysterious music he'd heard then?

He was on the brink of suggesting this but held back, his thoughts fast-tracking. Okay, so it's definitely not Lorna, but what if the house is home to some other spirit? Some other person? If so, who? Or what? And why? And how would Penny react? He certainly didn't want to cause her any upset. The last thing he wanted to do was frighten her, not that she'd seemed alarmed by what she said she saw last night. And whilst he was still trying to get his head around his jumbled thoughts, some semblance of order to how his brain was working at the moment, thought it best to say nothing. Not yet. It was all too unbelievable. Stupid, in fact. No, best to let it run its course. There has to be a simpler explanation. It will all sort itself out given time.

"Here, let me give you a hand." He scooped a pile of CDs up from the floor and passed them to Penny, who had begun restacking them in the storage cabinet.

"You must think me mad?" she said, the task finished.

"A little," he jested. "Mad to put up with me, that is."

"Madly in love, yes." She threw her arms around his neck and kissed him before scurrying off to dress.

"Best put on old trousers and wellies," he called after her. "After all the rain last night, it'll probably be exceedingly muddy where we're going."

Chapter 13

The atmosphere under the canopy of trees was humid, in places steaming where the sun's intensity had begun to evaporate the moisture and burn away the morning mist. The track through the woods was muddy, the vegetation dank. Gumboots made it cumbersome to walk, but Penny was glad she'd taken Harry's advice and worn them.

Clumping along the squelching trail, she swapped the tartan blanket from one arm to the other, a smile caressing her face at the thought of the blanket going with them. Whether on their long walks through the countryside surrounding the house, or ambling down into the valley below onto the Common, they would spread the blanket out, then sit and watch nothing in particular, often not talking for hours for conversation wasn't necessary, content enough being in each other's company.

But the blanket also had other uses. For those times when, certain they were alone and hidden from view, he would lay the blanket out on the ground and make love to her in the open air. She tingled at memories it evoked.

Sometimes on their walks the weather would change. Getting caught in the rain, arriving home thoroughly soaked but laughing, eager to share a hot shower or bath together, towelling each other dry before making love wherever the towels fell. There were many times she hoped it really would rain when they were out, for the pleasure of knowing what was to follow. She looked up at the clear sky. Was today going to be one of those days?

"Keep to this side of the track. It's drier here," Harry suggested, pointing out where to avoid the worst of the mud.

In places the path narrowed, forcing her to walk behind him. The claggy mud made the going hard, especially uphill. She stopped to catch her breath. In front of her, Harry slithered, nearly falling over. He looked so comical she had to contain herself not to laugh.

"Are you sure I can't carry anything else? That rucksack

looks heavy," she called.

He regained his balance. "There's only our picnic in here. A few salmon sandwiches, a bowl of strawberries and a bottle of wine, although at the back of my mind I have a niggling suspicion I've forgotten something."

"Keys?"

He shook his head.

"Mobile?" She would have been cross if it went off, disturbing their time together today, and hoped he'd remembered to turn it off.

"Nope. I purposely left it at home."

"Answerphone, then?" Not that she wanted him to miss any calls, business was business, after all.

"I double checked it was on. And made sure the doors were all locked."

Something rustled in the undergrowth, halting her in mid stride. In a blur of grey fur, a squirrel shot out across the path in front of them and scampered hurriedly up the trunk of a nearby oak tree to disappear out of sight. She turned to Harry, smiling widely to show him how happy she felt.

The house was far behind. Out amongst the trees and fresh air there was no music in her head, only the chirping songs of birds and the swishing of leaves on the trees in the breeze.

A few yards ahead Harry came to a halt and held out a hand, waiting for her to catch up.

"Come, take a look."

Through a gap in the tree-lined escarpment both Severn bridges were clearly visible, the sun reflecting off their high girders in flashes of white; the old bridge tall and majestic, the new one curved in a gentle arc, its structure echoing giant sails billowed out in the wind. Beneath the bridges, the wide silver waters of the river stretched onwards to the Bristol Channel in the distance.

"Wow!" She struggled to catch her breath only to have it swept away again by the view before her. Far below in the distance Bristol stretched out, the tall spires of its many churches clearly visible, the communications tower at Fishponds unmistakable. Further away, the Mendip Hills were a purple mound on the horizon. Casting her gaze to the far right, to the Welsh side of the river, the Brecon Beacons loomed through a misty haze. Words couldn't express her awe at the panorama.

"One of the best views in the county," Harry whispered, as if talking aloud would evaporate the scene.

She nodded in agreement, still gasping for breath.

"Not far now. Come on." He gave her hand a gentle squeeze. "I promise you won't be disappointed."

A little further along the path he pulled her to a halt and put a finger up to his lips. "Shoosh."

She stopped talking instantly and stood still, eyes widening in delight as she followed the direction of his pointing finger to a blue-and-pink jay perched close by in one of the ancient trees. The bird shuffled on the branch a few steps and stared back, seemingly unperturbed and unruffled by his fascinated watchers.

When she thought she could walk no further, the woodland cleared to reveal a grassy meadow, waist high and scattered with nodding scarlet poppies, moon daisies and bright blue cornflowers bobbing their heads above the tall stirring grasses.

On the far side of the meadow, set into an unkempt hawthorn hedge, a rusted iron gate hung precariously by one hinge. Harry heaved the gate aside so they could pass through.

The ruins of a large mansion lay in the field beyond. Transfixed, she stared in wonderment at an empty, broken shell of what once must have been a magnificent building. Its blackened, neglected stone walls towered in places three storeys high, other parts were collapsed to ground level. On the tallest crumbling walls, wild buddleias sprouted in a mauve flush of summer, a flotilla of butterflies and bees flitting from tiny flower to flower, a hum radiating from countless insects competing with birdsong from a nearby stand of trees.

The building was roofless, no trace of rafters that once

held it aloft. A wide gap in the decaying walls indicated where once had been the front door. What remained of the windows were glassless hollow voids draped with living curtains of ivy. On the remains of one wall wild honeysuckle entwined itself, festooned in yellow flowers. Their heady scent wafted towards her.

Inside the ruin, remnants of faded red, black and white tiles covered parts of the floor. Wild grasses and rosebay willowherb in resplendent pink glory grew in its many cracks and spaces.

She walked around the building, awestruck by the discovery. "This reminds me of photos of bomb sites in London after the war. There were buildings like this everywhere, derelict and destroyed and left to the elements after the air raids."

"This was no bomb damage," Harry said gravely, watching her eyes darting around in intrigued fascination.

"What happened to it?"

"Apparently, it burnt down a good hundred years ago, from what I can gather."

"How sad. And such a shame. I wonder if anyone was killed in the fire. It's such a large house there must have been lots of people living here. All wealthy and carefree. All the servants there must have been to look after them... No, wait... no, there were no servants here." Why should she think that, she wondered. It was more than a feeling – it was a sense of knowing.

She turned round and around, taking in every detail, each broken stone and crumbling window space, every wild flower and rustling leaf on the tall trees towering behind the decaying walls, trees that swayed in the gentle wind as if dancing to a music only they could hear and whispering stories about the great house they had to tell if only she would listen.

It all looked so familiar, a feeling of déjà vu wrapping her in a blanket of memory, yet she knew she had never been there before... and yet... and yet...

* * *

The last guests bid their hosts farewell before setting off into the winter cold, driven home in their carriages by patient liverymen and steaming black horses, allowing the von Engels to retire to their rooms for what was left of the night.

From the window, Liselle watched them go, wishing she, too, could take to her bed, but first the ballroom had to be cleared before any of the servants could catch a few hours' sleep.

In the kitchens, the scullery maids washed and polished with the utmost of care the lead-crystal wine glasses and white china plates, placing them neatly on trays ready to be carried back to the anteroom next to the ballroom, in readiness for another ball the next evening. Liselle helped to stack them away, then found another broom and helped the rest of the Schloss staff sweeping up the debris of the party.

It became an effort to lift her legs as she worked, exhaustion making her feel dead on her feet. In silence, she brushed away the many fallen petals from limp, drooping flowers that had decorated the room. Gone now was the idle chatter between Truda and herself, the sparkle in her chestnut eyes stilled like the flat, undrunk and wasted champagne. When the men, heaving and pulling on the rattling chains, lowered the two immense chandeliers and capped the candles, the heady scent of perfume, flowers and candlewax hung in the air amid the lingering odour of tobacco smoke and stale alcohol.

In the dimmed room, she noticed the young Count standing by the open door. He looked in her direction, smiled slightly, then strode across the room to her. She shook, barely able to hold the broom. Had she done something wrong?

"I am most pleased," he said. "You have done well. Thank you. You were by far the loveliest of creatures in the room. Far, far more beautiful than all those painted young ladies my parents invited tonight to be paraded before me." He took the broom brusquely from her. "You look tired. Go rest."

In all of her three months at the castle, no one had offered her a single word of thanks, or shown any sign of appreciation. Taken aback by the young Count's flattering words, she spoke out, forgetting herself.

"Sir, that is kind of you but I really must—"

"It is an order," he insisted.

"But, sir, I cannot, not until we all have finished." Why had he picked her out, she wondered. Never before had he bothered to speak to her, nor to any of the servants, so why her? Why tonight? She tried to look away from him, but he caught her chin in his hand, his fingers warm, soft, forcing her to face him again. She knew the other servants had stopped in their toil and were watching her and the Count, she could feel their eyes staring, burning into her back.

"Thank you, sir," she mumbled, "but the others would be upset. They have all worked as hard as me tonight and are equally tired."

The Count smiled as he pushed a strand of her mousy hair that tumbled in ringlets about her narrow shoulders away from her face.

"You are indeed a considerate girl. That is good. I can see now why Zdenek recommended you to my mother."

"Please, sir," she pleaded, looking about with eyes heavy from too little sleep to see if the others were still watching. They would be jealous, she was sure. "I don't want any special treatment. My uncle—"

"Of course," he interrupted, retreating back a step. "How thoughtless of me. We will speak again some other time. Until then, goodnight." He handed back the broom with a brief, polite bow, a gesture that made her mouth drop open in shock.

Baffled by his behaviour, she watched as Johann von Engels clicked his heels, turned, and in large if weary strides, walked away, his red and black cape flaring out about him.

In a moment of sheer madness she called out after him, "Goodnight, sir. I do hope you had a happy birthday."

He looked back over his shoulder and confirmed, "Oh it was, it was..."

Chapter 14

Penny shook her head, trying to make sense of the words and scene that had unfolded before her eyes, eyes wide open yet seeing another view, a different world where there were high mountains, swirling snow, red military uniforms. And people. She could hear their voices, understand their thoughts, feel their innermost emotions. They were not English, of that much she was sure, conscious the events in her mind's eye were taking place elsewhere, not here, not within these ruined walls as stood before her now.

She shivered, goosebumps rising on her flesh. She rubbed her hands up and down her arms to warm up.

"What is it?" Harry sounded anxious.

"Nothing. I had a weird feeling, that's all. A tingling sensation, the hairs on my arms and neck prickling to minute vibrations. There's an atmosphere about this place, Harry, I can feel it. Not in a spooky, eerie sense," she hurried to add, seeing his quizzical frown. "It's more a feeling of calmness. Solace. And a lot of happiness."

Again, her gaze swept around the building, but this time she felt a different reaction. There was tension in the air, anguish and extreme pain in complete contrast to the scenes she'd witnessed only moments before...

Graf Wilheim's determined footsteps approaching echoed across the empty expanse of marble floor. Johann knew instinctively his father was angry.

"I will not allow this," the elder Count shouted upon entering the breakfast room. "You must end this foolishness at once."

Johann looked across the table towards his mother, seeking her support. None was forthcoming.

"You speak to him, Maria," Graf Wilheim ordered his wife. "Make him see sense for obviously I cannot. We will become the joke of the court."

"I do not see why. Liselle is nobility after all," Johann ar-

gued.

"From the wrong side of the blanket," Maria interjected, putting down her knife and fork. "Your father is right, Johann, you have no choice but to end this silly infatuation. You have the pick of any of the ladies we have presented to you; why do you insist on pursuing this young guttersnipe?"

Johann spoke gently. "Because I love her, Mother. Surely you can understand that?"

Maria reached across the table and took hold of her son's clenched hand. "No, it is not love, my son. It is nothing but an obsession with a pretty face, that is all. We cannot give our consent, and nor will the Emperor. You have your family and position to consider. And your future."

"Then I will speak to Franz Joseph myself."

"Don't be foolish, boy!" Wilheim bellowed. "Either give her up, or give up any rights to your inheritance."

Maria's mouth fell open in shock. "Wilheim, you cannot possibly mean that. He is your only son."

"He gives me no choice. What would you have me do? Condone this madness and become the joke of the season? He brings nothing but scandal to the family. I will not have the Engels name made a laughing-stock. And as for Zdenek, he will play no more in this house. He will play no more in Austria, I shall make sure of that. I must have been mad to agree to such an arrangement as to allow his niece into this household."

Maria pushed her plate away. "Zdenek cannot be blamed for his niece's actions. Banish him from court and you will upset the Emperor; he is his favourite."

"He is already in agreement. Believe me, I have not reached this decision lightly."

Johann rose defiantly from his chair. "Father, I intend to marry Liselle, and nothing you can say or do will stop me. I cannot give her up. I love her."

The Count dismissed his son's statement with a broad sweep of his hand. "Then so be it. If you choose to disobey me, we are finished, and I can no longer look upon you as my son!"...

* * *

Puzzled by the vision, a house one moment full of happy vibes, the next of anguish and trouble that seemed to emanate from another time, a different place, Penny staggered to a nearby fallen tree trunk and sat.

Harry hurried over to join her. "Are you okay?"

She could only nod, trying to grasp the ramifications of what she had experienced, trying to make sense of what had flashed through her head. Taking his hand into hers, needing to feel the security of his warm, solid presence, she remained silent until back in control, back in the real world.

"Did you used to come here with Lorna and the children?" she asked when calmness returned.

He shook his head. "I found it last year, when out for a walk. I'd rarely ventured this far along the top lane before."

"Whose house was it, do you know?" Although still bewildered by what she had experienced, she was intrigued to know more. She wanted to learn everything about the place. Perhaps then she could fathom out why she had felt as she had done, why she had imagined those images, so intense, so real.

"I haven't a clue. I keep meaning to find out more about it but...," he shrugged, "...well, you know how these things are. I never got around to it. Always too busy. But this isn't what I brought you here to see. There's more."

"Whoever lived here was happy, Harry. This house was full of love."

He pulled her to him and ruffled her hair. "Woman's intuition?"

She pulled away slightly. "I'm serious. There's something about the place; I can feel it, sense it all around us."

Her attention was caught by something lying on the damaged floor of the building. She trod her way carefully across to where the object lay and picked it up. It was a small broken fragment, its edges sharp. As she wiped away the splatterings of mud, the sun glinted on its black surface.

"It's a piece of old gramophone record, an old seventy-eight. You can barely make out the grooves. Look."

She handed it to him.

He turned the shard over and over in his hand, studying its surface, then glanced about him at the ground, looking for more pieces.

"I wonder what was on it?" He tossed the fragment carelessly back to where it had lain for over a century amongst the rubble. "I guess we'll never know."

"It's funny," she said.

"What, the record?"

"No, silly, not that. The couple I saw dancing last night in Hill House."

He looked disappointed. "So, you *do* remember last night?"

"Of course I do, how could I forget? I was wide awake. I can recall every last little detail. And if I can remember details, I know I couldn't have been dreaming. I never remember my dreams. Who does?"

"The mind can play funny tricks when you're tired, though. Recalling scenes from books or films that in the dead of night can seem like reality."

"It's possible, I suppose, but somehow I don't believe that's what happened. And it doesn't explain the music I keep hearing."

"Are you trying to tell me you believe you actually saw ghosts? Last night? Ghosts dancing in our hallway?"

She shrugged. "Kind of... Yes. Nothing scary, mind. I wasn't afraid; I was more fascinated than anything else." She paused. "I know they weren't really there, yet in the back of my mind something told me they were alive once. That they existed."

"They weren't really there although you could see them. That doesn't make sense, Pen."

"I know. It's hard to explain. They were echoes from the past. I don't know how else to describe them. They were broken shapes, like distortion on a TV screen when it's not tuned in properly. A weak signal. Just brief glimpses of faces and shapes appearing amongst the fuzziness. A glimmer of a swirling skirt, faint glimpses of hands held in a dancer's embrace. A flash of black shoes, the rustle of a silk dress fluid in movement. Things fading from view before coming back sharply into focus for a moment, only to vanish once more into the darkness." But the dancers last night danced in different halls to those she had seen minutes ago. Of that she was certain.

Harry reached out for her hand, giving it a reassuring squeeze. "And you weren't scared by it?"

"Not in the least. There was nothing threatening. I know this might sound stupid, but I'm rather hoping I'll see them again."

His eyebrows rose. "You *do*?"

She nodded. "Which is why I know I wasn't dreaming. And if they weren't part of a dream, then they must have been..." The realization faltered on the brink of incredulity. "Then they must have been real, along with the memories... But whose?" She had no idea where the memories had come from, but they were certainly not hers.

"What about the music?"

"That, I really wish would go away."

"Can you hear it now?"

She shook her head, answering adamantly, "I never hear it outside, only in the house."

"Do you think the two are connected?"

"They have to be, although I don't know how or why. It's only that when I saw the dancers last night, the music was different, more complete. Not in the sense that I heard the whole thing, but it was more rounded. More... well... orchestrated. Oh, I don't know. I'm probably not making any sense, but it's difficult to understand, let alone explain."

She fell into deep thought, analysing last night's vision and what she had seen here among the ruins. What part those images played in it all. Trying to make a connection between them that wouldn't come. Perhaps there wasn't one?

"Come, let's move on," he suggested. "But watch your step, there's fallen stones and blocks scattered about everywhere."

She followed his lead, crossing what she presumed must

once have been a neatly manicured lawn, one now so over-grown with dandelions and thistles it was impossible to tell where it started or ended. Ducking under a warped metal arch festooned with a tangle of ivy and sagging, limp clematis, she could make out a series of dry-stone walls, mostly collapsed, running in a series of terraces down the side of the hill. All manner of garden flowers grew in wild, unchecked profusion among rampant weeds that adorned the bleached yellow stones along each terrace, growing out from every crack and tumbling crevice.

Harry swept his hand across the wide vista ahead. "This is what I really wanted you to see. I call it the hanging gardens of Stonecott Hill."

He led the way, clambering through unkempt shrubbery, many whose flowering season was long finished. She recognized several camellia bushes amongst the overgrown grasses. Rambling roses crawled everywhere; these were in flower, pink and fragrant on the warm breeze blowing up the valley, but many blooms had peaked and hung limply, their petals brown and rotting from recent rains. She had to watch her footing to avoid catching her slacks on spiteful thorns of rampant brambles that were taking over. In some places it was difficult to see which was wall, flowerbed or path.

"It must have been spectacular in its day," she said. In her mind's eye, a vision of colourful beauty flashed. For a moment she almost believed she had gone back in time, to when the garden bloomed in all its true glory.

"Mind these steps, they're loose." Harry reached out a helping hand to steady her. Some of the flagstones wobbled precariously as she stepped on them, treading cautiously over fallen stones and rocks to descend to the lower terraces.

Harry stopped and looked out over the valley. "I assume the house was built here because of this tremendous view. I fell in love with the mystery and magic of it all, as the owners must have done all those years ago. Of course, the bridges weren't there then." His voice effervesced with excitement over his discovery.

Shielding her eyes from the sun, she followed his gaze

across the broad valley. "Mmm, I can understand why. There's certainly something about this place. An aura."

Harry laughed. "You and your feelings... You'll be telling me next it's all about Feng Shui. But it certainly is a lovely place. Intriguing and fascinating all at the same time. Ravaged by nature and neglected by time yet beautiful. I wonder if—"

He was silenced by the rustling of leaves close by at his feet, then pointed down to where a tiny, pink pointed nose poked its way through a pile of dead leaves. A ball of sharp-looking spines followed the nose. "Seems we've disturbed some of the wildlife. Look, it's a hedgehog," he said, smiling.

She bent down toward the creature for a closer look. "You're out rather late this morning, little fellow." She stood upright, watching the animal waddle across the path seemingly unperturbed by their presence as it disappeared into the undergrowth. "I bet there's lots of wildlife here. An absolute haven for them completely undisturbed."

She walked on in front of Harry and stepped directly into a spider's large web strung out across the path between two overgrown shrubs.

"Arrgh!"

He rushed to her aid. "I hear the insect life here has reached monumental proportions," he joked, helping her brush the silken threads from her face and hair. "We'd better watch out."

On the bottom terrace ran an intact stretch of wall. In front of it stood an ornately carved stone seat patterned with yellow lichen. It was strewn with dead leaves and twigs. Harry swept them off with his hand before swinging the rucksack off his shoulders and exchanged it for the blanket, which he laid out on the seat for them to sit upon.

"The perfect spot. Would my lady care to join me for lunch?"

"Yes, please. All that walking has made me hungry." She undid the buckles on the rucksack and retrieved the box of sandwiches, removing the lid and handing him the open container before delving back into the bag and pulling out a bottle of pink Grenache wine and two glasses. These she gave to Harry to hold whilst she rummaged deeper into the bag but could not find what she was looking for.

"Harry, you've forgotten the corkscrew! How are we going to drink this now?"

He laughed. "Oh dear, I knew I'd forgotten something. Still, I can't be perfect all the time, can I?" Then with a laugh and a wink, he turned the cap on the bottle, breaking the gold plastic seal. "Aha, the wonders of modern technology – screw caps!"

She kissed him tenderly on the cheek. How she loved this man who made her so happy, so alive. He placed the bottle down on the ground, then took her hand in his and raised it gently to his lips, kissing each fingertip lightly.

"Shall we eat later?" he asked. "I've an appetite for something else first."

Love among the ruins; her heart missed a beat at his intimation. She pulled him to her.

Strolling back home, her arm linked through his, they turned off the lane and into the driveway of Hill House. Without warning, conversation stopping mid flow, Harry withdrew his arm, thrust his hands deep into his trouser pockets and strode on ahead of her as if in some great hurry.

Penny stared after him, wondering what was wrong, his demeanour causing her to think he was nervous about something, afraid even. As if something about the driveway had for some reason upset him. She looked back towards the gate. The gravel by the entrance appeared brighter than the rest, less weathered. She hadn't noticed before, it being in deep shadow from the trees flanking it most of the time. Thinking this was nothing more than a trick of the light, highlighting things usually in shade, she was about to continue walking on when something else caught her attention.

Close to the gate stood several tall sycamore trees some of which were blackened, damaged from fire by the look of them. One was leafless and looked totally dead, as if at some point in time it had been struck by lightning. She wondered why she hadn't noticed it before. The tree didn't look safe and ought to be cut down, she thought, before a high wind uprooted it. It could be dangerous. They must do something about it soon before it fell on someone or a passing car.

A flurry of wind rustled the leaves on the other trees and played in the high hedgerow. As she looked up, the smell of smoke wafted into her nostrils. She sniffed at the air.

"I can smell a bonfire," she called to Harry, already yards ahead. "Who around here would be crazy or selfish enough to light a bonfire on a day like today? And in the middle of the afternoon. You'd think they'd at least wait until after dark."

Harry stopped and turned around. "I can't smell anything, only the stink from across the lane. Jacob must be muck-spreading the top field; one of the glories of living next to a farm. Which reminds me, I must ask him if he can spare a few sacks for the roses. They could do with a bit around the roots again."

She hurried to catch him up. "Smells more like a bonfire to me. Autumnal?"

"God, don't say that; we haven't even had a proper summer yet."

Chapter 15

Nurturing the flourishing gardens of Hill House became the only place where Penny felt she could truly relax, contented to be out in the fresh air busy pruning, clipping and dead-heading the plants to encourage new blooms, teasing shrubs into shape or weeding out recalcitrant stragglers and suckers.

Come autumn, she would plant lots of crocus bulbs, she decided, hundreds of them, and swathes of daffodils and snowdrops for a fabulous spring show. Envisaging, too, a long sweep of acers and maples growing on the far side of the lawn opposite the morning room, how their colours would glow red and amber and golden. A fire of nature to warm dismal days.

After such a wet start to the summer, everything had begun to flourish in spite of the unseasonably cool temperatures of August. At least the garden hadn't disappointed her with its show of clematis and blousy, old-fashioned but heavenly-perfumed roses. The bedding plants she'd put in earlier in the season now bloomed in a riot of colours, and the herb garden had begun to recover from its soggy beginnings, the sweet smell of rosemary and hyssop drifting on the air as she brushed by them.

Delightful as the gardens at Hill House were, she coveted the hanging gardens in the grounds of the ruined mansion, wishing they were hers. The place extruded an atmosphere she couldn't drink in enough of, and whenever Harry suggested a walk, she would plead to go back there. He always agreed, enjoying each visit too. It seemed no one else had found their secret garden, and trusting they would be undisturbed, he would take her in his arms and make love to her out in the open, on the blanket, hidden by the shelter of the lower terrace wall.

More and more she felt she belonged there. That she knew the people who had lived there long ago, understood their thoughts, their aspirations, and felt their emotions, adamant in her head she really could see them all. Hear their voices, their conversations.

More vivid was the perception of lavish balls. Of flowing gowns and striking uniforms, flashing swords and shiny brass buttons; such wonderful soirées and dinner parties full of laughter from guests. The gleaming silver and sparkling glasses. At times, she could smell the candlelight, see the flickering flames licking crystal chandeliers with glimmering light.

Yet these balls and lavish parties took place elsewhere. Far away, in another country. How did she know that, she wondered. Considering she'd never been out of England, she couldn't make sense of why she saw them happening at the ruin? It was a strange feeling, one she never mentioned to Harry. He wouldn't understand such strong and wild, nay, fanciful notions.

As she plucked honeysuckle sprigs to put into a vase for the kitchen table, in her mind's eye she visualised how the hanging gardens would have looked in their former re-splendent glory. She even pictured the previous owners walking arm-in-arm amongst the pink roses, admiring the views across the valley, a white lace parasol held high to keep off the sun.

To her, these were real people; flesh on the bones of her imagination. The woman, pretty and graceful, possessing mousy hair that tumbled in ringlets about her narrow shoulders. Her escort in a military uniform – black flannels and a red blazer as cherry red as the young woman's lips – was dashing. Yes, that was the word she thought best described him: dashing. An exceedingly handsome character straight out of a Regency novel.

She plucked another red and yellow bloom, inhaling its sweet scent, realizing with much relief that lately her nights were uninterrupted, the music and dancing apparitions no more. She couldn't even remember the tune now; it had been so long since it had become stuck on replay inside her brain. Harry had all but convinced her she had dreamt everything. Sleepwalking. Nothing more than a settling-in time com-pounded by tension and worry over the divorce, which had now become absolute.

Only she wasn't fully persuaded, positive there was a connection between the disjointed, vague figures she'd seen, or thought she had, dancing in Hill House. Even now, without her eyes being closed, she could see images of the people in the ruined house. What precisely that link was, was difficult to pinpoint for the visions so embedded in her head felt as if they were her own memories. Memories from a past she couldn't remember yet somehow must have once lived.

Could she be a reincarnation, she wondered. Was *she* the lady in the floaty dress holding the parasol and strolling through the hanging gardens? Was that dashing soldier her husband? A lover from some distant past life? She laughed at herself for letting her imagination run away with her yet again.

Too quickly the mild summer melted into autumn, creating early morning mists that blanketed the valley below, leaving Hill House floating in the air like a magical fairytale castle. Darker evenings heralded approaching winter, and a chill north wind blustered in, shaking loose what little remained of the glorious autumnal display on the trees.

Harry felt at peace for the first time in several years, the horrors of his past slowly fading, the nightmares fewer and fewer. Now, at least when he shut his eyes at night, the blackened faces of his children no longer haunted him. And Penny wasn't plagued any more by music. He didn't believe in ghosts, but something odd *had* happened, there was no doubting that but, hopefully, it was all over. Whatever it had been had now finally left them in peace.

A flash of lightning lit the room momentarily before plunging it back into darkness. Hearing rain lashing against the window, he reached out only to discover Penny's side of the bed felt cold. He grabbed his dressing gown and went in search.

He found her seated on the bottom stair, her arms wrapped around her knees. She was swaying gently from side to side, staring transfixed at some point along the hallway. Gently, he eased himself down beside her and took her gently in his arms, cradling her head and kissing her hair. Wearing nothing but her flimsy nightdress, her skin felt icy cold.

Wide-eyed, she turned to him, acknowledging his presence with a smile.

"Oh Harry, they're so beautiful," she whispered. "Look, there by the wall, they're dancing again. Can you see them? Look how much in love they are. Tell me you can hear the lovely music."

He could see nothing other than the grey flagstones on the floor and the whitewashed walls of the house, and the only sounds he could hear were the steady ticking of the grandfather clock and the rain outside. He sighed wearily. It wasn't all over at all.

"Come back to bed, Penny, it's late. There's nothing to see, you're dreaming again." Gently, he pulled her to her feet; she offered no resistance. Holding firmly to her hand, he led her back upstairs.

"But I'm not dreaming, Harry, I did see something. They were there dancing again," she said as he tucked the duvet around her.

"Sure you did." He placed a delicate kiss on both closed eyelids – she seemed to have fallen asleep immediately – then sat on the edge of the bed, head in hands, wondering... Am I verging on insanity, going mad, he thought. Is this all some horrible dream I'm going to wake up from? And when I do, will I find Penny gone and everything has been an illusion?

He turned and stared at her sleeping form, her back towards him. Maybe he should take her away? He needed to protect her. Shield her. But from what? Certainly not some spiteful, evil spirit come to manifest itself in their home. But what if it became worse? And if he told Penny of these concerns she'd probably tell him not to be so daft. It wasn't as if she was scared by what she saw...

The more he thought about it, the more silly the whole situation sounded. What was it with this music and dancers? It had to be something. He didn't believe in ghosts, he told himself yet again, and as for any earlier stupid thoughts of it being Lorna come back to haunt them, that idea was so preposterous as to not even be worth spending any further time brooding over. Ghosts didn't exist. Period!

He let out another heavy, troubled sigh before climbing into bed and switching off the bedside lamp. There was so much uncertainty and fear swirling around in his head, so many questions needing answers, he doubted he'd be able to get back to sleep.

"Oh, Penny, darling. I love you so much," he whispered against her soft hair. "What if tonight I fall asleep forever? What then? Who's going to hold you? Keep you safe? Love you as I do?"

In the darkness of the room, he made up his mind what had to be done. Only he had to pick the right moment to tell her because he knew she wasn't going to like the idea one little bit.

Chapter 16

"Sell the house! But why?" Stunned by this unexpected announcement, Penny studied the expression on Harry's face while a million questions raced around in her head.

What had brought this on? What had made him reach such a decision? And why now, when everything had settled down and they were happy? They *were* happy together, weren't they, she asked herself, doubt beginning to creep in. And if he wasn't, why hadn't he said something about it before? Talked about it. But to come out with this bombshell!

"I thought you loved it here. I know I do, it's perfect." Apart from the music occasionally drifting through her mind, that is, and the odd days when she felt Hill House was the enemy.

Regardless of both, she didn't want to leave the world she and Harry had created there together, their way of life, all those beautiful moments. She couldn't imagine any other house ever holding the same meanings for her.

Her voice quivering, she finally managed to utter, "I don't want to move; there's no reason to. What about all our plans to redecorate? My ideas for the garden?" She knew she sounded like a petulant child, but she couldn't help it. Moving was the last thing she wanted.

"It's not fair of me to expect you to live in a house once occupied by another woman. It can't be easy for you despite what you say. I'm sure that's why you keep hearing and seeing things."

"But that's plain daft. It's no different from any other house." She reached for his hand. "You silly old fool. I don't mind at all; it's such a lovely place and so comfortable. How can it matter to me when there is so little here to remind me Lorna had once been mistress of the house and bed I now occupy? Of course, I don't mind about her. How could I? It's not as if she's some mysterious figure to be revered and held in awe. Lorna had been a real person, your wife, and you have a past as much as I have. I didn't know her, so it's not as though every time I pick up or move anything I feel as if I am disturbing her memory."

"But *I* feel it," he quietly admitted. "It's like she's still here. And the children. Hill House has served its purpose, and I think the time is right for us to move on. Together." He lifted her hand to his lips and kissed it delicately. "Sweetheart, trust me on this. We need to start afresh in somewhere we can call *our* home. There are too many memories of my own here. Too much of the past constantly reminding me."

A wave of guilt washed over her for not taking account of his feelings in all this, focusing on her own wants and desires and not thinking of his.

"I'm sorry, Harry, I hadn't thought of things from your point of view. That was inconsiderate of me."

Inside, she fought a giant battle between her head, which accepted Harry was right, and her heart. Leaving Hill House would be a big wrench after becoming so settled, but perhaps if she could convince him not to move too far away, it might not be so bad.

She smiled at him and tried to sound enthusiastic when she said, "Had you anywhere particular in mind?"

"The estate agent in Chipping Sodbury has several suitable properties on his books that look promising. There's one in particular I like. I went to see it yesterday, on my way back from Peter's. It's a wonderful place, Pen. Lovely views. It's old but has all mod cons. It's been unoccupied for some months, since the old fellow that lived there died, so it's a wee bit neglected, of course, and needs some work doing. Apart from that, it is structurally sound. I've had a good look around inside. It's perfect for us. You will fall in love with it the moment you see it, I know you will."

"Oh." She turned away from him, not wanting him to see how even more disappointed his admission made her feel. That he'd been looking at places and talking to estate agents rankled. He should have at least discussed it with her first. Before now.

As if reading her thoughts, he said, "I know I should have said something sooner, but I had to get this clear in my own head first. I know how much you love it here, which was why I didn't mention it earlier, not until I was certain this is right for us both. I didn't want to upset you if it was all a storm-in-a-teacup inside me, some mid-life crisis. I think, deep down, I'd hoped that by seeing what else was available, it might convince me that things were okay where we are. But they're not, Penny. Not for me. And nor are they for you if you're honest. And whilst I feel this way, I can't be the man I want to be for you."

She understood then that he really did have her feelings at heart, admitting to herself she would have probably done exactly the same thing if the tables were reversed. She could at least go and have a look at this place he seemed so enamoured with. After all, they didn't have to accept the first house they looked at together. It wasn't as if they were in any great hurry to move out.

"It's not as though we'd be moving far away. The cottage is about a mile from here. And still on the ridge. At least come and have a look. See what you think," he implored.

Not taking her eyes off the view from the sitting room window, she reluctantly agreed. "Okay, but I warn you, Harry Winchester, I'm not going to be coerced into making any snap decision. It will have to be something extra special I move into. Anywhere else will need to come up to some pretty high expectations to win me over."

He nuzzled the side of her head and whispered, "Even with the music? Even though you see things?"

She spun round to face him, scrutinizing his expression. "Is that what this is all about? I'm seeing ghosts and hearing music, and you're the one who's frightened?"

He shrugged. "Well, you do have to admit, something peculiar is happening to you here. To us. "

She sighed, torn between loving the house and its location one moment, and hating the very stones it was built from the next. One moment happy and content that the music had gone; the next driven to despair by it playing all the time in her head. Never really going away. Never stopping. And she had been sleeping badly again of late, too many disturbed nights and long, worn-out days.

She looked deep into his eyes, comforted by the knowledge he would never do anything to hurt her or spoil their relationship. She kissed his cheek.

"Maybe you're right, Harry. Perhaps it is time we moved."

Chapter 17

The troubles of the past year soon evaporated along with the fog lifting from the valley beneath a cold January sun barely skimming the brow of Stonecott Hill. Dispelled, too, were any remaining doubts over moving into Pond Cottage now the seemingly endless task of unpacking had started. And, much to her joy, Penny found she enjoyed finding a new place for everything; this in spite of the parched feeling on her lips and her mouth tasting of dust. In her arms, she held another pile of paperback books retrieved from the depths of the crate.

"Tell me where you want these put then I'll put the kettle on. Time for a drink I think, don't you?" A wisp of loose hair strayed out from beneath the red paisley scarf tied around her head. She tried to tuck it back in place but was hampered by her heavy load.

Harry stepped back from the low shelf in the alcove by the inglenook, where he'd been stacking books in order of height.

"I think it's my turn to make it. You sit down and take a break, sweetheart, you've been at it non stop since breakfast. Here, give those to me."

Kicking aside discarded newspaper wrappings and debris tossed to the floor, and stepping around packing crates still waiting to be emptied, he took the pile of books from her arms and put it down on the coffee table, pushing aside a bundle of scrunched-up newspapers.

She flopped onto the arm of a nearby armchair and nodded towards the crate she'd been emptying.

"That one's full of your books too, and all your boyhood comics. There are bundles of them in the bottom along with old biscuit tins full of cigarette cards and goodness knows what else. I thought you were going to sort them out?"

He gave an apologetic shrug. "You know me, I can't bear to throw anything out. It's like throwing away one's whole life."

"But where are we going to put it all?"

"The books can go over there for now." He pointed to the

shelf on the other side of the inglenook before surveying the clutter scattered about the room. "The rest can go up in the loft for now, I guess. Look, how about we abandon the remainder of this for now and go explore the garden instead?"

"Great idea. Yes, let's. What does it matter if the unpacking takes until next Christmas, we have all the time in the world." She leapt up from the chair. "Come on, then, I'm ready."

Laughing, he nodded towards her feet. "I suggest you change out of those white plimsolls first and put something decent on. You'll get cold feet."

Hidden from the lane by a high dry-stone wall and a stand of ancient oaks and knurled, ivy-covered sycamores and beech trees creating an air of seclusion from the outside world, Pond Cottage was a handsome, old stone house set in a natural depression on the escarpment. About half-a-mile from their previous home on the same ridge, none of the views across the valley Penny loved so much had been lost.

The cottage was a great deal smaller than Hill House, having only three bedrooms, four if you discounted the loft conversion, and one bathroom. "Who needs all that extra space, anyway?" Harry had said the day they signed the paperwork and collected the keys.

The cottage had been occupied up until the previous June, but the garden had been neglected for much longer, judging by how overgrown and wild it had become. Rambling brambles and straggly shrubbery grew everywhere. An untamed maze of tall brown grass was bathed in cold, yellow light. Saplings and whippy seedling trees crusted with frost grew in a leafless tangle amongst thorny rose bushes, creating a tortuous path down to the far reaches of the garden, a minefield of spiny leaves and clingy thorns to be carefully stepped over.

Harry pushed a low branch out of the way and held it back, allowing her to pass. It sprang back sharply when he let it go.

"Grief, there's a lot of work needs doing here," he said. "It will all have to be chopped back hard before the sap rises again. I'll have a word with Bob Dando from the village. I'm sure he'll come up and do the worst for the price of a few pints."

"Good idea," she agreed, "but not too much clearing, mind. We must wait and see what comes up first. We don't know what beautiful plants are here waiting beneath the soil ready to burst through." She kicked at the ground with her heel. It was frozen hard. A robin's tic-tic-tic called out. Looking up, she caught sight of the bird as it swooped down to the ground in search of a meal.

In her mind's eye, she could picture how the clumps of green shoots already poking through the ground would turn into banks of snowdrops, and sensed come springtime the garden would be full of flowers. That there would be drifts of primroses and daffodils and wood anemones and later, come May, the whole area carpeted in scented wild bluebells. She hoped so; it felt that sort of garden.

Beneath a clump of trees, the tell-tale signs of a badger's scrape were evident. She squealed with delight. She'd never seen a live badger before, although plenty of roadkills on the lanes. Finding a sett in the garden filled her with excitement, imagining balmy summer evenings waiting and watching for the black and white animals to sniff and grunt their way out of the hole on hunting forays.

Catching sight of a tawny owl studying them from a branch high up in one of the trees, its brown speckled feathers ruffled and puffed out to keep the winter cold at bay, Harry whooped with pleasure. The bird took flight at his outburst, settling again on another tree covered in rampant, unruly ivy close by. Harry pointed to where it had perched near a dark hole in the tree trunk.

"I bet that's his roost up there."

"This is like having our own secret garden. It's like the hanging gardens," she said, thrilled by the idea.

Harry nodded. "That's what I thought when I first saw it."

In a wide depression surrounded by tall, brown rushes growing unchecked about its perimeter, they came to the pond that gave the house its name. An ethereal silence surrounded the black water, a low mist dancing across the thin layer of ice that clung to its surface.

"Are you sure it won't overflow and flood the garden if it rains too much?" Penny asked, studying the dark and mysterious water.

"Positive. It's fed by rainwater running off the top of the hill in that narrow gully next to the house. Any overspill cascades down the escarpment to join the Frome river on the Common. There's no history of it ever causing a problem."

"It feels spooky here," she said, wrapping her arms around herself against the chill. Her feet felt damp inside her wellingtons, and so cold she wished she'd put on a further pair of socks.

"Nonsense! It's beautiful," Harry contradicted, smiling.

"I've always wanted a pond, but Alex refused to have one, for no particular reason other than to be cantankerous."

"Well, now you have your own miniature lake in the garden. I expect it's full of wildlife too, so I hope you like frogs."

"Love them. Especially fried!" she joked. Keeping back from the edge, she craned her neck to peer down into the blackness. "Do you think there's any fish in it?"

Harry stepped closer to the frozen water, unsure of his footing against the undefined bank. "Could be. If not, we'll have to buy some. Might be some newts in there, though."

She grabbed at his arm. "Oh, do be careful, darling. I don't want you falling in."

He laughed, swaying as if about to totter over the edge. "Well, you'd better let go because if I go in, so do you."

"Swine!" She gave him a gentle nudge, a playful attempt to push him in. Thankfully, his footing was on solid ground and he was quite safe.

"Brrr! I should have put gloves on." He rubbed his hands together against the chill as he looked about the frozen garden suspended beneath its sparkling frost icing. "Come on, let's go back indoors and get that coffee going, it's getting nippy out here. We can explore some more tomorrow." He grabbed hold of her hand. "Oh, Penny, it is going to be so wonderful here, I can feel it."

"With you, anywhere is wonderful." He turned at the intensity of her voice. "I'm sorry I made such a fuss about moving. The house is perfect. And the pond."

"No regrets?"

She shook her head. "None."

"Me neither."

She stood in silence surveying the water again before turning to Harry and asking, "Can we have some ducks for the pond? A few little ones?"

He smiled broadly, unable to refuse her pleading eyes. "I don't see why not. We'll have two and call them Easter and Christmas."

She stared at him blankly, before realizing he was teasing her, then punched his arm playfully. "Oh, you!"

Laughing, he said, "Of course we shall have ducks. We might even be lucky and find some wild ones settle here. Or we could go the whole hog and get a swan or two."

"Good idea. Race you back." She turned and set off at a sprint back up the garden towards the house.

"Hey, wait for me." He took a final look into the deep, fathomless water then gave chase, his heavy boots crunching and snapping twigs and dead branches underfoot as he ran. Halfway along the broken path, he caught up with her. She stood still, staring up intently at the house.

"Out of breath already?"

"No, I was looking at the cottage. It looks odd from here."

"What do you mean "odd'?" He gazed up at the building through the misty vapour of their breaths but could see nothing out of place. It all looked perfectly normal. "Don't tell me you've seen a mysterious face at the attic window? Dooo do, dooo do." He mimicked the *Twilight Zone* theme.

She swiped at his arm. "No, silly. Look, above the windows... they've all got different shaped and sized lintels. See how the one above the kitchen is different from the rest; it's much wider than the ones above the sitting room or bedrooms. Even the stone blocks are different. Some yellow, some grey, some square. Those over by the kitchen door are more oblong and black, charred looking. Others look like they've been pushed into the wall any which way or how."

He shrugged. "That's nothing unusual. These houses weren't always built from quarried stone, but often from the remains of other houses, or stones found in the ground as they farmed and cleared the land."

Her eyes widened expectantly. "Perhaps they came from our ruins?"

He pondered the suggestion a moment before answering, "It's possible, I suppose. I did hear something about the stones being removed and used to build other houses along the valley. I'm not sure if that's true or not."

"I expect it is. It's a well-known fact people pillaged and plundered other people's homes if someone died leaving no relatives behind to inherit. Even down to taking a dead man's boots. Waste not, want not. Only nowadays they call it recycling; a new slant on the old practice of reclamation. I'm sure the politicians think up these fancy names to boost their credibility. Oh, look at me saving the environment, I've invented recycling," Penny mocked in an exaggerated, squeaky voice.

Harry laughed. "You're not wrong there. The surveyor's report did say the cottage was added to over time."

"I wonder... Harry, we simply must find out. How romantic if it's true and Pond Cottage really is built from our ruin." She slipped her arm into his as they began walking, but she couldn't help staring up constantly at the house, stumbling over the wiry brambles in places as they walked towards it.

A shadowy face staring back down appeared at an upstairs window. Catching her breath in a sharp intake, she stopped short, pulling Harry to a halt.

"Oh my God! Harry, look. Someone's in the house." She pointed to the window.

His gaze followed the direction of her finger. "Can't be! I can't see anyone."

She shot him an incredulous look. How could he not see? When she turned back to the house, the face had gone.

"Stay here, I'll go and check but honestly, Pen, no one's in there." Harry ran off towards the back door and disappeared inside. A few moments later he reappeared in the doorway and beckoned. "It's okay, sweetheart, no one's here."

Hands tucked into her armpits, she trudged up the path and into the house, positive she had seen someone, or something, up there. That she hadn't been mistaken.

Chapter 18

Harry came up from the cellar after relighting the central heating boiler.

"That's the fourth time in a week it's gone out for no apparent reason. If it happens again, I'll call a heating engineer in," he said, washing his hands. "And it smells a bit damp down there."

"Do you think we ought to get it checked out, just to be on the safe side?" Penny spoke without daring to take her eyes from the stove, her arm never ceasing from stirring the risotto she was preparing.

"The surveyor did confirm everything is structurally sound and assured me it's never flooded down there. Still, might be worth getting it tanked out."

"There's no danger of collapse, is there?"

Hands dry, Harry hung the towel back over the rail at the side of the sink. "No, the house has stood here safe enough for centuries. But I think I'd better move some of the wine away from the lower racks down there, although the walls are completely dry. Better to be safe, though. We don't want our supply to spoil. I've some rather fine bottles of Chardonnay laid down for tomorrow night's dinner party." He crossed to the stove and leaning over the hot pan, took an appreciative sniff. "Mmmm. Smells good."

She dipped a teaspoon into the gently bubbling rice and tasted to check for seasoning. "Needs a touch more Parmesan, I think. Do you realize, it will be our first dinner party in our new home?"

"It will be our first dinner party, period. We never did any entertaining at Hill House, apart from Peter occasionally. Somehow we never seemed to get round to inviting anyone."

She gave him a quick kiss on the cheek. "That's because I didn't want to share you with anyone, least of all Elaine Frampton."

"Don't be too harsh on Elaine," he entreated. "I know she can come across as being a finicky fusspot, but that's her way;

even if she does drive me up the wall at times with her fussing. It's only because she's concerned for me."

"I'm always nice to her, but I still think she resents me. I can sense it every time she speaks to me."

"Well, she'll have to get used to it, won't she? Because I'm not giving you up for love or money, and especially not for Elaine. You're mine and here to stay for good, I hope." He gave her a squeeze around her waist. "I want to marry you, you know, Pen?" he whispered in her ear.

She turned her head sharply to look at him. *Marriage?* It was the first time he'd mentioned the word. She wasn't sure how she felt. Pleased? Flattered? Honoured? For the moment she was only too happy to spend the rest of her life with him, ring or no ring on her finger, but it was far too soon to consider marriage again. No, far too soon after all she'd gone through with Alex. She wasn't ready for such a commitment, as much as she loved Harry. She nuzzled into his cheek.

"Do I have to give you an answer now?"

He chuckled. "Certainly not! That wasn't a proposal, Penny Cornwall. When I ask you to marry me, it will be on bended knee with a diamond ring in my hand. The moment has to be right."

She laughed. "So I should hope!"

She continued stirring in silence a few moments, enjoying his protective arms around her middle whilst she plucked up the courage to say what was preying on her mind.

"I'm a little nervous over this dinner party, Harry. I've never hosted one before. Alex wasn't one to have company in. To top it all, this place is still in such a mess. There are boxes still waiting to be unpacked upstairs, the new three-piece hasn't been delivered yet and—"

"Calm down, pet. It will all sort itself out."

"But with all these people coming—"

"It's only the Smythes from across the lane. Merely a simple housewarming to get to know our nearest neighbours, and as a thank you to Pete and Elaine for helping us with all the packing for the move."

"I know, but I want to make the right impression." She

had been determined for the first time in her life she wasn't going to make do with other people's cast-offs. When she'd married Alex, all of their furniture and china, even down to the tea towels, had been donated either by her mother or by Alex's family or unwanted gifts given by someone else before being passed on to her. At the time, she'd been grateful for the donations, they didn't have a lot of money. Even moving into Hill House, everything there had been Harry and Lorna's, down to the last teaspoon and wine glass.

The move to Pond Cottage was a turning point in their life together, so everything had to be new. Her tastes, her choices, and Harry's, of course; a mutual agreement on decisions. This time, her home was going to receive the full treatment both it and she deserved. New home, new hopes and a new start, she vowed, sprinkling another handful of grated cheese into the saucepan.

"I simply want it all to be perfect. I don't want to let you down."

"Pen, you never let me down. You never will. And I think, too, it's about time I met your family. Especially your mother. We should invite her to stay for a few days."

Oh dear, could she cope with that, she wondered. She and Mum weren't exactly on speaking terms, hadn't been for some years. It wasn't that they'd had fallen out over anything in particular, more a case of not seeing eye to eye on several important matters. But Harry was right, of course. It was time they sorted out their differences, but she wasn't sure she was ready yet. She needed more time.

"Perhaps later in the year, when we're more settled," she said.

Harry laughed. "Okay. I'll hold you to that. Oh, did I tell you, Elaine positively bristled for joy when I told her Peter was now coming?"

"That's because she's got her beady eyes set on him now she knows she can't get her claws into you."

"You might well have an element of truth in that astute observation. I've seen Elaine in action too many times but, sweetheart, she can't compete alongside you. She and I were never going to be an item."

"Nor do I expect she and Peter ever will be. Do you? Mind you, he is a good catch. He's wealthy and available, and Elaine isn't one to miss an opportunity." She turned off the element under the pan. "I'm glad he's over that bout of flu, the poor man sounded so poorly last week over the phone."

Harry pulled her closer, sending heat and need rising, intensified by the warmth emanating from the stove. "It'll be rather fun watching Elaine perform her manhunter act. The evening's entertainment."

"Harry Winchester, you old devil, that's cruel. But I see your point." She laughed with him and kissed him again. "Now away with you and lay the table quickly. Lunch is ready to dish."

"Do you think I should warn Peter?" he asked over his shoulder, giving a playful smirk and wink as he pulled open the cutlery drawer in search of a couple of forks.

Jilly Smythe looked around the attic with keen interest.

"I keep telling my John we should be doing a conversion like this and putting in a couple of Velux windows, but he won't have it. Says we have enough room. But it would be nice to have the extra space for when the family visit." She walked to the far end of the roofspace, her heels tapping loudly across the bare floorboards. "It could be done up to be really nice in here."

"I couldn't agree more," said Penny. "We haven't really decided what we're going to use it for yet." She pointed to one side of the room where unpacked boxes were stacked. "As you can see, it's still full of bits and pieces we haven't found a home for yet, but it's way down on our list of priorities at the moment."

"Or a nursery and playroom perhaps?" Jilly suggested, a twinkle in her eye.

"Goodness me, no! I'm far too old to start thinking about babies." Having children was something she and Harry had never discussed; she didn't even know what he thought on the matter. After what had happened to his children she hadn't wanted to broach the subject, certainly not until he mentioned it first.

"Nonsense," Jilly protested. "Age doesn't come into the equation nowadays. You only have to look in the papers to read about women in their fifties and sixties, even older, having kids. You've plenty of time yet." Moving a pile of books from a rickety stool and placing them on the floor, Jilly sat down, pulled off one of her shoes and rubbed at her heel. "I must admit, I was most curious to see what had been done up here. I was surprised David was even allowed to do it, seeing as we're in a conservation area. When the Hargreaves down the lane applied for planning permission to extend their bungalow and make two dormer rooms, the local council refused."

Penny was about to reply when she thought she could hear music playing, sending a chill shiver through her. *Surely not, not here?* She walked back to the open door to listen, relieved to hear the sexy sound of a tenor saxophone from Kenny G filtering up from the sitting room. Harry had put on a CD. A roar of laughter issued forth. All sounds well downstairs, she thought, turning her attention back to her guest, who had put her shoe back on and was now flicking through the pages of a book from the pile on the floor.

"I don't think planning permission would have been necessary here, Jilly. The conversion hasn't affected the appearance of the house, and the gabled windows can't be seen from either the road or from lower down the hill. Over the years the house has probably changed several times, so who's to say what is the correct way it should look. Also, this isn't a listed building. We checked that out before we bought it."

Jilly closed the book and put it back down on the pile. "Mmm, I suppose you're right. The Ewells had the work done some years ago, a short while before poor Pamela died from a massive stroke. David became a bit of a recluse after that, so I never had the opportunity of coming in to have a little nose around. Mind you, we couldn't understand why he wanted to stay on here on his own, what with the garden and all the weird goings on."

Penny's ears pricked up.

"What do you mean 'weird goings on'?"

Jilly hesitated, seemingly reluctant to answer. "Oh, it was nothing really... I never honestly believed Pam anyway when she used to talk about hearing odd noises in the house. Then there were the funny smells she kept on about. And she didn't like the pond, said it felt creepy."

Fascinated to learn of this, yet at the same time nervous she had stepped from one house with spirits straight into another, Penny's mind raced with questions and notions. Eager to find out more, she asked, "Did she ever hear strange music?"

"Not that I can recall her mentioning. She was a funny old woman, really. I think she was a bit addled. She used to get muddled and ever so forgetful towards the end."

"Alzheimer's?"

Jilly nodded.

"What about Mr Ewell? Did he ever talk about hearing things?"

There was a look of mild amusement on Jilly's face. "Oh, there's many a tale I could tell you, but not tonight. Those sorts of stories are best kept for a winter's evening, around a roaring fire when there's nothing decent to watch on the telly. Suffice to say, Pamela never liked the house much, that's all, but I think that was because she missed her old home in Easter Compton. Always wanted to move back there, she kept telling me. The old woman was going senile, then she had that stroke and never recovered."

"How sad." Penny picked up a picture frame from the top of a packing crate and blew away the thin film of dust from its surface. She studied the picture of Sam and Elly for a few moments before putting it back down. "Did you know them well, the Ewells?"

Jilly shook her head. "Not really. David kept pretty much to himself. Pam used to like dropping in for coffee and a natter. She was a friendly old soul but a bit lonely, I think. That tailed off towards the end. She used to say—"

Jilly stopped talking and looked around the room, sniffing

the air. "Can I smell smoke?"

"It's probably the bonfire. We found so much junk in the house, especially up here. You know, broken chairs, newspapers, rubbish, empty cardboard boxes, that sort of thing. As today's been the first dry spell for a few weeks, we decided this afternoon to burn some of it. You mentioned weird goings-on with the Ewells. What sort of weird things?" Penny wasn't about to let the conversation drift onto something else. She wanted to know what Jilly knew about the house.

"Coo-eee! Penny, darling..." Elaine's high-pitched voice called up the stairwell. "The dinger thingy on the cooker is pinging. Do you want me to turn the oven off? I must say, whatever it is, it smells mighty wonderful."

Inwardly annoyed at the poor timing but appreciating it was hardly Elaine's fault, Penny called back, "Yes, please. We're on our way." She beckoned to Jilly, whom she thought looked relieved by the interruption. "Come on, we'd better go down and join the party or the menfolk will wonder where we've got to. I do hope you like beef carbonnade."

She let Jilly go down the stairs first, then flicked off the light switch, plunging the attic into darkness. By the landing window, she stopped and glanced outside towards the bonfire. A few odd sparks and flames licked the cold night air. Wet spats hit the windowpane. It had started raining again, dousing the glowing embers of the remains of David Ewell's possessions.

Intrigued by what Jilly had told her, Penny decided she must ask her over for coffee one morning soon to quiz her further about this Pamela Ewell woman. There was apparently much to learn about this house, and she was eager to find out all she could.

Chapter 19

Pond Cottage proved to be far more comfortable and less draughty than Hill House. It hadn't taken long to settle in and it soon felt as though she had always lived there, as if Pond Cottage was hers and always had been.

Nor did it take long to settle back into their relaxed, care-free way she had come to love. The lazy breakfasts, the shared walks exploring the gardens and woods surrounding the cottage, and together creating plans for the spring, when they would clear the pond, tidy all the extraneous overgrowth from its perimeter and rid the surface of the duckweed.

February winds took on a northern chill, threatening to turn the rain into sleet and snow. For weeks now it had rained incessantly, the gully by the side of the house flowing in torrents as rainwater rushed off the top of the hill. The worst floods on record were reported from all over the country. Bridges and roads washed away in Cumbria. Towns and villages cut off on the Somerset Levels. Homes ruined, lives wrecked. A railway line washed away in Dorset. Britain, it seemed, was sinking beneath the waves.

Each morning she put on a pair of galoshes to wander through the garden, delighting in the discovery of each new green shoot fighting its way through the soggy soil, inching ever higher, each little clump a promise of spring flowers. The walks always ended by the pond's edge, always drawn towards it. Some days its inky darkness seemed fathomless; some days the water reflected the grey sky behind her own reflection as she leaned forward to stare down into the murky depths. As the days passed, she was sure the level was inching higher and higher, tumbling with increasing force over the edge and down the escarpment.

Today, Harry had left the house early for a meeting in Wolverhampton. With the dishwasher quietly humming away in the background, Penny took out the ironing board, filled the steam iron with water and set about pressing the new red drapes for the sitting room window, her concentration on a lively debate in progress on the radio between two opposing MPs' concerns over the country's current education system.

The first curtain done, she threaded the plastic hooks through the loops in the header tape, then topped up the iron again, ready for the second one. The discussion on the radio became more and more heated as the two speakers disagreed with each other's comments, the interviewer trying to keep order between them. Riveted to the debate, she became aware of background music playing.

Thinking the station must be drifting a bit, she twiddled with the tuning dial. Pond Cottage was in a black spot where communications were concerned, Harry even had problems with his mobile phone in the house, but her tweaking made no difference. Disappointed and annoyed with the radio, she switched it off. The talking stopped the instant she turned the knob, but the music was still audible if faint, sounding like it came from outside the house, or from upstairs somewhere. Fading in and out of her hearing, the odd snippet of a refrain...

Da dee da, dee da de, da...

She froze.

No, this can't be happening! Not here, not after all this time.

Running from room to room in a frenzy she searched for its source but could find nothing. Every room was quiet. In each room she entered the music sounded as though it came from the one next door...

Da da dee dee... from the dining room... *dee dum dum...* the kitchen... *dee dee da...* no, from upstairs, the bedroom, the bathroom, the loft... *da dee dum...*

"Nooo!" she screamed out. "Stop it!"

With her hands clasped tightly over her ears, she fled from the house.

The moment he let himself in through the front door, Harry sensed something was wrong. Normally at this time of day, Penny would be pottering around the kitchen organizing their evening meal, the sound of saucepan lids clattering, the whirring of the food processor, but there wasn't even the merest hint of a warm hug of comforting smells as he opened the door. No aroma of roast chicken or a tasty casserole wafting to his nose. Nor was there any sound of music playing. Often he would come home to find her playing the piano or tapping away at the computer with a CD playing in the background. But today the house was silent. No faint tap-tapping from the keyboard, no Gershwin or Debussy from the piano.

It was a funny thing, he mused as he hung up his jacket, how since they had moved she had seemed inspired and could not stop writing. At times he had to drag her away from the computer to spend time with him, to go for a walk or enjoy a lazy bath together. He thought that was where she was now, soaking in the bath, all sense of time forgotten, but with no whiff of patchouli or vanilla bath oils scenting the air either, he felt uneasy. Things didn't feel or sound right.

In the kitchen he found the ironing board out, the iron hot. Thinking she must be in the bedroom putting things away, he went back to the hall and called up the stairs.

"Penny? Are you up there?"

Receiving no answer, he began to climb. From the landing window he caught sight of her in the garden, sitting on the rusty cast-iron seat they had found hidden in the undergrowth near the pond. She was huddled beneath her thick, knitted pullover, knees drawn to her chin, her feet up on the slats.

He hurried down the garden to her, avoiding the worst of the mud.

"What on earth are you doing out here in the rain?"

She looked up with a half-hearted smile, a smile which told him things were not right with the world today. As did her puffy, bloodshot eyes.

"I couldn't stay indoors," she said.

"Why? What's gone wrong?" He settled next to her on the wet seat.

"I thought I'd sit out here for a little while. I didn't realize what time it is. Or are you back early?" The nonchalant shrug she gave couldn't disguise she was clearly upset.

"If anything I'm a little late. Is that what's upset you? I should have rung but, well, you know how it is?"

She could contain herself no longer and burst into tears, her body racking with each loud sob.

He pulled her to him, wrapping his arms around her tightly. "What on earth is it, sweetheart? What's happened? God, you're soaking, woman! How long have you been out here, for goodness' sake?"

Glancing over her shoulder he noticed the pond was well risen. At the far side of the water, near the overspill, a large fallen branch was trapped across the edge. He was sure it wasn't there yesterday.

He pulled her even closer. "It's okay, I'm here now, sweetheart.

Eventually, her crying subsided. "Oh, Harry, it's back." She sniffed loudly, blurting out a heavy sob of despair.

Puzzled, he pulled away slightly, staring deep into her eyes where tears threatened to break again.

"What is?"

"The music! I heard it this afternoon. It filled the house and I can't go back in there." She began shaking; whether with cold or fear he couldn't be sure.

"But that's not possible."

"It is, I tell you. I know what I heard. The music has followed us here."

Whilst he didn't believe for one moment the haunting music had moved here too, clearly something had happened else she wouldn't have been so agitated. Further words failed him as he took in the ramifications if it were true the music had indeed followed them to Pond Cottage.

He cuddled her, soothing and raining gentle kisses into her hair. "Come on, let's get back inside and get you warmed up again before we both freeze."

"But—"

"Believe me, sweetheart, there's no music playing." Maybe not in the house, he thought, but a note of worry prodded his surety. Had the music enveloped his beloved Penny's mind so much that she would never be free from it? God, he hoped not.

His reassuring words were enough for her to let him lead her back up to the house.

Although still shaking, she followed him into the kitchen, into the dining room and through into the hallway. As he had confirmed, the house was quiet, calming in its silence. There was no music, the only sounds the familiar ticking of the old grandfather clock in its new home at the foot of the stairs. Everywhere peaceful. Normal.

"You must think me such a fool, Harry?"

"Not in the least." He rubbed a playful hand through her wet hair. "The subconscious is a funny thing; it plays tricks on us all. Now, let's say we put on our glad rags and eat out in style tonight. There's a little Greek restaurant over in Painswick Peter's been raving about. We'll go there, shall we? Why don't you go and have a hot bath and get ready, and I'll finish up down here. Go on, up those stairs." He shooed her away with a playful slap on her backside.

After she'd gone, he pulled the plug of the iron out of the socket, folded the ironing board away, then went to the sitting room where, yanking off his tie and tossing it over the arm of the cream leather sofa, he dropped into a cushioning armchair.

Deep in thought, holding the bridge of his nose between a thumb and forefinger, he sat, heavy-hearted and worried. Seriously worried. If the music had followed her to Pond Cottage then what was to become of her? Of them? He couldn't believe both houses were haunted; it was too much of a coincidence. It didn't make sense. Ghosts don't follow people; they stay in one location, one haunt, don't they? No, something else had to be the cause. But what? He wished he knew. He needed to find a solution, a logical answer, a rational explanation. There had to be one. Somehow he had to find the way to exorcise this musical ghost which wouldn't let go. But where to start?

He tilted his face to the ceiling, not looking for inspiration but staring up to where he knew she was undressing.

"Oh, Penny, what are we going to do?" he uttered aloud.

Chapter 20

"Harry, wake up, wake up! You must be able to hear it?" She shook him violently.

Bleary-eyed, he propped himself up on one elbow. "I can't hear anything."

"But the music..."

He looked at the bedside clock; it showed a little after one o'clock. "You've been dreaming, there's no music."

"But you must be able to hear it. Listen!" She kicked back the covers and leapt out of bed. "I can't stand it, Harry. Make it stop!" She tugged at the handle on the bedroom door. "Listen, for God's sake, it's there, I tell you. Don't tell me you can't hear it!" Naked, she ran down the stairs.

Da dee dee. Dee da da dee dum dum... But she knew she hadn't heard the music in her dream because, now wide awake, she could still hear clearly every nuance of note, every chord and beat as it drew her towards it.

More and more she found herself hearing the notes drifting about Pond Cottage. Some days it played consistently, over and over, tormenting her, driving her to despair and distraction. No matter how hard she tried, she couldn't ignore the snippets and refrains playing repeatedly.

Other days there would be nothing, and she would struggle to even remember what it was she had heard, to the point where she believed it really was all a trick of her subconscious, like Harry had said. A bit like that feeling she had after taking off her hat and it felt as though she were still wearing it.

Then, unexpected, the music would return to haunt her again. And slowly, day by day, a little at a time, she knew she was going insane; the madness creeping around the cerebral coils of her brain. Didn't Jilly Smythe mention that the previous owner went gaga? That Pamela woman. Jilly said she was always saying she heard things?

Was it the cottage causing it? But if that were so, why had she heard the same music inside Hill House too? And if that was the case, then it couldn't be the house causing it, she reasoned. So it must be her. It had to be all in her mind. Yes, there was no doubt about it, she was definitely going insane. Loopy; like Pamela Ewell had gone.

"Make the music go away," she pleaded to the air. "Tell it to stop, I can't bear it..."

Weeks went by in a daze. With Harry spending more and more time away from the house there never seemed a moment to talk to him – he was always too busy. She wanted to tell him he was wrong to make her move, that she hated the house, but he was never about whenever she wanted to discuss it. Even during weekends, he would find an excuse to work upstairs in the loft, which he'd turned into his drawing office.

Except the house wasn't the real problem, she admitted to herself, watching him pull on his jacket, it was the music.

He pecked her cheek hurriedly. "I'll be back about four."

"Do you have to go? Can't Peter handle the meeting by himself for once?" she pleaded, knowing her voice touched on hysteria. She didn't want to be in the house alone. If she had to spend another day there by herself hearing that pesky tune playing repeatedly, she didn't know what she would do, scared she wouldn't be responsible for her behaviour. *Why, oh why, couldn't he understand?*

"Darling, I have to be there, it's important. You've got the car now, take yourself off somewhere for a few hours. The garden centre, or go and have a coffee with Jilly like you usually do on a Thursday."

Yes, the lovely powder blue Lexus with cream seats he'd bought her last month. She kept forgetting she had it. "Well, I couldn't expect you to stay here all day on your own whenever I'm out for the day," he had said, removing his hand from her eyes that birthday morning.

Harry picked up his keys from the hall table, opened the front door, then turned. "Oh, and if you go shopping, we're out of Chinese five spice. I used the last in Saturday night's stir-fry. You know, you could always drive over to Elaine's if you're at a loose end? She'd be more than pleased to see you." He pulled her towards him and gave her a passionate kiss. "We'll spend all day tomorrow together, I promise. Now, I must go or I'll be late picking up Peter."

Another hurried kiss that left her wanting more, then he was gone, his car disappearing out of the drive and onto the tree-lined lane. She stood at the doorway listening to the throaty roar of his BMW fade as he zoomed off into the distance.

Silence filled the air for a few moments before a blackbird burst into song from a nearby tree. A flock of sparrows swooped low over the roof of the house, twittering and chattering amongst themselves. The sky was clear, not a trace of a cloud, and the sun already felt warm even though it was only eight o'clock. From somewhere a dog barked. A fat wood pigeon alighted on the chimney stack, cooing and billowing to its mate out of sight somewhere in the trees. A world that felt normal. Calm. She allowed herself a smile. *Perhaps today will be peaceful after all. Perhaps today there will be no music.*

By ten o'clock the house was clean, the evening meal prepared, another finished chapter keyed into the laptop. The rest of the day was hers to spend in the garden. There was still plenty to do outside, lots of weeding and tidying but, first, it was time for a well-earned cup of coffee, then give Jilly a call.

Not that Jilly had been much help about the goings on at the house. Oh, a nice enough woman and good company, she always enjoyed their chats, but every time she broached the subject about the house's previous owners, Jilly avoided answering, somehow always managing to steer the conversation away to a different topic.

All of which led her to think either Jilly was evasive on purpose or, more than likely, didn't know that much about what had bothered Pamela Ewell in the first place. Either way, it was frustrating to the point she'd given up even mentioning the subject. If Jilly really did know something, she was bound to bring it up again. She would have to bide her time on that particular source yielding any useful information, she told herself.

She carried her coffee through to the sitting room, intent on browsing through a magazine or two with her feet up for half-an-hour. Instead, she sat at the piano and tinkered idly on the keys. Slowly, it dawned on her that she was playing the tune she knew so well in her head.

Da da dee, dee dee dum...

Note by note, the melody sang out from the keyboard as her fingers worked each key and chord.

"That's it!" she shouted out triumphantly, leaping off the piano stool and rushing across to the coffee table, hunting for a piece of paper and a pen. She must write it down quickly before the tune went out of her head again. The only thing to hand was the back of a letter from the Emerson's Trust.

"Sorry, Harry," she apologized aloud, grabbing at it then hurrying back to the piano where, leaning on its top, she drew five parallel lines in biro across the white paper, followed by another five lines, and another.

Finally, her fingers returned to the keyboard. She played it again, slowly, note upon note, checking she had scored each one precisely. Why didn't I think of this before, she thought, it's so obvious.

D sharp for a count of three. She drew a crotchet on the improvised scoresheet followed by a bar, then an E for three, bar, an A held for three beats, no, six beats, bar then a D, an E, now F. On and on she continued to play and jot down the corresponding notes until, oblivious to the time, she had the completed melody scored in front of her.

Reading from the scrap of paper, stopping to make minor changes. A minim there, a semi-quaver here, slight alterations as her accomplished hands flew across the keyboard. Again, she played the piece, this time adding embellishments and chords, her memory serving to show where the strings came into play, the harp plucking, a violin in counterpoint, a coda.

Over and over she played until she no longer needed to read the score, she knew it in full by heart.

* * *

As he pushed open the front door a little after four-thirty, Harry could hear the sound of piano music emanating from the sitting room. Oh good, she's playing again, he thought, she must be happy. She's been looking so fatigued again lately.

From the hallway, he listened as he removed his jacket and hung it up, slipped off his shoes and pushed his feet into comfy suede moccasins. There was a vague familiarity about the piece she played, he noticed, but couldn't place it. He certainly couldn't remember having heard her play it before. He dwelt on this thought for a moment, trying desperately to recall that tune she liked to hum. Didn't it go something like that?

He opened the sitting room door. "Hi, sweetheart. That's lovely, what you're playing. Don't stop."

On hearing his voice, she looked up at him as she continued to play, a broad smile set on her face.

"Recognise it?" she asked.

"I'm not sure. What is it?"

"Three guesses."

"Sweetheart, you could give me fifty guesses, and I still wouldn't know."

She stopped playing abruptly and announced jubilantly, "Harry, this is *my* music!"

He saw the hand-scribbled paper propped precariously on the sheet holder. "You mean, you've written it yourself? How wonderful."

Swiftly, she removed the paper and pulled down the lid of the piano. It shut with a loud thud.

"No, I haven't written it! It's the music I've been hearing over and over again here in this house, the same as at Hill House."

Disappointed, he shook his head. That wasn't what he wanted to hear. "I thought that had all stopped now."

She shook the piece of paper towards him. "I've managed to write it down, every note and bar. Now I have something tangible. Now perhaps I can finally find out what it is. Maybe someone will recognize it."

"But are you positive it is a real piece composed by someone else? Are you sure it isn't something made up in *your* head that has finally come out? You know, like an author, stringing words and sentences together until, finally, he has a whole chapter in front of him." He knew he was making feeble excuses, anything so as not to accept the truth. A question of don't think about it and it will go away, it's not really there.

She stared at the score she had so meticulously scribed. "No, Harry, this isn't me."

"Play it again. Let me hear it in full."

Acquiescent, she opened the piano lid, flexed her fingers, wiggled about on the stool to get positioned properly and began to play.

Da da dum, da dee dee...

He came and stood behind her, his hands resting gently on her taut shoulders. The haunting melody tugged at his heart.

"It's beautiful," he said softly when she had finished. "It makes me feel I want to sweep you into my arms and waltz around the room with you."

She turned to him, her face pale. "Waltzing? Yes... Dancing around and around the room... Harry, don't you see? That's what they were doing, those people I saw in the hallway. They were dancing to music. This music." She stared hard at him. "Harry, I didn't write this, but I'm jolly well going to find out who did."

Chapter 21

It became a daily routine. A quick tidy of the house, vegetables prepared for the evening meal, a meat casserole put hastily in the slow cooker or a joint of bacon or a chicken set on automatic timer in the electric oven before she left Pond Cottage. The quest now a challenge.

Armed with her scoresheet, each day she drove to a different town. Yate, Thornbury, Tetbury – anywhere there might be a music shop. Any place where she thought someone might recognize the music she had rewritten so painstakingly, copying the scribbled draft onto a fresh piece of paper, carefully drawing each note in place, adding accompanying chords and ties, phrase and crescendo markers.

The helpful salesman in Mickleburgh's in Bristol said he thought it sounded familiar after she'd played the tune for him on one of their pianos; the hope filling her heart soon quashed when he said he was sorry but he couldn't recall its title.

In a Bath store, several customers gathered around, listening intently as she played the piece, only to be met with numerous shakes of heads.

"There's a new shop in Keynsham you could try," the assistant suggested. "Or there's one in Gloucester that sells sheet music. Maybe they could help you? I'll give you the address."

On and on she searched, on and on like the music ingrained in her mind, but no one could put a name to it. As the weeks past, she despaired she would ever know.

"Have you tried writing to Classic FM, madam?" the chirpy young salesman at Goodmusic in Stroud suggested. "Maybe one of the presenters could help, and they do have a good archive. Why not email them? You would get a quicker response that way, I'm sure."

"What a wonderful suggestion! Thank you." She felt like kissing the man. Hugging him. Why hadn't she thought of that before? "I'll go home now and do it straight away."

She drove faster than she should have, ignoring the speed cameras. If any had flashed, she had no idea, so intent was she in reaching Pond Cottage quickly.

Not bothering to remove her coat in her haste, she sat on the sofa with the laptop balanced on her knees. But where to email to? She didn't know the address. Finally, it dawned on her. The Internet, of course. Twenty minutes later her electronic letter was zipping through to the BBC. She sat with fingers crossed for nearly fifteen minutes, waiting patiently for a reply, hoping it didn't get lost in the ether. *This must work. It has to!*

Don't be silly, it isn't that quick, she told herself when all she received was an automated response acknowledging her query. She made a mental note to turn on the radio early tomorrow morning. She would listen all day, all week, all year if needs be.

Days waiting for a response slipped into weeks before she received a reply, the immediate high of expectation quickly reforming into disappointment at the brief missive: "Sorry, we are unable to help your search in this instance."

She spent hours searching through music clips on YouTube, playing short bursts of unfamiliar classical tunes in the hope of coming across it, all to no avail. There were far too many to play every item; it would take until eternity to go through the complete listings, and without a title, an impossible task.

She called Anita, hummed it down the phone to her, but her sister couldn't help either.

"Try Mum. I bet she would know," was all Anita could say. Hardly the starting point of a long-needed conversation with her mother, Penny thought. Too many questions would be asked. Too many explanations needed.

Callers to the house were greeted with a musical rendition, but in return only provided looks of astonishment, bemusement, and more shakes of the head. Jilly Smythe told her she didn't know a Beethoven from a Bach when Penny played it several times over to her. Even Elaine, whom she was sure would know, admitted when asked that she wasn't into classical music at all, much preferring to listen to the Eagles or Boyzone, the revelation of which took Penny by complete surprise. Peter also listened intently, but like all the others, shook his head dismissively. It was an unknown. A mystery.

She felt as if she had reached a dead end.

The acrid smell of smoke invaded her nostrils, choking her lungs, rousing her from sleep. Coughing, she sat up in bed and saw a red glow flickering under the bedroom door. Fearing for their lives, she shook Harry vigorously.

"Wake up! For God's sake wake up. The house is on fire!"

Shaken from his slumber, instinctively Harry leapt from the bed and made straight for the bedroom door.

"No, don't open it!" she screamed.

But he'd already yanked open the door. The landing was in darkness. No smoke, not even a faint whiff of it. No burning timbers or flames leaping up the stairwell. There was no fire, only blackness of night filling the silent corridor.

"But I did smell smoke," she whispered, reaching to turn on the bedside lamp. "I saw the flames licking—"

He studied her in the lamp's soft glow. There was no doubting she believed she saw something. Another bad dream? The third in a week. Despairing, he dropped back down on to the bed, his head in his hands, contemplating what had occurred. These nightmares were getting out of hand. He turned to her, trying to keep his voice even and calm as he spoke.

"This can't go on, Pen. Something's got to be done. You're shattered, I'm shattered. First, it was music you heard. Then last night, you were convinced people were downstairs arguing. Before that, you could hear a baby crying. I seriously think it's about time you saw a doctor."

Tears welled in her eyes. "Are you saying I'm mad?"

"No, that's not what I'm saying." He swung his legs up into the bed, then reached across to stroke her cheek lightly. "I don't think for one moment you're mad, but this obsession with this infernal music is not healthy. It's ruining our lives. It's taking over. Give it up. Let it go."

"I can't. I have to find out or else I *will* go insane. It's got to me, Harry. You don't understand!" With a huff, she pulled away, turning over to face the wall, and snapped off the light.

He so much wanted to understand, to help, to ease her suffering, and placed his hand on her shoulder, trying to pull her back round. She shrugged him off and pulled the duvet up over her head.

"I do understand, sweetheart, but listen to me. I'm beginning to think you might be ill. These nightmares worry me. It's not normal. To me, they're a sign something's wrong. Tomorrow, I want you to ring Dr Madison to book an appointment."

"But—" She sounded close to tears.

"No buts. If not for yourself, do it for me. Please. You look absolutely worn out. I can't bear to see you suffering like this. I love you, and I don't know what to do any more. You need help."

She sniffed loudly. "And just what am I supposed to say to him? 'Doctor, my partner thinks I've gone crazy. Please give me some pills because I keep hearing music and having bad dreams about babies and fire.'"

"What harm would a check-up do? It might be hormonal. Perhaps you need a tonic?"

She turned over and groaned. "You mean the menopause? Why can't you see this isn't anything to do with "women's problems'? This isn't something that can be wiped away with a few pills and a pat on the back. There, there, it'll pass along with the hot flushes and cranky tears, for goodness' sake. Anyway, I'm too young for that. And I'm not ill either. I know what I—"

"You don't know that for sure. Humour me on this one, sweetheart, and promise me you'll go. It will put both our minds at rest." He waited for her reply. When none was forthcoming, he added, "Else I'll drag you there myself, and that's no idle threat."

She let out a resigned sigh. "Okay, okay. I'll go. Perhaps

you're right. As you say, what harm would a check-up do, if only to prove to you there's nothing wrong with me?" The tone of her capitulation sounded weak. Unconvincing.

"Promise me?"

"I promise."

"Good. Now try to go back to sleep." But he doubted he would be able to. Not now. Not with so much whirling going on in his brain. The music hadn't seemed to plague her so much lately, but these bad dreams were becoming more and more frequent. And what had fires and babies got to do with it all?

Chapter 22

The moment he heard the car pull into the drive, Harry rushed down from his workroom, taking the stairs two at a time. When he reached the hallway Penny was already in the throes of tossing her jacket over the newel post, her high heels kicked off untidily by the table. He pulled her into his arms and hugged her.

"What did the doctor say?"

"Tinnitus!" she snapped, pushing him away. "Brought on by stress, the stupid man. I don't know why I even bothered to go. I wish I'd never let you talk me into moving. At least at Hill House I didn't have nightmares!" With that, she stomped up the stairs, slamming the bedroom door closed in her wake.

He stood by the bottom tread, looking up, torn between running after her or giving her time alone to calm down. Given her agitated state, he felt no matter which he chose, it would be the wrong one.

It was difficult to believe it was stress at the root of all her problems. Granted, she had been upset initially about moving, but he'd thought all that had been resolved. She loved Pond Cottage. She'd said so. Often. He pondered on all that was good about the house. Its warm, cosy atmosphere. No drafts like Hill House had been plagued with. And with all the new fabrics and furnishings, which she'd taken great delight in choosing, had given him the impression she liked it too. And how often had she readily admitted to everyone since that it was such a great decision to move?

As for the garden, why, every day she was impatient to see what had appeared overnight, waiting keenly to see if it would turn into a pretty flower or possess some intoxicating, delightful perfume. And enveloping all that was good, to him their love for each other appeared to be growing ever stronger, wrapping a blanket of serenity around them. So it couldn't be about the move. No. It was that ruddy music! That intangible, damned enigmatic tune cutting through their lives, pushing them apart and ruining their future. He had to put a stop to it, but he didn't know how or which way to turn next.

When Penny came down for lunch several hours later, he could tell she had been crying. She looked so sad and miserable, he blamed himself for her distress; after all, it had been at his insistence she visit the doctor. Was that the cause, or was she really ill? Had some terrible life-threatening illness been diagnosed that she was too upset to talk about? A million thoughts and scenarios filled his head at once, all scrambling for attention. Unable to bear the silence between them as they ate, he put down his knife and fork.

"What exactly did Doctor Madison say, sweetheart? About the tinnitus."

Penny shrugged and continued to pick at her meal, the pasta already going cold.

"Didn't he give you any idea?" he persisted. "Surely you asked him to explain. I mean, tinnitus is a constant ringing in the ears, isn't it? You've not mentioned anything like that to me."

Her fork dropped to the table with a clatter, her bloodshot eyes flaring as she looked up.

"He said sometimes a bad cold or flu can bring it on. Or drugs, like tramadol or morphine."

"And...?" God, this was worse than trying to get blood from a stone, he thought.

"And what?" Her voice rose by several octaves.

"You've not had a cold or the flu. You're not taking any drugs."

"I told you – stress! Don't you think with the divorce, and the move, and everything else, I've been under a lot of it?"

"Yes, of course you have. But ringing in the ears—"

"It's not only ringing or buzzing. There are other forms, apparently. He says I have an earworm, or more likely what he calls a musical hallucination."

"A what?"

She sighed heavily, as if he should know all about it. "When one hears music when none is being played. He says musical hallucinations have a compelling sense of reality and are often mistaken for the real thing."

Well, that certainly made some sense, he thought. Perhaps the doctor was right.

"Apparently, the sounds are heard as short fragments, the same as I've been experiencing," she continued. "And, according to him, it's often from music familiar from youth, especially from hymns and carols."

"But that's exactly what I said before. Remember? That day we first went to the hanging gardens, when you were sifting through all those CDs."

Penny looked him in the eyes. "Except in my case, I don't recognize the music, Harry. I've never heard it before. I know I haven't."

"Is there anything that can be done to cure it? Did he prescribe anything?"

Penny reached into the pocket of her jeans and pulled out a thin white cardboard packet which she tossed down to the table, the contents inside rattling.

"Valium and..." From her other pocket she extracted a small brown plastic bottle which joined the pills already on the table. "...these."

The bottle rolled towards the edge of the table. He caught it before it fell to the floor, then read the label.

"Sleeping pills. Is that all? Small wonder you're so upset." Doctor Madison had clearly dismissed her problems as something to be wiped out with a few tranquillizers; it hadn't been the diagnosis or the cure he'd hoped for. He knew he should have gone with her to see him. At least then he could have spoken to the doctor as well. Demanded something further be done. Tests. Something more concrete, but she'd insisted on going alone.

"What else did you expect?" she said. "That he'll certify me for the nuthouse? Is that what you wanted?"

He reached out to take her hand but she moved it quickly out of reach. "Of course not, Pen. But I thought he might have delved a bit deeper. Offered some sort of counselling or recommended you to a—"

"Shrink?" she interrupted sharply.

"A specialist, I was going to say. I only want what's best for you. I don't like seeing you like this. It's breaking my heart to see you look so lost and miserable."

She stared hard at him. "Then help me find out about the music. Don't you see, I know I'm not suffering hallucinations. This is real. Very real!"

"But Doctor—"

"Knows nothing. I have to know what it is. Once I do, I know it will all go away. God, have you never had a tune play in your head all day that you can't get rid of? Do you know how that feels? Well, imagine it twentyfold. Fiftyfold. A hundredfold, day after day, night after night, week after week. It's enough to turn anyone into a raving lunatic."

"Believe me, Pen, if I knew where to start, I would. But hearing music is one thing. It doesn't explain the nightmares you have. And why be angry at me when all I'm trying to do is help you the only way I know how?" He tried to keep his voice calm, but it was difficult knowing how to tame Penny's near hysterical voice without the conversation escalating into a full-blown argument; something they had never had.

She gave him a long, withering look before strutting from the kitchen, leaving him to clear away the congealed remains of their lunch.

He was avoiding her, whether by necessity or plan, Penny wasn't sure but, either way, Harry was away from the house during the day more and more often, using the pretext of looking for premises he and Peter could work from instead of both working from two places miles apart. She felt it was just an excuse to be away from her as much as possible. And when he was home, he hardly spoke, the evenings spent in an uneasy atmosphere of politeness, speaking out of necessity rather than want.

He might still share her bed, but it seemed he didn't want her body. Even the cherished cuddles had diminished. The way things were going it was only a matter of time, she thought, before he moved into one of the other bedrooms. It was as though he had given up caring. He hadn't even bothered mentioning her visit to the doctor again. Nor had she, she supposed, thinking about it, there didn't seem much point. Nothing had been achieved by it other than to feel as if she were walking everywhere on broken glass, whilst all the tablets did was to make her feel like a zombie during the day.

She rested her head against the windowpane as she stared out of the bedroom window. Through rivulets of rain running down the glass, she could see the pond. The water was high, spilling over the edge to disappear into infinity below. The rush of the water in the gully beside the house was clearly audible above the silence within.

Neither the beauty of where they lived nor the coldness of the glass could remove the ever-present music in her head. The nightmares and distance separating her from Harry stretched out in front of her, the love between them lost in a vast empty landscape, the horizon shrouded with hopeless misery. Never had she felt so empty. So alone. It wasn't meant to be like this, she reflected. The house was meant to be a new beginning, the move to Pond Cottage a fresh start away from the music. Now all that was spoiled.

The forlorn demeanour Harry exuded when he'd come home that afternoon told her that somehow they must try to rebuild that special something which had been lost between them. They had to rekindle the magic.

She blamed herself. She'd been selfish and stubborn. It wasn't his fault he didn't understand how irritating and soul-destroying it was to have a tune take hold of your head and refuse to let go, a persistent melody taking over your whole life. He hadn't done anything wrong. It was up to her to make the first move. She couldn't destroy his life again, or her own for that matter. They'd each been through too much.

He was still awake, she could tell from his uneven breathing, and was probably lying there in the darkness, eyes wide open. She loved him so much and couldn't stand the distance between them, let alone endure another night with his naked back turned towards her. She wanted things to return to how they had been when she first came to him, back to the fun and the laughter, the romance and sweet love-making. It was too soon for the bubble to have burst.

Gently, she climbed back into bed and tentatively pulled on his arm, nervous of his reaction as she silently persuaded him to roll over and face her.

"Oh, please, Harry, let's forget the whole incident and put it behind us. Let's go back to where we were and start again."

Without a moment's hesitation, he pulled her into his arms.

"Oh, yes please, my love. I need you so much. I hate how we've been. Will you forgive me? I know I've only myself to blame, I've been so foolish."

She kissed him tenderly. "What's to forgive?"

"A lot. I'm not the easiest of men to live with, and I only want the best for you. I thought coming here would solve both our problems. Instead, it's made them worse."

"Do you want to move again?" she asked.

"Do you?"

"No. I've run away once in my life because I couldn't face up to things and fight back. I'm not prepared to do that again. This is our life, Harry, and our home, and I will do all it takes to bottom this out."

He squeezed her tighter. "I've been so worried you were ill, seriously ill and not telling me, by the way you reacted over the doctor. I didn't know what to think. I didn't know what to do. I thought if I gave you space you'd tell me in your own good time. Is there anything I should know?"

She kissed him, long and full on his quivering lips. "Nothing, darling. I'm not ill. I haven't got some inoperable, incurable disease creeping through my body, but the music that's got hold of me is a good analogy. There must be a cure but so far I haven't found it."

"And the dreams? The nightmares?"

"The sleeping pills have stopped them, but I'm not taking any more. I don't like the way they make me feel. I have to fight this thing on my own."

Burying his face in her hair, he whispered, "You're not on your own. We're in this together."

"I know, but at times lately I've felt you're never here. I'm left on my own all day to brood while you avoid me."

"Sweetheart, you know we've been looking for offices. Peter and I need to give ourselves a more professional image, up the ante. The commissions are rolling in, and rather than turning work away we can grow. Take on more architects. Set up a full-scale drawing office. We can't do that working out of a garret and thirty odd miles between the two of us. We've found a place in Stroud that seems viable."

She remained silent. He had explained all this before, but she'd only been half-listening during their stilted conversations over a meal table, too caught up in her own problems to take in the ramifications.

"Your silence tells me you don't approve about us needing to work away from home." His voice was unable to hide his disappointment.

"No, quite the contrary. It sounds good. I shall miss you about the house during the day of course, but I've plenty to keep me busy." She could get back to her mission: to find out what the music is that has brought her to the brink of derangement and nearly destroyed all that was good between them. As much as she would miss him, she wouldn't stand in his way. There might even be a place for her in their new office. They would need a secretary. Someone to answer the phone. She could do that. All at once, her mind was a whirlwind of possibilities.

"I do love you, you know," he said, walking his hand up her thigh under her nightshirt. "I'd willingly tell Peter the deal's off if you don't agree."

Yielding to the feel of his exploring fingers, arousing her, awakening the longing for him inside her she'd missed so much, she whispered, "Don't stop."

Chapter 23

Penny's stomach churned, full of trepidation as to what her visitor would come out with next. Elaine always had an uncanny knack of making her feel ill-at-ease and uncomfortable. It was only because Harry had warned her Elaine would be calling in that morning to collect some papers that she was on her guard.

Elaine, perched on a kitchen stool, her legs swinging back and forth whilst she finished her coffee, finally put the mug down on the counter and said, "Did Harry tell you Peter took me over to see their new offices yesterday?"

"Yes, he did say."

"I suggested they need a secretary and that I was happy to oblige. Although I can't understand why you haven't offered. I told Peter if you do it, it would save on costs, whereas I would expect to be paid. But, then again, perhaps you don't type. A secretary is a skilled profession, you know. What did you say you did before you met Harry?"

Penny's skinned crawled. *God, the woman was at it again. Didn't she realize how patronizing she sounded? Small wonder she rubbed Harry up the wrong way at times.*

He and Peter had already made up their minds to employ someone from an agency, but obviously hadn't told Elaine yet, and she certainly wasn't going to. Not wanting to discuss the subject further, instead she offered more coffee, in the hope the answer would be no and Elaine would be on her way, so she could get on with what she had planned. A music shop in Cheltenham had rung earlier, advising that they might have located the music she was looking for. Consequently, she was anxious to be on her way. Much to her relief, Elaine declined a refill.

"Another time, perhaps," Elaine said, scooping up the large brown envelope from the counter and waving it in the air. "I have to get these to the solicitor in Bath before midday. We're drawing up a new contract with our sister charity in Germany. You know, I do believe this plan will work. It's such a good idea, don't you think? If we can persuade every adult in the country to donate one pound, a single pound mind, nothing more, we will have millions in the bank to fund national disasters worldwide. And if the States and the rest of Europe join in, who knows what good we can do."

"Commendable indeed, but didn't someone else try to get something like that off the ground once before? It never took off."

"It doesn't mean we can't try again. And the world has changed since then." Elaine appeared to hesitate for a moment before saying, "Actually, Penny... I do feel I owe you an apology."

Penny raised her eyebrows. "For what?"

"I was an absolute bitch to you that day after last year's charity dinner. I'm ashamed of myself for behaving as I did."

Penny was taken aback. That incident had happened over twelve months ago, she'd more or less forgotten about it. It was incredible to the point of disbelief to think it had taken all this time for Elaine to admit she'd been in the wrong.

"It's because I felt responsible for Harry," Elaine continued. "It was none of my business, I realized afterwards. I knew I'd overstepped the mark, but I couldn't help myself. You'd been such a shock, you see. One minute Harry was single, shut away in his work and then he arrives with you on his arm announcing to the world you'd moved in with him. What was I supposed to think?"

"Well, he did try to tell you when you telephoned to remind him about the dinner. As I recall, he couldn't get a word in edgeways."

"Can you forgive me?" Elaine beseeched, looking suitably embarrassed.

"Apology accepted. It's ancient history as far as I'm concerned." Regardless, she still couldn't warm to the woman. Stay calm and keep polite, she ordered herself, after all, she has finally apologized, and coming from Elaine that must have taken a lot of courage.

Elaine slid gracefully from the stool. "May I use your loo before I go."

Penny wiped down the counter and stacked the remaining dirty china into the dishwasher, keen to be on her way as soon as Elaine had gone on hers. She picked up a drinking glass from the worktop, humming as she did so.

"Good Lord!" Elaine said, returning to the kitchen. "Lorna was always humming that little ditty. Fancy you liking the same bit of music."

The glass slipped from Penny's grip, hitting the open dishwasher door and bouncing off to smash on the floor, sending slivers of sharp shards in all directions.

"Damn it!"

"Lorna was always at it," Elaine went on, oblivious to Penny's reaction. "Used to drive Harry mad, it did."

"Is that so?" She tried to keep her voice even and calm as she carefully picked up the larger broken pieces of glass whilst her innards knotted tightly at this revelation.

Tut-tutting, Elaine pushed her aside gently. "Here, I'll do that. Pass me a dustpan and brush before you cut yourself. You don't want blood on your lovely white trousers. Lorna always said it was one of those songs you couldn't get out of your head. I vaguely remember her saying she could hear it playing in the house on occasion."

As Elaine swept up the mess, Penny's mind was in turmoil. *What was she insinuating? Surely Lorna hadn't heard the music as well? This was* her *music,* her *dream. And her nightmare.*

Elaine looked up at her, a look of incredulity settling on her face. "You mean you don't know about their frequent arguments over it? Has Harry not told you?"

"He doesn't like talking about the past much, especially the accident." Penny's tone was blasé, but she could feel her whole body shaking. She retrieved a newspaper from the pile by the rubbish bin and handed several large pages of broadsheet to a kneeling Elaine, whose eyebrows rose in wide amazement.

"Well, that is strange, considering it used to drive him up the wall, hearing her lah-lahring all the time. It was her constant humming that caused that dreadful accident. They'd been rowing about it. She'd stormed off with the kids in the car and bang. Drove straight into an oil tanker turning into their drive. The car burst into flames and Lorna and those poor kids were literally roasted to death." Elaine sniffed loudly and wiped a tear from her eye with the back of her hand. "It was terrible. Utterly, utterly terrible. When I think..." She pulled a tissue from her cardigan pocket and loudly blew her nose, then continued to wrap the broken glass in a bundle before consigning it to the rubbish bin.

So why had Harry never mentioned this important fact to her? Stunned, Penny pulled a chair out from the kitchen table and sat, her head spinning with a multitude of questions needing answers. The music shop would have to wait.

"Elaine, how well did you know Lorna?"

Leaving the dustpan and brush on top of the bin, Elaine joined her at the table. "Very well. We were best friends, but you know that. She confided everything to me. It was such a tragedy her and the children dying like that. Poor Harry, he's never forgiven himself. But I am pleased he's found someone again."

"Did you never want him yourself?" A niggling, gnawing doubt was spreading itself around her again, making her feel uneasy.

Elaine blushed and fidgeted on the chair. "Well, he is rather... Look, I've always loved Harry, as the husband of my best friend only, you understand? Nothing more. Of course, had he made any advances on me, I admit I would have been flattered. Tempted, even. But he's got you now, and you've certainly brought the light back into his eyes. I seriously worried about him ever getting back to his normal cheery self."

Penny wondered how to phrase her next question without it sounding like she was paranoid.

"Did Lorna ever mention ghosts? Do you know if she believed in them?"

Elaine looked taken aback. "I don't think it's a subject she and I ever discussed. Whatever makes you ask?"

She shrugged. "No reason."

Elaine's eyes widened. "Why? Have you seen one? No... don't tell me there's one here? Yes, yes, I can tell by your expression there is." She clapped her hands together, clearly excited at the prospect. "Oh, how incredibly fascinating. You wait till I tell the rest of the gang. What does Harry think about it? Has he seen it?"

She grabbed at Elaine's arm. The last thing she wanted was for Elaine to go rushing off into the world outside announcing their house had a ghost. It would make her, and Harry for that matter, look exceedingly foolish, and she knew he wouldn't take kindly to such a statement being made public, especially after all they'd been through in the past few months.

"No, don't go telling anyone anything. There are no ghosts here, I can assure you. It was a silly question, nothing more. There's no such thing as ghosts. Forget I ever mentioned it."

Chapter 24

She flew at him the moment Harry entered the house several hours later. After Elaine's departure, instead of dashing off to Cheltenham as planned, she'd spent the rest of the day brooding, wondering what on earth Harry was playing at. It was thoughtless of him not to mention this fact about the music after all she'd suffered. It was selfish and, most of all, it hurt. It hurt like bloody hell to think he hadn't been completely honest with her. She could scarcely believe that after all that had gone on, at both houses, he'd said nothing. It was beyond comprehension. Wild, irrational ideas had raged through her mind as she'd waited to confront him

"Why did you never tell me about Lorna and the music?" Under her furious glare, Harry's face blanched. "Why have you kept it from me all this time? Were you ever going to tell me?"

"Of course I was. Come here." He reached out, intent on putting his arms around her.

She backed away. "Don't touch me."

He shrugged hurriedly out of his suit jacket and eased off his shoes. "It isn't what you think. I had my reasons."

"At this moment I don't know what to think."

"Then at least let me explain." He beckoned her to join him on the sofa in the sitting room, tapping the seat for her to sit next to him.

Shaking her head, she sat at the other end, straight-backed, tense, the empty space between them like a void opening up, ripping apart at their love. At this moment all feelings for him were numbed.

"What's been happening, Harry?" She spoke quietly, fighting down the anger and hurt inside. "I want to know the truth. I deserve that much at least."

"I only wanted to protect you, you know that," he offered, studying her face as if trying to gauge what her reaction would be. "At first, I didn't think you were hearing what Lorna always hummed. Then, after, I wasn't sure..." He hesitated again. "Look, I know I should have told you, but I was scared of losing you."

"*Scared of losing me?* Yet you've let me suffer all this time while all along you knew. How could you?" she screeched, aware she was in danger of sounding hysterical.

"Darling, that's the problem. The whole point. I didn't understand what was happening."

"You should've told me, not hidden it all. I feel deceived, Harry. Used and cheated. I never thought you would do that to me..." Her face crumpled, tears cascading down her face, mascara running in long black streaks.

"Sweetheart, I never meant to hurt you, but something was going on at Hill House, something I couldn't fathom or explain. I thought the safest thing was for us to move in the hope it would all evaporate and go away. I didn't want to lose you too."

"*Safest?* Harry, I wasn't in danger there! What I saw and heard wasn't going to harm me." She tried desperately to keep her voice on an even keel, not wanting this to descend into a slanging match.

"We don't know that. And after what happened to Lorna, I didn't want to take any risks. There was too much at stake."

"Then you had better tell me what actually happened to her that day. After all, you made a promise to once, remember?"

So he told her, every detail surrounding the accident. She knew each word he spoke pained him to remember.

"Lorna thought she was going mad. She thought I was trying to drive her insane, that I was making the music happen! And then, that morning, we'd had the worst argument of our lives about it. So of course it was my fault."

"And had you given her any cause to think such a thing? Had she caught you playing around, perhaps?" Those seeds of doubt had doubled and pushed through the mayhem in her head, a sense of foreboding riding on a mounting wave of suspicion. Was Harry behind all this? Had he bumped off Lorna in order to be with Elaine? Or some other woman? No! That's just plain stupid, she told herself, shaking her head. Else why would he be with me?

"Or had you bumped her off for the insurance money?"

What am I thinking? Of course he wouldn't do such a thing. No way could he have done anything like that... He'd loved his wife and kids. And it was me who'd moved in with him, not Elaine. Harry loves me. Me! Not Elaine. He's told me what he thinks about Elaine.

Harry looked suitably mortified. "No way! God, Pen, what are you saying? What do you take me for? It wasn't like that at all."

But gnawing away, writhing inside her, those seeds of doubt wouldn't stop growing as realization dawned on her that, deep down, she really didn't know Harry at all. They had kept so much about themselves secret, neither wishing to pry or delve into each other's memories too much, for both had their own baggage chained to their ankles, and now it seemed it was too late. Far too late to start.

She looked him full in the face. "Then what was it like, Harry? Tell me."

A tortuous frown creased his forehead before he buried his head in his hands and wept, his whole body shaking with misery.

She had hurt him to the quick, she could see that, but she hurt too. Hurt like he would never understand. There was no excuse for him not telling her about the music before, no excuse in the world. Had he done so, she might have been able to sort it out before everything became so out of hand. Before all the pain, the pills and the nightmares. His deception had cut her deeper and sharper than any dagger or sword, but seeing his misery now, she longed to hold and comfort him. To apologize for making such accusations, but fear kept her away. Too much doubt wrestled in her head, and she didn't want to touch him.

Finally, he rubbed his eyes with his fists and looked up.

"Is that what you think of me, that I'm some kind of fiendish monster? That I did her in to get her out of the way? And do you honestly think I would have let my kids suffer like that too? I can't believe you're even thinking like this. Has my love meant absolutely nothing to you after all this time? I would never have hurt Lorna. She meant the world to me, as you do now."

She believed him. No, he wasn't some wicked person out for the insurance money, playing some sort of twisted mind game in an effort to drive her to the brink of insanity, pushing her that little bit more over the edge. He had no reason to. Yet, by his omission, keeping things to himself, he had achieved the opposite, instead driving a wedge between them she didn't know how to remove.

"But you should have told me, Harry. I'm not some china doll that would break at the slightest touch. Why do the men in my life always think they have to wrap me up in cotton wool and control me?"

"Oh, sweetheart, what have I done to you? Believe me, I didn't know where to start telling you, because I didn't want to believe what was going on. I couldn't bear the same thing happening to you as happened to Lorna and the children. I'm too frightened of losing you, don't you see? I was trying to protect you."

"From what?"

He shuffled uncomfortably on the sofa. "I wanted us to move out of Hill House because I thought by being away from there you would be safe. That there would be no music at night and no people dancing in the moonlight, except ourselves. "

"Did Lorna see them too?"

He shook his head. "Not that I'm aware of." He reached out for her hand, but she withdrew further back, huddling into the arm of the sofa.

"Penny, listen to me. At one point I truly did think Hill House was haunted, but... well, there is something there, you have to admit. Lorna heard music there, as you did. In fact, now I think about it, so did Elly. Sometimes she'd wake at night saying the radio or the television had woken her when clearly there was nothing playing in the house. I don't think either of us equated the things she heard with what Lorna did. We never put two and two together."

"But still you did nothing?"

"I'd never heard anything... well..." He faltered, as if trying to remember. "I'm not sure. I did hear music once, that night we went to the Emerson's dinner, but it could have been my imagination. Or as I said at the time, a car driving along the lane."

"And Sam?"

"Sam never heard anything, leastways not that he'd said." He shrugged. "Perhaps it's a woman thing?" When Penny glowered at him, he hastened to explain. "What I mean is, perhaps only women are attuned to whatever it is but, then again..." His voice trailed away. "Elaine's never commented she'd heard anything either, and she used to be there a lot, especially and after I lost Lorna, so I don't really know."

Elaine... Of course! The seeds had grown in strength, taking over, becoming stronger by the minute.

"Elaine, then."

"What? Whatever are you on about?"

"It's Elaine! She's behind all this. She's in love with you, Harry. Always has been. And, having got rid of Lorna, she's now trying to drive me away as well so she can have you all to herself. It's all making sense now. So obvious..."

"Penny, have you any idea how ludicrous you sound? Of course it's not Elaine! She's not capable of such a heinous thing? And why involve the kids? She loved those two like they were her own. Really, Pen, I'm beginning to think—"

"They were an accident. Not meant to be in the car. Wrong place, wrong time."

Harry sprang from the sofa. "God, woman, this is crazy! You're not thinking straight. You're tired. You're upset. But to even think she or I—"

"Is it any wonder I'm mad? First the music. Then all the secrecy. I still don't understand why you didn't say anything before now. Why you felt you couldn't trust me with the truth. I'm wasn't frightened by what I've seen or heard, but it seemed you were. I thought you were stronger than that. So we moved because it was you who was frightened?"

Harry flopped down again, an exasperated look on his

face. "In a roundabout way, yes. But for you. Believe me, if I'd have thought for one moment it would have helped, I would have said so straight away. But I didn't think it was the same thing. To be honest, I never really believed Lorna could hear anything. I'm not saying she was making it up, but it all sounded so... so... stupid. Illogical. I didn't understand what was happening."

He sidled along the sofa towards her, hoping the gulf between them was closing again, but she thwarted his manoeuvre by standing up abruptly and moving away, edging towards the door. What remained of the trust left felt as though it were being crushed out of existence, her heart ripping apart and at the moment she didn't trust her own judgement.

"Things are spoilt, Harry. You've ruined everything." With that, she rose and fled from the room.

Harry opened the bedroom door to find Penny bending over an open suitcase on the bed.

"Pen, what's going on? What are you doing?"

"Packing." She crossed the room to the open chest of drawers, gathered up a pile of clothes.

"What on earth for?"

She stopped to glare at him, her lips closed in stiff determination, her outstretched arms loaded with underwear.

"I would have thought that was obvious, even to you. I'm leaving." She went back to the suitcase and tossed the clothes into it. "I can't stand another day in this house. What with you and that god-damn music playing in my head, I'm too scared to spend another moment under this roof. I still can't believe you let me suffer—"

"But I thought—"

"That's the trouble, Harry, you think too much. You try to do the thinking for both of us." She headed for the bathroom.

"Penny, wait! Let's talk about this." Foreboding filled the empty vacuum in the room as he remembered a similar conversation, years ago, only then it was with Lorna. On the day she died.

She came back into the room, a toothbrush, her favourite bath crème and items of make-up clutched in her hands. These she put into a toiletry bag on the dressing table then tossed the bag on top of the clothes in the suitcase and zipped up the case.

"There's nothing left to talk about, Harry. It's too late."

"But there's plenty to talk about. We have to work this through. You're stressed out. You're not well. You—"

"Stop trying to tell me I'm ill. I'm not! I'm perfectly okay."

He flinched at the hateful scowl she gave him even though he knew he deserved it. His own stupid fault. He should have listened to Peter, done what he said.

"Look, I know I should have been more open with you, Pen. It was my own selfishness and fear that stopped me." Fear that had prevented him and fear that lodged itself between them. Now panicking, he reached out for her arm. He had to stop her. "You can't go. You mustn't."

She pulled from his grasp. "Let go of me. You've spoilt it all by deceiving me. I can't trust you anymore. You frighten me. What else lurks in the corners waiting to jump out at me? What other truths are there to come creeping out from the woodwork. How can I ever be sure there's nothing else you haven't told me, or what other skeletons hide inside the cupboards? I can't live like this."

"But I love you." Tears filled his eyes, pain cutting his heart into two, into four. Into tiny pieces.

"I loved you, Harry. I still do, that's what makes all this worse. We had everything going for us but you've ruined it. I will not be treated like a child; I had enough of that with Alex. Whatever is going on in this house, I want no part of it. It's worn me out and ground me down. If you had only been honest from the start, but you couldn't do that; you merely sat there and let me fall in deeper and deeper. I thought you were different. I thought you cared about me, but it seems I was wrong. Now I feel only contempt for you for putting me through all this."

"You don't mean that." He tried to take the suitcase from her grasp.

She backed away, thrusting out her free hand to keep him at bay. "Let me go, Harry. It's got to the stage I hate this house. I can't bear to be in it or with you a moment longer."

She fled down the stairs. He chased after her, reaching the front door before she did and blocking her way. He had to stop her.

"I can't let you leave like this. What we have is too precious to walk away from."

She pushed him aside. He couldn't believe where her strength came from to heave his bulk out of the way.

"You should have thought of that before. As far as I'm concerned, you can go to hell and join Lorna!"

He stood at the open door, nonplussed. She didn't mean it, she was angry with him. It was understandable; he'd well and truly fucked up. But she couldn't go. Not like this. The sound of her car starting up jolted him into action. He ran out onto the gravel, oblivious to sharp stones cutting into his shoeless feet. Reaching the car, he pulled on the door handle, to no avail; she had locked it from inside. Powerless, he stood watching her blue car disappear between the gates, out into the hedge-banked lane, and accelerate away in a squeal of rubber.

"Come back. I love you!" he shouted. "Don't go! ... Please! Come back. I need you... I love you..."

Chapter 25

"You've got to help me," Harry pleaded. "I'm at my wits' end trying to think of what to do next."

Peter grasped him by both shoulders. Shook him. "You mean to tell me Penny wasn't too ill to attend last month's little dinner party? That's she's left you?"

Harry shrugged guiltily. "I lied. I had to. What else was I supposed to have said? I'd hoped it would all blow over and she'd be back before anyone knew. At first, I thought she'd come home the following day. That all she needed was a little cooling-off time, to calm down, reassess the whole situation. That she wouldn't stay angry with me for long."

"So how long has she been gone?"

"Five weeks."

"Five weeks! And yet you said nothing!"

Harry nodded. "Almost six now since she stormed out. Over five weeks of frantically scrabbling in my trouser pocket for my mobile every time it buzzes or dashing to the phone at home every time it rings. Five long weeks of hopes raised that it's the voice I crave to hear, only to have them crushed when it isn't. Every time the postman rattles the letterbox, I'm rushing to the door like a madman, hoping for a letter. A postcard. Something. Anything! A scrap of paper, even if it's only to say one final goodbye, but this silence is crucifying me."

Peter pulled him closer. Hugged him. "You should at least have been open and honest with me, of all people. As you should have been with her, then you wouldn't be in this pitiful mess. I did warn you. I tried, I really did, but you wouldn't listen. You've really messed up big time."

"You think I don't know that? My own bloody stupidity for letting the situation get so out of hand. I've no one to blame but me. And admitting it doesn't make it any easier to live with myself. I have to get her back, Pete. I don't want to go on without her; I love her too much to let her go. Say you'll help me?"

"Of course I will, but you should have told me a lot sooner. Me. Your best buddy. I wondered what was wrong with you, why you weren't your normal self. Why you insisted on working so late in the office lately whenever I do. I was beginning to think you didn't trust me to come up with the goods on my own."

That word again. Trust. That's what Penny had accused him of - not trusting her. Now Pete. Was not confiding in people a form of mistrust? Did he have to tell everyone everything all the time, or were they all plagued by insecurity and self-doubt?

"I'm shit scared something terrible has happened to her," he confessed. "An accident... Or worse. I couldn't bear it. I just couldn't. Not all over again."

Peter clasped his shoulder. "We'd have heard if she'd been in an accident."

"Why would we? How could we? There's nothing to equate Penny to me—"

"You're not thinking straight, man. If there'd been an accident, they would trace the car's registration, leading them back to you."

He hadn't thought of that during his hours of misery imagining Penny laid up in some hospital bed or... He shook his head, trying to vanquish the picture in his mind taking shape yet again.

"Listen, whatever it takes to get to the bottom of this, we'll find her, Harry."

He sighed with relief. "I hope you're right. I've been so lost. I can't stand being in that empty house on my own, it's like being bereaved all over again. I miss her."

"You know, I never could understand why you moved when you did, especially after Penny saying how much she loved Hill House. I believed you when you said it was because there were too many reminders there of the past," Peter added.

"That much was true. But don't you see? I didn't have any choice. The thought of leaving Hill House depressed me as much as it hurt Penny, but what was I supposed to do? Stay put and watch the woman who is now my whole life go slowly insane? That sodding music wasn't supposed to follow her!"

"We'll sort it out, I promise. I like Penny; you make a great couple and are made for each other. And I know she utterly adores you and misses you."

His eyes flared. "How? How do you know? Has she been in touch with you? Have you spoken to her? I beg you, tell me!"

"Calm down, old boy. I haven't spoken to her since the night of the housewarming dinner, when your neighbours were there."

Deflated, his shoulders sagged. "I'm beginning to think I'm going crazy like Penny..." His voice trailed to a whisper.

Peter's voice softened. "She's not crazy, Harry. She's suffering from a breakdown of sorts. Christ, man, any woman in that position would have fled, it's only natural. I don't think I would have hung around for long if it were me hearing music day and night. Seeing things that weren't really there. I'd have been out the door pronto and whoosh... up the M5 like a bolt of lightning. Penny's not crazy, she's frightened. And no doubt at this precise moment probably feeling exceedingly alone and vulnerable, and wishing you would call her to say sorry."

Harry sighed. "You're probably right, but she seemed to have it in her head I was the cause of it all. And if not me, then Elaine. That she or I were trying to drive her out."

"Well, you certainly succeeded in that, old boy. But why Elaine? Doesn't make sense. I take it you've tried calling Penny's mobile? Left a message? Texted her?"

"No, she left her phone behind. I'm assuming accidentally. She never went out of the house without it, especially if driving anywhere."

"Any idea where she may have gone?"

"To her sister's. I'm positive. From the moment I bought her that car she kept saying she wanted to go and see her."

"What about her mother? I take it she's still alive. Would she have gone there? Most women turn to their mothers in times of need. I know—"

He shook his head. "They weren't particularly close. No, it's to Anita she'd have gone to."

"Have you tried phoning this sister?"

"Of course I have," Harry retorted, remembering how he'd searched anxiously through the contacts list on Penny's mobile, not that there were many to scroll through. "At first Anita denied Penny was there, said she hadn't heard from her for ages."

"Perhaps Penny told her to say that."

"Maybe, but somehow I didn't believe it. I knew she was lying. I told her all I wanted to know was if Penny's all right."

"Did you try calling again?"

He nodded. "Several times. My suspicions were confirmed when the cleaning lady answered one morning and said Penny was out shopping. I've rung practically every day since, and each time Anita says she's gone out, or asleep. Makes all sorts of excuses. Says she'll ask Penny to call me back, but she never does. I keep trying, hoping every time it will be Penny who answers, but it never is. I even tried again this morning, and all I got told was to fuck off, the phone slammed down on me yet again."

"That's half the answer in itself, Harry. Her sister! To her, you are the devil incarnate. You're the one who took Penny away from her marriage."

"That's absurd, Pete! That marriage was over long before I came on the scene."

"Look at it from her viewpoint. You enticed her sister to run out on her husband to come to live with you buried deep in the Cotswolds, miles away from all her family. Then, to cap it all, Penny starts seeing and hearing things in *your* house, *your* home. To her, you're the one who's frightened Penny away, made her ill. So now the big ugly sister thinks she's helping Penny by shielding her from you. I expect she hasn't even told her you've been trying to get in touch. And I suspect poor Penny's sat there heartbroken because you've not rung once to see how she is, or to try to persuade her to come home."

"Penny could have at least rung me, don't you think? Even

if it was only to let me know she's okay. Safe."

"Think about it. Would you in that position?"

He contemplated Peter's question a moment before answering. "No, I suppose not. So what do you think I should do?"

"Bloody well ring again, man! Do it now. Demand to speak to Penny. Better still, go down there. See her. Tell her how much you love her and want her back. On bended knees if needs be."

He shook his head. "She won't come back to Pond Cottage, not ever. She made that more than clear."

"Then sell up. Move away. Find another place together, somewhere well away from Stonecott. Out of Gloucestershire if necessary. Even to London, if that's what it takes."

"But we've only recently moved there!"

Peter's eyes rolled, exasperation written across his face. "Look, do you want her back or not?"

"Of course I do. I love her and miss her like crazy."

"Then get up off your backside and go tell her."

"How about if you go to see her, Pete? She might listen to you. I'm worried she'll slam the door in my face and not speak to me." With that, he put his head in his hands, shattered and confused by the whole sorry mess. What had gone so wrong when he was finally happy once again? "Why, oh why, should this have happened to me? Is it punishment for a bad past life? My own stupid fault for not being honest enough to tell the truth? Justifiable penance for letting Lorna rush out that day in a temper, ending up with her smashing into that fuel tanker?"

Peter put a comforting arm around his friend's shoulder. "Harry, it's tearing me up seeing you like this. Haven't you been through enough already? But, well, I did warn you."

Teeth clenched, he looked up. "If you say that one more time, Peter Ballantyne, I swear I'll—"

Peter flapped his hands up and down. "Okay, okay, calm down, man. What we need to do is find the root cause of this music and get your two lives back together again. You're too good a man to be dumped on from a great height and Penny's too wonderful a woman to let down. If nothing else, she deserves to know the truth behind it all, and we have to find it. So, I'll make a deal with you. I'll speak to Penny first, test the water, but after that, it's up to you."

"Oh, would you? I was hoping you'd say that." Relief filled his heart as he picked up his mug of coffee and took a long, slow swig. It was less than lukewarm but he didn't care. Food, tea, coffee, alcohol all had no taste, the past few weeks he'd eaten and drunk for sheer survival, any pleasure long gone from the moment Penny had left. In many ways it was worse than when he'd lost Lorna and the children. Then, it was the numbness that they were gone forever which filled his days. Now, it was a pain that cut deeper, knowing Penny was out there somewhere. If he couldn't get her back, he didn't know what he would do.

Peter shook a finger at him. "But you've got to come with me, mind. Because if she agrees to see you, it has to be there and then. No namby-pamby make-a-date-next-week job."

"Trouble is, I don't know quite what I'd say to her. That's she'd even listen to me after all this time." He caught sight of Peter's expectant expression. "Okay. What have I got to lose?"

Peter's frown relaxed to a smile. "Everything if you don't, you daft fool. Come on, grab your jacket. Let's do it now. If we don't, all sorts of reasons for putting it off will creep into that thick skull of yours. Something will always stop you, like work or a telephone call. You can do any thinking in the car on the way, apart from which the words will fall into place the moment you see her, you mark my words."

"I hope you're right."

"Trust me on this one, old boy."

Before he could appreciate what was happening, Peter had zapped round the office flicking off the computers and lights, put the telephone to answerphone, and had propelled him out of the building with a frenetic energy such as if the place was on fire.

Next moment, he was seated in Peter's car with Peter driving well over the speed limit down the A420 towards the motorway.

"So where to, old man?" Peter asked as they approached the interchange.

"London. I know Anita lives there because her phone number's a zero-two-zero code."

"Good start. Any idea what particular part? Or do we search up and down each street? Where to start first, the A's? Sorry, can't think of anywhere in London with an A. Oh, yes I do. Acton? How about B for Battersea? Brixton? Can't hear an answer, Harry. Shall we say Chelsea? No? Okay, how about Catford?"

"Your sarcasm doesn't suit you, Peter."

"Well, where in London? It's a bloody big place."

"That the other half of the problem. I don't know where exactly her sister lives."

"Bloody hell, man!"

"I don't even know her surname. All I know is she works for some woman's magazine, and believe me, I've bought loads over the last few weeks, trawling the editorial listings trying to find someone named Anita, all to no avail."

"She may write under a pen name," Peter said, pulling off the slip road and onto the inside lane of the M4, then into the middle lane, foot pressed hard on the accelerator. "Oh well, means this trip's suddenly got a little harder."

Approaching the Bath interchange, Harry looked across to Peter concentrating on overtaking two loaded car transporters in the second lane. His best buddy was right, he should have told Penny the truth from the start, but it was no use dwelling on that mistake now. What's done is done.

A thought filled his head; one he hoped would pay off else he didn't know what more he could do.

"Peter, come off at the junction after Heathrow. I've had an idea."

Chapter 26

Banks of low grey cloud cloaked London in a damp, cold blanket of drizzle. Penny had no idea of the time or how long she'd been sitting there. Her backside was numb and her left foot tingled with the beginnings of pins-and-needles, but she couldn't be bothered to move.

The window seat had become her favourite place in her sister's house in Chiswick, content to sit for hours in the early mornings watching the birds in the garden. Over the weeks, the sparrows and blackbirds had become used to seeing her there, no longer flying off to hide in the tall Leylandii trees at the bottom of the garden whenever she appeared at the third-floor landing window. A robin flew down from the garden fence to the dew-soaked lawn, where he pecked and pulled at something between the blades of grass then darted back to the fence. A frequent visitor to the garden, Penny was always pleased to see him flittering around the shrubbery, or hear him twittering from his favourite perch – a tall bamboo cane holding up a bright red dahlia at the back of the flower border.

From time to time the window misted over if she got too close or breathed out too hard. Several times she had to wipe the cold glass clear, leaving a smeary swathe of oil from the cream she'd earlier rubbed into her hands.

The quietness of the house was disturbed by the rumbling drone of the washing machine in the laundry room on fast spin vibrating through the building. Shortly after, the vacuum cleaner burst noisily into life as Meg, Anita's daily help, began cleaning and tidying somewhere downstairs. The smell of fresh brewing coffee percolated through the house, a door slammed, a shower heard running.

She sighed wearily. Another long day of indecision and boredom facing her, destined to be no different to yesterday, or the day before that. Another day of introspection. Another week slipping by in idle contemplation of what might have been, what could have been. What should have been. And with nothing to take her mind off Harry, trying to make sense of what had gone on only served to depress her further.

Her heart ached for his warm touch, the pain growing stronger each day. She didn't want to admit it, least of all to herself that, in spite of all that had transpired, she still loved him. But she couldn't forgive him.

Which was a dilemma in itself. Why was she finding it so difficult to forgive the man she loved? To him, his reasoning for keeping secrets was sound. He hadn't meant to harm her, of that she was certain. And the more she thought about him, the more she longed for his presence. Had she made a big mistake in running away instead of facing their problems together?

Her love for Harry was no less diminished, but Harry, it seemed, no longer wanted her. After all this time there hadn't been one single word from him, no attempt to find her. If he loved her as much as he'd professed he did, why hadn't he come? Been in contact? Surely he would know this is where she would be?

Every time Anita's telephone rang, every day when the letterbox rattled or the doorbell rang, her hopes rose it was him come to ask forgiveness and plead with her to come back home. She would have welcomed him with open arms, but he never came. He didn't want her, it was obvious now, but it had taken many weeks to accept that fact. And it hurt more than any fist or punch or kick could do to her insides. To her heart.

A large tear slid down her cheek. She sniffed, wiped it away with the back of her hand.

Of course, there was nothing preventing her from calling him, and she knew she really ought to let him know she was okay; he was bound to be wondering. Worried. But how, after all this time, could she? She hummed and hawed, churning the debate over in her head, but decided she couldn't. Too much time had passed, and she was too scared of what he might say after her acerbic comments to him that day she'd walked out. She regretted telling him to go to hell for keeping things from her and, in truth, she did regret that it had actually come to this, this separation. This loneliness. This despair. Small consolation, she thought. It didn't stop the hurting.

The clack-clack-clack of Anita's swift fingers over the keyboard of her computer informed Penny her sister was already in her study off the first-floor landing, engrossed in her work as "Dearest Jennifer", agony aunt for *Today's Woman.* Anita's constant remarks and digs about Alex hadn't helped much lately either and were beginning to get on her nerves. Okay, so she'd made a mistake. Hadn't Anita ever made a misjudgement? Was Anita always so right in the advice she handed out?

When she'd first arrived, she didn't want to tell her much about the strange goings on in Gloucestershire, and was grateful for her sister's understanding and not pushing for an explanation, instead allowing her the space and time to try to put things into perspective before working out what to do next. It had been only in the last few days she felt comfortable enough to be able to confide the whole sorry story, able eventually to talk about the music and the dancers, and Harry's paucity of the facts.

Anita's reaction had been predictable.

"Don't even think of going back there. Trust me on this, sis," Anita had spouted. "You need to get a new life somewhere else, well away from him. Alex was only ever interested in having a slave, another mother to do his cleaning and washing. Sounds to me like this Harry's just the same. No, you're better off without him."

"But you don't know him. You've never met him."

"I don't have to. Merely by the way he's treated you, I know his sort. Why do you always fall for the rotten eggs? Don't look so downhearted, you know what they say: "third time lucky'. Only next time, let me pick a man for you. Let me do a psycho-analysis on him first before you go committing yourself again."

"Who says there's going to be a third time!"

If Anita thought she hid her smile of satisfaction at this pronouncement, she was way off course, Penny thought. Having been a regular reader of her sister's help column, it being Anita's usual stance to preach modern feminism, always urging a stand-up-for-yourself attitude, Penny had been expecting such a comment.

Her mother's voice rattled in her ears: *It'll all end in tears. He's only interested in what money you can earn.* Words as clear now as they'd been all those years ago when she'd announced her engagement to Alex. Later, when his affairs had come to light, and she'd confessed about his intimidating behaviour and bullying tactics, Anita had wasted no time in telling Penny to ditch him. Well, Anita might have been right about Alex, but she wasn't right about Harry. She longed to tell Anita this, but couldn't face another lecture on her lousy choice of men.

Why, oh why did I agree to stay here, she quizzed herself, shifting her position slightly on the window seat. She knew why. To escape from Pond Cottage and the music, to the only safe haven she knew.

Rubbing again at the misted window with her sleeve, she realized that, during all her time here, the music had dissipated into the ether and not returned. Away from the house, the tune had simply vanished. It seemed it was only inside Pond Cottage or Hill House that its lulling melody and soothing climax had invaded her head.

Similarly, there were no more bad dreams. No fires or babies crying in the night. No mystic dancers in the shadows. Perhaps Harry and Anita and the doctor were right after all. Perhaps she had been ill without realizing it. She had escaped and so had the earworm. The tinnitus, if that's what it was, had run away. Gone.

But she had run away from one stress package straight into another. Chiswick wasn't exactly the best place to recover from what had ailed her, and the claustrophobic atmosphere was hardly conducive to harmonious recuperation. It was too close to Heathrow Airport for a start for it to be anything but peaceful, but at least she felt free. Free of the music, but not free from Harry. And certainly not free from her sister's constant concern.

The fuss extended to her had at first been refreshing and

welcome, but now she felt smothered and choked by Anita's well-meant care. Long days spent trying to occupy her time until Anita finished her daily pounding in the study were becoming too much of a drag.

Anita worked from home, most days shut away in her little office. Meanwhile, Meg took care of all the cleaning and cooking and everything else around the house, which left little for her to do to earn her keep, instead sinking deeper into depression and the doldrums.

It's time to move on, she decided, wrapping her chunky cardigan tighter around her. There was life outside the four walls of thirty-seven Palmer's Walk. Time to be making plans to find her own life, because she couldn't stay with Anita and Nathan indefinitely. The thought of entering the wide world again filled her with trepidation. She had little money, no home and no friends. Where would that life take her? More to the point, where did she want to go?

Back to Harry? She thought long and hard again. She did miss the house and the beautiful countryside she had come to love, those wonderful walks they shared. She missed his passionate kisses, the feel of his warm skin against hers. Her body yearning for his touch, his lovemaking. Besides which, there was little laughter in her sister's house; Anita and Nathan didn't seem to laugh together, only at stupid, silly TV programmes. Harry had always been able to make her laugh with his inept jokes and funny comments; his smile enough to bring sunshine into any damp and gloomy morning.

In the study below, the telephone trilled loudly. It was picked up immediately, Anita's voice loud, but Penny couldn't make out any words, the conversation ceasing after a brief exchange; the phone slammed back down. Another wrong number or cold caller? Anita had complained she'd been getting a lot of those lately.

She swung her stiffened joints off the window seat, stood and stretched, wishing now she hadn't sat there for so long in one position. Her hands were cold. She blew on them, rubbing them together briskly as she ventured downstairs to seek out a much-needed cup of hot coffee.

In the hallway, she stopped at the radiator to warm her hands, her eyes drawn to the telephone on the table. Should she ring him? What would she say? What would he say?

It might hurt like hell the way Harry had disregarded her feelings, kept things from her, but her mind was made up. The future clear. Her hand hovered over the telephone. If only she had the courage to pick up the receiver and ask to come home. She wanted to forgive him. Yet she couldn't. It would be admitting he was right, and no matter how much she wanted and loved him, sometimes love had to lose out over sanity. It was one thing falling head over heels like a sixteen-year-old, it was quite another letting them get away with murder, in both senses of the word. Not that she believed he had instigated Lorna's death. If only he'd explained things properly from the start...

Eventually, she plucked up the courage and dialled Pond Cottage. There was no reply. The answerphone didn't engage. She put the receiver down, wondering if she would even have left a message had it clicked in.

If only she could remember Harry's mobile number, but it was on speed dial on her mobile; she could only remember the first four digits. If only she hadn't left it behind at the cottage in her haste to get away...

With a mixture of disappointment peppered with relief – she really didn't know what she would say to him – she sauntered into the kitchen.

Meg was there, busy whisking a bowl of eggs. "Morning. My, you look miserable! Don't let your sister see you like that, you know what she'd say."

Penny shrugged and sighed as she poured herself a coffee from the coffee pot. "I've been thinking—"

A loud ringing interrupted from the hallway.

"That's the telephone again. I'd better go answer it," said Meg, swiftly wiping her hands on her apron, leaving Penny staring into the swirling black liquid in her mug, her ears straining to hear the conversation from the hall.

Was it Harry ringing back? Perhaps he'd been in the shower when she'd rung, unable to pick up the phone, and he'd dialled 1471 to find out who had called. She put her mug down and stepped closer to the kitchen door, hope rising. She heard the receiver being put back down. Disappointed, she went back to her coffee.

"It was for Anita," Meg said, coming back into the kitchen. "That's the fifth time in as many days that man's been on the phone demanding to speak to her. You'd think by now he'd get the message that she doesn't want to know."

"Who?"

"One of her readers wanting some personal advice over the phone, she says. Oh well, I'd best be taking her coffee upstairs, it'll be getting cold."

"Here, give it to me, Meg, I'll take it. I need to tell Anita I'm moving on and today's as good a day as any."

Chapter 27

Harry focused on the semi-detached. It felt peculiar sitting outside the house again. He prayed he wouldn't see a glimpse of Penny peeking out from behind the greying net curtains.

As if reading his mind, Peter asked, "You don't think she would have come back to him?"

From the passenger seat, Harry shook his head. "No. I know Penny; she would never, ever come back here. Not to him."

"If he's a teacher, wouldn't he be at school this time of day?"

"It's half term," he enlightened him, not taking his eyes from the house.

"Well," said Peter, "are you going to knock and ask, or are we going to sit here all day?"

He turned to his friend. "I'm thinking what to do if he's not in."

"You won't know until you go and find out."

"But if he's not?"

"Then we wait. All day. All night if needs be."

"He might have moved and I've made you come all this way for nothing."

"That's a risk you have to take. If we're going to find out where this sister lives, you're going to have to go up, ring the flippin' doorbell and ask. This was your idea, after all. Now get out of the flaming car!"

Harry flinched. In front of his eyes the haunting faces of Elly and Sam screamed at him, flames licking around all them.

Peter, realizing what he'd said, placed his hand on Harry's arm. "God, man, I'm so sorry. I didn't mean to upset—"

"It's okay. I know you didn't, but sometimes it simply takes the odd word for it all to come rushing back." He shook his head, trying to rid himself of the images forming inside.

"Then let's put an end to it. Now. If he's not in, we go and grab something to eat and come back later. If he slams the door on you, tough, we'll have to think of something else. And if he swings a punch, be ready to duck, then throw him a right hook. But for goodness sake get out and try. That's why we're here."

Harry extracted himself slowly from the confines of the seat belt then hurried along the garden path. Caught by the breeze, discarded crisp packets and screwed-up bits of paper whipped about the front garden. Rubbish lay in the weed-filled border of the overgrown lawn, crushed cigarette boxes and discarded beer cans tossed carelessly over the hedge. The man certainly hadn't made any attempt to keep it tidy, Harry observed. It had all looked so pretty the last time he'd seen it, the day he and Penny returned Alex's car before he had any reason to accuse Penny of stealing it the day she fled to Gloucestershire.

As he pointed a finger to push on the doorbell, the door flew open and there stood Penny's ex, dishevelled and unshaven, looking as if he'd only crawled out of bed a moment ago.

"What the fuck do you want?"

Taking a step back, and keeping a surreptitious eye on Alex's free hand, so he wouldn't miss any warning signs of an impending punch coming his way, he introduced himself and briefly explained the reason for calling. All the while his eyes darted to and fro at the houses either side, half-expecting a net curtain to twitch as a neighbour peeked out.

Alex's scowl morphed into a smug grin before he answered with venomous gloating.

"Well, well... So the bloody marvellous Harry Winchester hasn't turned out to be so wonderful after all, now there's a surprise. What you really mean is, she's left you!"

Goodness, what on earth had Penny ever seen in this man? It definitely wasn't his charismatic charm, thought Harry.

"No, it's nothing like that. She felt she needed a break, that's all. We're having problems with the house and—"

Alex cut him off. "And you honestly think I'm going to help you after you had the gall to take my wife from me?"

Infuriated by the man's arrogance, he stood tall, not that he'd expected the man's co-operation, but he certainly wasn't going to let Alex get the better of him.

"Let's be honest here; your marriage was already over long before I came on the scene."

"I loved her."

The words were spoken with such honesty, for a moment he almost believed him. "Then you had a funny way of showing it to her, that's all I can say."

Alex took a step closer and prodded him in the chest, snarling, "Listen, you don't know a damn thing about—"

"I know enough!" He pushed Alex's hand briskly out of the way. "Look, whatever you think, whatever happened between you two, this isn't helping to find her. Will you tell me Anita's address or not?"

"No. Now fuck off!" At that, Alex stepped back and slammed the door shut.

"I take it he didn't want to know, then?" Peter said when, shaking with anger, Harry climbed back into the car.

"My, you are full of wit and wisdom today. What has got into you because you're not helping much? You're supposed to be supporting me."

"I thought that's precisely what I was doing. You haven't exactly made things easy for yourself and if you had listened to—"

Harry glared at him. "Look, I don't need you to rub it in. You gave me my lecture this morning. Come on, let's get away from here. This place is depressing me."

Peter started the engine. "Okay. Where to now?"

"Anywhere. ...I don't know; I'm trying to think."

"Let's find some coffee whilst you're doing it, then."

Peter slipped the Mercedes into drive and was about to pull away from the kerbside when a loud thumping on the car roof jolted him to an abrupt stop.

The tinted passenger window slid open silently when Peter pushed a button on the centre console, allowing enough room for Alex to thrust a folded scrap of paper through to Harry before stooping to speak through the open gap.

"Here, take this. It's Anita's address, though why I should be helping you is beyond me when I really ought to be punching your lights out good and proper. A for your darned cheek, and B for pinching my missus. We had a good marriage until you came poncing along."

"If it was that good, Harry nor anyone else would have been able to entice Penny away," Peter threw across to him. "She wouldn't have looked twice at any man."

"Who the bloody hell asked you?" growled Alex.

"Look, mate, bullies like you—"

Anxious to end the altercation and get away before things got out of hand - he could tell the man was sparring for a fight - Harry butted in.

"Shut up, Peter. We got what we came for, now let's go." He waved the note at Alex. "Thanks. What made you change your mind?"

Alex stepped back from the car. "I guess because I suppose I still care about her. And because you're a much better man than I am."

"Meaning?"

"Meaning you have the courage to chase after her whereas I did nothing and lost her for good. But I'm warning you, when you find her, don't you dare hurt her or else I'll—"

"Or you'll what?" said Peter, making to unbuckle his seat-belt.

"Listen, I love Penny," Harry said. "Far more than you could ever imagine. She'll be taken good care of, I promise." He didn't take his eyes off Alex, even though he could sense Peter was ready to bail out of the car and square up to him.

"Just take it as a warning, Winchester." Alex stuffed his hands into his pockets and retreated into his garden without looking back.

"Strange man," Peter commented, indicating again to pull out, watching in his wing mirror for a gap in the traffic zooming by. "Right, where to?"

Harry unfolded the crumpled piece of paper torn from an exercise book.

"Chiswick. Palmer's Walk."

Chapter 28

Penny knocked gently on Anita's office door before entering. The small room looked cluttered but cosy bathed in a pale glow from the desk lamp by Anita's computer. Reference books and piles of magazines filled every available shelf.

Anita looked up at the intrusion. Smiling, she put down the letter opener and took the proffered mug. "Thanks. You were up early again."

It sounded more of an accusation than observation, Penny thought. "Sorry if I disturbed you."

"You didn't."

"I've been thinking—"

"I can tell by that expression on your face what you're thinking," Anita interrupted.

Was it that obvious, Penny wondered. "I am grateful, sis, but it's unfair on you and Nathan me being here all this time. Staying here was only meant as a stop-gap. A bolt hole until I worked out what to do. I need to get myself a job. I can't afford to run the car much longer on my own, and I need my own space. I can't go on living off you two."

"Why not? It's what families are for. You can stay for as long as you want, you're not in the way."

"Your boys are home from Cambridge soon; they don't want Aunt Misery moping about the house all day."

"Nonsense. And you can worry about money when you're fully recovered."

"From what? God, Anita, it's not like I've been ill or anything!"

"No, but you need time to rest and pick up the pieces of your life before you go rushing headlong into another disaster." She handed Penny yet another pamphlet to read about depression and self-help therapy.

Appreciating Anita only acted out of sisterly concern, as well as in her professional capacity dolling out advice, trying to help, Penny took the document. And not wishing to upset her by ignoring it, she unfolded its triple-folded pages and pretended to read its no-doubt informative information. When Anita's attention refocused on the computer screen, she quickly refolded the pamphlet, running her fingers down the folds, sharpening the creases, before returning it surreptitiously to the pile on the desk.

"Mmm... sorry," said Anita, without looking up. "I'm going to have to leave you to your own devices again today. I've a deadline to meet, you know what it's like. If I don't finish on time the magazine withholds payment. We'll chat about this more over dinner."

She was sure her sister's remark wasn't meant to be barbed, nonetheless it made her feel guilty. She was taking up Anita's precious time by keeping her from her work, discussing her problems when she ought to be solving other people's.

Anita peered at her over her half-rimmed spectacles. "Mind you, if you are getting bored, you could give me a hand to write my column for the magazine."

"Get real, Anita. How can I be expected to do that when my own life is in such an utter mess? I'm hardly the person to be offering advice to others, am I?"

If trying to solve other people's problems was meant to be another of her sister's so-called therapy sessions, it was futile, Penny thought. Other people's problems paled into insignificance compared to her own. No one could be suffering the same emotional roller coaster she rode at the moment.

"You might find some answers for your own problems hidden amongst these gems I have to deal with."

"The chances of that are pretty remote, even you have to admit that," she threw back.

"I'm not expecting you to come up with the answers, Pen, but you could at least help read the postbag, there's a mountain this morning. You know, fish out the real juicy ones, or ones which are different from the usual "Dear Jennifer, my wife doesn't understand me' or "My husband's having an affair with the milkman, what shall I do?' That sort of thing."

The thought of doing something useful was tempting, but after a moment deliberating, she shook her head. She'd already made up her mind what she wanted to do today.

"Actually, sis, I only interrupted you to bring you your coffee, and to tell you I've decided to go and visit Mum for a few days."

For some unfathomable reason she couldn't explain or understand, she wanted her mother. Needed her. It wasn't an ideal solution, for staying with Mum meant she wouldn't be able to do precisely what she wanted when she wanted, or eat when and what she liked. What it would be was a change of scenery. And it would go a long way to make amends for the guilt she felt at not having visited her mother long before now.

"Do you regret not having children?" Anita asked unexpectedly, seemingly ignoring her announcement.

Whether this was by accident or design Penny couldn't be sure. And even though Anita's question had caught her off-guard, she didn't have to give it a moment's thought before answering.

"No. You know me, I never was one to go gaga every time I saw a baby, or drooled over prams and pushchairs."

"Only I wondered with this dream thing, hearing babies crying and what have you, whether it's an inner emotional cry to become pregnant before it's too late. The old biological clock ticking. Time running out."

"And you analyse everything too much. You know I never wanted children. I'm not the motherly kind."

"Are you sure it wasn't because Alex didn't want babies and you went along with him for the sake of the peace? Didn't he always say it was never the right time?"

"It was both our decision. He worked with children all day, teaching. He didn't want them under his feet of an evening as well."

"Typical selfish thinking on his part."

"In any case, it's rather late in the day for me to start pining for babies, isn't it?"

"Not if you really want one."

"I don't!" The words blurted out before she had time to think whether that was indeed the case. She would have liked to have children if she were completely honest with herself, but considering how things had ended up between her and

Alex, she was glad none had been involved; it had made the separation and divorce so much simpler.

"What about Harry? Did he not want more children, particularly after what happened to his own?"

"It was something we never discussed. He never spoke much about his kids. You make it sound as if by having more they can replace those he lost. Would you go ahead and have more children if anything happened to your sons?"

"Nothing could ever replace my boys."

"My point exactly."

"Look, Pen, I love you dearly and when you hurt, I hurt too. As does Mum. We all feel for you, and believe me when I say no one understands more than me what you're going through at this moment. You're torn between wanting this Harry and wondering whether to forgive him. If you do, you're a bigger fool than you've already been. He's a bastard of the first sort. No, I'll correct that, of the second sort. Alex is still number one bastard in my books. Forget Harry, forget Pond Cottage and make a fresh start."

"It's not that easy."

"No. It's hard. But you've taken the first step by leaving him. The second step is always harder, not knowing which one to take next, but you're single again. You're still attractive, and have everything going for you. I could probably even get you a job on the magazine if you want, but you've got to stop dwelling on the past. It's over. Move forward. There's a whole big world and life out there if you pulled yourself together and go for it."

"Finished?"

"For now, yes. Look, I only want to see you happy. I hate seeing you mope about the house all day. You need to do something."

"That's why I'm going to see Mum."

Anita rose from her chair, went to her and gave her a big hug. "Good. Grieve for Harry yes, because it hurts like hell when a relationship turns sour, but there comes a point when the anger and grieving must end. Let that time be today."

"Thanks, sis. Thanks for everything. I owe you." She

made for the door.

"Hey, where are you going? I thought you were going to help me?"

"I'm going to ring Mum now. See if it's okay if I come today." It was only to be a visit, certainly no more than a few days; she wouldn't be moving in.

By noon she was packed and ready to go.

"I've been expecting this for days," Anita said, helping Penny carry her bags downstairs. "But are you sure about going? A visit to Mum sounds a good idea, but there's nothing to do there. You'll be as bored there as here. Goldstoke is hardly the buzz town of Bucks, it's in the middle of nowhere. I know Mum'll be pleased to see you but—"

Penny lifted her suitcase into her car's boot. "Exactly. It will be good for us both. I've never seen her new house, and we've a lot of catching up to do." She checked her handbag. "Now, have I got everything? Purse. Credit cards. Keys."

Anita threw a hand to her mouth. "Gosh, I forgot! You don't know the way. It's one of those villages that if you blink, you'll miss it. You need a map. Hang on, I'll write out the directions."

"I do have satnav," Penny said, exasperated by her sister's constant fussing, however well-intended. "Stop worrying, I won't get lost. And even if I do, it will be an adventure."

Anita sighed. "As long as you're sure this is what you want? You know you're always welcome here." She hugged Penny. "Drive safe. Give my love to Mum."

"Will do. And thanks again for putting up with me all this time."

"Will you be coming back here after?"

"We'll see." At the moment it was difficult moving from one day into the next; she didn't want to plan that far ahead.

Harry watched from the car while Peter spoke to a woman in her late fifties, short-cropped greying hair, feather duster in hand, standing in the open doorway. *That couldn't be Penny's sister, surely?* The woman shook her head, several times, in answer to Peter's questions. The front door to the four-storey house closed. Peter got back into the driver's seat, his dour expression telling Harry he'd received no joy.

"We're too late, we've missed her," Peter told him. "Apparently, she packed this morning and left shortly after lunch."

"What?" He punched the dashboard. "I can't believe after all this time she chose today of all days to leave! Did she say where she's gone?"

"Said she didn't know. Sorry." Peter studied the disappointment written over his friend's face. "Sod's law, old boy. Hey, you don't think she was trying to fob us off, do you? I mean, what if Penny's in there now watching us from an upstairs window?"

Harry looked back towards the house, wanting to see a curtain move, hoping to catch a glimpse of Penny's face peeking out between the gaps in the vertical blinds.

"Do we even know that was the housekeeper and not Penny's sister pretending? Have you ever met her?" Peter asked.

"Penny said there was only a few years age difference between them. That woman was a lot older, so no way could she have been Anita."

"I did suggest we call back later when her boss was back," Peter told him, "but she said not to bother, and that she was under strict instructions to send you away if ever you called."

"Didn't you explain—"

"Of course I did, idiot. I'm not that stupid. At first, she didn't want to say anything, but I think she felt sorry for us when I told her we'd driven all the way from Gloucestershire this morning. She did seem pretty genuine."

Harry shrugged. "So, what to do now? Go home?" Inside, his heart had nose-dived into the pit of his stomach. He'd been so full of hope and certainty Penny would be there.

"What! You're giving up? After we've come all this way?"

"Of course I'm not giving up. It's simply that I don't know what else we can do today. How *do* you find someone who doesn't want to be found?"

"So we've failed plan one. There's always plan two."

"Which is?"

"I'm working on that one. Let's go grab a bite to eat and drink, I noticed there was a pub at the end of the road. We'll come back later. There has to be a way of finding out where Penny's gone, and my money's on the mother. We could always go back and ask the ex where she lives."

"And that, Peter Ballantyne, would be really pushing our luck. Somehow I don't think he'll tell us."

"I think you're right there, mate. What if you report to the police that Penny's car's been stolen? They might locate it and her for you."

Harry glared at him. "And wouldn't that go down like a ton of bricks with her! No, there has to be another way. I only wish I knew what that way is. No, the evil sister is going to tell us, whether she likes it or not. I'm not giving up. Come on, Let's go grab that pint."

Chapter 29

With each passing mile, Penny worried how she would cope with living under the same roof as her mother, even if just for a little while. Theirs had been a strained relationship for many years, no longer the mother and daughter affection between them that had once been so strong.

It hadn't always been like that, she brooded, negotiating the complex of roundabouts through Milton Keynes. She supposed that was her own doing. Another pang of guilt swept through her. She should have visited her mother long before now; there'd been ample time to make up their differences. She hoped it wasn't too late.

The clouds dissipated and the sun burst forth, lifting her mood. A wooden sign, set into a neat flowerbed of multi-coloured petunias at the side of the road, proclaiming "Welcome to Goldstoke. Please Drive Carefully" came into view. The narrow, gently winding road with its neatly clipped grass verges led her to a sleepy backwater with one shop, a small petrol station, and not much else from what she could see until the road curved to the right, went over a little humped-back bridge, and the village proper came into view.

Keeping her speed to 20 miles an hour, she drove by man-icured lawns and neat, pretty gardens of the ancient thatched cottages and bungalows strung out along the road, thinking that it all looked overly-neat. Unreal. A place where no discarded crisp packets or empty drinks cans lay in the gutter or verge and no weed dared grow amongst the dahlias and rose bushes. No plastic bags or bits of paper blowing about. Where shrubbery was clipped into perfect mounds of symmetry, and no doubt the concrete garden ornaments were the height of good taste; no garden gnomes or plastic meer-kats here, she thought with a wry smile. And every bit as quiet as Anita had described. Too quiet. Not a person to be seen. If she hadn't seen the sign she would have sworn she'd driven straight into Brigadoon.

As she neared a centuries-old looking pub, the disembodied voice of the sat-nav announced: "You have reached your destination." Nervous and weary from the long drive, she pulled up in front of a small row of cottages and turned off the engine. Immediately, a door to one of the cottages opened. She saw her mother step out, waving like mad, the smile on her face as wide as Penny could ever remember. Arms outstretched, her mother rushed to the car.

"Penny, darling. It's so wonderful to see you."

The tight hug and greeting kiss were as warm as the butter-coloured stone building, telling her she needn't have done all that worrying. All was well between them. Her mother ushered her quickly indoors.

Sitting in the tiny dining room, she watched her mother pour tea into a delicate china teacup with matching saucer. She still used a teapot, Penny noted, remembering her mother's statement of long ago: "A teabag dipped into a mug doesn't taste the same. Tea has to be made properly. It has to have time and room to brew."

Gazing about the room, at the unfamiliar sideboard against one wall, a small mahogany unit tucked into a corner, she saw nothing to remind her of her childhood home. None of her parents' furniture would have fitted in here anyway, she realized. The cottage was small, no hallway, with stairs leading directly up from the dining room. It was all so different from the large house and garden she grew up in overlooking the Thames at Richmond. Barely enough room to swing a teapot let alone a cat. Yes, definitely bijou in size, but bright and cheerful, with a warm, homely feel.

"What did go wrong between us, Mum?" she asked, as Anna cut a wedge of fruitcake, carefully placed it on a matching teaplate, and passed it across to her. The cake was shop bought. She'd probably rushed out to buy it the moment she knew I was coming, Penny thought. Years ago, there had always been home-baked cakes or buns in her mother's tin.

"It's all so irrelevant now, my dear. Let's not dwell on it." Anna handed her an ivory-handled cake fork.

"But we used to be so close when we lived at home." Penny remembered with fondness those days when their laughter frequently filled the old house. "All the jokes we shared, and those silly pranks we used to play, especially on Dad."

Anna laughed at the memories. "Your poor father. What he had to put up with in a house full of women. You were always goading and teasing him."

"And the days out in Richmond or Kingston, when the three of us went shopping together. Always on a Saturday."

"We were certainly a force to be reckoned with. I miss those times," Anna said wistfully.

"They were fun days, Mum. What changed it all?"

"Alex."

Her mother's curt reply was no more than she expected. Her parents had always disapproved of her choice of husband but to hear it voiced now, so emphatically, hurt.

"So why did you and Dad never try to prevent me from marrying him?"

"What good would it have done, Pen? You were always so headstrong and determined. You always thought you knew better, so I'm afraid we simply let you get on with it."

"I seem to recall words from Dad like 'your bed, you go lie on it'. I can imagine how he gloated and ranted how right he'd been about Alex. How I should have left him after that 'dreadful time'. I can hear his voice right now telling me, 'I told you so.'"

"He only wanted what was best for you. We both did. He didn't want to see you get hurt."

She sighed glumly. "Poor Daddy. I do miss him."

"So do I," her mother whispered, her grey eyes shining from welling tears.

From where she sat, Penny could see into the compact but modern kitchen at the rear of the house. The back door was ajar, opening onto a small courtyard garden no wider than four large paving slabs and surrounded by a rough-stone wall. From the gaps in the stonework aubrietia tumbled down in mauve cascades. Along the top of the wall monkey-like faces of yellow and blue pansies nodded in the breeze. Fresh air blowing in carried with it the sounds of birdsong and farmyard smells from the cornfield beyond.

"Don't you get lonely here, Mum? It does seem rather isolated."

Anna smiled. "Not in the least. I have plenty to keep me busy and I've made many friends here. The village is a magical place to live, I couldn't have found better. The only thing I do miss is seeing my two girls often enough. More tea, dear?"

"No, thanks. Two's plenty for me. But what do you find to do all day? Doesn't it get boring stuck out here, miles from anywhere?"

"Boring? Goodness me, no. There are never enough hours in the day! I'm secretary for the parish council, that's a full-time job in itself. You'd be astounded at how many people move into the village from towns looking for the country life and then bemoan the tractor trundling through the village in the early hours, or the muck and mud left in its wake. I've even had someone ask me to do something about the cows mooing, that it wakes them up too early. Or could I silence the cockerel from cock-a-doodle-doing at the crack of dawn."

"You have got to be kidding me?" She was amazed at the effrontery of some people.

"Oh, I'm serious. With all that going on, I don't know where I find the time to sit on the village entertainment committee and be a member of the board of governors for the village school. And as if that wasn't enough to fill my day, I chair the floral committee and help with the flowers in the church. Always busy, busy, busy. Always rushing somewhere. I never have time to be bored or lonely."

Penny put down her empty plate. The cake, although light and moist, wasn't anywhere near as good as her mother used to make.

"Finished, dear?" Anna asked. "Then let's get your bags in and I'll show you your room. It's yours as long as you want it. I do hope you're not going to go rushing off after the week-end, we've so much catching up to do."

A swift tour of the cottage revealed it was larger upstairs than Penny expected, with two ample-sized bedrooms, the largest of which had French doors opening out onto a narrow balcony, where several large blue pots of bold-red geraniums nestled against the wrought-iron railing.

"I turned this room into a sitting room so I can enjoy the views across the open countryside behind the house. The guest room's up in the loft, again commanding glorious views from its dormer window," Anna told her, leading her up another flight of stairs. Do you think you'll be all right up here?"

"Wow! It's lovely. However did you ever find this place?"

"Oh, quite by chance, dear. I became lost on my way to see a house for sale in Olney. I'd only stopped at the shop to ask directions. The lady behind the counter mentioned that this one was up for sale. I fell in love with it from the moment I stepped through the front door. It might be small but it suits me to a T."

"But why out here? Anita and I could never understand why you wanted to move so far away from London after Dad died, away from everything and everyone you knew."

"Because I need a fresh start. Something different. A new beginning."

"I can understand that. I know how I felt when Harry and I moved to Pond Cottage." She crossed to the window to admire the view then turned around to face her mother.

"Mum, do you still knit?" She didn't know what made her ask that. Perhaps she was still looking for something familiar and comforting in her mother, she had changed so much since Penny had last seen her. Even her hair was different. It never used to be so dark nor as short, but the loose, free style suited her. "You always had a pair of needles in your hand or a crochet hook, I seem to remember. Dad bought you a knitting machine and then grumbled all the time about the noise it made and how much room it took up in the breakfast room."

"God, yes. He did go on about it, didn't he? Always grouching, but he was grateful for the new jumpers I made him. Sadly my eyesight isn't as good now, and with only me to knit for there isn't a need. One can buy equally good sweaters and so much cheaper in the shops nowadays. Now, tell me all about this Harry fellow? Do you want to tell me what's gone wrong?"

Penny smiled pensively and shrugged. "It seems I have this uncanny knack of choosing the wrong man, according to Anita. I thought Harry was the man of my dreams, but the dream turned into a nightmare, I'm sorry to say. He didn't love me enough to trust me. He thought I couldn't handle the truth."

"The truth about what?"

"What was behind the cause of the deaths of his first wife and their two children. That he was to blame."

Anna looked horrified. "You mean, he murdered them?"

"As good as, according to him. But it wasn't what you think; it was an accident."

"Then I don't understand—"

"I've been through hell the past few months, Mum. Full of nightmares and music and visions. And all the while Harry knew what was happening. It had happened before, you see. To his wife. Yet he kept it all from me. He lied to me. Let me suffer." Tears welled in her eyes, trickling down her cheeks as the memories and the heartache inside overwhelmed her again.

Her mother pulled her close into a warm, tight hug. "Oh, my poor baby. Then you have done the right thing by leaving him."

"The trouble is, Mum, I still love him."

Chapter 30

Any remaining wariness evaporated as Penny settled in, relishing the time spent sharing stories and anecdotes with her mother, catching up with all those lost years. Reminiscing.

Two days soon evolved into a fortnight; far longer than she had planned to stay. In truth, she liked living there, the past few weeks enjoyable. And, much to her relief, Anna had refrained from asking how long she intended stopping or what her future plans might be.

Even though the house was small, Anna had managed to afford her daughter ample space, respecting and allowing her privacy. For this, Penny was grateful, and for her tactfulness in not quizzing and questioning or further probing for every minute detail as to what had gone on with Harry.

In return, she tried hard not to interfere with her mother's hectic but ordered lifestyle, as Goldstoke proved every bit as lively as Anna had extolled. It seemed a friendly little place, where everyone knew everyone else, and where something was always going on: coffee mornings, sherry parties, charity events, weekly readings in the village hall, the forthcoming village fete. She hadn't appreciated her mother led such a busy life.

But was Goldstoke where she wanted to stay, Penny asked herself. Could she ever settle there? There was no reason why she couldn't, she supposed, and the Buckinghamshire countryside was as beautiful in its own way as Gloucestershire, even if she were to admit she missed the rolling hills and wooded valleys of the Cotswolds. Was that a good enough reason to move on? She shook her head. No, it wasn't. It was an excuse, and a feeble one at that. One that skirted the real reason she still felt lonely and isolated. It was the simple fact she missed Harry, the enforced distance between them doing little to reduce the want or need for him.

For the outside world, but mainly for her mother's benefit, she tried to appear carefree and bubbly, always smiling, confident she hid her feelings well. But her smiles were false, the laughter hollow, her eyes wet with fought-back tears. She carried her heart like a heavy iron ball, its chain taut, cutting deep. By day, as long as she kept herself busy, she could cope, her brave face a mask she hid behind. But when no one was looking, she allowed that mask to slip.

Most nights, unable to sleep, she tossed and turned in bed, imagining she could hear Harry's voice whispering on the breeze blowing through the gently billowing lace curtains, calling to her. Her body ached for his touch, her lips burned for his sweet kisses. Try as she might, she couldn't stop wanting him with a love and passion that was now unrequited. And for the first time in her life she knew what real unhappiness was. It seemed the further and longer she was away from him, the more painful it became.

Perhaps rushing out had been foolish, but the pain and torment he'd put her through whilst he singularly knew what was happening incensed her still, raging away inside like a trapped, angry wasp. She felt betrayed. She felt lost, wishing instead it would all return to how it had been. The clock put back. But could she ever go back to Pond Cottage, she asked herself a thousand times more? And would the ghosts, if that's what they were, ever be gone? The nightmares exorcised? She doubted it. Somehow there would always be another presence lurking there.

"You never know what you've got till it's gone." Words to a song rattled through her head, reminding her of what had been between them, all the loving and the fun, such happiness. True words indeed, but they offered little comfort to her suffering, no easement of her pain. She knew what she had at the time, but now it was gone. Lost. Never to come back. Yet he still held a grip on her heart, tugging and pulling at her emotions. Oh, why wouldn't he let go?

Elaine Frampton draped her arms around Harry's neck the instant he opened the front door of Pond Cottage.

"I'm so sorry," she whimpered. "It simply slipped out. How was I to know you had never told her about Lorna and the music? Please say you'll forgive me. When Peter told me

184

that Penny had in fact left you, I was beside myself. I feel so guilty. He said you and he have been up to London on a wild goose chase to find her. I've come to apologize and make amends."

Furious, Harry thrust her arms away from him. The merest touch of her skin and the overpowering perfume in his nostrils made his skin crawl.

"You had to open your mouth, didn't you? You just couldn't let it drop."

"But it wasn't like that—"

"No? Then what was it like? Frighten Penny off so that you could try to wheedle your way into my affections? Penny was right about you and—"

"No, no, you've got it all wrong," she pleaded. "This proves she didn't really love you if she's run away after one small, tiny argument?"

He tried to close the door, but Elaine's foot prevented him.

"I'll do all I can to help you this minor hiccup, because that's all this is. A little hiccup. Harry, listen to me—"

"No, Elaine! I've done enough listening to you over the past three years. You've interfered in my life once too often. What were you hoping for? That I'll come to you, sob in your arms and you'll kiss it all better for me?"

Tears streamed down her cheeks. "The last thing I want to do is hurt you, Harry, darling. This is clearly your vented anger. I can understand your bitterness but—"

He didn't give her an opportunity to finish the sentence. "Just go, will you? Leave me alone." This time no amount of tears were going to make him relent. He pushed the door extra hard.

Elaine extracted her foot rapidly, screeching, "You wait and see, Harry... In a few weeks' time you'll have calmed down. It's for the best, you know. Call me if you need anything, won't you, Harry? Harry?"

Leaning with his back against the front door, he tried not to listen. That woman! She was enough to drive any man to drink. What was wrong with her? No, Penny was definitely right about that one. Why hadn't he seen it before?

"Oh, Penny," he wailed into the silent hallway. "Where are you? If you'd only let me know you're okay?"

He had not lost count of the weeks since his impetuous trip to Chiswick with Peter, all with no word from her. Not one. He had hoped Anita would relent, seeing him standing on her doorstep pleading, begging her to tell him, but nothing would shake her resolve to remain silent. But the reception he had received at Palmer's Walk, when he and Peter had returned that day they went in search, was enough to convince him he wasn't welcome, but he lived in hope.

He had to hope. It was all he had left.

Chapter 31

Anna's order of the day was a pattern Penny fell swiftly in step with. A light breakfast, a quick tidy up of the house and a flick of the feather duster, followed by a stroll around the village. Lunch would often be taken in the Lamplighters next door, before her mother dashed off to some meeting or other, leaving her on her own for the afternoon. She didn't mind this, anxious not to intrude any more than necessary into her mother's many committee meetings and circles.

If the weather was too inclement to be outside, she filled the time curled up on the sofa upstairs with a book or watching an afternoon movie on television, preferably a good weepy so she could indulge in tissues and tears. Other days, she much preferred taking long walks in the open countryside surrounding the village, each time striding out in a different direction, eager to explore more of the village's environs.

Heading back home after visiting the little church on the hill, wandering amongst the old, lichen-encrusted tombstones and reading all the inscriptions, she walked with a smile of mirth on her face, wondering how much Anna's hand had in keeping Goldstoke the way it was. A typical, quintessential English village waiting for the preservation order to be slapped upon it, she thought, and wouldn't have been amazed if it had been done so already.

With its idealistic roses-around-the-door country living, the village possessed a unique charm, a charm that had stealthily entwined itself around her, offering security within its tight-knit community, and stability in the humdrum pace of everyday life.

For the first time in months a feeling of peace settled over her, an overwhelming sense of calmness as her unhurried footsteps took her along the narrow main street, home in sight. At first, she couldn't fathom what had brought on this reaction, until the sun slipped back out from behind a fluff of cloud and bathed the pavement ahead in golden sunlight. Then she knew. It was the village. Goldstoke had worked its magic. In that moment she knew it was a place she would never want to leave.

Did this mean she was over Harry? She searched her heart, waiting for the flutter that usually came whenever she thought of him.

It didn't come.

She had her answer.

Armed with this revelation, she stopped outside the village shop to read the advertisement cards placed in the front window, as she did whenever she passed – a habit she'd learned many years ago from her mother. A postcard can tell a thousand stories, according to Anna, and an astute way to keep abreast of what the neighbours are about. Or, if you were lucky, you might find a good bargain for sale.

One card in particular caught her attention, a part-time position behind the counter. She went inside to find out more.

"As I've decided to stay in the village, I've also decided to take a job. As from next Monday, I shall be serving in the shop a few days a week," Penny announced to her mother over supper that evening.

"There really is no need. I—"

"There's every need, Mum. I need something to do, apart from which, I can't expect you to feed and house me forever, and I don't want to be an extra burden on your pension. I felt uncomfortable enough as it was living off Anita and Nathan. I need my independence. And it's only right to offer something towards the upkeep of the house and my food whilst I am here."

"But I'm your mother; I can't take money off you."

"I insist. And I've also decided to sell the car. It's too expensive for me to run on my own, especially the insurance."

"Do I gather from that, you intend stopping here?"

She hesitated, unsure from her mother's tone whether there was a subtle intimation that, if she did intend staying in the village, she should find a place of her own.

"No, Mum. You've found your niche here and have your

own life to lead. I must find mine. It was never my plan to stay here long, and as soon as I can find somewhere else to live, I'll leave you in peace. But I do intend to settle in the village, if that's all right with you."

Anna put down her knife and fork, then folded her hands under her chin, elbows on the table. "I was rather hoping you would stay here. With me."

Her heart swelled. "Do you really mean that?"

"I wouldn't say it if I didn't. I love having you here. It's comforting."

It was all the words she needed to hear. She leapt out of her chair and rushed across to give her mother a hug, followed by a kiss on her cheek.

"Oh, thanks, Mum. I was foolish not to come to you sooner; I should have known better. We'll be okay, but promise me you'll say if you've enough of me, if I outstay my welcome. Or if someone else comes into your life. You mustn't let me stand in your way. We have to be honest with each other."

Anna wiped a tear building in her eye then patted Penny's hand still gripped firmly to her shoulder, a slight laugh of relief in her voice as she said, "I promise."

Selling everything from a loaf of bread to a can of oil for someone's bicycle chain, a constant flow of people came into the lively little shop for their papers, a pint of milk, a book of stamps or a gallon of gossip, and for a small sleepy backwater there was gossip aplenty. Penny was privilege to it all...

"Did you know Abigail's son is coming over from Canada?" "What, the one who married that pop singer?" "That's the one." "I heard tell Freda's husband has been promoted." "So soon? Why, he's only been with that company for four months." "Apparently, that Jack Godall is having an affair with that widow who's moved into Sceptre House." "Really? Who told you?" "I've seen him myself. Creeps out of the house in the early hours, he does." "I wonder what his wife will do when she finds out, and her expecting their fourth in October." "Well, I never..."

Accepted now as part of the village community and not merely as someone passing through, Penny enjoyed listening to it all, regaling in retelling the daily news to her mother, and frequently finding out Anna had already heard about it from someone else. Not that that mattered; she delighted in sharing gentle chit-chat, observations and comments and, best of all, finally able to put names to faces as they talked, laughed and joked together.

Before long, Thursday and Friday evenings found Penny also serving in the bar of the Lamplighters, and at weekends working at the Weeping Willow, the small hotel and restaurant on the edge of the village, where she helped to change the sheets, clean rooms or arrange fresh flowers into vases with blooms picked from the hotel's small rose garden.

Occasionally, when the restaurant was busy, the owner would ask her to put in a few extra hours waiting on tables. As if this wasn't enough, whenever she could spare the time, she also helped out Francis Fyfield in the village hall, which served as the library, play school, and community meeting room.

When the cellar-man at the Lamplighters tripped on the cellar stairs and twisted his ankle on his way to change a barrel of ale, Tom, the landlord, offered her a job helping his wife in the kitchen weekday lunch-times whenever she could in order that he could spend more time running the bar. She accepted readily, grateful for the extra money.

Anna objected. "You'll wear yourself out."

"It's what I need. Keeping busy blocks out thoughts of Harry, sending him and Pond Cottage into the past. I don't have time to think of him, no time to miss him."

It had taken far longer than she had expected, but she was getting there without him. She felt proud of herself. She had survived. And if she was over this hurdle, she could survive anything life now threw her way.

The Lamplighters was exceptionally busy for a Tuesday evening. It seemed the whole of Goldstoke had turned out to watch the darts match between the village and their arch-rivals in the league.

Penny didn't know the tall, handsome man that came up to the bar and plonked himself down on a bar stool.

"A pint of best bitter, please, seeing as you've taken over my job," he said.

"I beg your pardon," she replied, indignant.

"Working here."

"Oh, I see. I'd be happy to step down if you want your job back. I'm sure Tom would be—"

"No, no. This is only a flying visit. For the darts." He handed over a twenty-pound note and waited for his change. "No, that's not quite true. I teach English in Turin. I'm back with a group of children on a month-long exchange programme, so decided to look up a few old buddies whilst I'm here." He smiled widely as she counted the change out into his hand.

A nice smile, she thought. Friendly. Cute. Not that she was interested in him.

"You're on next, Marc!" someone called out.

He winked at her. "My turn. Catch you later. Perhaps I can walk you home when you've finished?"

"I only live next door!"

"You want to watch that one," said Mandy, nudging her arm after he'd walked away. She hadn't noticed the landlord's wife standing next to her, pulling a pint and listening to every word. "Marcus Ford's a well-practised charmer of the worst order who thinks he's God's gift to women. The village heaved a sigh of relief when he left, I can tell you."

"Oh, I don't know. He looks pretty safe to me." She watched as Marc took his place on the oche and aimed his first dart, throwing it with an expert, precise shot. It flew into a treble sixteen. With no further interest in the game, she picked up a cloth. Maybe Mum is right, she thought, as she wiped up spilt beer from the wooden counter. Perhaps I do have to put the past well behind me and start again.

"Mandy, is Marc married?"

"Why do you ask?"

"Just curious."

She didn't catch Mandy's response; it was lost when a customer banged on the counter for attention.

"Are you serving, or what? I asked for two pints of pale ale and a packet of pork scratchings, please."

She turned to the impatient man standing at the end of the bar, one of the opposition.

"Sorry. Coming right up."

Chapter 32

"Peter, why have you got your head up the chimney?"

Harry watched as Peter extracted himself from the fireplace in the sitting room of Pond Cottage.

"Clues, Harry. I'm looking for clues."

"Who do you think you are? Inspector Morse? I can assure you, you're not going to find Penny there. This isn't one of your gory murder mysteries that gets solved in Chapter Nineteen. It was the butler what did it, officer! I haven't done her in, if that's what you're thinking."

Peter brushed away the powdering of soot and dust from his hair with his hand. "I never thought for one second you have. Although it would certainly help if we did find a few old bones up there. It might explain one or two things."

"Such as? No one's died here. No one's been murdered."

"Ah, but are you sure? Can you be absolutely certain? This house is old, anything could have happened here in the past."

Peter turned his attention to the carved stonework surrounding the narrow window between the sitting and dining room, tracing around the arc of the stone arch with his forefinger.

Harry observed him intently, wondering what on earth his friend was up to now.

"Have you ever thought of contacting one of those house detective programmes they sometimes have on television?" Peter asked, his ear pressed close to the plasterwork as he rapped on the wall with his knuckle. "They have historians and researchers trained in looking up the history of houses. I've heard there's a new series being made. I bet they could sort out what's going on here."

"For goodness' sake, the last thing I need is a load of people and cameramen crawling all over the place. Most of what they find out anyone with an ounce of sense could learn for themselves anyway."

Peter spun around, brow furrowed. "I'm shocked by that

supercilious attitude, even from you. If it were that easy, those programmes wouldn't be made, would they? God, you're such a grouch lately."

"Is it so surprising?" Harry muttered. Too often it had been easier to feel like giving up, but that was when he was in one of his black moods. And more than once he had nearly rung the police, as Peter had suggested, to report Penny's car stolen and hang the consequences if it meant finding her, find out if she was all right. Safe.

"In fact, I'm finding it increasingly difficult to maintain our relationship with the mood you're in lately. I've ignored the comments but I can't contain myself any longer, and whether you like it or not, it's time for a few home truths."

Sighing heavily, Harry slumped into an armchair. "Here it comes... another lecture."

"Too bloody right! Look, I can understand how miserable and depressed you feel, but you're not even trying to help. Don't you want to get to the bottom of this? Don't you want Penny back? Because the only way she's going to come home is if you pull your finger out and get it sorted. Like you should have done with Lorna because, Harry Winchester, there are some days I feel like knocking your head against the wall. You're a fucking bloody idiot. You've found the best thing to have happened to you in God knows how long, and all you've done is let her slip through your fingers, all because of your own pig-headedness. You've shoved your head into the sand and hoped it would all go away. In one way it has – she's gone. And whether you like it or not, one way or another we're going to find out what's been going on here. Got that?"

He glared at Peter, the air between them static as a nervous flicker crossed his friend's lips, making him wonder if Pete was waiting for him to explode with a tirade of abuse and be told to clear off and leave him alone. Not that he was about to, because Pete was, as usual, talking absolute sense whilst he was being an utter idiot. A stupid fool who at times felt so sorry for himself it was a miracle Pete hadn't told him where to get off. He needed to snap out it. And pronto, if he were to have any chance of getting to the bottom of this and, more importantly, in finding Penny.

"You know, Pete, you're dead right. I've been stupid beyond words to let things get this far out of hand. And equally foolish for not appreciating what a good friend I have in you." He leapt up and clasped his friend firmly around his shoulders, pulling him towards him in a bear-hug of brotherly love. "Thanks, mate. Once again, I don't know what I would do without you."

Peter looked relieved. "Right, well, I'm glad that's sorted. At least she's not been back to collect the rest of her things. That's got to be a good sign, hasn't it? It means she intends coming back at some point, otherwise she would have sneaked in and removed everything when you weren't here."

"Like we did with her ex." His mind flashed back to the day they'd let themselves into Penny's old home after first checking Alex wasn't at home, the day they returned the car. He'd felt like a thief hanging about downstairs on lookout whilst his accomplice raided the drawers and cupboards upstairs.

"Look, I'll do all I can to help you two get back together; you know that. I like you, and I also like Penny. A lot. She's so right for you, only a klutz head like you can't see it."

"I can, that's the problem."

"Listen, I've been talking with Elaine about all this. Don't roll your eyes like that, Harry, she feels dreadful about all this."

"So she should!"

Peter shook his head. "She's suggested looking on social media. You know, Facebook and Twitter."

"But Penny wasn't into any of that stuff."

"No, but apparently there are a couple of groups out there especially aimed at finding missing persons. What if we put up a photo of Penny and a few details? You never know, someone out there may recognize her."

Harry scratched his head. "It's not something I would have thought of. But, okay, let's give it a go."

"Good, because I've already suggested to Elaine she sets it up." Peter nodded toward the wooden beams across the ceiling; they were thick, solid and black. "Let's try this one," he said, pulling a stool underneath the central support. Intent on continuing his search, he climbed up and ran his hand across the timber's surface.

Relieved the atmosphere between them had lightened, Harry watched, determined to see this through to the end, no matter the outcome. No matter what Peter uncovered. Meanwhile, he couldn't afford to lose the only friend he had, least of all by falling and breaking his neck on his living room floor.

"Be careful, Pete. I don't know if that stool will take your weight."

"Strange. I thought these timbers were just painted black, but they're not. They're more like burn marks or smoke damage."

"Probably accumulation of soot and dirt from the open fire over the years. Just what exactly are you looking for?"

"I don't know. Clues... Anything that can help tell us about this place or its past residents."

"But it's just your normal run-of-the-mill cottage, probably some tenant farmer's accommodation. There's nothing spooky or remotely interesting."

"But what do you actually *know* about who lived here before?"

"The last owner lived here all his life. He died in South-mead Hospital according to the agent. Nothing funny or suspicious to make ghosts..." He hesitated a moment. "Come to think of it, Jilly Smythe did mention something in passing to Penny about his wife never really feeling comfortable in the house. But neither of them were strangled in their beds or pushed down the stairs by a madcap axeman disguised as the postman."

"And before him?"

"In truth, I've absolutely no idea. How could I possibly? We'd have to check on the deeds."

"Or the electoral rolls. Censuses. This house is certainly a mish-mash of styles," Peter observed, getting back down from the stool and returning it to its place next to the fireplace.

"That's nothing out of the ordinary. Lots of houses had extras added and extensions built on over the years. This place is no different. That's what people did before. They didn't go out and buy a bigger house when little sonny Jim the sixth was born. They built more rooms, adding another storey, extended the scullery or built into the loft. Like people do nowadays instead of moving, keeping the likes of you and me gainfully employed." Harry was pensive for several moments, remembering the day they moved in. "Penny thought the house looked like a jigsaw puzzle with bits slotted in here and there wherever they would fit."

"Well, she's right there," Peter said readily, rubbing a hand across the rough stone of a wall that had never been plastered over. "Nothing's of one period throughout the house. It's all jumbled up. What else do you know about the place?"

He shrugged. "Very little."

"Too little for you to consider it worth investigating? Because I don't. It might be all we have to go on but, as they say, every house tells a story. We merely have to find out what this one's is. First stop, search the census records. We need to find out who had lived here before the old chap you bought the place from. I've also been thinking... I have a friend at Bristol University, an archaeologist. He's offered to come and look over this place."

"An archaeologist? Are you being serious? What possible use is an archaeologist going to be? We're talking nineteenth century here, man, eighteenth at most, not ancient Egyptians and buried bloody treasure."

"Wrong! We're talking about Penny. She's the treasure you want to find, isn't she?" Peter brushed his hands together, wiping off the film of dust that had accumulated on them.

"And what do you think this chap's going find? Specifically, I mean. Knowing the house's history is hardly going to make Penny come rushing back home."

Peter sighed wearily and shook his head. "Don't you want to find out why she's been hearing music here? The Prof may find the answer."

"How do you figure that out?"

"Well... he also has a keen interest in unusual phenomena. He loves solving mysteries and investigating things. If anyone can unravel what's going on here, he can."

He stared at Peter, hardly able to believe what his friend was suggesting. Did he really want this professor poking his nose into his house, his problems? He looked around the room again, considering his options. There weren't many. If he said no, he'd never hear the last of it from Peter. And if he said yes...

"Well," said Peter, interrupting his train of thought, "do I phone him or not?"

Chapter 33

The tall stranger, sporting a green, leather-elbowed tweed jacket that looked two sizes too big, strode across the driveway, his hand outstretched to greet Harry as he extracted himself from his car.

"Hi, I'm Professor Filton Shields."

In his mid to late forties, Harry guessed, eyeing his visitor cautiously as they shook hands. With wire-rimmed thick glasses and unruly salt-and-pepper long hair, Professor Shields looked every bit the archaeologist he envisaged one would look. Even down to the creased pale blue shirt with a badly pressed collar, and the ancient black Morris Minor parked on the drive.

Harry shook the man's hand. "I hope I haven't kept you waiting too long? Sorry I'm late. My meeting in Bristol overran somewhat."

"No, no. It's fine. I knew you'd be back soon enough. I took the liberty of wandering around the house and gardens in your absence; I trust you don't mind?"

"And did you find anything of interest?"

"Oh, plenty," said the professor. "A curious mix of stonework for a house like this. Even your gatepost is a lintel from another building, although I do find that a lot. Happens all over the country. Lots of farmers use ancient marker stones as gateposts, on account of how durable the stone is, especially the type we have in these parts. Used to be hundreds of them dotted all over the place, particularly across the moors indicating the way and distance between towns." He pointed to the cottage. "Take your house here... if you look closely, you can see that the sitting room and the room above it are much later additions—"

"Nothing unusual in that."

"No. But the stones used are from a much earlier period. Mid to late sixteen century, judging by the way they've been worked."

Harry shrugged. "Lots of places are built from reclaimed

stone. How do you know that's our sitting room?"

Shields coughed sheepishly. "I took the liberty of peeking through the windows. And I agree about houses made of old materials, but it's the sort of thing we would expect to see on earlier constructions. Many alterations were made to manor houses following the Dissolution of the Monasteries, free building material up for grabs thanks to good old King Henry the Eighth. And when castles fell into disrepair or blown to smithereens in the Civil War, that sort of thing. But this place is different. It is unusual to see so much use of reclaimed timber and stonework for such a humble dwelling. Peter tells me the other house you lived in was like this too? Is that near here?"

"It's further back along the ridge, about a mile or so, right on the bend in the lane as you get to the top of the hill. You would have driven right by it."

The professor nodded. "The late Georgian one? I re-membering seeing it. Impressive building."

"Alterations there are not in evidence so much that one would notice. The odd stone or two in the walls. More replacement or repair than additions."

"Mmm, interesting. I should like to see inside now, if I may?"

Allowing the professor free reign to wander about the rooms of Pond Cottage, Harry busied himself making coffee for them both. He could hear the man's heavy footfalls clumping about in the rooms above, crossing from the landing to the bathroom, from bedroom to bedroom, the creak of the staircase up to the loft. A short while later, the footsteps started back down the stairs, stopping midway for several minutes, before continuing slowly. Eventually, Professor Shields joined him in the kitchen.

"So, have you found anything?" Harry asked, not expect-ing to hear anything he didn't know already.

Filton Shields scratched his head. "Whoever did the alter-ations made good use of what was to hand, a good example of late eighteenth-century rural craftsmanship. As I said, it's unusual to see so much use of reclaimed timber and stonework for such a small dwelling. None of it has come from any religious building or castle. I also noticed some of the stonework is cracked, the sort of damage that only intense heat causes. Tell me, has there ever been a fire here?"

He shook his head. "Not to my knowledge, no." But the professor's question reminded Harry of the night Penny had woken up imagining that the house was on fire. "If there had been a fire here, would that explain why my partner sometimes thought she could smell smoke?"

"It's a possibility." The professor put his open notebook down on the kitchen table for him to look at. "I've made a few sketches. All we need do now is find out where the extras came from."

"And you think that will solve my problem?"

"Not in the least. You want to know about the house, I'll tell you as much as I can. After that, it's up to you how you use the information. Peter told me you were having problems with ghosts. Is that true?" The expression on Professor Shields's face was unwavering, no look of disbelief or amusement at the mention of apparitions or spooks.

"Not ghosts *per se*. Ghosts don't actually exist, do they?" He noticed the professor shake his head, confirming to Harry that the man agreed with him. "But my partner often thought she could hear music playing in Hill House. And she was always humming some little ditty. The same here. She believes the music's followed us from there." He purposely spoke of Penny in the present tense; unwilling to accept she was resigned to being yet another sad memory in his life story.

"And you?"

"Never. Well... perhaps once. I'd pretty much dismissed that occasion as my being mistaken."

Shields stroked his bristly chin. "Interesting. I should like to inspect Hill House if I can. Do you think the present owner would mind if I pay a visit?"

"Feel free to ask. I'm sure they won't object. But I suppose you can always view it from the outside if they do."

* * *

The summer night was hot and sultry, the warmth of the day clinging to the walls. Even though the window was wide open, the room was airless. Unable to sleep, Penny threw back the sheet and crept downstairs in search of a drink of orange juice to quench her thirst. In the fridge she found the half-drunk bottle of Grenache left over from supper. As she began pouring herself a glass, she stopped, head jerking up at a bizarre sound coming from outside.

What on earth was that?

Goosebumps rose instantly on her skin, a prickly sensation of alarm and fear. There it was again. A distant, animal noise. A vixen's bark? She listened. The sound came again. No, it sounded more like... like a horse snorting. Yes, that was it, a horse sound. But at this time of night whoever would be messing about with horses?

The sounds grew louder. She could hear faint whispers, voices so low she couldn't tell whether they were male or female. Horses' hooves clipped across stone, sounding as if coming from the courtyard at the back of the cottage where the cars were parked. She flicked back the lace curtain at the kitchen window and peered out.

The courtyard was silent and empty except for her Lexus and a red Jaguar parked against the far wall. Bathed in soft moonlight, the colour looked more blue than red but she knew it was their neighbour's car; he always parked it there. Noticing, too, how the pansy flowers poking out of the stone wall took on an eerie, luminescent quality. They nodded delicately as if laughing at her.

The horse sounds and voices faded away, in their place the overwhelming stench of horse manure filled her nostrils. She stood for several minutes in the stillness, trying to make sense of it all, before letting the curtain fall back into soft folds.

Eventually, she reached the conclusion that someone must have ridden past the house along the road, the buildings and atmosphere distorting the direction of the noise, and the pungent odour swept in on the heavy night air. She could still smell it. She picked up the glass of wine to take back upstairs, thinking that no doubt in the morning there would be a pile of horse muck outside at the kerbside. An odd time of night for anyone to be out horse riding though, she considered. Perhaps, like her, they couldn't sleep either.

"Arrh, that'll be the Goldstoke Ghost," old George Rycroft said the next evening, draining the dregs of ale from his glass in the Lamplighters. He wiped his mouth on the back of his hand. "Happen you must have heard it."

Penny wished now she'd never mentioned the incident to him. The last thing she needed was another ghost plaguing her life. She continued stacking clean glasses onto the shelves.

From his usual place propping up the far end of the bar, Frank Pearce tutted.

"Take no notice of that silly old codger, Penny. Ain't no such thing as ghosts. It's only a lot of silly superstition."

"That's your opinion," retorted George. "'Ere, girl, another refill please and one for yourself. 'As no one told ye about the ghost of Goldstoke before? Well, now," continued George, watching intently as she pulled his pint, "'tis said that one of those conspirators of the gunpowder plot escaped being captured, but was thrown from his horse not far from here. 'Tis said his ghost still rides these here roads and that anyone who looks out on him will die a grizzly, horrible death. Be warned, girlie, be warned."

She looked across to Frank, who winked back and said, "Is that so, George? Have *you* ever seen him?"

"Nopes, else I'd be pushing up daisies by now, wouldn't I? But I've heard them horses many a night, I can tell ye."

Frank shook his head and thumped his empty glass down on the counter. "A load of old codswallop, it is, and I ain't talking about the beer. Ghost, my arse."

Letting herself into the house after saying a swift goodnight to Marc, Penny could see her mother's dark silhouette sitting outside in the small courtyard at the back of the house. The summer night was warm and still.

"I'm out here, dear," Anna called to her on hearing the

front door close. "Come and join me. It's too nice a night to sit indoors. There's fresh tea in the pot if you want one, or there's a bottle of wine opened in the fridge. Was that Marcus Ford's voice I heard outside?"

Penny tossed her cardigan over the back of a dining chair and walked through the kitchen to join her mother. She dropped a gentle kiss on Anna's head.

"It was. I don't know why, but he keeps insisting on walking me home. He hangs around outside whilst we clean up the bar. That's the third night in a row. It's not as though I've far to walk. The pub's next door, for goodness' sake."

"He's trying his luck, that one. You want to watch yourself with him. He got quite a reputation."

"Mandy's already warned me. Not that I'm interested in him. Or any other man, for that matter. Twice bitten and that sort of thing. Thank goodness he goes back to Italy next week."

She disappeared into the kitchen to fetch herself a glass of wine then settled down on the empty cast-iron garden chair next to her mother.

"The stars are fabulous tonight, aren't they," Anna said. "Such a clear sky. I saw a couple of shooting stars too just before you came in."

"Mum, have you ever heard of the Goldstoke Ghost?"

Anna turned to her, a smile on her lips. "You've been listening to old George Rycroft, haven't you? Take no notice of him, Pen. He likes winding up newcomers to the village. It's his way. He regaled me with that story the day after I moved in here. Ghosts indeed! There's no such thing."

Chapter 34

"Are you ready yet?" Peter called up to Harry.

"What time did you say we'd be there?" Harry yelled back.

"Ten-fifteen. That only gives us twenty minutes to get to there."

"At the speed you drive it will only take us ten!" said Harry, coming out from the bedroom and making his way downstairs. "You know, it's been two weeks since your professor friend called and I haven't heard a thing back from him. I'm beginning to think the whole exercise was a complete waste."

"Patience, dear boy, these things take time. Right, let's go."

As Peter drove towards the small market town north of Stonecott, Harry pondered on his dilemma. It had occurred to him that Pond Cottage might not have ever been officially registered, or that nothing untoward had ever happened there. And if that was the case, how on earth were they ever going to find out its history? And if they did uncover anything, how would or could it help him find Penny?

"I just hope this proves more fruitful than the census search we did. Not one of those records we trawled came up with anything," he said.

"It was worth a shot, and an obvious place to start. I'm pretty sure today's hunt will throw up something useful."

"I wish I could share your optimism."

"Think positive thoughts, Harry, stirred up with a strong dose of determination. Somehow, somewhere, there has to be an answer."

The archive room was housed in an upstairs room of the old town library, a building of Elizabethan origin with gabled windows jutting out precariously over the main street of the town. The curator led the way up the narrow, wooden stairs with care. They were slippery with age and sagged in the middle where a thousand footfalls must have trod their way over the centuries. The latch door at the top opened with a creak, filling the darkened stairwell with sunlight.

Wrinkling his nose at the fusty smell emanating from ancient undisturbed dust and ageing paper, Harry followed the old man into the room, Peter a few steps behind. Around the room stood floor-to-ceiling bookcases filled with large, leather-bound tomes protected by heavy-looking leaded-glass doors. In the centre of the room stood a solid-looking wooden table with heavy bulbous legs. Harry gazed about him. There were no chairs so it looked as if they would have to stand the whole time.

The curator handed him a long brass key. "Make sure you lock 'em back up when you're finished. You'll find gloves in the table drawer. No food and drink up here, and no smoking either," he added as he left them alone to their search.

Peter pulled at a drawer in the side of the table; it was stiff and took two hands to yank it open. Inside he found a bundle of white cotton gloves.

"Mustn't get our sweaty little paw prints over the documents, must we?" he said, tossing a pair to Harry.

Harry caught them, pulled them on, then turned to study the first shelf. "How far back are we searching?"

"Well, you've certainly changed your tune. For a while, I was beginning to think you weren't interested in solving our little mystery. Let's try eighteen hundred and work back from there." He shuffled along the bookcases, seeking out where to start. "Ah, this will do. Here."

Harry took the heavy ledger Peter handed to him and gently placed it down on the table. Cautiously, he opened the book, admiring as he did so the craftsmanship of its gold tooling on the cover and spine.

The second ledger Peter pulled from the shelf looked as heavy as the first one. He carried it to the opposite side of the table and put it down with a heavy thump, sending a cloud of dust into the air.

Harry turned his attention back to the ledger in front of him and began searching its lists, his curiosity kindled. Even if all this research didn't bring Penny back, he hoped he would finally be able to chase away the ghosts from inside his head.

Ghosts of the guilt he felt. Guilt for what happened to Lorna and the children, and guilt for not taking Penny more seriously. They should have done this in the first place, back when it all started. But there was no way he could put back the clock. What happened, happened. What was done, done. A life full of ifs, buts and maybes.

"What precisely are we looking for, Pete?"

"Any references to Pond Cottage, Hill House or of any other building on the hill back then. I'm thinking castles or manor houses."

"The hanging gardens. I wonder..." said Harry.

Peter looked up at him. "What on earth are you talking about?"

"It's an old wreck of a place on the ridge Penny and I often took a walk to. She loved the terraced gardens there. Lovely views. There's practically nothing left of the house, it got burnt to the ground donkey's years ago, but the gardens are still there though, completely overgrown and neglected. Penny often wondered if bits of Pond Cottage were taken from the old house. She had this rather romantic notion she could see for real the grand balls and parties that must have been held there. We found a bit of old gramophone record there once."

Peter pursed his lips. "Any idea what the place was called? If we can find some old land plans, they should have the house marked."

Harry shook his head. "No, but there must be maps and drawings of it. A house that size would have been noted somewhere."

"Well, get to it. Start hunting."

Harry closed another ledger with an air of resigned defeat, breaking the silence of their labours for the first time in three hours as they sought their goal.

"Well, that's it then, right back to the start of the seventeenth century. What a disappointment. I was certain there would've been some mention of the house or its owners. Absolutely nothing. Zilch."

"So frustrating! Several mentions of Hill House, even some of the farm cottages are marked up, even Pond Cottage, but that's about it. Let's put these back and go have a beer. Work out what to do next." Peter started closing the volumes around him, inspecting the titles before putting them back on the shelves in the right order.

Harry peeled off his gloves and tossed them into a waste-basket by the desk. "I'll ring the Land Registry office in Gloucester tomorrow morning, see if we can make an appointment. There must be something held on record there. One little clue is all we need."

He locked each glass door securely, his mind all the while on Penny, wondering where she was, what she was doing, if she missed him as much as he missed her. A vast empty chasm existed in his life that only her return would fill. He remembered the envelope waiting to be opened on the hall stand back at Pond Cottage.

"A letter arrived for Penny yesterday, did I tell you? It was from the BBC," he told Peter.

"Why would the BBC be writing to Penny?"

"She'd emailed them ages ago, and later sent a copy of the score she'd written down, hoping someone there might know what the music is. She always thought once she knew, it would go away and leave her alone."

Peter's brows raised. "So... what did it say?"

"I don't know, I haven't opened it." He stared at Peter, expecting a rebuff.

Peter eyed him back. "Are you thinking what I'm thinking?"

"I'm two steps ahead of you. Come on. Let's get out of here."

"Any joy?" enquired the curator, when Harry handed him back the key at the library counter downstairs.

He shook his head glumly.

"Of course, we've only partial records here. Those moved from the old register office before it closed back in the early seventies. What with constant boundary changes, first Gloucestershire, then Avon, then South Gloucestershire, who knows where you need to check. Probably all of them."

"Excuse me, but I couldn't help overhearing," interrupted an old man waiting by the desk. "I know quite a bit about local history. What exactly are you looking for?"

Harry briefly explained.

The old man shook his head. "Can't say as I'm familiar with that place. Have you tried searching through old newspapers? If a big house around here caught fire, it must have been reported?"

"Might be worth checking out local birth, death and marriage records too," the curator offered. "'Course, it'll all be on microfiche now. As long as you've some idea of a date, I'm sure you'll find something. I can—"

"Thanks, we'll have to look another day," said Harry, impatient to leave. He didn't want to appear rude, but he was anxious to get home and read the letter, find out what it said.

"Have you tried the Internet?" asked the old man. "You'd be astonished what information you can glean from there. My grandson swears by it for his research. Apparently, you can trace your family tree and census records. You'll find the local council even has a site listing tombstone dedications in the county."

"How bizarre," Peter exclaimed. "Who on earth thinks of these things?"

Walking across the car park, Peter said, "You know, for a wizened old goat that fellow in the library's right. We hadn't thought of searching the Web."

"Come on then, what are we waiting for? I'll read the letter, you search. Deal?"

Peter zapped the key fob in the direction of his parked car. "Only if supper's on you tonight."

Harry opened the letter with care, slitting along its top with his silver letter opener, a Christmas present from Peter many years ago.

"I don't feel right doing this, it's like spying. It is addressed to her, after all."

"And it's for her we're doing this, remember? I'm sure she

won't mind. If it has the result she's been looking for then your problems are solved."

"Correction. One problem. I still have to find Penny."

"True. Well, ... come on. What does it say?"

Harry read the letter aloud. *"Dear Miss Raines—"*

"Raines? I thought her surname was Cornwall?" Peter interrupted.

"That was her married name." Harry stared at the letter... *Raines. Raines.* The word jumped out at him. "Bloody hell! She must have reverted to her maiden name when she wrote to them. I never realized. Never even gave it thought." He looked up at Peter and grinned. "You know what this means..."

Peter laughed. "I do indeed. If Penny's maiden name is Raines, then so is her mother's...unless, that is, she married again."

Harry shook his head. "I don't think so, least not that Penny said."

"So... go on." Peter urged.

With shaking hands, Harry looked back down at the letter, hardly unable to contain his excitement. Finally, he was getting somewhere.

"Dear Miss Raines," he began again. *"We have searched our extensive music libraries and are sorry to advise you that nothing remotely resembling your score is on record. Please contact us again if we can be of any further help. Good luck in your search. Yours blah blah blah..."*

"Damn!" Peter kicked the table leg in annoyance.

Glum-lipped, Harry folded the letter and put it back in its envelope, his heart sinking to the pit of his stomach. "Well, I guess that's it, then. If they don't know, no one does."

"Not necessarily. We don't know how old that tune is. It might not be a classical piece. It might be from a film. John Williams or Sondheim or—"

"We've been down that route, Peter. If the BBC can't find it, it must be either so obscure or not exist at all. There's no point in—"

"At least we have another name now to go on with our

search for Penny. That's got to be a good thing."

"And what if her mother, even if we do manage to locate her, is as obstructive as Penny's sister? What then?"

Harry looked around the room. It felt bleak and desolate. And empty. Coming home and not finding Penny waiting eagerly for him was as bad as those dark days in Hill House. There was no life in the house without her. He was grateful for Peter's support, even envied his enthusiasm in trying to solve the mystery, but the weight of despair and the feeling of hopelessness he felt only served to crush him further.

"You seem to give up hope at every obstacle. I thought you were made of sterner stuff than that."

"Is it any wonder, Pete? I don't think I can take much more. Was I such an evil man in a past life to deserve such misery? First Lorna and the kids being taken away, then Penny running out on me. Can you blame me for feeling like giving up?"

Peter gave him a brotherly hug. "I know, mate. I've been there too. Life stinks at times, but we can't give up on this. Not now. You mustn't give up on Penny. And think what a great plot this will make for that novel I've always been meaning to write. Damned good blockbuster."

He knew Peter was only joking about the book, trying to make light. Cheer him up. "Huh. No one would ever believe such a thing. Anyway, what makes you think the story's all yours? I might want to write it myself one day, when all this is sorted... If it gets sorted..." Harry sighed. "I'm going to find us a beer."

"That's the most sensible suggestion you've had all day," Peter quipped, pulling his chirping mobile from his trouser pocket. He read the text message. "It's a text from Filton. Says he wants to meet us tomorrow evening."

Chapter 35

Filton Shields was fifty minutes late when he pushed opened the door of the lounge bar in the Stonecott Arms public house, his eyes searching around the crowded bar for Harry and Peter. He found them seated at a table in one of the bay windows.

"I'm sorry," he said, sounding harassed and out of breath, "only my car conked out coming up the hill. I had to abandon it and walk the rest of the way. I couldn't phone or text you either. Battery's dead on my phone."

Harry rose to shake the professor's hand. "We were about to give up on you and leave. Let me buy you a drink, you look like you need it."

"Thanks. A beer shandy would go down a treat," Filton said, taking up the empty chair at the table.

"I'll get it, stay there, Harry, and talk to the man."

"So, what have you managed to find out?" Harry asked him hopefully, while Peter headed off to the bar.

Looking pleased with himself, Shields pulled a small white rock from his jacket pocket and passed it to him.

"This is limestone. From the Cotswolds. The hills are made from this form of rock. It's called oolite, but often referred to as eggstone, because of the small round granules that make up each piece."

Harry turned the stone over and over in his hand, studying its intricate patterns of tiny spherical particles, feeling its rough, grainy texture, then held it close to his eyes, squinting to see.

The professor handed him a magnifier. "Here, use this."

Harry peered through the thick lens. "It looks like fish roe. Here, take a look at this, Pete," he said to Peter, returning from the bar.

Peter took the stone and magnifier, gave the rock a cursory gaze then put both items down on the table. "Fascinating. So what's this all about?"

After gulping down half of his shandy, the professor wiped

his mouth on his sleeve before speaking.

"As I'm sure you know, rock from the Cotswolds has been used for drystone walls for centuries, but much has been quarried for building material and—"

"And Pond Cottage is made from this stuff; we know that." Harry wondered where all this was leading.

Peter shushed him. "Let the Prof finish, man."

Shields extracted a second stone from his pocket and set it down on the table next to the first piece.

"I took the liberty of extracting one of these from your cottage, Harry, from where it wouldn't be noticed or cause any damage. I had a geologist at the university test it against the other one. It appears Pond Cottage, along with a few of the other houses scattered along the ridge, are built, rebuilt or repaired at some stage with blocks removed from Whitestone—"

"There's no such place around here," Harry interrupted, sitting back and folding his arms across his chest. "I know this area like the back of my hand. None of the quarries hereabouts are called that."

The professor shook his head. "Whitestones isn't a quarry. It was a large house on the ridge, close to where you live."

"Whitestones..." Harry muttered. "So that's what it was called!" He picked a stone again and rubbed his thumb across its surface. "The hanging gardens... so now we know... Penny was right in her assumption." He looked at the professor. "So how did you find out its name? Peter and I spent ages searching the local records office yesterday and didn't find a single mention of it."

"Stefan, a colleague from the university, recalled doing some research on the area back in the early eighties. He'd come across an old map from the seventeenth century along with a few books that had been donated to the university by a retired lecturer years previously. In one of the books, part of what looked like a letter was found. It mentioned a house of that name on the southern edge of the ridge."

"What a stroke of luck," Peter said, with a clap of his hands.

"Indeed," Filton agreed. "We still had the map in the archives. After checking, between us we put two and two together and concluded the building shown on that old map had to be Whitestones. And once we had a date and the name of the building, we could extend our search. Of course, it could be that in its history the building had its name changed by new owners at some point. It did happen occasionally. With so many country estates in the region and land often passing hands, it's not surprising records are sometimes vague," he added.

"Did you find out anything else?" Harry was all ears now. At long last he was getting somewhere.

Filton nodded. "One of my students found a newspaper article, thank goodness for microfiche, from March 1902 stating that the house had been destroyed by fire."

"That much we knew. In fact, it's about *all* we knew. Admittedly, we didn't have any idea of the date."

"I knew the Prof here would come good," said Peter. "Was anyone killed in the fire, did the report say?"

Filton shook his head. "We assume not. The newspaper quotes the house as being empty and abandoned."

"Any idea how it started?"

"There was only speculation... a lightning strike being the most probable cause."

"Did it say who owned it?" Harry asked.

"There was no mention of names, no."

"What about that letter found? Whoever wrote it must have been connected to the house in some way, no matter how tentative. It might give us the clue we need. A name they could check out."

"That we don't know," Filton told him. "Sadly, the start of the letter is missing, and the signature is difficult to read. It's smudged. Looks like water damage and we can't make it out. What we do know is the letter is written in German."

Peter's eyebrows rose. "German?"

Harry picked up his glass and looked forlornly into it. Just when he thought he finally had some answers, they were already slipping away from him again.

"Do you think that old ruin could be something to do with the music Harry's girlfriend heard?" Peter asked.

Filton shrugged. "Who knows, but I'd say there's a strong possibility. Stefan and I have several theories on such matters. To that end, he and I have been doing further investigations to see if we can garner more information. But there's something else..."

"Which is?" Peter asked, wide-eyed. He glanced at Harry, lost in his own thoughts again. He gave him a nudge. "Harry, are you listening to all this?"

He blinked several times, coming out of his reverie. "Sorry, but we've not really learnt anything new. I'm beginning to feel this is all a complete waste of everyone's time and effort." He picked up his glass and took a mouthful.

"But I haven't finished telling you everything yet," the professor enthused, leaning his elbows on the table, chin propped on his hands. "This whole thing is utterly fascinating, has the faculty buzzing, and Stefan is as intrigued as I am. You see, apart from our own specialist fields, his is in geology, we're both parapsychologists and—"

Harry spluttered on his beer. "Para- *what?*"

"Ghost hunters, for want of an easier word, although we prefer to call ourselves unexplained phenomena investigators, because we investigate anything unusual or strange, occurrences that can't be explained away by normal means. You know, things like UFOs, jumping clouds, second sight, reincarnations."

Harry spun his attention to Peter. "Did you know about this? About this ghost hunting malarkey?" The more he heard, the more irritated he felt over the direction this conversation had taken. Having the house investigated from an archaeological perspective was one thing; ghost hunters quite another.

Peter shrugged. "I knew he had an interest in ghosts and such, that's why I thought he might be able to help."

"But we haven't got a ghost!"

"What you have is paranormal activity, Harry," the professor said. "Odd things goings on. Strange music you can't explain. Someone seeing things. It all falls under the para-normal umbrella, things that Stefan and I take great interest in."

"So you're saying now you *do* believe my house is haunt-ed!" Was he really to believe this professor, an intelligent, well-educated man actually believed in the supernatural?

"To all intents and purposes. However, I've already stated, Stefan and I are of the firm belief all paranormal activity can be explained away by natural forces, the landscape playing a major role in most events. We've drawn some interesting conclusions through our various explorations and investiga-tions, although much more still needs to be done. As scientists, we believe there has to be a scientific, logical reason for everything that goes on around us. It's finding the right explanation that's the difficult part."

"Then you'd better explain on because, so far, you've told me nothing we haven't or couldn't have found out for ourselves eventually."

Peter shot him an incredulous glare. "Well, he's certainly found out a darned sight more than we have. Give him a break, Harry."

Unperturbed, Filton continued, "These pieces of oolitic limestone here... Well, Stefan and I have this theory—"

Filton and Peter jolted upright, clearly taken aback when Harry banged his fist down on the table, sending the stones bouncing and the glasses shaking.

"Theory, bah! That's all I hear is theory. I've plenty of theories of my own, thank you. This whole thing is going nowhere. What I want are facts. Concrete evidence. I want answers. What I need to know is what is really going on in my house, not some hypothesis by some ghost-hunting Sherlock Holmes."

"Look, Mr Winchester," snapped the professor, "whether you take me seriously or not is up to you. Okay, so I can understand your scepticism; a perfectly normal reaction by most people over such matters. Your friend here has asked me to investigate this problem, and that's precisely what I'm doing. Whether you believe me or not is neither here nor there. I can't force you to believe; that's your prerogative. Apart from which..." Shields nodded in Peter's direction. "...your friend here is paying a hefty fee by way of a donation to my faculty for my opinion, so at least give me the courtesy of allowing me to finish."

Harry glared at Peter. "You never said anything about this. How much?"

Peter sheepishly shrugged. "The sum is immaterial. I don't believe in using people's professional expertise for free because they happen to be a friend. Advice is one thing, their time and expenses incurred are, of course, another. That's what I'm paying back to the university, for the use of their facilities."

"Well, put like that—"

"Exactly," said the professor. "By the same token, it has also made for an interesting case study for my students. A double whammy. Now, if I may continue? Unless, that is, you want to end this conversation now." He reached for his tweed hat on the table and moved to stand. "In which case, I'll be on my way."

"Stay put," Peter urged, waving for him to sit back down. "Of course we're interested, aren't we, Harry?"

"Good. Because having come this far, I'm too intrigued myself to call time on this investigation. I want to know the outcome even if you don't, Harry."

"Sorry, yes. Yes please, do go on," said Harry, feeling guilty over his outburst. "I *am* interested. But it's this whole concept of ghosts—"

"Scares you? It shouldn't, you know," Filton said, giving him a reassuring smile. "There's no recorded incident of anyone ever actually being hurt or injured by ghosts."

"No, not scared, as such. I admit there have been times when I thought Hill House was haunted by my dead wife, but I put that down to lack of sleep and shed loads of worry. In fact, I had grave doubts about my sanity at the time. Let's just say I've yet to be convinced ghosts exist."

Filton smiled a knowing grin. "I've no problem with that. What is a difficult concept to understand is what actually constitutes a ghost. Flapping white sheets? Rattling chains? Things that go bump in the night? Headless grey ladies? Most of these can be explained away by science. Now... take Stefan. Stefan is an expert in the stone tape theory."

"The stone tape theory," repeated Peter, punching the air jubilantly. "That's it! I've been trying to remember what it was called. Harry, do you recall that film we watched one evening many years ago at university, written by the same chap who wrote *Quatermass*? The one where they were renovating a stone mansion where several women had died and people could still hear the screams long after it happened? Caused quite a stir when it was first shown on TV back in the 1970s, apparently."

"Nigel Kneale!" Harry surprised himself at plucking the name out of the deep recesses of his memory.

"That's the fellow!"

"But that was pure science fiction, Peter. Stones can't do that. The whole thing was ridiculous."

The professor's expression told him he didn't agree. "You know, it is actually now a widely accepted theory among us scientists."

"You're kidding me!" Harry said, shocked.

"Not at all," said Filton. "It's believed limestone, oolite especially, is one of the primary causes for these sorts of phenomena. The Cotswolds is made up of oolite, as is the bedrock beneath York. And York is famous for sightings of Roman legions walking through the foundations of many of its buildings and walls, is it not?"

"But we didn't see anyone walking through walls."

Peter coughed. "We didn't, no, but Penny did. Remember? You said she thought she saw people dancing." He pushed his stool back, pointing to the two empty glasses on the table. "Time for another drink, I think. Professor?"

"Nothing more for me, thanks, I'm driving. That's if my old Morris Minor starts up again, that is."

"Don't worry, old chap, I'll see you get home okay, even if I have to call a taxi or give you a tow myself."

Harry stood, his empty glass in hand. "Sit down, Pete, I'll

get these. It must be my round."

Whilst Harry fetched the drinks, Peter leaned further across the table, beckoning the professor to come closer.

"You'll have to forgive Harry's little outburst just now, only he gets incredibly tetchy at times. Under a great deal of stress and desperate to get his girl back, as I've told you. He's anxious to hear what you've uncovered, but at the same time he's reached his own conclusion that no matter what the answers are, he's probably lost Penny for good. He's having difficulty coping with that fact, let alone ghosts and stones and fires. Blames himself all the time for everything that's gone wrong in his life, he does."

"I do understand," Filton said, nodding. "It's a difficult situation to find yourself in, and for the record, *I* don't believe in ghosts."

Chapter 36

Clearing away the remains of their supper, Anna Raines was not easily fooled by her daughter's charade at playing happy ever after. Penny had hardly touched the delicious lamb casserole prepared so meticulously that morning, left all day to braise in the slow cooker. It had always been one of her daughter's favourite dishes. Today's addition of an extra dash of red wine had given it a special little lift, but it appeared wasted on her today.

"No appetite again?"

"Sorry, Mum. It's lovely but, well... I'm not feeling hungry. Perhaps later."

It wasn't the fact of yet another meal being thrown away; it was more concern about Penny's weight. It was dropping, and the bright spark that had always been so effervescent in her eyes had lately dimmed. For the past few weeks she had watched without comment as Penny kept herself busy and seemingly cheerful, her concern growing as her daughter gradually withdrew more and more into herself, saying little, never wanting to talk further about Harry.

She didn't like to pry, but to her, the reason for her daughter's unhappiness was clearly apparent – she was still madly in love with him. She'd said so the day she arrived in Goldstoke, but this self-enforced separation was breaking her daughter's heart, and at the same time breaking her own to see Penny so miserable.

As for working every hour God sends, she knew it was not the way to forget. Experience had taught her it was okay to start with, being too busy to think about things. But things have a habit of catching up, and when you're tired, that's when misery hits you full in the face. You want comforting as well as sleep, as Penny needed now. She could read her daughter like a book, the tell-tale signs there for her to see.

"Go back to him," she said, putting a cup of coffee down in front of Penny.

Penny's head lifted with a jolt, staring at her for a moment as if trying to register the outrageousness of such a suggestion.

"Christ, Mum, it was you only a few weeks ago telling me to move on with my life. Start again. And that's precisely what I'm trying to do. Now you're telling me to go back to him. How can I? Especially after all this time. There's no going back. I simply can't."

"Can't, or won't? From what little you've told me, his wife and children's deaths were an accident. He can't be held responsible."

"No, but he is responsible for keeping the circumstances of it from me. Then there was that music. He should have told me. Trusted me. Look, Mum, I'm over him."

"Perhaps he cared too much for you. Perhaps he was frightened of scaring you off if he told you the truth. Men like to bury their heads in the sand and hope the problem will go away. They don't see things the same way as we women do. As for being over him, I don't believe you."

"If he cares so much, why hasn't he tried to find me? Why has he never telephoned? He knew I would have gone to Anita's. Or you. That I had nowhere else I could go, so why didn't he come?"

"His pride."

"I have pride too."

"Yes, dear. It was pride that made you stay married to Alex for so long. And it was stupid pride that caused you to run away from Harry, the only man who ever really loved you. And it's still only your foolish pride now that prevents you from picking up the telephone and calling him. It's getting both of you nowhere."

Penny glared at her. "You clearly don't understand, do you? How can I—"

Anna sighed, interrupting. "I understand only too well. Believe me, whatever happened, it's not worth the two of you ruining your lives over. You need to talk to him about it, sort it out. Anita's told me about the music, there has to be some logical explanation for it, but unless you go back and face it, you will never know the truth. You will spend the rest of your life wondering what it was all about and blaming Harry. Life's too short for that sort of waste."

"No, Mum, I cannot go back, not now. It's been too long."

Anna shook her head. "I think you're making a huge mistake."

"Anita doesn't think I am. She says I—"

"Huh! What would your sister know? Have you ever read that column she writes?"

"Yes. She talks a lot of sense."

"And I expect she told you to walk away from him too, to keep well away from him. That's her answer to every problem: walk away from it if it's too complicated. She may be full of advice, but she doesn't know what real love is."

"Oh, how can you say that? Of course she does. You only have to look at her and Nathan to know how much in love they are."

"Go back to Harry. It's what you really want, if you're honest with yourself."

"It's too late." Penny's words were little more than a whisper.

Anna placed her hand over her daughter's and gave it an affectionate squeeze. "It's never too late if you love someone enough. In this life we don't get many second chances."

"You sound as if you speak from experience."

"I do."

Although Penny refrained from asking what that experience was, from her expression Anna could tell she was curious to know.

"As I see it," Anna said, "you have two alternatives. Go back to him, or find yourself another man. A decent man, and not that Marcus Ford either, he's a well-known womaniser. Apart from which, you're too young a woman to spend the rest of your days here with me."

"Are you saying you don't want me here? I thought you were happy—"

"I'm not asking you to leave. But if you stay on here indefinitely, what's going to happen? You'll end up some shrivelled old maid who has to wet-nurse her mother in her dotage. I don't want that for you."

"I don't think I want to be involved with another man for the rest of my life. Twice is enough."

"Those are words you will come to regret with age."

"What about you? What if another man comes along and sweeps you off your feet, would you so eagerly go with him?"

Anna laughed. "Don't be absurd. What man's going to want a wrinkled-up old woman like me? In truth, I wouldn't want another man. I loved your father dearly. He was a good, loving man and a brilliant father. I know what I had. No one could ever replace him, nor do I want to."

"Then you can understand how I feel."

"No, I can't. Your father and I had our life together, you and Anita became part of that life, and Ralph and I were happy. My memories keep me now, good memories. But you? You have only grief and anger inside your heart. There needs to be love. When a man offers you that love, you must grasp it with both hands and hold it close. Never let it go."

"But love means trust."

"You keep using that word. What is trust? Trust is faith. Trust is hope and conviction. Love also means forgiving, ignoring the faults. It isn't a perfect world we live in, and unless we forgive and forget sometimes, we never find happiness. Love is all about helping each other over the hurdles of life and holding the other's hand to guide them through the emotional minefields life throws at us." Anna's eyes filled with tears. "I can no longer bear to see you so unhappy. You're my daughter and it pains me to see you pining so much."

"Is it that obvious?" Penny asked, picking up her half-full wine glass and gulping down its content.

Anna knew then she must do something positive before it really was too late.

Penny stood. "I'm going up for a shower. Tom's asked me to come in early tonight as there's another darts match on. Thanks for the meal, and sorry I couldn't eat it. Don't throw it away. I'll probably have it for supper later."

Waiting until Penny had left for work, secure in the knowledge she wouldn't be back for several hours, she pulled open a drawer in the sideboard, took out a sheet of pale blue writing paper, then sat at the dining table to write.

A few lines down the page, she stopped, ripped the page from the pad and screwed it up into a crumpled ball, telling herself it was wrong to interfere.

No, it isn't.

Yes, it is.

As she picked up the pen again, the argument in her head raged on.

Chapter 37

Harry returned to the table with Peter's half-pint of best bitter and a double whisky for himself.

"Cheers, mate. The Prof here's been telling me he doesn't believe in ghosts, do you, Filton, old boy?"

"But you said—" Harry began, sliding back into his chair.

"I don't believe in spirits, ghouls and ghosts as most people perceive the paranormal to be, no," Filton confirmed. "Nor do I think they are the unjust dead seeking retribution for all the wrongdoing against them or have become trapped between the present and the hereafter. Ghosts are not spirits of dead people unable to move on to the next world. There *is* no next world. Death doesn't work like that. When the body dies, the flesh dies, the organs die. People can't talk from beyond the grave."

"So what do you believe, then?" He leaned back in his chair and took a mouthful of whisky, staring at the man with suspicion. This had better be good, he thought, or else he was off. He'd heard enough for one evening.

"For centuries people all over the world claim to have seen and heard things that go bump in the night," Filton began. "Some people see Roman soldiers marching through walls. Others see spirits or orbs gliding across rooms, while others can hear voices, whisperings, chains clanging, that sort of thing."

"Why only some people? Why not everyone?" Peter asked, leaning forward, not wanting to miss a word.

"Because some people are more sensitive than others. They're more attuned to such vibes, especially in places where something horrific happened. In castles or dungeons, for example."

"But surely that's people's imagination," offered Harry, "knowing a murder or battle took place there. Surely the power of suggestion alone is enough to make them think they can actually see or hear things from the past."

"I agree that might be so in a lot of cases, but what we have to remember is that all these tragedies involve enormously high emotional energy, and energy is an electrical impulse. It's our theory... in fact, many reputable scientists have come to the same conclusion."

"More theory... This is getting beyond a joke... Don't you people have any evidence? Surely after all this time science would be able to prove one way or another?"

"The science is fairly new, Harry. And given that many religions have for thousands of years believed in an after-life, a world beyond this one, we've only recently started to look at things in a new way."

"Fair enough. What is this theory?"

"That electrical energy bursts can become embedded into the very fabric of buildings."

Harry raised his eyebrows.

"I know, I know," said Filton. "Sounds improbable. Impossible even. But we honestly believe this has been going on from the year dot. Think of all those Druids and New Age people, those that claim they can feel something magical at Stonehenge and Avebury and other sites around the world. I think they really *do* feel something."

"Hang on a minute," Harry interrupted, "we're talking about ordinary houses here. Simple homes. There's nothing to even hint anything awful happened, not one single report of someone dying, either at Pond Cottage or Hill House, much less any murder or hangings or gruesome goings-on."

"No, but something dreadful did at Whitestones; it got burnt to the ground. Even if Whitestone was empty at the time it caught fire, it had a history. People must have lived there at some point. Who's to tell what occurred there?"

"What about the smoke Penny could smell in the cottage? Smoke isn't an emotion, so how do you explain that, Prof?"

Filton smiled. "That's an easy one, Harry. Take a sniff of the wall behind you. No, a long, hard sniff. What can you smell?"

"Stale cigarette smoke."

"Exactly, but no one in here is smoking, are they? Nor have they since the smoking ban was enforced several years ago. And, judging by the colour of the ceiling and walls, this place hasn't been decorated since long before then. Tobacco smoke is a strong energy. Its nicotine and tar molecules linger, attaching themselves to everything they touch, be it cloth, wood—"

"Which can be washed out," Peter interrupted.

"But not from stone. I doubt even a good sandblasting could eradicate it completely. Smoke in strong enough concentrations, like that created in a hot, scorching fire, is powerful enough to infuse itself right into the heart of a solid object. And if charred bits of Whitestones found themselves into Pond Cottage, I think it goes a long way to explaining why Penny thought she could smell smoke there."

"Sounds feasible," Harry agreed.

"It doesn't take much for the brain to put images together to make sense of an odour," Filton explained. "The brain is still working when we sleep, as is our hearing. And when you put the pieces together, the brain creates its thoughts as a dream, a nightmare, or an image of the real thing. A memory, perhaps? And sometimes it goes into self-preservation mode, causing the poor person to wake up believing there really is a fire."

Harry pondered on this as he took a swig of his drink, remembering all those disturbed nights Penny and he had endured. Could the answer be that simple?

"You look doubtful, Harry. Okay, let me give you an example. There's a large country house in Wiltshire where people often report being able to smell pipe tobacco burning when clearly no one is smoking in the house."

"I've heard about that," said Peter. "Most people think the smell comes from somebody having a crafty fag outside the building, the smell wafting in through an open window."

Filton didn't look convinced. "One of the building's earlier occupiers was known to be a prolific smoker, of a particular brand of tobacco that you can't obtain any more, yet at times the smell of it is overpowering. The answer can only be explained by the fact that smoke was ever-present there, so much that the essence of eau-de-Ogden's Nutgone has engrained itself into the wooden panels, the plaster, floor-boards, marble fireplaces. Everything. And under certain conditions, the building releases those fumes back into the atmosphere."

Peter nodded. "That sounds perfectly plausible, don't you think, Harry?"

Harry pursed his lips. "I can all accept that, yes, but Penny saw things too..."

"In all of the documented sightings of paranormal happenings, two things are invariably present," Filton said, "one of which being oolite, along with several other minerals. It's thought together they may also be able to record scenes from the past. A stone video for want of a better description. An echo. A momentary fraction of time in history caught on a stone tape. The walls have captured the image and when given the correct sequence of triggers, play those seconds back, hence people walking through walls. *Et voilá*, your ghostly apparition."

"What about music? Your theories make some sort of sense, I suppose, but they don't cover music."

The professor leaned back in his chair. "Oh, but I believe they do, Harry! Emotions are energy outbursts, likewise music, and equally the voice. Music – all sound – is a burst of energy that travels in waves. And if, as in your case, the wall has been torn apart and the pieces jumbled up or separated, the video plays back disjointed images and sounds. A flicker there, a flash here. A few notes over there, a discord over here. All conjecture and hypothesis, I grant you, but it's the best we've got. And I'm perfectly willing to hold up my hand and say we could be wrong. Very wrong."

Harry picked up a stone again and sniffed at it. It didn't smell of anything. Placing to his ear, he listened as one would a shell from the shore. *Isn't it said if you do that, you can hear the sound of the sea?* What was he hoping to hear from a stone from out of the ground, he asked himself. He noticed Peter and the Prof staring at him and immediately felt stupid.

He put it back down. "So explain how this lump of rock here can do all that. I'm finding it rather hard to believe."

"If the mixture of minerals and conditions are right," said Filton, "they attract sound waves like magnetic tape. Somehow, and I admit here this is only speculation, because we're not sure how it works, but *somehow* the oolite traps the waves, recording them like miniature tape recorders. Hence, the stone tape theory."

"And sensitive people have the ability to hear these stones playing back sounds," Peter reiterated, making sure he'd understood the professor correctly.

Filton nodded. "Only there needs to be an energy source, a catalyst to make it work, a form of electrical energy, as would a tape recorder need to be plugged into an electrical source in order for you to play back the recording."

Harry shook his head, disbelieving. "But this is all pure conjecture, isn't it? You've no real, solid evidence."

"Oh, come on, man," bellowed Peter. "It's the best conclusion we've had. Why do you always doubt so much? Have you any better answer than the Prof here?"

"Think about it," said Filton, unperturbed. "If these stones do – and you are correct, there's no scientific proof yet – but if they *do* record sounds or feelings, the thoughts at that moment before death which must charge the air around them with such a force, the stones attract and trap that emotion. Can you imagine the emotional backlash of being trapped in a fire? The horror and fear transmitted from those poor creatures."

Images, dreadful images filled Harry's head. The screams from his children, the fear and panic they suffered, the horror that must have filled his wife's head at the moment of impact. He thrust his head into his hands. Were their echoes etched into the gravel that filled the driveway at Hill House? The screams imprinted on the trees nearby? Was the music Penny heard the music playing on the radio at that terrible moment of impact? Could it really be the past she saw and heard? *God, this was too awful to contemplate...*

He felt Peter's hand on his arm, shaking him.

"Harry? Harry, are you all right? You've gone deathly pale."

His eyes flew open. Peter and Filton were staring at him again. "Yes, I'm fine. Stop fussing me." He gulped, took a hurried swig of whisky. Gulped again. "Sorry... you were saying, Prof..."

"I said that fear is a powerful emotion, one of the strongest electrical impulses created by the brain. The survival instinct. Fight or flight. This is what we think sensitives hear, and likewise when they see ghosts."

Peter looked in awe around the bar area. The pub, too, was built from stone blocks and old, blackened wooden beams. "I bet there's a ghost or two in here even," he commented.

"Most old pubs can lay claim to a ghost. It's good for trade; it brings in the punters," Harry responded.

"I can't blame you for being sceptical," Filton said, "but I wouldn't be at all surprised if some of the stones in this pub found their way here from Whitestones too. There's probably a whole host of history in here trapped in the walls or the cellar. Many hostelries served as meeting rooms or court-rooms years ago. The Bloody Assizes and the Spanish Inquisition are well documented as having taken place in inns like this. All highly-charged meetings where someone's life hung in the balance. All creating particles of emotional electrical energy to become trapped in the walls."

"Wouldn't you be emotionally charged if you were about to have your head chopped off, Harry?" Peter put in. "Wouldn't you rattle your chains like crazy if you were about to be tortured to death? Wouldn't you moan and groan if some sadistic, hooded fiend was about to shove a red hot poker up your backside? I know I would."

Harry sighed heavily. "Admittedly, those are all hugely disturbing influences, which, I can appreciate, generate currents of fear, but music doesn't do that. People dancing doesn't create fear and panic. If music is such a strong influence then why aren't we hearing the walls play back the Rolling Stones or the *Moonlight Sonata* all the time?"

Peter laughed. "Perhaps the walls can do but we can't hear it. Well, most of us. Who's to say what music the Albert Hall would play back given the right set of circumstances, the right sensitive person in the building. Right, Prof?"

Harry ignored him, his attention focused on Shields, who was nodding in agreement with Peter's observation. "So if all this electrical energy is flying about my house, why don't *I* see dancers or hear music?"

Filton held Harry's gaze. "It's a well-known fact women are by design more sensitive to the feelings and emotional side of the human psyche than we men. They are able to open up their minds more, thus they are more susceptible to picking up the waves emitted by the stones. As are children, because their minds haven't been polluted by technology and us adults. Walls have ears; I think they also have mouths with which to speak. And I firmly believe those stones from Whitestones present in your cottage *are* emitting strong enough signals in the right conditions for someone to tune into. More to the point, Penny wasn't the first person to hear music on Stonecott Hill."

Harry sat bolt upright. "What do you mean?"

"We've come across several newspaper archives from before World War Two. Apparently, there were several reports from various homeowners on the ridge who heard music playing in their homes or claimed to have seen odd things. One chap going so far as to sell up shortly after moving in, because his wife was so convinced it was haunted and refused to stay there a moment longer." Filton paused, waiting, watching Harry's reaction as the enormity of the words sunk in.

"But that doesn't explain anything," Harry eventually said. "Ghosts – if that's what we're labelling this – ghosts normally frighten people. Penny was never frightened by what she thought she saw or heard. Quite the opposite, in fact."

"And there's no reason at all why she should have felt scared or threatened. After all, no one has ever been harmed by a ghost. Maybe one or two have died of fright, but that's about all."

"That's not quite true," Peter interrupted, wagging his index finger. "I've seen plenty of programmes on TV where people have been scratched or attacked by entities. Poltergeists and such like."

"And if I'm not mistaken, most of those programmes are made purely and solely for, and I quote, "entertainment purposes only', particularly those from the States. Most can be classed as fakes," Filton countered.

"He has a good point," said Harry. "I've seen a few of those myself. They're a load of tosh."

"Tell me, Peter," asked the professor, "from all those shows you've watched, have you ever seen a spirit actually do anything? Is there photographic evidence? Anything caught actually happening on camera?"

"Well, yes, as a matter of fact. I've seen several where you see real welts and scratches appear on someone's back or arm."

"But is the camera focused on them the whole the time? I bet if you study the footage carefully, you don't see the person moments beforehand. For all we know the victim in question scratches his own arm seconds beforehand and then the camera zooms in as any marks materialize on the skin. Those shows are so well edited there's no way the viewers can tell."

"Remember the famous Enfield poltergeist, Peter? That turned out to be the child herself causing all the mischief and mayhem," added Harry.

"Precisely," said the professor. "Most people who claim to have seen something are more frightened by the fact that they can't put a rational explanation on what they've seen or heard rather than by the actual phenomenon itself." Filton paused to take a drink of shandy.

Harry waited until he'd put down the glass before saying, "You said a few moments ago there were two things always present, one being oolite. So what's the other?"

Filton pulled out a handkerchief from his trouser pocket and wiped his perspiring brow. "The other thing is water."

Peter's eyebrows rose. "*Water?* Why water? Wouldn't that cause a short-circuit, blow the whole thing to smithereens?"

Filton shook his head. "Think about water diviners and

the methods they use. Water creates its own electrical fields which run to earth. Water also creates magnetism. Diviners are able to feel this energy through their bodies, causing the rods in their hands to turn. What we believe happens is that water penetrates the stones and creates a circuit, thus charging it with enough electrical impulse to switch on the playback mechanism and Tada! There are your spooks. Your sounds, your whispers, your rattling chains and footsteps. Voices."

"And music!" Peter slapped his knee triumphantly and turned to Harry. "It all makes sense, don't you agree?"

Harry remained quiet, deep in thought as he took in the professor's words. Was this what was really happening at Pond Cottage? Questions tumbled in his head, spinning and churning. *Was it possible? But hang on a minute...*

"Okay, accepting the water in the gully running alongside Pond Cottage might – and I emphasize *might* – have such an effect, there was no water present at Hill House, and Penny often heard music there. She was always humming it. She saw people, spectres dancing there. So how do you explain that one away?"

Chapter 38

"Rain," said Filton, sounding as if the answer should have been obvious to them. When Harry cocked his head, giving him a look of incredulity and disbelief, Filton hurried to quantify his statement. "Rain. Pure and simple rain. Lots of it. Torrential. Non-stop for days. Floods. Not the odd shower or thunderstorm but deluge after deluge."

"Exactly like the lousy summer and bloody wet winters we've had lately!" trilled Peter. "Harry, this has to be it!" He fell silent, as if processing this information hard, then his grey eyes widened as if a monumentous revelation had uncovered itself to him. "Harry, this is a long shot, but when *exactly* did Penny hear music?"

Harry didn't have to consider his answer, his response was immediate. "At any time, day or night. Sometimes all the time, over and over again. For days on end. It wouldn't go away."

"No, no, what I mean is, was it at any particular time of year?"

"I told you – any time."

"What was the weather doing at the time? Can you re-member? Was it summer? Winter? Was the sun shining?" Filton asked.

"What the... I can't recall."

"Then think, Harry boy. Think!" Peter shouted. "It's im-portant. Had you ever heard any unexplained music?"

Harry dragged his mind back, trying to remember. A vague recollection sprang to the fore.

"Come to think on it, I do recall once hearing music play-ing. I thought Penny had left the radio on." He pondered on the incident a moment, trying to recall everything about that occasion. "We were about to go out. It was the day before the Emerson's dinner at the Beverley. We were still living at Hill House then, she hadn't long moved in. We were on our way out to buy her gown... No... no, we weren't. It was when she came down dressed for the do; she looked so beautiful...

Peter, why are you asking me all this?"

"Because it's fucking important, man, that's why. Haven't you been listening to a thing the Prof's been saying? Was it wet when you heard the music? Was it raining whenever Penny heard it?" Peter's voice was insistent.

Harry looked at Filton who nodded rapidly, urging him on. He thought of all those nights he'd awoken to an empty bed, to find her seated on the stairs staring at a blank space on the wall in front of her. Was it raining then? He couldn't say. As far as he could remember it rained most of that year, a complete washout.

"And what about at Pond Cottage?" Filton asked. "When did she first start hearing it again? Come on, Harry, you must be able to remember."

Harry tried to cast his mind back. *When was it?* "There was a time when the boiler kept going out when we first moved in. I'd been down in the cellar. It was damp. She was worried in case the rain undermined the foundations; the gully was in full flow." He fell silent again, thinking, trying desperately to recall the sequence of events. Wasn't it the following afternoon he'd come home to find her shivering to death outside in the garden because she was too scared to go back indoors?

"Yes, yes. I remember now," he shouted, jubilant. "It *was* raining. It rained for weeks on end last spring. She would hear the music for days on end, too. Then it would stop. Yes, yes, yes... it was raining every time. Bloody pouring down!" His relief at this epiphany bubbled over, making him want to prance around the crowded room with joy as the black cloud lifted in his head. "So all I need now is to find Penny and tell her." He looked at Filton. "I don't suppose your para-wotsit friend has any theories on how to help me find her?"

Filton laughed. "You know, I'd like to meet this young lady when you do find her, and I'm sure you will. I would love to have a chat with her about all this. Hear her views on what she's experienced. And my students would be fascinated to hear her story too. As would Stefan."

"*If* I find her," Harry muttered.

Peter grabbed the professor's hand and shook it rapidly. "Thanks, Filton. You've been a great help, and I believe every word you've said. I have one question, though..."

"Which is?"

"Has there ever been a case you couldn't explain by scientific or natural means?"

Filton Shield smiled and gave a slight shake of his head. "Not yet."

"Well, that's good to hear, isn't it, Harry? Harry?"

Harry already had his jacket on and was heading towards the door.

"Harry, where are you going? Hang on..." Before he gave chase, the professor tugged at Peter's sleeve.

"About that lift?"

Chapter 39

The next morning, in Pond Cottage Harry brewed coffee whilst Peter sat at the kitchen table, trawling the Internet on his laptop, searching for more information on the stone tape theory.

"Did you get any sleep last night?" Peter asked, not looking up from the screen.

"Not much. Spent most of it going over what the professor said. Wanting to believe him one moment. Dismissing the whole thing as bunkum the next. I still don't know what to make of it all."

"Well, there was a lot to take in. I didn't realize quite how much the Prof was involved in paranormal research. With a bit of luck and—"

"Yes, but even if I do manage to locate Penny, how on earth am I supposed to tell her all this and, more to the point, would she even believe me?"

He looked about the sitting room, wondering how such an innocent little house could hold such vivid echoes. The bright evening sunlight streamed in through the window but he wished it would rain. Rain so hard he could hear the walls speak to him. Huh! Like that was ever going to happen.

"Listen to this..." Peter said, hardly able to contain his excitement. He read out the words on the screen in front of him. "There is a strong belief in many academic circles that certain people have the ability to hold objects and read their history—"

"Penny never did anything like that. She never had anything to hold."

"Will you shut up a moment and let me finish!"

From the glaring look Peter gave him, Harry could see he was annoyed, a glare which sent him skulking away from the table to the sofa.

"Thank you. Now let me read on. 'There are some sensitives who can even read letters sealed inside envelopes.'" He looked across to Harry. "You obviously don't have that power."

Harry stuck out his tongue, then mouthed an obscenity. Grinning, Peter turned back to the screen.

"Well," asked Harry, impatient with Peter's protracted silence, "what else does it say?"

"Hush, I'm reading."

"Well, read aloud."

Peter rolled his eyes heavenward then, following the text across the screen with his index finger, read out: "All these theories and ideas were dismissed as hokum until the beginning of the middle of the twentieth century, when scientist Stefan Marsham, aided by Professor Filton Shields, formed the Faculty for Psychical Research at Bristol University. Whilst they have found no evidence of true hauntings, the faculty notes many places they have investigated do have a creepy atmosphere about them—"

"Bah! Nothing creepy about this place. Depressing at the moment, but not creepy."

Peter ignored his jibe, continuing, "These places are said to have a black mood hanging over them, often causing depression in those living there. Marsham believes voices can and do imprint themselves into certain buildings built with stone containing a strong mica content." His voice rose an octave. "In order to investigate and test his theories further, in 2012 Marsham developed and patented highly-sensitive recording equipment which he believes can capture these phenomena..." Peter stopped to draw breath and take a swig of coffee.

"Is that all?" said Harry. "It doesn't tell us much more than what Shields said last night."

Peter scrolled further down the website, clicked on a link and another webpage shot up in front of him. "There's quite a bit on this one. A whole string of places Marsham and Shields have investigated. Here's one: 'Graffiti discovered on inside walls of an ancient outside toilet at Heligan consists of many signatures along with a single date, August 1914. All these names were also found inscribed on a war memorial in the local churchyard. All fell in World War One and all served in the same regiment. They were all gardeners at Heligan. Several exorcisms have been carried out in the grounds of Heligan, but the feeling of melancholia still hangs over the gardens especially in the vicinity of the lake, where people have reported seeing an ethereal black cloud hovering over the water. Others have reported hearing singing. Apparently, the gardeners all sang in the church choir and,' listen to this, 'they would often sing whilst in the privy.'"

Peter scrolled down again, paused, scrolled on. "Listen to this one. It cites Chingle Hall in Lancashire as being reputedly the most haunted house in England. People have reported seeing monks, although there was never a monastery in the area. It is, or was, surrounded by a moat."

Intrigued, Harry crossed the room to stand looking over his friend's shoulder. Was there more to all this than he first thought?

Peter turned to look at him. "You know, if stones have been removed from monasteries and churches and used elsewhere in other buildings, Filton's theory could well explain why a lot of ghost sightings are often of monks in places totally unrelated to them."

"Makes sense," said Harry, "if this stone tape theory is for real. Any more?"

Peter continued reading out the vast list of supposedly haunted buildings and sightings, each having one element in common: water – be it moat, river, lakeside or underground streams.

"Peter, there's a lot there that makes sense now but also an awful lot of questions which still need answering. I think—" At which point Harry's mobile phone rang. "I'd best get this, excuse me a minute."

He took his phone out of his trouser pocket, clinging to the hope it would be Penny, and stepped into the hallway, closing the door behind him. When he saw the caller's number, his heart sank. Moments later, he went back into the kitchen.

"That was Elaine. Says she's tried ringing you numerous times but can't get an answer. Said to tell you you're late. She didn't sound too pleased."

"Oh heck! I'd forgotten," said Peter, looking up from the laptop. "I'm supposed to be taking her out for dinner this evening." Peter patted his trouser pocket, then shrugged. "I must have left my mobile in the car."

"She never gives up, does she? You don't fancy her, do you? I mean, she's—"

"A pain in the butt at times, I know. But she's also a warm and lively, intelligent lady. And when you get to our age, it's nice to share a meal and a bottle of wine with a good-looking woman. You of all people should know that. Do you have problems with this?"

Harry slapped him across the back. "You carry on, pal, because at least whilst she's got her painted talons in you, she's leaving me alone and not making it her life's work to look after me."

"That bad, eh? You know, she feels pretty dreadful about saying what she did to Penny."

"So she should."

"Come on, man. She didn't mean any harm and you know Elaine, she's loyal to Lorna and, well... you've only got yourself to blame. You should have told Penny at the start, then none of this would have happened."

Harry scowled. "Thanks, like I need reminding."

Peter glanced at his watch. "Look, I've got to go, Can't keep the lady waiting any longer." He studied his friend for a few moments before taking his jacket from the back of a chair. "I'll see you tomorrow. Get to bed, you look haggard."

Harry led him to the front door. "Do me a favour tonight, Peter?"

"What's that?"

"Tell Elaine I'm sorry."

"I think that's something you should be telling her yourself, don't you?"

Chapter 40

It had been three days since his discussion with Filton Shield in the pub, three nights and days of being no nearer to finding Penny. Seated at the kitchen table, he scanned through the newspaper as he sipped his morning coffee. There wasn't much news to grab his attention, only the usual political slandering and back-biting, some overrated and overpaid mega pop star being involved in a wild drugs party, more refugees being pulled out of the sea near Turkey.

Flicking through the broadsheet, his attention was caught by the advertisements page. What if he put in an ad for Penny, he thought, something along the lines of "Lonely architect begs forgiveness" or "Please come home, Penny, the ghosts have been exorcised." Would she read it? Would she even realize it was aimed at her? Was he really that desperate to write to the lonely hearts column? Yes, yes and triple times yes, he told himself. Anything to reach out to her.

The letterbox rattled. From the kitchen, he saw a pale-blue envelope skim across the flagstones as the postman's chirpy whistle faded. He rushed down the hallway to pick it up.

The neat handwriting with its wispy curlicues and flourishes wasn't familiar, the postmark blurred. He ripped it open, read a few lines, then the signature. In sheer disbelief and utter joy, he collapsed into the chair by the hall table before picking up the telephone.

"Peter, listen. I won't be coming in today. You'll have to manage on your own. ... No, I'm not ill. ... No, I'm perfectly okay. I'm going up to Buckinghamshire."

"Whatever for?" Peter's voice on the other end of the line sounded confused. "You can't. Patrick Holden's coming in, remember? We have a meeting and I need—"

"Sorry, buddy, you'll have to handle him on your own today. I've had a letter."

"From Penny?"

"No, from her mother, believe it or not. Apparently, Penny's living there with her. Has been for some time."

"Good luck."

"Thanks. I'll keep you informed."

"Do that."

"And, Peter..."

"Yes?"

"Thanks for putting up with me through all this."

"Bugger off and go get her, you silly old lovesick fool."

Harry put the phone down and grabbed his car keys.

"Please, please, please be there, sweetheart," he begged aloud into the air full of dancing specks of dust agitated by his enthusiasm.

Anna ushered him into the dining room.

"Come in off the doorstep. We're quite safe, Penny's out."

Harry held out a hand-tied bunch of flowers. "Here, these are for you."

She took the proffered bouquet and sniffed at the partially opened yellow lilies nestling amongst bright red gerberas and white gypsophila.

"They're beautiful. Thank you. Let me go and pop them in some water. I won't be a moment." She disappeared into a room beyond, calling out, "Tea? Coffee? Did you find us okay?"

"Coffee would be lovely, thanks. Your map was fine, didn't even need the satnav," he answered, gazing about curiously at the small interior of the house, noticing the limewashed stone of the party wall, sure if he stretched out his arms he would be able to touch both sides of the room.

Carrying a tray loaded with cups, milk and sugar, a plate of biscuits and a full cafetière, Anna came back from the kitchen.

"Here, let me." He rushed forward, taking the wooden tray from her, and turned to place it on the dining table.

"No, no, not there. Up there." She pointed to the highly polished oak stairs. "It's more private up in my sitting room. If anyone looks through the window, you won't be seen. We don't want to spoil our surprise, do we?"

He followed her lead, carefully carrying the tray.

"Mrs Raines, I can't tell you enough how grateful I am for all this. If only you knew the heartache I've been going through these past months."

"As has my daughter." She indicated to the glass coffee table in the centre of the room they'd entered, a room Harry's architect's mind immediately concluded was originally designed as a bedroom. He put the tray down, and at her invitation made himself comfortable on one of the armchairs, and watched as Anna poured coffee. When she offered him a biscuit, he refused.

"Right, Harry. Now, I think you had better tell me all about it and what drove my daughter away from you?"

So he explained about the accident that had killed his children and wife, how guilty he felt over it, how helpless he'd been. About the nightmares he'd suffered before Penny had stepped into his life, and how he'd thought the nightmares were over. That was until the music started.

He'd been such a fool not to tell Penny, he admitted, but he'd been so frightened of losing her, he didn't want to accept what might be going on so had kept it quiet, never realizing the wedge he was driving between them until the truth came out. But by then it was too late, the damage done. Before he could comprehend what was happening to them both, Penny had left, and he'd been broken hearted ever since. He spoke of Peter and of Professor Shields, and of their findings. Now all he wanted to do was find her, beg forgiveness and pick up the pieces of their lives he'd been so stupid to let slip through his fingers.

"I don't pose any threat to your daughter, Mrs Raines, I love her. I want her back. I would never harm or hurt her. I really do love her."

"There's no hiding the emotion and love in your voice and heart," Anna told him, studying his pained expression. "And I appreciate your honesty. It's a rare man who would readily admit to his future mother-in-law he'd made a mistake and was wrong."

"Future mother-in-law? But—"

She held up a finger. "Let me finish. I can guarantee that

you and Penny will be back together before the week is out and that this is all going to end with wedding bells. Having met you, listened to your side of the story, I am more certain than ever. Penny still loves you, even though she denies it. A mother senses these things."

"But how can you be so sure? I don't know what I'm going to do if she refuses to see me."

"Would you blame her if she does? After all, you've not made much of an effort yourself to find her."

"But that's not true. I tried telephoning your other daughter countless times. I knew that's where Penny would have gone initially, but her sister always denied she was there."

"Anita never said," Anna responded with a frown. "I've spoken to her on numerous occasions and not once did she mention you calling; I'm sure she would have mentioned something as important as that. Anita kept me constantly informed during Penny's stay with her. Did you never think to write to her there instead?"

"I couldn't, I didn't know where to write. In the end, I went cap-in-hand to Alex. He gave me Anita's address but when I got there, the housekeeper told me I was too late and that Penny had left." Harry hung his head. He hadn't thought of sending a letter, he admitted. Reflecting now, it seemed such an obvious thing to have done. "Would Anita have even passed on any letters if I had?"

Anna huffed. "After what you've told me, probably not." She shook her head wearily. "But why would my daughter stop you seeing Penny? I don't understand."

"Because Anita thinks I'm the big bad wolf. She left me in no uncertain doubt of that the day I called back to see her."

"Then Penny must have convinced her you were."

"Do you believe that?"

Anna's response was immediate. "No, Harry, I don't. Penny wouldn't do that. Oh my, I am sorry. That was terribly wrong of Anita to keep the two of you apart. The stupid girl! All this hassle and heartbreak could have been so easily avoided if she'd had the gumption to bring you two back together to sort out your problems. That's typical of my Anita.

Always thinking she knows best, thinking that she can read people's emotions. One degree in family psychology and she thinks she's the world's expert on relationships. At the first opportunity, I'm going to ring that interfering madam and give her a piece of my mind, daughter or not."

"I suspect she was only trying to protect her sister, believing she was doing the right thing. But if Penny loves me I can't understand why she never called or wrote to me."

"I can answer that for you. Her pride."

"Pride?"

"Yes. It's a silly thing us women have. We don't like admitting to the men in our lives that they *are* sometimes right. And if you want my advice, you'll move right away from that house. Well away. If what you tell me is true, this thing will follow you both if you stay in that area. Who knows what other houses might be affected."

"I've already thought about that, but Pond Cottage is such an idyllic place. I'm rather hoping now we know the root cause of the phenomenon it will go away. There must come a time when it fades away completely. Like a record that's played all the time, again and again, it will eventually become worn out."

"Yes, but how long will that take? And can you afford to wait that long?"

He shrugged. "Unless I buy a brand new house, who's to tell if it won't happen elsewhere? Take this house. It isn't new by any standard—"

"No, but nothing has ever happened here, least not to my knowledge. This place was an old barn before it was converted, the back a stabling yard and next door the smithy, yet I don't hear horses from the past whinnying or neighing. I don't hear cartwheels and wagons trundling by my windows in the dead of night, although there are some in the village who talk of a ghost rider."

He sighed. "Perhaps you're right, Mrs Raines. I'm not thinking straight half the time. This whole business has worn me to the ground. Until I have won Penny back I can't be practical and logical."

245

"Love's a funny thing, Harry. It addles the heart as well as the brain."

"Do you think Penny will see me?"

"I'm sure she will as long as it's not left any longer. There's already some other chap trying to muscle his way into her affections. I know she's still in love with you, but she's vulnerable. Marcus Ford is a nice enough man in some respects but will readily break her heart as the next woman's; he's that sort."

"And you think I won't? Haven't I hurt her enough already, yet you still have faith in me?"

"Listen, I pride myself on being a good judge of character, so I know you're not that sort. A lesser man would have given up on her. They would have accepted the love affair was finished and moved on to the next, but not you. And having met you, I can understand why Penny is so confused and hurt. What woman wouldn't fall for you and that wide, enigmatic smile, your deliciously blue eyes. You're a heart stopper." She sighed. "And I'll tell you something... if I were thirty years younger I'd be setting my sights on you too. You're a handsome catch, far too good to let my daughter allow to escape."

Harry felt himself blush, flattered and embarrassed by Anna's statement. He had poured his heart out to this woman and she'd believed him; now all he had to do was convince Penny and persuade her to come back to Gloucestershire with him.

Anna looked up at the wall clock. "She'll be home soon so I suggest you disappear for the time being. As I said in my letter, there are always rooms at the hotel across the way, you can't miss it. Book yourself in and park your car at the back, well out of the way where Penny won't see it, and tomorrow morning I'll make myself scarce." She escorted him back downstairs and opened the front door.

He shook her hand fondly. "Don't you feel guilty doing all this?"

"Not in the least. It's natural instinct for a mother to meddle if it means protecting her young, as much as it's natural to want what's best for your children even if they cannot always see it, especially when it's right in front of them." She reached up and kissed his cheek. "Writing to you was the right move; I only hope Penny sees it that way. I can't make her see sense so it's up to you now. Till tomorrow then. And good luck."

"Thanks. Something tells me I'm going to need it."

Chapter 41

"And what have you been doing with yourself?" Penny asked, arriving home from her afternoon stint behind the till in the village shop.

"Oh, enjoying a quiet afternoon listening to the radio and catching up on some mending, that's all. Nothing exciting." Anna could feel the flush on her face. She didn't like deceiving her daughter and hoped Penny wouldn't sense something had been going on behind her back. She tried to react normally, innocent. "And yours?"

Penny kicked off her shoes and threw her jacket over the banister. "That Francis Fyfield, what a dragon! Do you know, the woman even had the effrontery to tell me not to call her Francis until such time as she gives me her permission, when she thinks we're better acquainted. Can you believe it? How long have I been living here, for goodness' sake! You'd think by now we were acquainted enough."

"Yes, she can be a cantankerous old spinster. That's what happens when you live on your own too long without a man in your life." The gibe was directed more for Penny's benefit but Anna doubted her daughter would pick up on the point. "A cup of tea, dear?"

"I'll do it." Penny continued chatting from the kitchen. "Oh, by the way, Edith said to remind you... Oh, what lovely flowers!"

"Aren't they?" Anna called back. "Someone I've done a little favour for popped in with them." At least that bit wasn't a lie, she thought with a wry grin. "By the way, I'm going into Milton Keynes tomorrow. There's something I need to do."

Penny carried two cups of tea back into the dining room. "Fine. What time do you want us to leave? We could go in early, do our shopping, and have lunch there for a change."

"I'd rather like to go on my own this time, dear, if you don't mind?"

"Oh. Okay. No problem." Although feeling let-down by her mother's insistence on going to town alone, she didn't question her reasons. If Mum had something to do on her own, so be it, she wouldn't encroach or argue. They were getting on too well to let a simple shopping trip spoil their relationship. She hadn't felt so close to her mother for a long, long while and didn't want to upset things. "I'll tidy the place while you're gone. The fish van calls tomorrow. Shall I see if he's got any fresh salmon cutlets for our tea?"

"That'll be nice, dear, or some trout if they look sparky." Anna could sense her daughter's disappointment. Their shopping trips together each week were always enjoyable, but this time it couldn't be helped, Penny needed to be at home.

Her mother having left the house early to catch the bus into Milton Keynes, Penny slipped into her jeans and pulled on a sweater, not bothering to shower first or do anything with her hair. She would do all that after the housework was done, and then go for a walk.

With the radio tuned to Classic FM, she turned up the volume, fetched the vacuum cleaner from the landing cupboard where it was stored with all the other cleaning equipment, and was soon lost in Pledge and Schubert's *Fifth* when the doorbell rang.

"Harry!" Her heart leapt into her throat at the sight of him.

He stood in the doorway, wringing his hands nervously, clearly unsure of the welcome he would receive.

"Hi," he said after a moment.

The sound of his voice, that one little word, set her pulse racing. "What are you doing here?"

"We need to talk."

She wanted in that instant nothing more than to be swept into his arms, that old familiar tugging on her heartstrings imploring him to reach out to her, but as he stepped forward as if reading her mind, she took a step back, reluctant and scared to let him back into her life. The pain and hurt still resided in her pounding heart.

"There's nothing to say," she snapped.

"May I at least come in off the street? Hear me out, that's

all I ask."

A tantalizing whiff of his aftershave caught in her nostrils, reminding her of their romps in the fields, breakfasts in bed, and all those passionate nights beneath the sheets; all the things she craved and missed so much. At first hesitant, she finally beckoned him inside and closed the front door.

His presence seemed to fill the whole dining room. Feeling her knees buckling at the closeness of him, she grabbed hold of the back of a dining chair for support. He still had the power to collapse all her resolve.

"What do you want here, Harry? I don't need this. Not now. Not after so long. Oh why, why now?"

"Penny, we need to talk. Civil this time. I have so much to explain. I've found out things—"

She cut him off mid sentence. "How did you find me? Did Anita tell you I was here?" When he didn't answer, she second-guessed. "Mother, then? The scheming shrew. She promised me she wouldn't interfere."

He reached out and touched her arm lightly. "Don't be cross with her. She was only doing what she thought best. She hates seeing you so unhappy. I've come to ask you to come back with me. I've missed you so much."

She snatched her arm away, trying desperately to ignore the hot sensation his fingers brought to her skin. "No. Never! I can't go back there. I can't come back with you."

"Peter and I have discovered what's going on there and—"

"Harry, don't you understand? It's over between us." Her dry mouth and floundering heart told her a different story.

He shook his head, disbelieving. "No. I'm not leaving here without you. I need to explain—"

"Like you did before? You don't get it, do you? For all you proclaimed that you loved me, you couldn't tell me everything from the start. You had to hide it from me. Let me suffer. Suffer so much I was this close..." She held up her thumb and forefinger, emphasizing how near to the brink of madness she had been. "... this close to being locked up as a psychotic nutcase."

"Penny, I'm begging forgiveness. I was so wrong. What we

had was good; we can't throw it all away over a misunderstanding."

"A misunderstanding!" she shouted at him. "I wouldn't call—"

"Would it help if I said I was sorry?"

Her voice softened. "That's too easy a word to say, considering..."

"But one that's dreadfully hard to express."

"If you truly felt sorry, why has it taken you so long to come?" Unless he came up with the right answer now it was definitely goodbye Harry, she decided, no matter how much it hurt.

"You weren't exactly easy to find," he said. "And your sister didn't help much either, making sure she kept us apart. Telling me every time I phoned that you weren't there. That she didn't know where you were. Look, Pen, I know I handled everything all wrong, I can see that now, but at the time I was only doing what I thought was best. Deep down, I didn't want to accept what was going on. I was foolish to even begin to think I could hide the past. In my own idiotic way I thought I could protect you. Believe me, I never meant to hurt you; it was the complete opposite."

"I felt I couldn't trust you any more. That..." She stopped, his words sinking in. Registering. "Hang on... Anita said *what?*"

"She told me she didn't know where you were. I didn't believe her. Ask her." He pointed to the telephone on the sideboard. "Ring her now if you don't believe me."

"So why didn't you come for me if you knew where I was?"

"Because I didn't know where she lived! I had to go cap in hand to Alex to find out. When—"

"You went to *Alex?* And he told *you?*" Boy, he must have been truly desperate to ask for Alex's help, she thought.

He nodded frantically. "I didn't know what else to do. When I finally got to your sister's, I was told you had left. That very same morning!"

"You made me feel like everyone was talking behind my

back. Keeping secrets. Whispering about it."

"Our friends were doing no such thing. Peter constantly nagged me to tell you everything. He was right, I should have. Aren't I allowed one mistake?"

She pulled a chair out from the dining table and sat, trying to take in the enormity of his words. Hadn't she made mistakes in her past? Like Alex for example? And yes, Harry was right, what they had was good. Better than good. And she believed him when he said he'd been trying all this time to find her. He'd even gone to Alex for help. That must mean something.

Just hear me out, that's all I'm asking," he pleaded. "If you don't like what you hear, fine, I'll go. For now. Like I said, I'm not leaving without you, no matter how long it takes."

The determination in his voice flipped her heart. He really meant it. How could she ever not forgive him? But along with the thrill of realizing how much he cared, how much he loved her, hesitation still sat on her shoulder. He had come all this way too, so she had to listen to what he had to say, she owed him that much at least. What harm would listening do? Listening didn't mean she was committing herself, and at least then she would know what happened else, as her mother had said, she would spend the rest of her life wondering. Whether that was before or after she killed Anita, she wasn't quite sure.

"I'd better put the kettle on then. It sounds like this may take some time."

Seated at the dining table, she let him talk, explain things. Things she had no idea about. She listened, and in the long gaps of silence that interspersed the one-sided conversation, she delved into her thoughts, trying to come to grips with her turmoiled emotions. Had she over-reacted about the whole thing? Thought the worst through a mind confused and tired? Was all of this heartache all her own fault? Her doing? Jealous of another woman when, in fact, it was purely a case of self-doubt and fear of losing him.

Love smouldered beneath the surface ready to burst into flame at his touch but so far he hadn't attempted to touch her again. He hadn't even held her hand let alone attempt a kiss.

She didn't know if she was glad or disappointed, her thoughts were so mixed up, as jumbled and disjointed as the music she'd often heard in her head. Was he frightened she would back away again? She couldn't blame him, but seeing him there on the doorstep had been such a shock. So unexpected after all this time.

Inwardly she cursed her mother, angry she'd gone behind her back, yet at the same time pleased she had. It had needed that force, that impetus to confront the situation she had been too weak and stubborn to make the first move to amend. She looked at Harry seated opposite as he spoke. He looked drained, physically and emotionally. Then her ears pricked at something he said.

"When the professor found out other houses on the ridge had reported the same phenomenon, that was when the connection was made. I realized there had to be some truth in the matter."

Her eyes widened. "You mean, it wasn't only me who heard music?"

He nodded. "There have been numerous reported incidences of strange noises and sounds heard going back decades."

The immediate relief at hearing this came as a warm wave washing over her, sweeping away all the self-doubts and torment. The news was music to her ears, a confirmation that she wasn't hallucinating or imagining any of it.

"Then perhaps poor old Mrs Ewell wasn't as mad as Jilly made out, and she had been hearing things in the house too all along," she said.

"Something paranormal is definitely going on there, and the professor thinks your beloved ruin is the cause. He's found out the house was called Whitestones. We know it burned down, but we don't know why. We haven't got to the bottom of it precisely. But, Penny, if you come back home we can continue the search together. There's nothing to be frightened of."

She sat upright. "I never was frightened, Harry. Only of you. Of Elaine, come the end."

"And now?"

"I need time."

"For what?"

She shook her head. "I don't know... To think... To sort this all out in my mind."

"You've had plenty of time to think, Pen. Do you still believe I'm such a fiend? That I'm the big bad wolf to be avoided? That I'm dangerous? I'm not. I love you and I need you. I can't function without you. And having now found you, I'm not letting you go."

She stared into those deep, alluring eyes that reflected so much of his innermost thoughts. Knowing his body longed for release wrapped within her. Tense. A coil waiting to be sprung the moment he sensed she had forgiven him even if she never uttered those precise words. There would come a point, she knew, when he could stand the waiting no more and would catch hold of her, pulling her towards him. She wanted him to, to make it all better, and yet she was scared. Scared she wouldn't be able to prevent him, and scared of her own wants and desires.

"I've missed you," he said again, quietly.

Her heart pounded against her ribs. "And I you."

"Am I forgiven?"

"Am I?"

As he enfolded her in his arms, his head and heart exploded with relief. Tears flooded his eyes. He'd found her at last, and he would never, ever, let her go again.

Her lips tasted hot, her body wilting against his touch. He wanted nothing more than to lift her from her feet and carry her upstairs but refrained, enjoying instead the kisses and warmth that wrapped around him, wanting the moment to last forever.

Finally, unwillingly, their lips parted.

"So you'll come back home?" he uttered against her hair, knowing he couldn't bear it if she said no?

Her body stiffened as she pulled away. "No, Harry."

His world plummeted. "But I thought now we know the

truth—"

"But that's the point," she interrupted. "We don't. Not fully anyway. Things there are not resolved and won't be until I find out what that music was. What it was called. I *need* to know. More so now with what you've told me. Until I do, I won't be able to settle there. I'm sorry, Harry, that's the way it is. I can't go back to Pond Cottage."

His body sagged, his heart falling into the pit of his stomach. Just when he thought it was all over and their life could go back to normal. What more did he have to do, to say, to persuade her?

"Penny? I... We..." He couldn't think straight. So many thoughts, ideas, scenarios churning inside his brain. "At least come back with me for the time being. We can move to a hotel. Stay with Peter. Anywhere you want. We don't have to stay at the cottage. I know with you there the truth will out; you're the key. Come back with me, please. You don't have to stay but at least give it a try, at least until we find out the full truth, an explanation. What Professor Shields has unearthed is only part of the story."

"And when it's over and we know the answers? If we ever do find out—"

"We can sell the cottage. Find another house away from the ridge."

"What's wrong with you living here?" she asked. "Goldstoke is equally as beautiful as Stonecott and the ridge."

Taken aback by a solution he hadn't contemplated, he couldn't answer. This needed thinking about. He liked the West Country, Gloucestershire in particular. Then there was the business to consider. The new premises. But did it matter? Something could be worked out with Peter. Okay, the northern reaches of Buckinghamshire were alien to him, even the soil a different colour, but if it meant not losing her again, he'd go to the ends of the world if it meant she was with him. He'd been to hell and back already and he'd no intention of descending that path again. So could he stay here, not go back either? The answer came instantly. Yes, yes, and a thousand times yes. Anywhere, as long as she was with him.

He was about to speak when she looked up, a faint flicker of a smile, a gentle sigh.

"Okay, Harry. I'll come home. I have to face this thing, no matter what it is, and I can't do that from a hundred miles away."

Delighted beyond his hopes, he pulled her into his arms once more. "We'll face it together, sweetheart. And I meant what I said. We'll sell the cottage and move elsewhere, anywhere. To the moon and beyond, if that's what you want."

Chapter 42

Pond Cottage felt strangely odd as she walked inside ahead of Harry. Familiar objects seemed starkly out of place. Not moved in the physical sense, more a feeling of being out of context, out of time.

"We'll be okay," Harry tried to reassure her. "It will sort itself out."

"Not until I know the full story it won't."

"Can you hear the music now?"

Penny tilted her head, listening. "No. Nothing."

"That's because it hasn't been raining."

She looked at him in confusion. "What's that got to do with anything?"

"Everything, apparently!" He led her to the sofa to explain the professor's theory on stone tapes again as best he could, and how the effect of water upon the stones could, given the right set of circumstances, play back the past.

"And you really believe all this?" she asked when he'd finished.

He nodded. "I didn't at first, no. Crazy as it sounds, there is scientific evidence, according to Shields. I think he's right. He knows what he's talking about. He can explain it far better than I'm doing. All I ask is that you listen to what he has to say. Also, I am glad it isn't raining today because I've a special treat in store for you this evening. One I'm sure you'll enjoy. I'm taking you out to dinner and a show."

She looked at him quizzically. "Oh! Where?"

"It's a surprise." There was a hint of mischief in his eyes. "I thought it would take your mind off the cottage this evening, and help us both to relax. I'm kind of hoping we can regard it as a date."

"But how did you know I would come? I might have said no and stayed in Goldstoke."

"I took a gamble."

"I'd better go shower and change then," she said, softly kissing his cheek.

"It's nothing posh, mind. Jeans and a warm sweater is de rigueur for where we're going."

The red stone of Berkeley Castle glowed like amber fire in the early evening sunlight, the fields below swathed in a glorious orange hue. Beneath the towering walls, people queued patiently to enter the turnstile into what was once the jousting field, where re-enactments now took place, according to the literature Penny had read with mounting excitement during the taxi drive to the oldest inhabited castle in the country.

"Wouldn't we see better sitting over there to the left a bit more?" she suggested, when Harry dropped the tartan blanket and waterproof sheet to the grass.

He agreed, gathering up all the paraphernalia again and moving it to the spot she had indicated. Penny threw the two large cushions, the only items he'd let her carry from the car, down onto the blanket. He held out his hand to help her sit.

Once they were settled, he opened the wicker food hamper and started laying out its contents. Out came two plastic plates filled with smoked salmon and thin slices of buttered brown bread, neatly cut into quarters, and lemon wedges; these he passed across for her to remove the clingfilm. Next came a plastic box holding some dainty little pastry savouries and canapés filled with ricotta and spinach, and prawns in mayonnaise. A bowl of potato salad followed. The basket seemed a never-ending cornucopia of goodies, including a sealed plastic tub full of hulled strawberries and a handful of little individual pots of cream.

"Cutlery?" She peered into the hamper.

"Of course. I've remembered everything. Even down to a bottle of wine and glasses." He lifted up a stainless steel vacuum flask for her inspection. "And hot coffee for later, plus brandy miniatures to go with it."

The canvas bag alongside the hamper contained metallic stakes, hooks and lanterns with tealights. These he set around the edge of the blanket ready for when it grew dark. He'd even brought a torch, he told her. Indeed, he had indeed thought of everything, making her smile contentedly, even though she was still baffled by his organization at such short notice.

"Actually, it was Peter who prepared everything," he confessed. "He and Elaine had planned to come tonight, but when I spoke to him earlier, to tell him the good news you were back, he offered me the tickets instead. He thought you would enjoy the concert more than Elaine would anyway."

"Now I feel guilty," she said, "spoiling their night."

He took her hand, kissing her fingers one by one. "Don't. They know the score and understand we need time to ourselves to get to know each other again."

"As long as it doesn't give her another reason to despise me."

"She doesn't despise you. Quite the opposite, in fact. She was beside herself when she found out that you'd left me. Apart from which, she isn't really a classical music fan. Apparently, she was only too happy to forego the event. Peter's taking her to the theatre instead. So..." He kissed her fingers again. "Let's forget about them for now and enjoy ourselves."

"Yes, lets. I'm glad they've become an item, though. I'm pleased for both of them. And I'm so sorry I thought and said those awful things about her."

"It's all forgotten. Now, shall we start? What would you like to eat first?"

As she ate, she gazed around, taking in the whole spectacle, savouring the excited atmosphere building up around her. Laughing, carefree groups carrying deckchairs or folding garden chairs along with their bags and hampers were settling to enjoy their picnics too. She wondered if they were in as much eager anticipation as she was for the show to start. On the large stage at the end of the field, two men were testing the lights, another three moving chairs and music stands into place.

She watched as a group of six dinner-suited men carried stacked chairs and a trestle table between them and set it all down on the grass a short distance away. Bemused, she could hardly believe her eyes when one of them, white-gloved and wearing a penguin suit, covered the table with a white linen cloth then proceeded to lay out china, glasses and domed-covered platters of food along with two huge silver candelabra complete with tapered white candles. A party of women befrocked in elegant full-length taffeta evening dresses crossed the field to join them. The candles burst into flickering light. Battery-powered, Penny realized with a smile.

She nudged Harry, also watching what was going on. "That looks so much fun."

"Doesn't it? I'll see what I can arrange for next year, shall I?" he replied with a wink. "Have to admit that's the first time I've seen anyone dressed for dinner like that at one of these picnic concerts. What a hoot!"

Unlike the dinner-suited party laughing and enjoying themselves at the dining table, everyone else wore jeans and t-shirts or sweaters, she noted, and had carried in jackets and fleeces or wraps with them, in anticipation of any evening chill that might whistle in later. Rain hadn't been forecast, it was a glorious summer's evening, so why, she thought, did everyone also bring umbrellas, especially all those big colourful golfing types.

Harry offered up a dish of Pringles. "Quite a sight, isn't it? Have you never been to one of these picnic-concerts before?"

"Heavens, no," she declared, taking a handful. "Alex wouldn't dream of coming to something like this. He couldn't stand picnics, less still, the very idea of sitting in a meadow, eating cold food and listening to boring classical music and opera filled him with distaste. "Two thousand years of civilization and people want to sit out eating in damp fields," he'd say," she mocked. "He was the same with barbeques. Thought them stinking nuisances that the Government should ban."

"Well then, my lady, you are in for a real treat tonight. Poor Alex doesn't have a clue what he's missing in life. More wine?"

"Please." She lay back in her chair, replete and content. A smile creased her lips at a naughty thought crossing her mind...

If only we were here on our own... I know what I would want Harry to do to me... here, on our blanket.

After topping up her glass, Harry read through the programme he'd purchased at the entrance gate, leaving her lost in her thoughts again.

How could I have ever have doubted him? My running away wasn't the answer.

Setting aside all her misgivings when he'd arrived on her mother's doorstep yesterday, she was glad he had found her.

I'm glad Mum did what she did... And it's true... despite it all, he is the best thing that's ever happened to me... I love him so much.

She sat upright, turning towards him. "Harry, I—"

"It says here," he spoke at the same time. "Sorry, you were about to say..."

She laughed. "No, it's okay. You go first."

He pointed to the pamphlet. "It says here that after the intermission there's to be a medley of waltzes by Straus, Chopin and a composer I've never heard of - Zdenek Fibich."

She frowned, puzzled by the name. "No, I've never heard of him either. Does it say anything else about him?"

"Only that he wrote several tone poems and operas including *Sarka,* and over two hundred piano pieces and songs."

"I'm none the wiser," she commented. Spontaneous clapping from nearer the stage made her turn her head. "Oh good, the orchestra's coming on."

The musicians took their places, filling the stage swiftly, shuffling and fidgeting in an effort to get comfortable, rearranging their music stands - a little bit more to the left, no that's not correct, a bit more to the right - and began tuning their instruments with squeaking moans from violins and low, single note trumpet blows that filled the expectant air.

Her skin prickled with excitement as the audience erupted into applause when the conductor took his place, bowed to the crowd, then turned and tapped his baton on his music stand. A moment later, the cloudless sky above the castle filled with the sound of strings, drums and clarinets as the orchestra struck out with an opening selection of Grieg and Rimsky-Korsakov.

"Enjoying it?" Harry asked, pulling her closer to his side.

"Mmm, immensely." With all the worries and troubles of the past months pushed aside, for the first time in months she felt totally relaxed and happy, enraptured by the food, the wine and the music. And, of course, by Harry.

The orchestra moved on to play Vivaldi's *Summer* movement from the *Four Seasons*. As if on cue, a flock of starlings swooped low over the roof of the stage, dipping and diving in perfect time to the music, as if choreographed, much to the delight of the audience who showed their appreciation by applauding the impromptu display.

All too soon, thought Penny, it was time for the final session before the intermission.

"Watch this," Harry said, "this is the bit everyone loves."

The moment the opening bars of the *Sailor's Hornpipe* started, the crowd was up on its feet, swiftly followed by a plethora of multi-coloured umbrellas opening. Umbrellas and people bobbed up and down in time to the music, everyone clapping, stamping and stomping with gusto. And when the pounding beat of *Rule Britannia* resounded, umbrellas were swopped for Union Jacks and red St George's banners, held high in the air, waving to and fro as people swayed in rhythm. She'd never seen such a splendid sight.

She turned to Harry and laughed. "So that's what all those umbrellas were for!"

The music led straight into *Land of Hope and Glory*; the tune always brought a lump to her throat, tonight more so. She yanked Harry to his feet and began singing the chorus as loudly and raucously as everyone else. The encore was sung even more enthusiastically. And still she wanted more.

"More! More! More!" the crowd shouted.

The day's light had tipped unnoticed towards dusk and overhead the first of the evening stars twinkled one by one into view. Peering over the cavernous black roof of the stage, a bright, full moon inched its way up. It seemed so close

Penny felt she could reach out and touch it. In the gathering darkness, a multitude of small lanterns slowly lit up around each party sitting in the field, flickering spots of candlelight that helped create the magical atmosphere around her.

Had the castle ever witnessed such a beautiful evening as this, she wondered, staring up at the majestic building now bathed in floodlight casting long flickering shadows up to the battlements. Horror and murder had taken place inside those walls, but tonight a serenity swept down across the meadows and beyond to the waters of the River Severn somewhere out there in the night.

Intermission over, the familiar introductory music to *The Blue Danube* began. As the melody gathered pace, people nearer the stage stood again, and in the clear spaces, waltzed to the tune.

Penny pointed to them. "Look, Harry, they're dancing. Isn't it wonderful?"

The *Danube* flowed into the *Kaiswerwalzer*, which in turn faded into *Wo die Zitronen blüh'n*, and the dancers twirled and glided in a synchronized display of Viennese dance. Effortlessly, seamlessly, the music changed...

Da dee dee, dee dee de da dum dum...

She froze! Blood throbbed in her ears, her heart beating wildly in rapid triple time.

"Harry," she screamed. "That's the music!"

His head jerked round to her. "What? It can't be!" He picked up the discarded programme, anxiously scanning down the page, but couldn't read the tiny white lettering against the blue background; there wasn't enough light.

"Penny, are you sure?"

Da dee da, dee dum dum, da da dee...

"Of course I am. Hurry, what's it called? I have to know."

"It's called... I can't see properly. Pass me the torch. ...It's called... *Poème.*"

"*Poème,*" she whispered, listening, recognizing each nuance and note. Unable to prevent them falling, she burst into tears, a feeling of freedom coursing uncontrollably through her veins, making her lose her composure. She was free...

Free from the heavy burden that had weighed her down for so long. Free at last! She wanted to shout it to everyone. And she wanted to dance. Dance for joy, dance for pleasure and dance for release. At last she knew. The unknowing finally over.

Harry pulled her into his arms, kissing away the salty tears, covering her mouth with his hot passionate lips, while the music ebbed into a softer, gentler interlude. Swathed in its surrealism, she cuddled against him, her head resting on his shoulder as they gently rocked to each romantic melody the orchestra played. Every now and then another salty tear trickled down her cheek, which she brushed away with a finger.

When the rapturous applause around them died down, and the dancers had returned to their seats, the conductor announced the finale. A collective groan emitted from the audience, causing people to laugh.

Music from *Star Wars* began. To the mounting, pulsating beat, fireworks shot up into the black sky, bursting forth in orchestrated loud bangs, rocking the field. Huge rockets whistling and whooshing as they shot upwards and exploded into different coloured showers of reds, blues, greens, yellows and golds. Another, another, and yet still more shot skyward creating multitude specks of light that drifted down slowly above the audience.

Penny loved each noisy bang and colourful exploding display. To her, they mirrored her escape from the blackness of the past, of being set free and bursting forth into light as the music neared its climax.

Harry said something. She couldn't hear him above the ever-increasing loudness of the music and wizardry pyrotechnics.

He shouted louder. "I said, will you marry me?"

"Pardon?" Unable still to understand what he said, she cupped a hand to her ear.

"Will you marry me?" he yelled at the precise moment the music came to a lull.

She heard him that time, not fully believing she had understood him correctly. The music had risen again in volume, the closing crescendo nearing its climax. She was about to answer when a gentle tap on her shoulder made her turn her head. A man stood behind her, a broad grin on his face and a twinkle in his eye.

"For goodness' sake, tell him yes. We're all waiting to know."

Glimpsing behind, she could see his fellow revellers were not watching the show lighting up the night sky, they were watching her and Harry, giving her eager nods and encouraging signs, goading her on. She turned back to Harry; he was down on one knee, his hands tightly grasping hers.

"Will you marry me?" he asked again.

She knew then she could never let him out of her life. This was her second chance. The love of a man like Harry Winchester wouldn't come her way again. She threw her arms around him as another super-duper, whiz-bang firework burst above his head in a spectacular display of gold and silver stars echoing the shape of the Death Star. The lights hung there seemingly motionless for several seconds before falling slowly in a dazzling shower, petering out before they reached the ground.

"Yes, yes. A million times yes," she cried out.

When Harry pulled her to him and kissed her again, she heard a loud cheer erupt from the party behind.

Chapter 43

Pond Cottage was afire with light blazing from every window shining out into the darkness. The explosions and music still pounded in her head as, curled up alongside Harry on the sofa, Penny read and reread the concert programme, hoping to see something more, some tiny detail they may have missed about the obscure composer, but there was nothing further to be gleaned.

"We have to find out more," she said anxiously. "But how?"

Both pairs of eyes fell on the laptop. Harry beat her to it and switched it on, waiting for what seemed an aeon for it to boot up and flicker into life. He called up Google and tapped in the composer's name.

Hitting the first site on the list that appeared, a glimpse of the life of Zdenek Fibich unfolded on the screen. There was a black-and-white photograph of him in profile: broad-chested, sharp nosed, high forehead, stern-looking, but was there a softer side hidden beneath his full beard, Penny wondered. The information read, Harry surfed entry after entry, zipping from one site to the next, as eager as she to garner as much information about the elusive composer as possible.

"Slow down, Harry, you're going too fast. You're not giving me enough time to read everything properly."

"I'm sorry, but I haven't seen anything yet to link Fibich or the music to Whitestones. Nowhere does it mention anything about the background to his work. Are you sure it was definitely the same piece we heard played tonight?"

"How can you even think to ask such a question? Of course I'm sure. I know that music inside out, note for note. Remember? I can hear it in my head even now. No, not like that. It's as though hearing it this evening has indelibly printed it in my brain, but differently. Complete. *Da da dee, dee dee dee, daa dee daa dee dee dee.*" She sang the notes. "I know it's the same. No doubt about it."

Harry yawned, stretched his aching limbs and glimpsed at

his watch.

"Jesus, look at the time! It's well after midnight. Come on, sweetheart, let's go to bed. We're not going to find out any more tonight." He moved to shut down the computer.

Her hand stopped him. "No, wait. I'm too excited to stop. I won't sleep. Not now. You go on up if you want, but I have to keep looking. There has to be something more here."

"And if there's not?"

She waved the concert programme at him. "There's enough information here for me to start again. With the orchestra, the BBC, score sheets. And Fibich must have family in the Czech Republic we might be able to contact. Perhaps your professor friend can help. Or the university."

He nodded. "I'm sure, but not now, it's the middle of the night. Come to bed, you'll feel better for it. I'll ring Shields first thing in the morning." He slid his hand down her back, teasing his fingers up and down her spine, then inching his way under her sweater. As he did so, he bent his head and kissed her neck.

As Penny reached up to kiss his mouth, his free hand flicked the switch on the computer and the screen turned black.

Sleep wouldn't come despite the satisfaction of Harry's fervent lovemaking making her feel deliciously content. Beside her, Harry slept. It had been too long without him by her side.

Fibich's melody played over and over again in her head, but this time there was pleasure hearing every note, every chord. Music so dear to her heart it was as if it had been written for her. Instead, she tossed and turned, restless, too excited by the evening's events and the monumental result.

Gently so as not to disturb Harry, she slipped from the bed. A shaft of moonlight through the window fell upon his face. Poor man, she thought, he needed the rest. He'd looked so dejected and tired when he'd appeared on the doorstep in Goldstoke, the pressure of the last six months ageing him. He looks so relaxed now, a smile upon his lips.

Quietly, she dressed, tiptoed from the room and crept down the stairs. In the hallway, she put on a pair of walking shoes, shrugged into her fleece, then picked up the flashlight from the hall table.

Listening at the doorway, checking she hadn't woken him, she left the house.

Chapter 44

A short distance from the cottage, a fox's bark from the woods made her jump but didn't stop her in her tracks, such was the yearning need to be at the ruins. At Whitestones. Something intangible was pulling her, drawing her along the lane towards it. Without understanding or questioning why, she simply knew it was vital she went there.

The night was clear, the moonlight enough for no need of the torch. Above her, she could see stars in their trillions twinkling and blinking like diamonds scattered across black velvet. A barn owl's silent flight across her path a few feet ahead startled her momentarily before she smiled at the sight of the beautiful creature now quartering the top field.

Unheeded in her footsteps, the tune in her head repeated itself, as it had on so many occasions, but now she could appreciate the full beauty of its melody, secure in the knowledge that the music was real. That she hadn't made it up in her head. Someone *had* composed it – Zdenek Fibich – a real man, not some figment of her imagination.

But why was this man and his music bound to Whitestones? And how? She needed to know, to find the answers otherwise the unknowing would haunt her for life. There needed to be a finale. An end.

What was more difficult to grasp was the professor's notions that the stones from the house still held on to snippets of the tune. Incredible, as was his belief that water could make the stones play the music back. And why could only she hear it? Why not Harry? After all, men were sensitive creatures too. And what about children? Young and innocent, they more than anyone should be attuned to such phenomena. *Wasn't it always children poltergeists were drawn to?*

Ahead lay the Whitestones, a black shadow looming into view through the trees as she neared. To lesser women out on their own in the darkness they might have been terrified, imagining all sorts of scary things lurking in the undergrowth, Penny thought. But not her. Here, she knew there was

269

nothing frightening. Quite the opposite. A sense of calmness emanated from what remained of the house, of happiness, laughter and love amongst the ruins, emotions so strong she was convinced they were her own. Yet she knew these feelings came from another time, another place.

She looked around for somewhere to sit. Spying a fallen tree trunk amongst the long grass, she made her way to it. Once seated, she looked out across the hill. In the distance the lights of Bristol glowed, an orange fazed halo over the city, bright strings of yellow lights marking the motorways. A flashing red light, static, a beacon hanging in the air, whilst above it, moving across the sky a smaller blinking light caught her attention. An aircraft coming in to land at the airport on the far side of the city. Silent, steady, gradually moving nearer the ground.

The view reminded her she was not alone. Out there, the world carried on as normal, as on any other night of the year. People sleeping, others working the night shift. So what was she doing out here, she asked herself. She should be at home, in bed, cuddled close to Harry. What had called her out here on some fool's errand in the middle of the night?

Although conscious of the dead tree she sat upon, of the night air around her, she could smell lavender and roses scenting the air, hear birds singing in a garden far away from Gloucestershire. Captivated, she sat motionless as a hundred years or more peeled away from her eyes, revealing images so real she felt she could reach out and touch the lives of the people unveiling before her. Stepping back in time to another country, she could see mountains, rugged, snow-capped. Back to an era when gallantry and honour meant something; where a man gave up everything for love against all odds. A soft breeze rustled the grass and gently blew strands of her hair across her face. She brushed them away...

At the sound of someone approaching through the herb garden, Liselle turned and, seeing Johann, waved out to him, hope in her eyes. He ran to her, took hold of both her hands, kissed her cheek delicately.

"Your face tells me your father disapproves," she said, observing with a crestfallen shrug of her shawled shoulders. "I knew this was madness. I shouldn't have let you do it."

"He refuses to listen to me. That man has no heart. If I marry you, it will be without my parents' blessing and I shall be forced to leave. He talks of sending you and your uncle back to Bohemia."

"Then it was foolish of us to even think they would agree. I cannot allow you to give up everything for me. I won't let you."

Johann pulled her into his arms. "Darling Liselle, I would give up my life for you. No one, including my father, least of all the Emperor, is going to prevent me from marrying you."

She pulled away, her hazel eyes wet with tears. Inside her heart was breaking. "No. Your father is right. We are not meant to be. Maybe it would be best if I went away from here. You will soon forget me, find another, someone whom your family approves of. I would rather go back to scrubbing steps and floors in the tavern than allow you to give up everything for me. I cannot ask you to do that. I bring nothing but trouble to you. It is simply not meant to be."

"You do not believe that any more than I. True love cannot be brushed aside on the whim of a power-hungry, weak old man in the pockets of a puppet king."

She thrust a finger across his lips and looked about nervously. "Hush, my love, someone will hear you. It is wrong to talk of the Emperor like that."

"Then we must leave the Schloss. We must run away. Escape. I will not allow anything to come between us. I love you too much."

She shook her head. "Johann, this is foolish talk. We cannot—" The sound of voices and footsteps drawing nearer halted her words.

Graf Wilheim appeared beneath the far end of the rose pergola, heading in their direction. At his side strode the Emperor.

Hastening to flee, hoping they hadn't been spotted, she grabbed Johann's hand.

"Quick, come. I have a thought. My uncle, he might be able to help us. He has many contacts; he will know what to do."

Johann pulled her to a halt. "No, I cannot let him do that. He will get himself into further trouble. You go, I will stay here and face them. I am not afraid. We will be together, trust me. Now hurry..."

A loud crack filled the air. Sounding like a snapping tree branch, Penny snatched her head around towards the ruin bathed in an ethereal glow of silver moonlight. In spellbound fascination, she watched as the house on the ridge created itself before her, stone by white stone tumbling down as if poured out from the clouds by some unseen giant JCB in the sky.

As the walls rose, red, white and black tiles drifted down to the floor of the ever-growing building, each one slotting neatly into position in a complicated geometric pattern ordained by some greater being. Colonnaded concrete columns of a portico erected themselves in front of the tiled floor, a dark, wooden double front door appearing from out of nowhere.

Tall sash windows came next, falling into place in the gaps left in the stonework, and as still more stones and more windows followed, the walls grew higher and higher. The cascading stones morphed into grey pantiles, interlinking themselves in steep-angled rows and valleys to form the roof. The final item to take up its position was the chimneystack, and then Whitestones stood before her in all its splendour.

The doors to the house stood open. Through them, she could see into a large room on the ground floor, a glorious waft of lily of the valley scenting the air. A man, his back towards her, sat at a grand piano in the corner of the room, his fingers swiftly moving over the keyboard in accomplished style. Instinctively, Penny knew this man was Fibich.

Tall white candles glowed from silver candelabras scattered about the room. Bathed by their shimmer, Liselle and Johann waltzed around and across the floor to the music, Liselle's peach dress swirling about her. Was this the couple she had seen dancing in the hallway of Hill House, she wondered.

She could hear every sound, every word they spoke, criss-crossing from one to the other, hearing every note that issued forth from the piano. Every shuffle and glide of feet across the wooden floor. Every swish, swish of Liselle's beautiful gown.

But she could do more than see and hear. She could read their innermost thoughts intermingling with her own. With each elegant footstep danced she sensed every feeling, every intense emotion that poured out across the spaces between the two dancers, filling the voids. She was part of them, part of the light-hearted conversation taking place as they danced, listening in like a fly on the wall, and all the while the music played, music so familiar she hummed aloud to Fibich's skilful playing.

Once, twice, a third time he played the tune in its entirety, and when he finally stopped, she watched as Johann pulled Liselle into his arms and kissed her passionately, unashamed-ly...

Laughing, Liselle pulled away from him, her hair bouncing around her shoulders, flashing highlights of gold cast across her dark ringlets. Woven into her hair small sprays of lily of the valley nodded gently.

"Stop it. You'll embarrass Uncle," she said.

Johann, moustached, tall and standing proud, and every inch a soldier by his stance, although his clothes were casual, dark trousers under a maroon quilted smoking jacket, turned to his benefactor at the piano, the joy in his face evident.

"I do not think your uncle will mind in the circumstances. And I must thank you, Zdenek, you have done more than enough. I don't know how we can ever repay you." He clipped his heels together and bowed in gratitude and respect.

Turning to speak, Zdenek swung one leg over the stool in order to look at him. "Seeing your happiness is enough for me. I am only sorry you had to give up so much, but seeing the love in your eyes, and knowing it is in your heart, perhaps all will end well. It may be that one day your father will be able to find it in his heart to forgive."

Giving a soft kiss to Johann's cheek, Liselle went to sit with her uncle on the piano stool, fluffing out the fullness of her dress about her, persuading him to shuffle up a little more to make room. She put her arms around him and kissed his cheek with affection.

"And thank you, too, Uncle, for all you have done for us, and for such a wonderful wedding present. It's perfect. You must teach me how to play it before you leave."

"Alas, my dear child, I fear there is no time. I must return to Vienna by Friday, which means I must leave in the morning."

Liselle looked disappointed. "But you cannot leave us yet? You have only recently arrived."

"It grieves me as much as you that I cannot stay longer, but your Johann's father has given me no choice. If I do not arrive in time to play at the Count's anniversary party on Monday, I fear I will lose his favour and be forced back to Prague." He stroked her cheek with the back of his hand. "Don't look so sad. I will do all in my power to persuade the Count to change his mind. When he hears how good a wife you are to his son, I am sure he will change his mind and accept you."

Johann's face fell sullen. "Nothing you can say or do will make him change his mind, I fear. He made his thoughts more than plain to me the day he banished me from the Schloss. It is futile to put yourself at any further risk on our behalf."

"He was angry. Disappointed. It will pass in time," Zdenek offered.

"It is no excuse. By sending me away he has hurt my mother also. What he does to me is of no consequence, but I cannot forgive him for hurting her. Ever."

Liselle rose sharply from the stool. "Enough of this sorrow," she ordered, close to tears. "I have brought this grief on you all. It is all my fault."

"No, Liselle," Johann contradicted. "It is no one's fault. You cannot stop love when it comes for you. You either embrace it or turn your back on it. That is nature. And for me, I embrace it wholly, so come back into my arms and we shall dance more. Today is our wedding day and we are here to celebrate. If Zdenek must leave tomorrow, then let us enjoy what is left of this fine day. Again, Uncle, I beg you, play the music and we shall dance until daybreak. We shall dance until our feet can carry us no more, and then we shall dance in our dreams." Johann held out his hand, beckoning his bride to join him.

Liselle kissed her uncle's cheek again before reaching out to her handsome husband. How she loved him. What other man would give up so much for such a poor servant girl as she? It was the stuff of dreams and fairytales, and hers had finally come true...

Her eyes flitting this way and that, Penny could feel all the pride and pleasure inside Fibich as he flexed his long fingers, ready to play the tune again...

A smile of self-satisfaction crept across his lips as he struck the first chord and watched fondly over his shoulder as his beloved niece and her new husband danced to his music. Would they never tire of dancing this night? He had done all he could for them, and was sure his little Liselle and Johann would find peace and happiness together, even if it was in this strange, damp country of England, so far from home, so removed from their families.

Indebted now to the Earl of Kendleshire, owner of this grand house, whom he'd met years before whilst studying in Paris, he wished he had time to visit his old friend. Renting this house for these two young exiles was costing him dear, but seeing the love on their faces, he knew it was worth it. He would have to work harder, write more music, sell more to pay the bills. And Johann would do all in his power to pay him back in due course as promised. He had no doubts; Johann was a man of honour.

And they would be happy, he felt, adamant in the knowledge that before the year was out, Liselle and Johann would have their own family; that it wouldn't take long for this strong young man to create a new life. An heir. And he was even more certain that when Graf Wilhelm heard news of a grandchild, all the bitterness and hate would melt away like the snows in spring.

He would do his utmost through the Countess to convince the Count to allow his son back into his life. He would have to be subtle, choose his moment with precision and care; but what mother ever could resist the love of her son or her first grandchild? With gentle persuasion Maria could force the Count to change his mind about anything.

As the young couple laughed and danced, his memories drifted back over the last few years since his wayward cousin had died, recalling every detail of that awful night as if it were only yesterday when he had sat helplessly by her bedside, holding her hand, bathing her brow as she lay dying so painfully.

In those precious last moments of her ebbing life he had vowed he would look after her daughter, the young Liselle, a child so happy and so unaware of the scandal surrounding her birth, but the bastard child of a wily nobleman was doomed to a life of hardship. It was not the girl's fault, and although he hadn't been a man of means, he thought he had done well to eventually find her a position with the von Engels; he wasn't to know Liselle would fall in love with Graf Wilhelm's only son. They had tried to prevent it happening, deny their feelings for each other, but as the months passed and winter had turned into a glorious spring, their love had blossomed amid the Osterglocken until they could hide their love no longer.

He had tried his best to persuade the carefree young man and Liselle to end their liaisons. They all had, but he, too, had tasted illicit love and well understood how the heart rules the head. If his darling Liselle could find happiness and security in the arms and bed of Johann, who was he to interfere? How can you stop love? So now, here they were. He'd kept his part of the bargain; the future now was up to them.

Liselle caught his gaze. "Tell me, Uncle, what is this wonderful music called you have composed in celebration of our *marriage? Truly such a beautiful piece."*

Smiling, Zdenek replied, "I have not named it yet. You must choose one."

"Poème," she said gaily, "for already I know the words."

Zdenek laughed at her whim. "But I have not written any words."

She patted her chest. "They are here in my heart already, Uncle. They speak in this room, in the air. It is as if they were written for us and are captured in your music."

"Then say them to us," Johann asked, turning his wife in a graceful spin and leading her back down the room. "Sing them to me."

Liselle's eyes never left his as she sang.

*"Are you real or are you an illusion
in my world like a dream tracing a path
straight to my heart?
Are you real or are you an illusion
captured in moonlight forever..."*

Penny heard and understood every word Liselle gently sang, as if standing in the room right next to her. Evocative words, at once sad and happy, the intensity mirroring her own love for Harry.

Involuntarily, she uttered a loud shuddering sob and turned her face away, the white mist of her breath drifting up like the fire's smoke from the chimney into the night air.

Chapter 45

Waking to find the empty space next to him in the bed, panic rose in Harry's chest. Frantic, in case the worst had happened and she had decided to leave him again, he ran through the cottage calling her name, seeking her out. He noticed her jacket and shoes were missing from the hallstand, so pulled open the front door.

"Penny? Are you out here?"

The light from the hall fell onto both their cars parked on the drive. Relief flooded through him. At least she hadn't driven off somewhere. Thinking she must be in the garden, sitting down by the pond watching the stars, he ran back upstairs, threw on a pair of jeans and a sweater, then swiftly raced back down. Dashing into the hall, he grabbed for the torch. It was gone. She must have taken it.

The moon had transformed the garden into an ethereal wilderness, but thankfully its light was adequate for him to make his way along the path. His heart sank as he neared the pond. She wasn't there.

"Penny, where are you? Can you hear me?"

A rustling in the trees made him look up. Another rustle from the undergrowth and then a blackbird hidden in a nearby tree burst into song, heralding dawn's slow approach.

Flummoxed, unable to locate Penny, he plonked himself down on the garden seat by the water, trying to think where she might have gone. Surely not for a walk on her own in the dark through the lanes?

Rubbing his eyes with his fists, he looked out across towards the far eastern horizon. The sky was lightening, the blackness of night streaked with a paler blue and thin orange fingers of cloud edging into the west. He turned his head in the other direction, towards where Whitestones lay.

Instinct told him that was where she had gone. Breaking into a run, he made his way back up through the garden, into the house, snatching up his car keys from the hall table. He'd drive across the ridge and look for her there.

Leaving the car near the broken gate of the field, he made his way through the thick stand of trees hiding the house from the lane, until he came to the clearing. Across the dew-soaked meadow, he spied her silhouette outlined against the horizon. Not wanting to frighten her by his unexpected appearance there, he held back, watching her for a few moments. Seemingly oblivious to his presence, she was staring up at the ruin.

Hesitantly, he stepped a little closer. He could hear her muttering but the words were incoherent. Meaningless. Then slowly more audible words issued from her mouth. They sounded foreign. German? He couldn't be sure, but it certainly wasn't English. He didn't even know she could speak another language. Whatever it was, the words were poetic in their delivery.

He could contain himself no longer and called out.

"Penny, are you all right?"

She turned, smiled and waved, beckoning him over.

"What are you doing out here?" he whispered, settling himself beside her on the log.

"I'm so pleased you've come. I should have woken you, but you looked so peaceful."

He put an arm around her shoulders, drawing her closer. "What you were saying when I arrived; it sounded like a poem. A song or something."

She turned her head slowly to look at him, her puzzled face pale in the diminishing moonlight.

"It wasn't me, Harry, I never uttered a word. *She* was saying them. Liselle." She pointed to the house. "And if you heard her, then I'm not imagining all this; it really is happening."

He stared at her, perplexed. "Liselle? Whoever are you talking about? It was *you* I heard talking; your voice. There's no one else here but us."

"But they are here, all of them. Liselle and Johann. And Fibich. Look, there in the drawing room." She pointed to the house. "There! Can't you see them?"

He followed the line of her finger. Whitestones was as dark and ruinous as ever. She was obviously sleepwalking, he thought, yet she seemed so lucid, so awake. It was creepy seeing her so animated like this, convinced she could see things. More than creepy. It was downright frightening.

What to do? He would have to lead her, try not to wake her; it could be dangerous, so he'd been given to understand. It could send people over the edge if they wake up and find they're not in their bed, but somewhere else. If Penny said she can see people there in the moonlight then he'd best play along.

For one crazy second he felt cheated, wishing he too could experience what she saw. He wanted to see ghosts, something paranormal, share the moment instead of having to sit back and watch the reaction it had on her. Because to Penny, something tangible was actually happening in front of them in Whitestones; he could tell it in her face, her eyes and changing expressions.

He shuddered, looked around the field, to the distant city waking up, up to the sky, and realized there was one important factor missing in all this. The one thing, according to the professor, that made it all possible.

Harry's worried expression told Penny that he couldn't see Johann or Liselle, let alone Whitestones rebuilt before them. He couldn't see the piano player or hear his wonderful music. He could see none of the things she could.

As she tried to describe what was happening before her eyes, he shook his head in apparent disbelief. She could hardly believe it all herself. What strange science made it possible for her to feel the deep devotion between Johann and Liselle creeping out from the walls and flood the space between the floors and elegantly plastered ceilings? From doors and windows, stones and mortar she knew were no longer there. Scenes playing out that made her feel elated, yet knew she should be scared she could see images from a past so real she could reach out a hand and touch them. Because, if they were real, Harry would be able to see them too.

"It doesn't make sense," he muttered.

"I know, but that doesn't mean it's not happening."

She could still see into the house, only now she was upstairs. It was night, the windows covered by draping swags of deep-red velvet curtains. Liselle sat on a wooden stool beside a nursery crib, rocking it gently to and fro. After a few moments, Liselle stood, leaned over the crib and kissed the baby's head then left the sleeping child, quietly closing the bedroom door.

But she was more than seeing, she *knew* these people, felt their every emotion, drew their breath. *How could she explain all this to Harry?* It wasn't only what she saw, it was everything else surrounding them. All the sensations, the smells, all the sounds, the thoughts. All the love and music transcending the barriers of time. That professor fellow may have made a plausible case for the defence, according to Harry, but all those hows and wherefores lacked any credible explanation as to *why* she could glimpse into the past, and that glimpse was no ghost; it was part of her.

She didn't want to say any more in case the spell broke apart. In case Harry thought she really had flipped this time.

"Don't go quiet on me," he implored. "Talk to me. Tell me what's going on. What's happening? Can you see anything now?"

She sensed he felt uncomfortable by the way he tugged on the neck of his sweater, pulling it away from his throat as if trying to stop it from choking him.

He moved to stand up, saying, "Perhaps we should call it a day for now. It's getting light and neither of us has slept well. Let's come back later? Bring the professor with us?"

"No!" She grabbed his hand, pulling, trying to persuade him to sit back down. "Wait. Listen. I know this sounds incredibly crazy but I'm being shown this snapshot of time for a reason. I cannot leave until I've learned why. I've come this far, Harry, I have to know what happened to them."

"I thought once you knew what the music was all this would be over." He sounded exasperated. "Don't do this to yourself. To us. You know the music now. The search is at an end. Let it be." He tried to pull her up from the log. "Enough now."

"Harry, please, there's still so much more here, I have to go on. It seems so unfair, to be banished by his family, losing his inheritance, and allowing nothing, not even his father's threats, to stand in their way. I have to know what happened to them. Did they live happily ever after? Did the child unite the family again? I *have* to know."

"What child?"

"Their child. Johann and Liselle's."

He studied her face for a while, as if trying to make up his mind, then sat back down. "How do you know all this stuff?"

She shrugged. "It's imprinted on their minds and in their hearts and somehow, don't ask me how, it's become imprinted on mine. I know their history, as unbelievable as it all sounds. They can't rest until it's told."

"Why? They are nothing to do with us. It's not like it's *our* history."

She smiled. "But it is. It's what's made you and me the people we are. It's affected our lives for months, as it has everyone else that has touched upon this place. It's touched on Peter, Elaine, Lorna even, and on Professor Shields and his students. Anyone at all whom we've talked to about this. And what about people like Dave Ewell and his wife who lived in Pond Cottage before us? And those before us at Hill House?"

"I don't like this idea. Something's happening to you again, something weird, and it's frightening me, Penny. I think this is all too much and you're letting your imagination run away with you."

She patted his hand. "Trust me, darling. I'm quite safe here with you. And how can knowledge be a bad thing? If I don't follow this through, here and now, it will be gone forever. And then I shall never know what happened next, and their story will always haunt me. It will be forever hanging over us. You want to exorcise this as much as I do, I know."

"Ten more minutes, that's all. Then we go." She could sense his reluctance in agreeing.

"It will be enough."

She looked back to the house, delighted and relieved to

find Whitestones still there in all its proud and complete glory. Instinct told her that in the few minutes her attention had been focused on Harry, within Whitestones time had moved on again. She couldn't tell if it were seconds or minutes. Days or weeks or years. But there was no mistaking the shift.

The house stood silent against a dark night sky. Nothing stirred. Then, as she thought nothing else was going to happen, a wisp of smoke puffed out from one of the chimney pots, reminding her of those email Christmas greeting cards people liked to send nowadays instead of the real thing. All it needed was snow for the image to be complete, she thought.

The thought had no sooner entered her mind when a gentle snow started falling, slowly coating Whitestones in a white dusting. She felt the damp flakes kiss her face; she brushed them away, then held out her hand, palm up.

"It's snowing, Harry."

"No," he argued, shaking his head. "There's no snow. It's the middle of summer, for God's sake."

Snow or no snow, it wasn't relevant. What mattered was what was happening in front of her. Inside the house a log fire burned brightly in its hearth, red and orange flames licking the bark, filling the room with the heady, resinous smell of elm and oak.

Quiet at first, then increasingly louder, music filled the building once more, filling her head with its romantic sounds. There was no sign of Fibich. She listened, a strange noise coming from somewhere within the house – a baby's cry...

"I must go to him, he is unsettled tonight. Perhaps he is cold," Liselle uttered, rising from the chair at the walnut writing desk. "I'll finish this letter tomorrow. Another day isn't going to make any difference."

"Of course. It is such a pity your uncle never lived to see him born. Zdenek would have been besotted by Rolfe."

"It is more the pity your father wouldn't listen to him, and now our son is to be denied also."

Johann pulled his wife to him and kissed her passionately.

"But he will never be denied our love. That will make him richer than any money, jewels or lands could ever."

She eased away from her husband's arms, sensing his reluctance to let go, and fled the room, lifting her flowing skirts in order not to trip as she ran up the stairs to their bedroom and the crying child.

Johann crossed to the phonograph on top of the closed piano, and lifted the needle arm, silence filling the room. He removed the large black disk and slipped it into its brown paper sleeve, put it down next to the phonograph. Crossing to the marble fireplace, he pushed a log into the back of the fire, and then followed his wife, closing the door firmly behind him.

In the ensuing backdraught, the log rolled forward, rocking on the embers before it finally tumbled out of the dog grate, rolled across the hearth and onto the wooden floor...

Penny blinked, and in that instant erupted a thousand hot tongues of heat. Flames licked at the windows. The panes cracked and burst out from the sashes in noise-filled explosions, making her cower for cover, fearful of being hit by the flying, lethal shards of glass. The wooden frames darkened, smoke billowing out in all directions, filling the ever-lightening sky with papers from the desk, some blackened scraps, others whole and white rising in the grey plumes towering above the treetops.

The fire burned more fierce, eating away the wooden staircase, smouldering the carpet runner, dancing in and out of the newel posts, crackling and spitting like a fire goblin from hell inching its way higher and higher until it reached the landing.

She couldn't see properly, the smoke hot and dense, and shied back from the intense heat.

"The house is on fire! Help them," she called out, in panic. "We've got to help. Please let them wake up, there's still time to get out." She reached out to turn the brass doorknob, but it was hot, burnt her fingers, the smell of searing flesh filling her nostrils.

"For God's sake, help them, Harry," she cried out, leaping to her feet.

Harry jumped up from the log. "Enough!" He grabbed her hand tightly in his own, restraining her, trying to prevent her from rushing forward into the burning building.

She struggled against his firm grip, pulling away.

"Let me go, Harry, let me go. I have to help them."

"No! Stop. Come back," he shouted.

Chapter 46

He pulled her into him, wrapping his arms around her.

"Sweetheart, there's nothing you can do..." He raised her hand to his lips, kissing her fingertips.

She winced.

"I couldn't save them," she whispered, tears streaming down her face. "I couldn't save them, Harry. I'm too late..."

"I know, I know," he soothed, pulling her tighter to him, holding her quivering body against his own. He kissed the top of her head. "I know, sweetheart, I know."

Staring back at what remained of Whitestones, she felt nothing but emptiness, a cavernous hollow where once Liselle and Johann and Rolfe had lived. Now they were gone.

The depth of loss filled her with grief, for such was the power of love between this tragic couple in those few brief moments, she had experienced every emotion they had gone through. Every joyous minute and every painful heartache, in love and in death. If what the professor said was true, such was the strength of their love that their bond had been captured in the stones of the house to travel down more than a century of time, and would probably last for centuries longer.

Was her love for Harry that strong, she wondered, now that everything had finally fallen into place, piece by piece, interlocking like parts of a jigsaw puzzle to form the whole picture?

Harry held her face in his hands, tilted her head and moved to kiss her trembling mouth. As their lips touched, a gentle wisp of air brushed between them.

Imagining the final breath of Johann and Liselle's love touching them both, she smiled as Harry's hot mouth smothered her own, knowing as she closed her eyes, hers and Harry's was also a love that would last. They too would write it in stone.

"Come on," he said gently. "I'm taking you home."

* * *

After breakfast, whilst Penny showered and dressed, Harry went back to the computer, intent on finding the particular website they had read last night before going to bed, anxious to find out more about the people Penny was so convinced were at the centre of a world that no longer existed.

His search drew a blank, unable to find many links to the composer other than to multitude music shops worldwide selling copies of his scoresheets. Another site led him to the details and location of Fibich's grave and memorial in Prague, but nothing mentioned him ever visiting England.

He was beginning to wonder if Penny was wrong in this being the elusive music, the right composer. He shuddered at that thought. If she was wrong, then they were back to where they started, and the music would continue to invade their lives. Then what? His thoughts were interrupted by the phone ringing.

"Mind if I drop by today?" Filton Shields asked. "I've found out something interesting I thought you should know as soon as possible."

"Can't you tell me over the phone?" He really didn't want their day disturbed, least of all by visitors. It had been a long, stressful night, and he and Penny needed time alone together; they had a lot to discuss and sleep to catch up on.

"It's something you both should hear. I gather from Peter, Penny's back with you. I would like to talk to her too, if that's okay?"

He thought for a moment. Perhaps the Prof could help shed more light on the strange happenings of last night; it would be interesting to hear his interpretation. And the sooner they could all resolve this, the better.

"Sure, come on over."

"See you in about an hour."

By the time Professor Shields rang the doorbell, Harry felt confident today would see closure, and he and Penny could move forward in their own world uninhabited by spirits from the past.

When he introduced Professor Shields to Penny, he noticed her demeanour alter: she physically tensed. Was she frightened Shields would explain last night's events as nothing more than hysteria? Hallucinations? He glanced down at her hands.

Filton refused the offer of coffee. "Perhaps we can walk up to Whitestones and discuss this along the way?"

"No!" Penny's immediate response was adamant. "I don't want to go back there. Not yet. What occurred last night is still too raw in my head."

The professor's bushy grey eyebrows rose quizzically. "Why? What happened?"

"I think you need to sit down," Harry said. "We've had quite an interesting twenty-four hours, to say the least."

"So have we," Filton said excitedly. "We've finally found out who owned the house. We've come across another press notice. It turns out we'd been looking at the wrong timeline. The fire actually occurred during December 1901, only nothing was known about it until March the following year."

"But that doesn't make sense. A huge fire like that would have created much more interest when it happened. People on the ridge would have seen it go up in smoke."

"Not necessarily," said the professor. "The house is well hidden; it can't be seen either from the lane or from the Common. I've double checked. The trees hide it from view."

"Agreed, but there might not have been any there at that time, or at least they would have been a lot smaller. Plus it was winter. They would have been bare."

"Granted, but you know yourself the area around here is more farmland than residential. And back then there would have been fewer people living hereabouts. Plus, if the fire happened during the night, one assumes most would be trying to stay warm indoors, behind closed curtains. Asleep. They simply wouldn't have been aware of it. And probably knowing the house was empty, no one had any reason to be concerned."

"But it still doesn't explain why it took three months before it was discovered," he argued.

Penny, who'd remained silent during his exchange with Filton, her eyes flitting from one to the other, interrupted.

"Because of the snow, Harry. It started to snow the night of the fire. Remember?"

Filton shot her a puzzled stare. "Quite." He turned back to Harry. "It was a bad winter that year. Apparently, deep snow set in for several weeks..." He spun to Penny again. "Hang on... how do you know it was the same night? No one knows the actual date it happened. It wasn't until the thaw set in that the demise of the house was discovered."

"I know because I saw it happen. We were there," Penny said.

Filton's mouth opened to say something but Harry quickly intervened. "What she's trying to say is that—"

"Are you saying something else has happened?" Filton interrupted.

"Oh yes. Indeed it has."

Filton's gaze swept around the room. "What, here?"

Penny shook her head. "At Whitestones. And it's going to take quite some explaining. I hope you're not in any hurry."

"No, I've all day if needs be." Filton leaned forward in the armchair. "So tell me... I'm all ears."

Chapter 47

"I'm not sure where to start," Penny said, looking to Harry for guidance.

"We went to a concert yesterday evening," Harry began for her. "One of the pieces played Penny recognized as the music that's been haunting her all this time. It turns out it was written by some Czechoslovakian composer we've never heard of, which probably explains why it was so obscure."

She nodded, taking her cue from Harry. "That's right. After we got home, we searched the Internet and found out more about him. I was looking for a connection between the music and Pond Cottage, all the while knowing there had to be a link to the ruin. I had so much buzzing around in my head, I couldn't sleep. The next thing I knew I was heading up there. I don't know why I felt compelled to go, I only knew for some reason I had to be there."

With help from Harry, she tried as best she could to explain to the professor what had followed on from her trek to Whitestones in the middle of the night.

With pursed lips, concentrating on everything she told him, the professor listened, at the same time making notes in a spiral notebook he'd withdrawn from the inside pocket of his jacket. Any thoughts he might have on her story he kept well hidden, she thought, for his face showed no reaction to anything she said. Occasionally, she looked to Harry for confirmation, who nodded repeatedly, with the occasional "That's right" added.

"I know it's impossible, but somehow I could read all their thoughts. That's when I found out Fibich had rented the house from the Earl of Kendleshire, whoever he was."

Filton's eyes lit up. "This is absolutely astounding. You do realize what all this means?"

Harry shook his head. "No. What?"

"That I'm not hysterical or making things up?" she said sourly, wondering if indeed even now, regardless of all she'd said, the professor would dismiss it as nothing more than imagination. Too much wine. Wishful thinking...

The professor laughed. "My dear, I never considered for one moment that you were. You could never have plucked that name out of thin air or made the connection to Whitestones on your own. In fact, I'd go so far as to say impossible. You see, the Earl of Kendleshire died in October 1902, penniless and with no heirs. He was the last of the line and died without leaving a will. He went owing thousands of pounds to many debtors. We only made the connection when we came across the second newspaper report about the fire."

Harry leaned forward. "Are you saying he is to blame for it?"

"That was our initial thought, yes. Burn down Whitestones – no longer wanted or used, so no loss to him – and claim on insurance, pay off bills. Sorted. But that wasn't the case here."

"If Kendleshire had set the house alight, he would have been guilty of murder. The fire was accidental," said Penny, "because three people died in that blaze. They burned to death and there was nothing I could do to save them." She put her hands to her face and sobbed. Feeling Harry place a comforting arm around her shoulder, she leaned into him, shuddering with further tears.

"Absolutely tragic," consoled Filton. "But that is what I came to tell you. It transpires that after the thaw set in, a couple of local lads found the house burnt out, told their parents and it seems some of them went to see what they could rescue or purloin from the spoils. Whilst they were rifling the debris, they came across three bodies. Two adults and a small child found huddled together. It turns out those poor souls are buried together down in the village churchyard, in a grave marked only by a small tombstone with the words: 'Herein lies those unknown who perished in Whitestones.'"

She stared at him, stunned. As was Harry, she noticed.

"No one knew who they were," the professor continued.

"But surely after they were found, this Lord Kendleshire would have made it known this hapless couple was living in his house?" said Harry.

"Oh, he did," said Filton, "but he had no idea who they

were either. Said something along the lines of he'd rented it out to a friend for his family. He never said who the friend was. We assume he advised this friend of the ensuing tragedy. Stefan wonders if that was what the scrap of letter found was all about."

"What about Kendleshire's accounts? Are there any records pertaining to this?" asked Harry.

"When he died his home was sold off to pay the debtors. What records existed at that time were lost, destroyed probably."

Penny lifted her head and looked at Filton. "But we *do* know who they were. The woman was Liselle, Fibich's niece. The other body was that of her husband, Johann, the son of Count Wilheim von Engels of Austria. Wilheim disowned Johann because of his love for Liselle, a servant at their castle. The child was their baby, born after they married. They'd named him Rolfe. And I can tell you how the fire started too; I witnessed it."

"You did?" For the first time, the professor sounded astonished.

She nodded, feeling tears brim her eyes at the memory. "They perished in there, including the little baby. Can you imagine the horror of it?"

"Indeed I can," said Filton, nodding.

She held Harry's hand tightly. "I felt all their fear, their panic and their distress amidst all the undying love they held for each other and that infant."

"Which is precisely what we think is imprinted into the walls of that building, pieces now scattered across other homes including here," the professor extolled, sounding more than pleased. "This proves our theory that what we have here is a classic stone-tape case."

She sank back into the sofa. "But it wasn't only fear and death I felt. If stones from the house were removed and placed elsewhere, I can fully understand why I only saw and heard snippets and flashes before, but last night much of what took place was complete, the whole shebang. Your theory doesn't make sense."

"Emotions," Filton said simply. "Emotions so strong, so powerful they imprinted themselves onto everything they touched. The walls, the floors, every item of cutlery, clothing, jewellery. Love is one of the strongest emotions anyone feels, is it not?" Filton looked at Harry, who nodded agreement with this statement. "In fact," Filton continued, "I'd even go so far to say *the* most important. Those intense, wonderful warm feelings we experience in the heat of passion, at the moment of sexual climax, aren't they as strong as the feelings of fear and death? Perhaps even stronger. Don't you think they could evoke high energy levels capable of being zapped around the room to become trapped in the walls?"

"Or the intense emotion of two people very much in love," she muttered.

"Gosh, that's right." Harry raised her hand to his lips and kissed her fingers as he looked into her tear-soaked eyes. "I seem to recall you saying something like that the first time you saw the dancers. You said how they were very much in love. And you said something similar the first time I took you to see the ruin."

"And passionate love is as highly charged as fear and death," the professor reiterated.

She rose from the sofa and walked to the window, staring out across the garden and the wide valley beyond. Everything the professor said was grounded in a perfectly logical explanation to the events, but something still wasn't right. Something in his theory was missing. She turned to him.

"What you've said makes some sort of sense even if I don't understand it all, but it still doesn't explain how I managed to understand everything they thought or spoke. More to the point, your theory doesn't explain how I could see what took place hundreds of miles away from here. Johann came from Austria, Liselle and Fibich from Czecho-slovakia. I saw what went on in Austria. None of that could have imprinted itself on Whitestones, it didn't happen there. Nor did they speak English, yet I understood every word they said."

"They were memories," the professor answered. "Their

memories."

She frowned, puzzled by this answer. "Are you saying memories, as well as words, can be imprinted into stone?"

Filton nodded. "If they are strong enough, I see no reason why not. It is said your life flashes before you in those seconds before your death. These two wretched people shared many of the same memories, a bond strong enough to create such an echo."

"And my being able to understand them? I don't speak German, Austrian or any other language. How could that be?"

"Have you ever heard of cases where people come out of a coma being able to speak another language they never could speak before? Or being able to play an instrument? Anything is possible where the brain is concerned. This may sound far-fetched, Penny, but you may have ancestral Austrian or German blood in you. You might know a language without ever having realized it."

"God, that is a long shot," exclaimed Harry.

Filton's eyebrows rose. "I agree, but it's the best I've got for the moment. However, it might be worth checking out your family history, Penny. Connections may be tenuous but the link could be there. If you do, I'd be eager to know the results because... You look puzzled, Harry."

"Well, yes, I am. You said before that..." Harry rubbed his forehead. "You said before that water is needed to trigger the stones to play back what they have captured. But last night, there was no water, no rain. There's not even a stream up by the house to cause Penny to see what she did? How do you explain that?"

The professor shrugged. "It rained here the day before yesterday, and what with all the rain over the past two years, the aquifer beneath the ridge must be full, the ground around and beneath it soaked. There may be deep underground channels and chambers full of water seeping up into the foundations of what remains of Whitestones. Also, I am sure somewhere in the grounds of the house there must be a well."

Harry laughed.

"Okay, I confess, I don't have all the answers," Filton said, hands held palms open in acquiescence. "I'm guessing. And a lot of what I've said is as yet unproven. All I will confirm is that other people's memories, other people's dying thoughts as their lives flash by just before death, happy thoughts, sad thoughts, love and panic, fear and regret can be caught in stone and held captive until that one magical moment when one special person has the key to unlock them." He looked at her and smiled. "In this case, Penny, that was you. How does that make you feel?"

She shrugged. "Privileged, I suppose, to a degree. Honoured that causes unknown have given me an extraordinary and unique gift. Something rare and precious, yet at the same time wishing it wasn't me. That it never happened."

"You should be proud," said Filton. "Proud you've brought further proof to the piles already collected on such phenomena. Our work is often laughed at, sniggered and scoffed by those who feel it is a lot of mumbo-jumbo. I'm kind of hoping here you would be prepared to give us more of your time. Help us in a few experiments. I'd like to do some more research up there."

"What sort of research?" Harry's question sounded guarded.

"Ground surveys and tests, that sort of thing. I'm pretty convinced there are geophysical movements that also play a part in all this. My students are currently working on several incidents and ghost sightings around Stroud. There's far more to all this than we know at this point in time."

As Penny opened her mouth to speak Harry intervened.

"I don't think so, Professor. I think Penny's been through enough. We need to put a stop to it all now. There needs to be an end, and this is it. No more. It's time we moved on in our lives and began to enjoy each other as God meant."

But this wasn't the end. Not quite. There was something she had to do first.

"Hang on, Harry. I would like to help him. He's brought us this far, perhaps in a few weeks' time when we've settled again and had time to think about all this, the professor could come back. It would make it feel like Johann, Liselle and little Rolfe didn't die in vain."

Harry looked deep into her eyes, squeezed her hand. "As long as you are sure, sweetheart."

"I'm sure. And there is one thing I'd like to do first, if you don't mind?"

"Which is?"

She took a deep breath before speaking. "I want us to arrange a proper headstone to mark their graves. One that bears their names, and mention of the music. They shouldn't be left as unknowns now. That wouldn't be right."

Harry smiled widely. "I think that's a lovely idea, don't you, Prof?"

Filton nodded. "Fitting. Very fitting indeed." He rose from his chair to take his leave.

"Just one more thing before you go," she said. A plan was forming in her mind, a delicious, mad, crazy idea that set her heart and thoughts racing.

Filton sat down again.

"Do we know who now owns Whitestones and the land around it, including the hanging gardens?"

"Now we have names and dates, I'm sure we can eventually find out. The Land Registry must have some idea even though Kendleshire's records are exceedingly vague."

Harry frowned. "Why do you ask, Pen?"

"Oh, just curious," she answered.

"Do you think Liselle and Johann will ever come back?" Harry asked after the professor had left.

Penny looked at him. "I hope so, but I doubt it. Some inner sense tells me it's over, and that they and the music are gone. Purged by rain and evaporated into the ether."

He pulled her into his arms. "So, Mrs Winchester, what do we do now?"

She laughed, then reminded him jovially, "I'm not Mrs Winchester yet."

"Okay. So, future Mrs Winchester, do I take it you are happy to continue living here now the mystery of the music has been solved?"

"I'm not sure. That's why I wanted to know who owns Whitestones now. This may sound daft, even a fantasy, but..."

"Go on..."

"How would you feel about us living there? At Whitestones. You know how much I love it there, and always wanted those fabulous hanging gardens for myself, and—"

His eyes widened, his brow creased. "But the place is a wreck! And what if Liselle and Johann haven't gone? This could go on for years before the stone record wears away. Could you honestly live with that?"

"But what if we remove all that remains of the house, pull it down totally and build a new one in its place? That way there would be nothing left to yield up any ghosts or phantom music, pain or grief. We could fill it with *our* love, *our* memories. You're an architect, Harry. You and Peter could design a fabulous new home, a new Whitestones. Oh please, please say yes. Tell me you think it's a marvellous idea."

Chapter 48

Penny turned this way and that in the mirror, checking every angle, pleased with the design, fit and colour of her dress. Anita brushed out a fold in the back of the peach-coloured wedding dress.

"You look lovely, Penny. The colour matches your complexion completely."

"Thanks. You were wrong about Harry, you know?"

Anita laughed. "So it seems. And yes, he is gorgeous and Mother loves him, so he must be okay. But I was only doing what I thought best for you. I didn't want to see you hurt again."

Penny kissed her sister's cheek fondly. "I know, but in future, I do what I think is best for me. And do me a favour. If I ever come running to you for cover again, kick me straight out of the door back to Harry."

"Go get him, sis. Hey, but that Elaine's a rum one, though."

"Elaine's okay when you get to know her. It took me time, and her me. Looking back, I can understand her reservations about me in the beginning, and despite anything she might say or admit. I think deep down she really was in love with Harry. I don't know which came as the biggest shock – the news that during my absence she and Peter Ballantyne had become an item, or the fact that they jumped at the chance to buy Pond Cottage from us when we're ready to sell up once the new house is finished."

"What about you? Do you think you and Harry will be happy living there after all that's happened?"

Penny smiled, adamant in her response. "We'll be happy no matter where we are. When we're settled in you and Nathan must come and stay. As must Mum."

"We'll look forward to it." Anita hugged her then gave her wristwatch a quick glance. "Right, it's time to go, although there's still time to change your mind if you want."

Even on her wedding day her sister still couldn't get out of her agony aunt hat, Penny thought, smiling. "Change my mind? Anita, I've never been so sure of anything in my life."

"Good, that's all I wanted to hear."

"Darling, you look divine." Elaine rushed to greet Penny with an affectionate kiss at the foot of the grand staircase in Berkeley Castle. "I wouldn't have missed this for the world. You have no idea how good it makes me feel seeing you and Harry back together. I felt so responsible for it all."

"Well, it's all sorted now, and it wasn't your fault what happened. Now, what's all this about you and Peter? I hear wedding bells are in the air too for you two."

Elaine's face beamed as she clapped her hands. "Yes, in three weeks' time. When he proposed there seemed no point in waiting. I'm so happy. You and Harry will come, won't you? You will be back from Barbados by then?"

"Of course we'll be there. But do you think you'll be happy living in Pond Cottage, what with its ghosts and all that?"

"Darling, I positively love it there. It's so pretty. And do you know what I'm looking forward to most? To being in bed at night waiting to hear the music. It must be so dreamy, so romantic, I can't wait to hear it. We couldn't believe our luck when Harry told Peter you were selling up. He'd already made up his mind to sell the mansion, it's far too big for the two of us and, like you, we wanted a fresh start, not in somewhere that holds memories for Peter."

Penny laughed. "So, he's swapped one set of ghosts for another? Makes sense."

"The odd ghost or two doesn't worry me, Penny dear, but I can understand why you and Harry have gone for a new build, one with no history or horror stories attached."

"Ahh," said Anita, mischievously. "The trouble is, you never know what's buried underneath."

Penny nudged her sister playfully in the ribs. "Behave."

The melody would never make itself known to Elaine, Penny knew. And if moonlight dancers were to ever sashay across the hallway of Pond Cottage again, she knew full well Elaine would either have an attack of the screaming habdabs or tell them in no uncertain terms to go and waltz in someone else's home.

"Right, follow me, girls," ushered Anita, leading the way into the anteroom. "We've time for another glass of champagne before we go in."

As she walked down the aisle, Penny's heart swelled, her eyes filling with tears of happiness. They'd found their love again among the ruins of Whitestones, and knew their love would also stand the test of passing time, as had Liselle and Johann's.

The registry book signed, photographs taken, she and Harry started their walk back down the central aisle of the crowded hall. The quartet up in the minstrel's gallery burst into tune.

Da dee dee, da da da, de dum dum...

She pulled him to a stop. "Oh, Harry, listen. They're playing Fibich's tune."

Smiling widely, he turned to look at his beautiful wife. "Yes, it's our tune now. Our love poem." He offered a hand. "Will you do me the honour?"

"With pleasure."

To the amusement of their families and friends, she bobbed a curtsey, and laughing, allowed Harry to lead her in a waltz down the rest of the aisle and out into the bright sunlight flooding the garden terrace.

In the many months that followed while the planning permissions waited approval and later as the demolition works progressed in tearing down the remains of Whitestones, Penny busied herself in the hanging gardens. The terrace walls were repaired, shrubs cut back and tidied. Even though she could only imagine what it looked like in the past, she felt sure its re-emergence would do justice to the time and effort she put in. She'd never felt so happy.

"Come and see what we've found. The professor was right," Harry called to her from the top terrace.

She brushed the wet soil from her gardening gloves and made her way up the terraces. "Right about what?"

"There *is* a well! And a deep one, at that."

"Oh my! Where? We've never come across it."

"In the cellar of the house. It had been covered with flagstones for some reason but never filled in. We didn't know until the digger ripped up half the floor. Come and look."

She stood near the edge of the gaping hole, peering down. It was brick lined as far down as she could see before it all become lost in the darkness. "I wonder how deep it is."

Harry picked up a nearby stone and dropped it in. After hearing it clatter against the walls a few times, silence ensured for several seconds before they finally heard a faint splash.

"It's deep," he said.

"What are we going to do with it?"

"It needs to be properly investigated and surveyed first before we can decide, but I don't think it will make a lot of difference to the plans of the new house. I'm hoping we will be able to fill it in. It depends on how deep it actually goes. I'm assuming it won't affect the watercourse off the hill if we do. We'll need to check."

She looked back down into the darkness. "It would be nicer if we could keep it, don't you think?"

Harry scratched his chin. "Well, it does lie outside what will be the new foundations. I suppose we could make it into a feature as part of the garden. I never gave that a thought. There's still a lot of extra groundwork and surveying to do first because of it, but I'm sure it'll be fine."

"We could make it a wishing well," she enthused, excited by the prospect.

"Good idea. We could even rename the place Wishing Well House..."

She glared at him. "I thought we'd agreed on New Whitestones?"

Harry laughed. "It was only a thought..."

Eighteen months later summer rolled lazily into autumn, the leaves on the trees painting the Cotswolds in hues of burnished gold and fiery reds. New Whitestones had risen from the ashes of its past into a high-tech, state-of-the-art modern house, with hints and nods here and there to the vernacular honey-stone architecture of the other houses scattered along the ridge.

Built with new, man-made stones, seasoned timbers that hadn't been reclaimed from anywhere, and rooms untouched and uncluttered by memories, the new house possessed no mysterious history, no ghosts, and no peculiar smells other than the odour of fresh paint and new carpet. From the moment they moved in, peace and contentment cloaked their new home.

In the darkness of their bedroom, Penny lay awake listening. From somewhere within the depths of the house she thought she could hear the distant but happy sound of someone singing.

Beside her, Harry slept soundly, exhausted by their impassioned lovemaking, the covers over him rising and falling gently to the steady rhythm of his breathing. Outside, a gentle October rain fell. She shook him several times.

"Harry! Harry, wake up. I think the professor was wrong!"

THE END

AUTHOR'S NOTES

Zdenek Fibich

Born in 1850 in what is now the Czech Republic, Zdenek Fibich was a prolific composer of classical chamber works, symphonic poems, symphonies and operas. Although popular in his native country, sadly he is little known in the UK, and his beautiful works rarely heard or played here. His father was a forester for a Czech nobleman, his mother an ethnic German Viennese. Fluent in both languages, his educational years were spent in Germany, France and Austria in addition to his native Bohemia. Fibich died in 1900 aged 49 and is buried in Vysehradsky Cemetery, Prague.

He was the first to write a Czech nationalist tone poem (Záboj, Slavoj a Luděk) which later served as the inspiration for Smetana's Má vlast, and the first to use the polka in a chamber work: his quartet in A. He composed some truly beautiful music including the romantic piece Poème Op.41 No.6, the inspiration for this novel. The piece was also the original melody for "My Moonlight Madonna", popular in the 1930s, with English lyrics by P.F.Webster and sung, among others, by David Whitfield and Richard Tauber. Lyrics to Poème used within this book are, however, the author's own.

Various sites on the Internet list his works in full and give accounts of his life, loves and tribulations. There is, however, no recorded note that he or any of his family ever visited the UK during his lifetime or that Op.41 was dedicated to any member of his family, and any inference is of the author's own making in this work of fiction.

To hear the music that inspired this novel, visit:
https://youtu.be/YeNUV9_sCrM

The Stone Tape Theory

"The Stone Tape" is a television play written by Nigel Kneale (writer of *Quatermass*) first broadcast in December 1972 on BBC television. Critically acclaimed at the time, it is still regarded as Kneale's best and most terrifying of plays. The

story centres around a team of scientists who move into a renovated Victorian mansion with a reputation for being haunted with a view to determining if the stones of the building were acting as a recording of past events. Their investigations unleash a malevolent force far darker than they presumed. The play is available to view on the Internet viaYouTube.

Since its broadcast, the hypothesis of residual haunting has been referred to as the Stone Tape Theory, and accepted by many paranormal investigators as being a possible explanation for ghosts despite not being an exact science. No one yet has been able to prove or disprove the theory, just as no one has yet proved ghosts do or do not exist. The Stone Tape Theory suggests that buildings and materials can, given the right set of circumstances, absorb some forms of energy from living beings, be it human or animal. It is thought magnetic fields and natural electrical energy also play a part and that if climatic and humidity conditions are the same as those which occurred when the recording took place, it will be played back. This would also cause a repetitive playback of the same recording.

The idea that water is always involved, as expanded and discussed in this novel, is the author's own addition to this subjective debate.

Hill House

The Hill House depicted in this novel is fictitious, as is Stonecott Hill upon which it is set, but based on a Georgian mansion perched high on the edge of the Cotswold escarpment in southern Gloucestershire where the author resided for several years. Although no ghosts were ever seen or heard during her time living there, there were stories of a frequent guest at the house who claimed to be able to hear piano music playing in the dead of night on occasion. The source of the music was never established.

ABOUT KIT DOMINO

Kit Domino grew up in West London, England during the 1950s and 1960s, before moving to Gloucestershire in 1972 where she still resides with her husband, whom she met in 1976. A trained secretary, her working career has always involved books, copy-editing, proofreading and typesetting, and for 10 years ran her own word-processing agency. During this time she began writing her first novel as well as poetry, several of which were published. Later, becoming office manager and company proofreader for a large planning consultancy near Bristol, she continued to write in her spare time.

In 2004, she was shortlisted for the Harry Bowling Prize for a London novel with *Every Step of the Way*, published in 2013, fulfilling her life-long ambition. Writing in several genres including timeslip, paranormal, and social history fiction, she's held a life-long fascination with the paranormal, and whilst not believing in ghosts per se, is willing to accept there are strange forces that we still have yet to discover or explain.

Following redundancy in 2010, she decided and help other new writers achieve publication by setting up her own small, independent publishing house. Despite always being busy, she somehow manages to also find the time to work as an editor for several established authors.

If all this wasn't enough, Kit is also an internationally-selling artist and art tutor working in acrylics, as well as an avid gardener and food blogger.